A TOWN
THAT TEMPTED FATE

Farewell
RABAUL

BASED ON TRUE EVENTS

ALAN B. PIERCE

First published in Australia by Aurora House
(http://aurorahouse.com.au)

This edition published 2025
Copyright © Alan B. Pierce 2025

Typesetting and e-book design: Amit Dey (amitdey2528@gmail.com)
Cover design: Donika Mishineva (www.artofdonika.com)

ISBN number: 978-1-923298-35-4 (paperback)

A catalogue record for this book is available from the National Library of Australia

DEDICATION

To the members, past and present, of the Papua New Guinea Association of Australia, who are dedicated to the collection and preservation of material relating to Australia's role in the development of Papua New Guinea and to enhancing the relationship between both countries.

Be on guard! Be alert!
You do not know when that time will come.

Mark 13:33

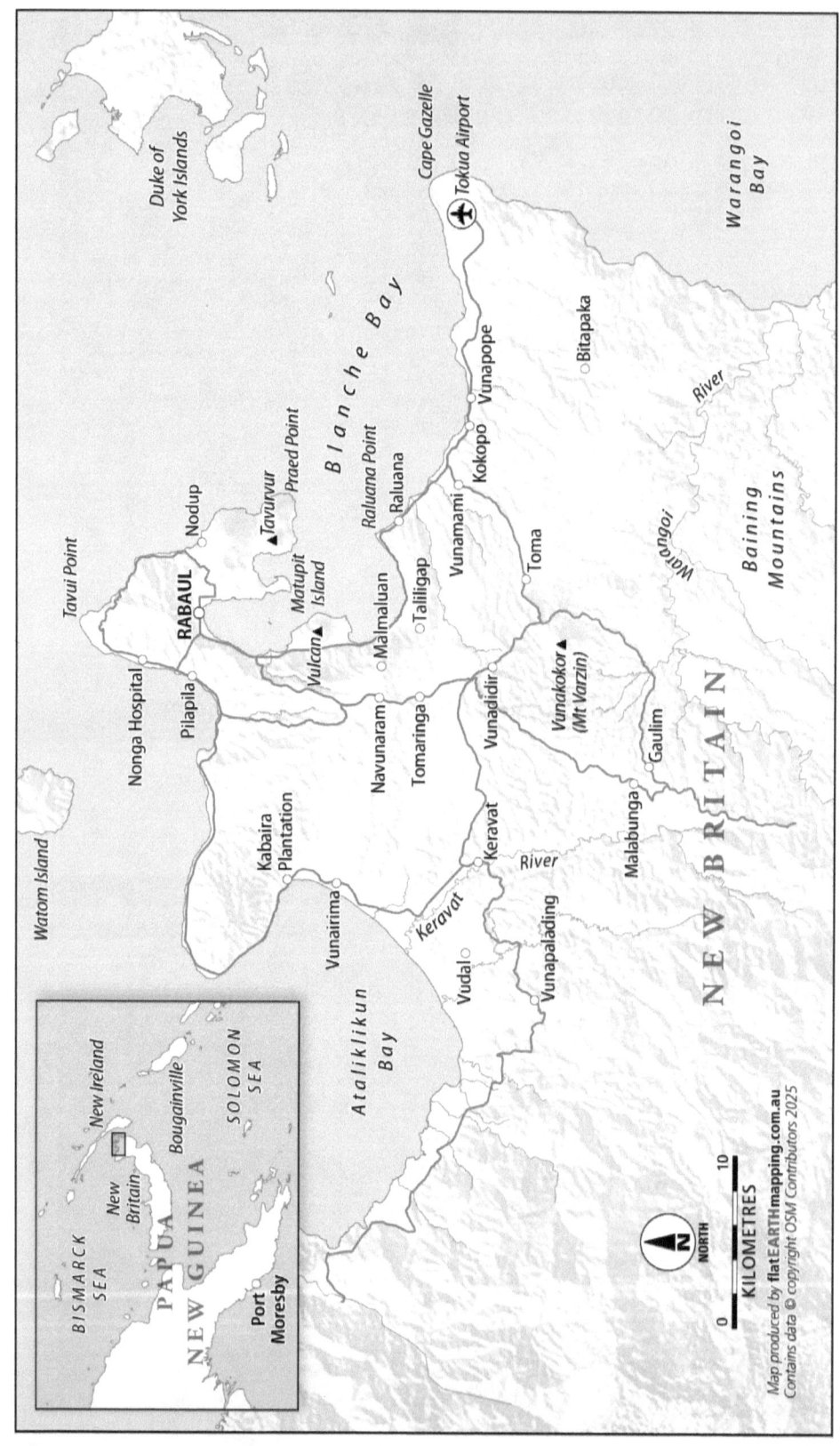

Map produced by flatEARTHmapping.com.au
Contains data © copyright OSM Contributors 2025

KILOMETRES

NORTH

0   10

PROLOGUE

Lester Chettle's family home, one of a row of Victorian-era workers' cottages on a ridge in Sydney's Greenwich, overlooked a bay and the oil refinery tanks at which oil tankers docked.

His parents, Charles Chettle and Kitty Kettle, were born and married in London. Charles, a functionary in the civil service, was soon posted to the British Customs Service in Hong Kong. Five years later, in December 1941, the Japanese invaded the British colony.

Kitty and many others were evacuated to Australia well before the invasion. Charles spent more than three years in a Japanese internment camp for civilians on Hong Kong island. Internees had to fend for themselves and scrounge for food.

Kitty, pregnant with Lester when she landed in Sydney in late 1940, had no friends, no relatives and no home. She had enough money to rent a small apartment, found work as a seamstress and was looked after by her church community. She brought up Lester alone.

Lester was nearly six when Charles arrived in Sydney. Cadaverously underweight and in poor health, his only thought was to return to Hong Kong, but the post-war civil service in Hong

Kong rejected him. He found work with a shipping agency in Sydney.

Given that Greenwich conjured up the London borough famous for its maritime history, and with harbour views from the ridge, Charles, unsurprisingly, determined to settle there. He bought the cottage when he still had a job.

After leaving the agency he moved into the loft and converted it into an office, with prints of sailing ships and photos of merchant vessels on the walls. Most days, he visited nearby vantage points, logging the movement of ships, even barges and ferries, in the harbour or the Parramatta River beyond. This pastime became an obsession.

This was the father Lester remembered, a gaunt and angular man, gazing across the water, sombre and silent. Charles Chettle was always like that—with him and yet absent at the same time.

Charles died suddenly when Lester was fourteen. Kitty was left to pay the mortgage and look after Lester, at least until her father, Reg Kettle, arrived from England to help her. Kitty continued work as a seamstress and Reg, a carpenter, found enough casual work to contribute his share. It was a constant struggle to make ends meet, but they sacrificed their comforts for Lester's sake.

Through his primary school years, Lester spent lengthy periods at home recovering from chest infections. During high school his health improved, and he found ways to earn money by running errands and delivering pamphlets. With no father, no siblings, no relatives beyond his grandfather, and few school friends, he spent much time reading, fishing in the harbour and wandering the shore.

A year after his father's death he met a neighbour, Rebecca. They were both fifteen. Rebecca was pale, Gothic in style and ethereal. During their final school years, they shared a passionately chaste relationship. One day she moved away without saying goodbye. A year later he heard she'd fallen ill and died.

Lester was bereft, hearing this news so soon after his father's death. Gradually he withdrew, convinced that life was a succession of unhappy events that could be avoided only by erecting a protective wall against them.

At school, he studied hard and won a scholarship to Sydney University. He had no idea of what to do with his life until a teacher said, 'If you're clever and can't do anything else, do law.'

That hadn't been a long-standing ambition, but after his first year he joined a firm of Sydney solicitors as a law clerk. He earned an honours degree and was made a junior associate on a meagre salary.

He found his work no more stimulating than his life at home. Although pleasant and cooperative at work, he never sought friendships or contacts, and he rarely travelled beyond Sydney.

Nor did Kitty or Reg; they lived their lives in Sydney as a transplanted patch of England.

Lester believed this was to be his life: a slow progression to nowhere in particular. This view was nurtured by reading the works of authors who generally struggled with a bleak assessment of human existence: Patrick White, Russian writers Pushkin, Turgenev, Goncharov, then Sartre and even Nietzsche.

But then he struck up an acquaintance with Patricia Knowles, an accountant with his firm. They had rarely spoken until a harbour jaunt on the launch of a senior partner brought them together one afternoon.

He'd had rare girlfriends from his student days, usually just as bookish and reserved as himself. Patricia—Patsy—was different: nearly four years older, sophisticated and outgoing. She owned an apartment and drove a sleek new sports car. Her gift of appearing to be sincere whenever she spoke meant people wanted to believe her. With lush golden locks, a generous mouth, a willing smile and classical proportions, men found her very attractive.

As their relationship flowered, Lester often wondered how she could be attracted to him, but he was determined to enjoy the relationship while it lasted.

Despite Patsy's humdrum occupation, she loved restaurants, theatres and concerts. They enjoyed each other's company for nearly two years and even talked about living together.

Patsy answered exclusively to partners in a part of the business dealing with investment companies. As their relationship matured, so did his willingness to help her and become a money-maker for the firm. He yearned for a lifestyle to match hers.

He might be named as the company secretary on company documents, or buy newly issued shares, then sell them back to the partners. Though there was nothing particularly unusual or illegal in these activities, money streamed mysteriously into Patsy's bank accounts.

Lester dared not follow the stream to its source. At times, a slip of the tongue by Patsy might raise doubts in his mind, but he wouldn't risk his career by taking on the partners alone when others were silent. He knew he trod a fine line between ignorance and involvement.

It was only a matter of time before officers from the Criminal Investigation Branch raided the law firm, revealing a world of shelf companies, offshore trusts and tax havens. The law practice was shut down amid allegations of insider trading and money laundering.

Early one morning, police came to Patsy's apartment and took her away for questioning about her lavish lifestyle and suspected involvement. Lester, present in her bed and wearing only his boxer shorts and a Rolex wristwatch, was unable to convince the investigators of his innocence. He too was scooped up in the net.

This disaster caught him unprepared, resurrecting his soul-destroying fatalism. His only option was to resign and lie low.

For the next few months, he dressed for work and set off each morning, returning in the evening, pretending to Kitty and his grandfather that he'd been at work. He spent most of his time in libraries, an honours graduate still studying law, hoping for a miracle to resurrect his career. Meanwhile, Patsy was charged with being an accessory to the partners' criminal activities. A jail sentence was inevitable.

The miracle came eventually in the form of a postcard from a law school acquaintance. A glossy photo of white sands and sapphire-blue sea fringed by coconut palms. On the reverse side it bore a stamp from the Territory of Papua and New Guinea and the following:

> *Come up to Port Moresby and join the Department of Law. Get ten years' prosecution experience in two. Murder trials on your first day in court. Good pay, cheap living. This is the view from my office window.*

When Lester arrived a month later in Port Moresby, his friend had already left it behind.

And the view from the office windows was of shanty settlements climbing Port Moresby's dry and scrubby hills.

PART 1

Rabaul 1969

1

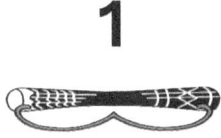

As the aircraft door opened, searing midday heat forced its way on board. Lester Chettle hesitated, daunted, reluctant to leave the cabin's airconditioned comfort.

On the walk to the terminal the tarmac was soft under his feet, a veneer of melting liquorice. Sweat was already dampening his shirt. Nose-twitching, throat-tickling sulphur fumes caused him to glance beyond the airport at a small volcanic cone emitting puffs of gaseous steam from vents on one bare, grey flank. All around was a succession of cone-shaped hills, densely green, circling a shimmering blue harbour.

This, at least, was the extraordinary vista he'd been promised, far removed from the dusty, down-at-heel suburbs of Port Moresby. When he was posted to Rabaul as an assistant crown prosecutor, someone in the Department of Law had warned that the town was a Finnish sauna by day or night, but no glossy tourist photograph could reproduce the sweltering heat.

It was too late to turn back. He'd volunteered—no, begged—for the transfer.

He retrieved his luggage and guitar case. The terminal building emptied. He looked outside, half-hoping someone might meet him. No bus to town and no taxi in sight—only PMVs, utility trucks known as passenger-carrying motor vehicles, but the drivers ignored him.

'Mr Lester? A message for you.'

A slight, wiry New Guinean in shorts, long white socks and a white shirt had materialised silently beside Lester and handed him a note.

> Gabriel will take you to the Ascot Hotel. See you at the office tomorrow. Flanagan.

'I'm Gabriel Toporo,' the man said. He picked up Lester's bulging suitcase, gauged its weight, put it down, picked up the guitar case instead and turned to the exit. 'I have a truck outside. Please come.'

Lester squeezed into the cabin of a PMV alongside Gabriel and an elderly man in a laplap and faded T-shirt. The man grinned, his lips and teeth stained a vivid shade of red. He was chewing buai, or betel nut.

'My uncle,' Gabriel said. 'He's a councillor.'

'They'll spit betel juice all over you,' Kolchev had warned. Kolchev, a Russian émigré, had occupied the room next to Lester in a government hostel. He'd worked in Rabaul for six months with the Public Works Department.

Lester's knowledge of the Tolai people of East New Britain had been gleaned entirely from Kolchev in the week between hearing of his posting and landing in Rabaul.

The Tolais were Melanesians like most of the population, better educated than most, numerous, settled in their villages, Christianised, proud and aggressive. They'd come from New Ireland, ruthlessly displacing the Baining people, the former inhabitants, and settling in an area known as the Gazelle Peninsula.

They chewed betel nut which, when mixed with leaves of the betel or *daka* plant and lime, was a mild stimulant and produced bright red spittle. Kolchev didn't like the Tolais. Then again, he didn't seem to like anyone.

No sooner had Gabriel driven onto the main road to town than he turned the vehicle onto a side track that led to a causeway and a small island jutting into the harbour. The island was a fringe-suburban outpost, closely settled in haphazard fashion with simple tin and fibro homes among sparse palms. The volcano loomed nearby.

'Is the hotel here?' Lester asked, alarmed.

'This is Matupit, my place,' Gabriel said.

Coming to an open village square, Gabriel stopped to pick up waiting passengers, collecting fares through the cabin window. 'They're going to the *bung*,' he said.

'The *bung*?'

'The market. It's near the hotel.'

They drove into the town and along a wide main street lined with modest, modern buildings, shops and offices, all disappointingly utilitarian, without the elegant colonial buildings or homes with broad eaves and ornate, railed verandahs he'd seen in Queensland and imagined he'd see in Rabaul.

The passengers alighted at a bustling marketplace, a cornucopia of fresh fruit and vegetables. Gabriel's uncle climbed out, grinned again at Lester, spat a mouthful of red liquid onto the pavement and disappeared into the throng.

Gabriel dropped Lester off at the Ascot Hotel. He was shown to a room with an air-conditioner that clattered like worn tappets in an old car engine. He unpacked the work clothes that his letter of appointment had mandated for work in the tropics: two pairs of dress shorts, two pairs of knee-length white socks and two white short-sleeved shirts.

For court appearances, the instructions added a long-sleeved white shirt, a barrister's collar bands, dark trousers and black patent leather shoes. Antimalarial tablets and a mosquito net stayed in his suitcase.

He downed two whiskies with ice at the deserted bar, showered away the day's sweat and slid gratefully under the sheet. Rabaul's humid heat would take some getting used to.

'Welcome to the branch office.'

John Flanagan, the Senior Crown Prosecutor for the New Guinea Islands region, in charge of the only outpost of the Department of Law, rose from his desk to shake Lester's hand.

In Port Moresby, Lester learnt of his mission in Rabaul: to relieve Flanagan of appearing in run-of-the-mill Supreme Court criminal cases on the New Guinea Islands Circuit.

The second-floor office in the two-storey Australian Administration building resembled a campaign room. Maps and admiralty charts adorned the walls. On a large colour map, Flanagan's finger traced the Supreme Court Circuit route, jabbing at fragments of green in a vast blue expanse of Pacific Ocean. New Britain, Manus Island, New Ireland, New Hanover and the Admiralty Islands: romantic names that Lester had heard about, a string of islands along the Bismarck Archipelago. The fraying edges of a colonial empire.

'The New Guinea Islands Circuit will be your main responsibility,' Flanagan said. 'Depending on the cases to be tried, you might be away for two weeks at a time. Oh, here's your office.'

Lester was guided into a room half-partitioned with glass, no outside view and barely able to hold a desk, a cupboard and two chairs. He sat down, placed his briefcase on the desk and surveyed the prosecutors' domain.

Between Flanagan's office and his own was a woman typing at a desk.

'Gloria Chan,' was Flanagan's offhand introduction.

Gloria, honey-skinned, sloe-eyed with straight black hair in a bun, smiled thinly at Lester then looked away.

By the main door at another desk sat Gabriel, brow furrowed, studying a newspaper photograph.

Lining one wall were metal filing cabinets and a collection of legal textbooks and law reports. Further afield were wide windows that looked out on a carpark, adjoining streets and jungled hills rearing up behind the town. Air-conditioning purred softly through the building.

Sometime later, Flanagan sat down in the spare chair and dropped an armful of manila folders on Lester's desk.

'Settling in? Sorry I left you to find your way. I've been talking to the Secretary for Law on the phone.'

'I'll be happy here,' Lester said. 'It's air-conditioned.'

'Had much prosecuting experience? I heard you were a solicitor in Sydney, so you're not from Queensland. That's a pity; we apply the Queensland Criminal Code in New Guinea.'

'I'm afraid my firm's practice was largely commercial. I've been reading up on the Code. It's basically the common law, so it's not a foreign language.'

'It's a foreign language to the locals.' Flanagan paused and looked at him carefully. 'I've read your file. You're twenty-eight and still single. I hope you'll prove less trouble than the last fellow they sent me.'

Flanagan slid the folders across the desk. 'These are for you. On top are indictments for Manus Island, that's all for this month. The judge is coming next week. I've arranged a six-seater aircraft, an Aztec twin-engine, for the court party. Let's see how you go.'

In Port Moresby, Lester had heard rumours about Flanagan, a former Queensland policeman who'd studied law while in the force. A competent, hard-edged prosecutor who enjoyed a drink. He owned a yacht and mercilessly bullied anyone who dared sail with him. On no account should Lester agree to crew. The description melded well with Flanagan's solid build and florid appearance. An open-neck shirt revealed a nest of ginger hair. A pugnacious type, Lester thought, with little time for niceties.

He wondered what had happened to the last occupant of his office. No trace of him remained. After Flanagan left the office, he asked Gloria. She looked down at her hands and said she didn't know.

Over the following days, Lester awoke with the sunrise and walked the town streets around the foreshore. In the windless cool of early morning the harbour was mirror-smooth, reflecting the sky. The Beehives, two conical ash cones, a remnant of ancient eruptions, rose from its centre like crumbling pyramids. At the far end of town were the wharves, shipyards and warehouses of the coastal trade.

He bought a booklet on the history of Rabaul and read it at night in his hotel room. The town, he learnt, was born as the administrative centre of the German colony of New Guinea in the late nineteenth century. After the defeat of Germany in the First World War, the colony became a Mandated Trust Territory under Australia's control. One legacy of German rule and passion for order was the grid of broad, straight streets with colonnades of giant rain trees, mango trees and casuarinas backing onto hillsides behind.

Were it not for the magnificent harbour around which the town was built, it could have been, like a score of other towns on Pacific Islands, a somnolent backwater lazing under the tropic sun. Instead, it became a bustling trading hub, a port for coastal shipping and the export of tropical products.

As the townsfolk of Rabaul asserted, it was the only town in the world built in the crater of a volcano. That was both its blessing and its curse. As in history and opera, beauty and tragedy were bestowed in equal measure.

Simpson Harbour, a safe and deep anchorage, was a massive volcanic crater formed more than 1,000 years before by the collapse of adjoining volcanoes and breached by the sea. The township grew up in a bowl formed by the crater walls that were themselves the cones of smaller and dormant volcanoes, now steep and forested hills. Europeans named them as the Mother, North Daughter and South Daughter, respectively.

Two less-quiescent volcanoes were nearby. Tavurvur, beside the airport, was one. On the harbour's far side was the other, the smooth mound of Vulcan. Both erupted together in 1937, not long before the Pacific War. Volcanic ash buried the town and many of the surrounding villages, killing hundreds. There was much talk afterwards of moving the town, but while the talk went on, buildings were rebuilt and the war came.

The town was thus at the mercy of earthquakes and volcanic activity all around. Every so often, eruptions of steam from Tavurvur and minor earth tremors, known locally as *gurias*, reminded locals of how precarious their tenure was.

According to the booklet, the town's heyday had been in the 1920s and 1930s, before the volcanic eruption of 1937, and before it was occupied by Japanese forces and destroyed again by American bombing in the Pacific War. Pre-war photographs showed gracious buildings and rambling gardens; the Coconut Tearooms, the New Guinea Club and the Regent Theatre. Snapshots of the colonial establishment stiffly posed: men in colonial whites, women in elegant long dresses, no doubt perspiring in the heat. Though its glory days were gone, its incomparable setting remained.

At the office, Lester was left to read the bundle of files he'd been given: committal papers for the trial of crimes in the Supreme Court. They came from the resident magistrates in Rabaul as well as part-time magistrates, often administration field officers known as *kiaps*, in smaller island centres.

He read the indictments, the formal charges prepared and signed by Flanagan for presentation to the court. Sometimes there seemed little to connect the charges to the flimsy records of evidence in the files.

Flanagan was preoccupied with strategy meetings. Police and admin officers came and went throughout the day. Apparently, matters of great urgency and consequence were being debated in Flanagan's office in an aura of secrecy. They had to do with recent political developments in the Gazelle Peninsula. Flanagan refused to explain them.

Gabriel spent much of his time running errands. Gloria spent hers battling with an old typewriter, either furiously typing on it, cleaning it or remonstrating with it in an unintelligible tongue and untangling jammed keys. She paid no attention to the occupant of the little walled-off office space beside her.

Lester wrote to Kitty in Sydney.

I can't tell you how happy I am to be in Rabaul, rather than Port Moresby. Tonight, a deluge is drumming on the hotel roof, washing over gutters and sluicing down massive culverts along the streets. Outside the air is cool and smells of jungle and flowering frangipani. This is the real South Pacific.

Tomorrow, I fly to the farthest reaches of the Bismarck Sea, my first ever flight in a light plane. They told me in Port Moresby that crown prosecutors on circuit have a shorter lifespan than fighter pilots in the Battle of Britain. Luckily, this flight is over the sea all the way, and we'll have life jackets. I can't wait.

2

'This is my story,' said the defendant, Porman Palas. As a village elder who knew the value of solemn and measured oratory, he paused to look gravely about him. 'We were all together that night in my house. That is how it began.'

Arthur Prest, a judge of the Supreme Court, sighed. A case of incest was particularly troublesome in a place where records and relationships were so often nebulous. He removed his horsehair wig, the symbol of his authority, his talisman, his magic, a chain of office, and placed it before him on the bench. It lay crumpled like a small dead animal, yellow with age. He dabbed at his forehead with a handkerchief and scratched irritably at his balding pate. His face was warming to the morning's work. By day's end, his complexion would match his scarlet robes.

The courthouse in Lorengau, the largest settlement on Manus Island, was a Quonset hut, a long half-barrel of corrugated iron already baking in the mid-morning sun. From a distance the structure seemed a silvery shimmer, uncertain of its form.

Lester sat at the prosecutor's table. Beneath his black gown and white, long-sleeved shirt, beads of sweat followed a trail over his chest and down to his waist like wandering ants. There were no fans in the courtroom and not a breath of wind outside. He fingered the cloth bands at his collar. He wanted to take them off, undo his collar button, open his chest to the air. But no, the court's dignity had to be maintained.

Torpor had settled over the room. A police constable slumped in a chair, fast asleep. At a table in front of the judge's raised bench sat the judge's Associate, Mr Broad, a pensioned Englishman, his head bowed and his long, sombre face hidden. Sitting next to him was the interpreter, a young teacher at the local school, self-conscious in a short European-style skirt and nervously clutching at her exposed knees.

While the judge and counsel conversed in English, the witnesses and the defendant spoke Melanesian Pidgin. At another table sat the defence lawyer, Evans, a Welshman assigned to this remote court Circuit by the Public Solicitor in Port Moresby after drawing the short straw. A black folder propped up before him concealed an open paperback from the judge's gaze.

On benches behind the lawyers sat a cluster of villagers, most of them related to Palas or to the witnesses, and behind them a District Officer, the local *kiap* representing the administration, together with a few other Europeans, likely to be residents drawn by curiosity or idleness.

Porman Palas surveyed the audience with satisfaction. This was his trial, his day in court.

'I will tell you what happened.' He stopped to look around, to draw attention. 'My daughter Napipi was sleeping on the verandah with her friend Nari. It began to rain. They came under the big mosquito net inside, next to me and my wife and the little boy. I was next to my wife. Those girls were next to her.

'My wife went outside to pass water. She came back and lay down on the other side. I was next to that girl, Nari. Later, I thought I would like to have intercourse with that girl. Then I heard her go out, too, to pass water. At least I thought it was her, but perhaps it was my daughter. These women kept getting up and coming back and changing places.

'My boy went out and came back. Then I got up, went out and came back. The kerosene lamp went out and it was dark and raining. I was asleep. I felt a woman next to me. At first, I thought it was my wife. I wanted her. She didn't speak. She didn't turn around. I was dreaming, I didn't wake up.'

'So, you thought you were having intercourse with your wife?' Evans asked, now alert, placing a bookmark in his novel.

'No.' Palas shook his head. 'A young woman is different from an old one.'

Muttering from the onlookers on the wooden benches. The police orderly woke up and turned to berate them. The interpreter, who had become increasingly distressed during the course of the case, murmured her translation.

'What was that?' the judge boomed at her. Although Palas spoke in Pidgin, the judge perfectly understood. 'Something about young women?'

The interpreter began to cry. Lester and Evans exchanged glances; Judge Prest was inclined to harass interpreters.

'So, you knew it was your daughter?'

'No, I thought it was Nari, her friend.'

'Yes, he had sex with me,' a young woman called from the benches before she could be hushed.

'An honest mistake, your Honour,' Evans said to the judge. 'That would be a defence.' He thumbed through a worn edition of the Queensland Criminal Code, the circuit lawyers' bible, looking for a precedent.

Lester shuffled again through the witness statements. No mention of Nari, the friend. The police hadn't bothered to inquire about how many bodies may have lain under the mosquito net, nor about their comings and goings.

'My Code, Mr Broad.' The judge leaned forward. The bowed head of Mr Broad didn't move. The judge picked up a heavy book and dropped it onto the table in front of his Associate. Broad grunted awake and stared wildly about the courtroom. He fumbled among the books and papers on his desk.

Judge Prest studied the law.

'The other girl looks underage to me, too,' he mused. 'Does it make any difference? The defendant didn't commit one crime because he thought he was committing another?'

'He wasn't charged with that one,' Evans said.

'And too late to do it now,' the judge sighed, acquitting the defendant of the charge of incest.

Porman Palas rode his bicycle back to the village. The residents were bemused. After months awaiting the trial, the affair would have to be settled in the village after all. Before leaving, Palas walked over to Lester and, from a ragged shoulder bag, produced a document—a blue certificate with a coat of arms and the court's seal upon it, mounted in a carved wooden frame—apparently a trophy from an earlier trial.

It read:

Be it remembered that Porman Palas came to the Supreme Court of Papua New Guinea and acknowledged to owe Our Lady the Queen the sum of $10; to the use of Our Said Lady the Queen, Her Heirs and Successors; upon condition that if the said Porman Palas shall keep the peace and be of good behaviour for the term of three years from the date hereof then this recognizance shall be void....

Palas smiled proudly. 'The last judge to come here gave this to me. It is a letter from *Missis Kwin*. It says that I am a good man, a man of peace.'

Before coming to Manus, Lester had read about the anthropologist Margaret Mead. The village where she'd lived and theorised about nature and nurture was close by, only an hour by outboard-powered canoe through a maze of reefs and islets. What would she have made of the shambles of his first criminal case?

The *kiaps* had a ready explanation. The wife had made the complaint of incest in revenge for her husband's dalliance with her daughter's friend. The villagers had been incensed, not only because Palas walked free, but because the interpreter spoke out on matters of intimacy when she, as an unrelated, unmarried woman, was forbidden by custom to do so.

Village confidences should not be broadcast to a wider world. That is what angered people about Margaret Mead.

With time to spare, Lester strolled around the little settlement of Lorengau, through a shady grove of rain trees, past a line of sailing canoes drawn up on the beach near the jetty and the market, and past the row of rusting Quonset huts used by the Public Works Department. Along the foreshore of grand Seeadler Harbour were twisted, tortured strands of steel, red brown with rust. Parts of trucks and engines. Tank turrets, protruding from the sand like the trunkless legs of Ozymandias in the desert.

The American army juggernaut swept through the Admiralty Islands in 1944, filling the broad reaches of the harbour with ships. It annihilated the modest Japanese occupying force, flattened the land, built a temporary city for hundreds of thousands of men, nourished them on hills of ice cream and lakes of Coca Cola, and reached out to retake the Philippines. Then it bulldozed the lot into the sea and departed as abruptly as it had appeared.

Lester was shown photographs at the Europeans' club: lines of jeeps and tanks, the harbour teeming with landing barges, Japanese bodies beside the road bloated and tight-skinned like barbecued sausages. It was the way the war was fought, said the old ones who remembered and who'd been there ever since. Now, there was only the soft pulse of the ocean, washing at Lester's feet in the still, pink evening, licking patiently at the remaining, stubborn scars.

Next day the court entourage set off for the airport, a bone-jarring ride in the District Officer's truck. The judge shared the cabin with the driver. The others shared the open back with the judge's suitcase packed with robes, legal tomes and court records. The road hugged the winding coastline, squeezed between a rainforest and a breezy sea. Waves dashed against the shore, soaking the hapless passengers. The jungle smell was strong and moist ahead of an advancing rainstorm.

A police wagon came speeding to the airport less than twenty minutes before the weekly Fokker Friendship flight from the New Guinea mainland was due. The police brought a man who'd flouted the law while on a good behaviour bond and was to be sentenced to jail. It would be many months before a judge would come again.

The chartered Aztec for the judge's return to Rabaul had not yet arrived. A makeshift court was set up in a *haus wind*, an open-sided waiting area with thatched roof and bare concrete floor, across from the airport buildings. The judge claimed to have seen papers, years before, declaring it a court for just such an occasion, a flying judicial visit. He changed into his robes in the airport's toilet block.

Lester stood at a desk carried over from the airport manager's office, reading rapidly through the police papers. The prisoner looked hopefully at the sky. One never knew with Europeans; he might yet get to fly in one of those sleek, white aircraft. From overhead, suddenly, came the whine of the plane's turbine engines.

'For God's sake, hurry up!' Judge Prest bellowed at Lester. 'We mustn't be seen out here in a shed!'

The man was sentenced and bundled back into the wagon as the Fokker taxied to the terminal. The judge lifted his robes and, prancing on crane-thin legs, fled across the grassy apron heading for the toilet block to change his clothes.

Lester peered down from the Aztec's side windows as it gained height over the Bismarck Sea. The Admiralty Islands, of which Manus was the largest, were now a straggle of freckles on the earth's blue cheek.

Below was a faint white thread, the wake of a government trawler. Evans was on that boat, Lester knew. It was the way he travelled if he could get away with it. A deckchair placed under an awning at the stern where he could put his feet up on the stern rail. A good book and a packed coolbox of South Pacific lager, enough for the two-day journey to the mainland.

Strung out behind, a lure of chicken feathers for wandering skipjack tuna danced in the wake. Every so often a flash of silver. A wriggling skipjack would be hauled in, cooked and eaten on the spot with rice from the hot stove. No meal, Evans avowed, could taste better.

Mr Broad was at the plane's rear, head slumped, eyes closed, his hands shaking. According to Evans, he was recovering from a mild heart attack. It had happened during the last court Circuit on the mainland.

A scientific research vessel had collided with a pilot whale in the waters off the town of Madang. The dying mother whale had a young calf by her side. The scientists caught the baby and put it overnight in the hotel's saltwater swimming pool. Mr Broad, a guest at the hotel, fancied a midnight swim after finishing his daily ration of whisky. As he slid gratefully into the cool, dark water the snub-nosed, curious calf had surfaced beside him. This was the story as Evans, the Welshman with the voice of Dylan Thomas, told it. Lester was unconvinced.

Beside the Australian pilot, Judge Prest stared rigidly ahead, a poor passenger. In this land of jagged limestone ridges and towering, thundering banks of cloud, small planes were terrifyingly puny and fragile. Sinews on the judge's neck stood out like fencing wire. The young pilot beside him had a Disney comic propped up on the control stick as he chewed an apple.

A judge worn down by travail, a decrepit English Associate, a Welshman whose heart had never left the soft, green valleys of home. What were they all doing here? Lester gazed from the window at passing clouds. Were they no more than performers in a travelling sideshow? They had come to a remote speck in the Pacific, played their parts to an uncomprehending audience, then vanished, just as the American soldiers had done.

Ahead, inching over the horizon into a low haze were grey-green pimples, volcanic cones, the sentinels of Rabaul.

3

Gabriel was at the airport on Lester's return. A car and driver awaited the judge and his Associate. In the balmier air of Namanula Hill, a high ridge above the steamy town centre, were superior houses for senior administration officials. One house was set aside for visiting judges. Judge Prest had telephoned ahead to reserve it for a day or two's rest before flying on to Port Moresby. Though rarely occupied, it was Flanagan's duty, or rather Gloria's, to see it was kept spotless by a resident servant and cook.

But no such treatment for Lester. In the back of Gabriel's truck were Lester's luggage and guitar from the Ascot Hotel.

'What's going on?' he asked.

'Mr Flanagan says the hotel is too much money.' Gabriel gave an odd, embarrassed giggle. 'I'm taking you to a cheaper place.'

This turned out to be a compound for unmarried European men. Lester was shown a toilet block, a cafeteria that doubled as a common room, and a row of dilapidated, hut-like, wooden buildings, colloquially known as dongas, bordering a grassy area the size of a tennis court.

'This palace is yours,' the compound manager said, pointing. 'I'll come round later to fix the door so that it closes. Most of the blokes here are from Civil Aviation or Works, paper-shufflers or mechanics. How about you? A lady called Gloria booked you in. She said you were a lawyer from Port Moresby.'

'That's right.'

'We've got four lawyers in Rabaul already. That's four too many. You're the first lawyer to stay here. The others aren't so hard up.'

Lester brought his belongings inside and looked around at shuttered windows, an iron-framed bed, plastic furniture, a sink, a bench-top stove with one rusty plate, a ceiling fan and a carpet reeking of stale beer, heavily stained and patterned in a violent clash of colours.

That evening in the cafeteria, a blowsy manageress from Brisbane served burnt chops and coleslaw followed by a dessert of cold custard and fruit sludge.

She seemed anxious to please. 'Was the meal all right?'

'Delicious,' Lester said.

The three other diners ate silently and alone. The manageress waved her hand around the cafeteria.

'Have you met the others yet?' She pointed to a thickset, elderly man with the large, gnarled hands of a farmer. 'That's George. He's with the Works Department. He's a foreigner. Over there, that fellow with the funny face is Milo. He's a foreigner too, and he's with Posts and Telegraphs. The two of them get up to mischief together. They fight and then they're friends again. Been here for years. The one down the end, he's a young bloke, a clerk somewhere. He keeps himself to himself.'

As she spoke, the three men rose and left without a word, a look or a smile between them.

'That's all your lodgers?' Lester asked with some disappointment.

'There's a Chinaman, too. He runs a trade store. He's called Fong. He doesn't eat with us. He cooks his own food: rice and such and dried fish. His donga stinks to high heaven.'

Back in his own donga, Lester switched on the fluorescent tube light and sat down heavily on the bed. The donga had gluttonously absorbed the day's heat so was like an oven. He turned on the overhead fan. It whirred, sputtered and stopped, emitting a sharp, burnt wiring smell.

He took a pillow under his arm and towed the mattress and a sheet behind him onto the grass outside. He lay down and looked up at the clear night sky. The faintest of night breezes bore the sweet fragrance of frangipani and an aroma of dried coconut from the rambling sheds of the Coconut Products factory down by the main wharf.

The door to the donga beside his own creaked open. A pale Chinese face was caught briefly in the moonlight before the door swiftly closed. It opened again as Lester watched. Fong's wafer-thin figure, clad in the loose black clothes of an old-time coolie, shuffled out past him, not pausing to look. Pattering, slippered feet sped towards the darkened toilet block.

He didn't see Fong scuttling back to his donga. As he was about to doze off on the grass, he heard an annoying sound nearby. Like the fabled king in his counting house, Fong was adding up the takings from his store. Night after night, for as long as Lester stayed there, he suffered the maddening click-clack of Fong's abacus.

'Comfortable at the compound?'

Flanagan sat down heavily in Lester's office. His presence in the small space was overbearing.

'Couldn't be better,' Lester said.

'Did you expect a welcome from the mayor and a brass band? A house with a harbour view on the hill? There's a hierarchy in this town, and you're right at the bottom.'

Flanagan had more case files for him, this time for Rabaul. A judge would arrive from Port Moresby in two weeks. There was a large detachment of experienced European police officers in Rabaul, Flanagan said. Crimes were thoroughly investigated, and the evidence carefully assembled. It was different on the outstations, where exhibits to be presented in court often disappeared before a trial was held, many months after a crime was committed.

'You might even get a conviction this time,' Flanagan said with a brief, sardonic smile. 'Get runs on the board.'

'I need to learn Pidgin,' Lester said.

'Start at the market. Take Gabriel if he's free.'

He studied Flanagan's Pidgin-English dictionary at night in the donga, a trade-store fan on the table whirring beside him. He turned first to the language of the *bung*, so he could buy and cook his own meals on the donga's stove.

Under open-sided sheds the sellers, predominantly Tolai women, displayed their wares on banana leaf matting. It was a colourful, vibrant and noisy gathering place for gossip. They spoke the local Kuanua language, mellifluous and vowel-rich, but Pidgin or *Tok Pisin*, the *lingua franca* of New Guinea, was understood by all.

He spent hours at the market in those first weeks, mingling with the villagers. Gabriel, when he came, seemed to know everyone, introducing him to relatives and acquaintances alike as *loia bilong gavman*, a description received with a knowing nod and little enthusiasm.

He learnt most Tolais came to town only when necessary to sell their produce or handcrafts. The name *Rabaul* was a Kuanua word meaning place of the mangroves, with obvious connotations of mosquitoes and illhealth. The town area had never been favoured by the Tolai as a place to settle permanently.

He bought a small wooden carving of a leaping dolphin for his office desk. Along the main shopping strip on Mango Avenue he bought cooking implements, a coolbox, toaster, kettle and the groceries he needed to avoid eating in the cafeteria again.

When at night he could absorb no more of the donga's heat and the strange and often amusing logic of Pidgin—*wilwil* for bicycle, *bagarap pinis* for broken beyond repair—he would sit outside on the step and softly strum his guitar.

From a nearby donga came classical music played loudly on a gramophone, and often sounds of George and Milo arguing or fighting. They'd both arrived in Australia from central Europe as refugees and drifted northwards until they could go no further. To Lester, they were fine examples of the human flotsam that ended up in the administration's compound for unmarried men.

Police Inspector Macleod rang about a file on Lester's desk. Coolidge, a planter and member of the New Guinea Club, had thrown an empty glass at a waiter. Later, at the hospital, a dozen stitches were sewn into the waiter's cheek. A case of assault for the magistrate's court.

'We don't want to prosecute,' Macleod said. 'Coolidge says it was an accident. We'll run the file past John Flanagan, just to confirm we can close it.'

A hint of arrogance in the crisp, clipped accent. The product of a recent recruitment drive to secure white police officers from South Africa for the local police force. Their reputation in apartheid South Africa preceded them.

'John's in Port Moresby. I'll look after it. Do you believe Coolidge's version?'

'No, but there was provocation. The *boi* was insolent and refused to serve him.'

There was a statement on file from Anthony Cherry-Apsley, a doctor at the Nonga Base Hospital beyond the town. Lester rang the hospital. Eventually, a cultured English voice answered the phone.

'I was actually in the club when it happened. A great white *bwana* shouted at the waiter and hurled his glass. It hit the waiter on his cheekbone. Blood and glass were everywhere. I drove the waiter to the hospital. Distressing, really.'

'Why didn't you say that in your statement?'

'I was told there were enough witnesses already. I told them about the treatment, that's all.'

'Would you be happy to make another statement?'

'If you really want me to. I'm terribly busy, you know. But I would like to see justice done.'

Macleod rang again the next day, sounding peeved. 'I've just been talking to Cherry-Apsley. So, you're pressing on with this?'

'Yes. Why didn't you get his account of it before?'

'I was told he didn't see it. The police weren't called to the club; the hospital reported it.' There was a pause. 'My chief says you're new to the job. He says leave it until Flanagan gets back.'

'John's away for two weeks. I'll prosecute the case myself. Try and get a date for the court next week.'

The Rabaul Yacht Club had a certain ambience: European maleness, tarnished trophies, fading honour boards, cigarette smoke and the smell of beer. Lester was signed in by Macleod, then, unsurprisingly, ignored. He knew no one among the groups at the bar. He took his drink to a table in the garden where he could see the harbour. Gusts of male laughter wafted from the interior.

A dozen yachts lay at anchor off the Yacht Club jetty's end, among them grand visitors on their way around the world, decks cluttered with extra spars and ropes, wind gauges and self-steering vanes. Over the next few months more yachts would come from Tahiti, Samoa or Fiji, helped along by the southeast trade winds that blew from May to October.

In Rabaul they rested, waiting for the monsoon weather that would take them on towards the coast of Africa. Lester imagined the restlessness in these beautiful craft tugging gently at their anchor chains.

'All alone and palely loitering?'

A middle-aged man in a rumpled, collarless shirt of Indian cotton stood at Lester's table. The shirt strained against the bulge of his stomach. A red bandana hung loosely around his neck.

'We're the only two out here, so we may as well talk to each other. I'm Darryl Cleary. Two 'R's as in Sir Darryl Lindsay the artist.'

'Lester Chettle.' Lester stretched out his hand. The hand that took his was soft and smelled faintly of turpentine. 'You're a painter?'

'Not a painter—an artist.' Cleary made a face from his rubbery features. 'Lester Chettle—what a wonderful name you have. There's a ring to it, an ancient lineage perhaps. It's a pity you're a lawyer. I can tell any man by the way he dresses. What I see is thoroughly bland, not a hint of extravagance. Isn't it terrible? We can't disguise our true selves, however hard we try. You've been driven out of the bear pit, too. I sense a kindred spirit.'

'I've just arrived. I don't know many people.'

'I've been here a long time and know too many. That's why we're in limbo together.'

Cleary set his beer glass on the table, brought up a chair and sat down.

'I'm teaching, by the way, at Nodup over the hill. I've been there for years. My ex-students are everywhere. The men wear a hibiscus flower behind the left ear; you must have seen them.'

'You're right. I'm a lawyer, a prosecutor for the administration. Someone must've told you.'

'They did. So you've come to bolster the forces of law and order? A last, desperate gamble by the *ancien régime*. The wheels are falling off, so they've sent for reinforcements.' Cleary raised his glass. 'Welcome to the death throes of colonialism.'

'I hear there'll be a demonstration soon at the admin building—something to do with a new Tolai resistance movement. It seems they don't want us here."

'You mean the Mataungans? They have a point, don't they? We weren't invited in the first place. Nor were the Germans, nor the Japanese. These people have been Christianised, colonised, starved, bombed and told what's good for them for a century. Now they're telling us it's time to go.'

'Just how dangerous is it around here? I've overheard talk...'

'At the bar?' Cleary laughed. 'Oh yes, you'll hear it all in there. Vigilante groups, death lists, women and children to the lifeboats. I live in a village in a cloud of hash. It all goes over my head. Another drink?'

'I'm in the magistrate's court tomorrow. I have to prepare.'

'Aha! That must be about the waiter from the New Guinea Club. It's all around town. You've laid siege to hallowed ground.'

'What else could I do? There was an assault. The laws are no different in a white man's club.'

'Well! That's not what I heard. This town was built on different rules for different races. I suppose clubs are the only places where that still applies. The last refuge of the white rulers. Some people might think you've gone a bit too far.'

'You don't believe that, do you?' Lester smiled and rose to leave.

'Me? I've been stirring the possum for as long as I can remember. You're going? Best of luck with the case. And talking of waiters, isn't the young man behind the bar gorgeous? I think I'm in love.'

The town's courthouse was the Masonic Hall, an old wooden building now owned by a Chinese businessman. Beneath a rusting iron roof, weatherboard walls shed pale green paint like dried skin. Tired awnings drooped on leaning poles. In heavy rain it was impossible to hear the witnesses.

With Chinese practical good sense, it served also as a hall, a Masonic Lodge, a catering establishment and an art gallery. For months after an exhibition, paintings unsold and abandoned by their creators would decorate the courtroom's walls.

As Cleary foretold, the case generated interest. The court-room filled. Some faces he now recognised: the pharmacist, a bank manager, the newsagent, police and admin staff, the resi-dent reporter from the national newspaper.

Nipa, the waiter, had come with moral support, *wantoks* who were friends and relatives from Morobe, his home district on the mainland. They sat at the back, behind seats reserved by long custom for Europeans. Gabriel Toporo led in a small group of Tolais. Lester felt a moment's irritation—why wasn't he look-ing after the office?

Walter Colston, one of Rabaul's two lawyers catering to the business community, turned to Lester beside him at the bar table.

'There's still time to withdraw.' His voice rasped from a trou-bled throat. 'It's my client's word against the waiter's. I know who'll be believed.'

He was wizened and grey-haired, with eyes that were bul-bous, challenging and unblinking. However, Lester had been tutored by police on what to expect from his opponent. Colston was a bluffer who'd shy away from a courtroom fight.

Nipa's evidence, delivered in Pidgin and translated, was plain. Coolidge had been drinking all afternoon. He demanded an imported beer from the coolroom. Nipa refused; no such beer was available. Coolidge, with a face like a bright red pep-per, shouted 'lazy bastard' and threw a glass that broke against Nipa's cheek. He could hardly see for the blood in his eye.

Colston, cross-examining, called Nipa a liar. Nipa had dropped a glass on the floor. In picking up the broken glass, he clumsily cut his face.

This was Lester's cue to call upon Cherry-Apsley. Lester had expected an older man, a reticent witness, but Cherry-Apsley seemed thoroughly at ease and barely older than Lester himself. He was dressed in the tropical kit of an earlier generation of

Englishmen, a white long-sleeved shirt and cream linen trousers. He placed a white Panama hat at a rakish angle on a knob
projecting from the witness box and leaned back in his chair
with languid assurance, then smiled pleasantly at the magistrate, pushing back a lock of fair hair. Lester was immediately
struck by a sharp pang of envy.

Cherry-Apsley, at the club as a guest, had witnessed the
encounter. He answered Lester's questions with no hesitation
or uncertainty in a quiet voice that hushed the courtroom. He'd
driven Nipa to the hospital himself. Coolidge had been drunk
and abusive.

Colston whispered to Coolidge behind him. He rose to
address the magistrate.

'Your worship, Mr Coolidge wishes to change his plea to
guilty.'

Lester's heart leapt. The sweet thrill of victory.

The magistrate looked at Colston. 'Do you want to speak on
your client's behalf?'

Colston straightened slowly, wincing, turning to the public
behind him. It paid well, he'd discovered, to play up his ailing
health. He shook his head sadly, a sign that they were all witness
to a minor tragedy.

'I've known Neville Coolidge for twenty years. He's been a
member of the New Guinea Club for all that time. He came to
New Guinea when people like him were respected. He came to
expect those standards even in these troubled times, if not in
the street, then at least in the sanctuary of his own club. There
are conventions in a club and membership entitles you to some
respect. That's why you pay your dues.'

European heads nodded in agreement. Colston paused,
looked about him, flourished a handkerchief, blew his nose
noisily, apologised and continued.

'Your Worship, my client was under great stress. There are squatters on one of his plantations, and daily confrontations with unruly mobs, that's the only way to describe them. We've all been under stress in this town since the troubles began, since one or two public nuisances we all know about have been stirring up trouble in the villages. They encourage insolence and insubordination.

'You can forgive a man who has spent his career building up his plantations, and this beautiful town, for a momentary lapse, for which my client tells me he is truly sorry. I can say with confidence that Nipa will go back home wearing his scar proudly. For these people a scar is a decoration, a tribute to manliness. No one has suffered.'

Colston's plea was rewarded. His client's fine was a paltry sum with no conviction recorded. The crowd escaped gratefully from the sweltering courtroom. Colston and his client, mates together, left to have lunch with Inspector Macleod and the magistrate at the New Guinea Club.

Lester caught up with Cherry-Apsley as he strode towards a mudspattered utility truck.

'My thanks to you, Doctor.'

Cherry-Apsley smiled as he climbed into the driver's seat.

'My pleasure. A victory—I hope not a pyrrhic one. I have to go. When you need a breath of mountain air come up to Taliligap. I live in a bungalow all alone.'

The sweet taste of victory did not last long for Lester. Resting afterwards in his donga, he read his mother's latest letter again and put it down on the bed beside him.

...I was so proud of you going off to work each morning in a suit and a different tie for every day of the week. I told friends at church that, being a lawyer, you helped those less fortunate by fixing their problems with land- lords and such. I can't imagine what it must be like in Rabaul where I've been told almost everyone has malaria. We never thought you would end up there. I hope it's like a holiday and you can come home soon...

A familiar refrain. Kitty portrayed herself as abandoned. He felt guilty he'd left her in such haste, although this was waning. He still sent all he could afford from his monthly salary, something he'd done since he first started work in Sydney.

The carpet, a pizza square of tomato-paste red and melted mozzarella-yellow, glared in the harsh light. He rubbed his eyes and dabbed away sweat at the base of his neck. The northwest monsoon lingered longer than usual; breezes died away and thundery rain persisted. The nights were still and humid. He paused to listen to noises of the night: a dog scuffling under the hut, the strains of Beethoven's music from Milo's donga, the clicking of Fong's abacus next door. He wished he had earplugs to banish them.

Even given his mother's flair for dramatisation, the letter was upsetting. Loneliness stalked the admin compound. It awaited him in hotel bars and at the office. He hadn't been prepared for the stark cultural adjustment, the racism, the iso- lation. It was a tough, unfeeling little town, far from the world he'd known.

4

Rabaul was awakening to a rising tide of Tolai discontent. In the weeks since Lester's arrival, there had been an undertone of unease. In shops, clubs and homes, rumours were circulating that newly elected members of the House of Assembly in Port Moresby, the forerunner to a national parliament, were less tolerant of what were seen as long-standing injustices over land alienation and the sidelining of traditional village government.

In Port Moresby, colleagues had scoffed at his posting to Rabaul by offering him a hammock in which to laze away his days among the coconut palms. Instead, the local Prosecutor's office had become embroiled in the politics of law and order. Flanagan's working days began early and extended beyond the short, sharp tropical sunsets, and he was now rarely seen at the Yacht Club, an imposition on his free time he loudly lamented. His yacht, swinging idly at anchor, was visited only by seagulls.

A large crowd of Tolai villagers gathered in the carpark outside the admin building. Lester, looking down on the scene, listened to the speakers and read the waving banners. A local politician in sunglasses and a bright Hawaiian shirt harangued the crowd.

Megaphones spat out a staccato torrent of Pidgin. Gabriel, at Lester's shoulder, interpreted when asked, but the message, in English on banners and placards, needed no translation. The Tolais wanted self-government. They wanted foreigners to leave. They wanted the return of land stolen from them. They didn't want Europeans on their local government council. They wouldn't pay their council tax. Roars of approval rattled the office windows. Their sweat and anger mingled in the sun.

The District Commissioner, commonly called the DC, came next, leading his deputies and assistants. They formed a team of *kiaps* in white shirts, shorts and knee-length socks, exuding discipline and solidarity.

The DC's Pidgin was clear and measured, as if he were addressing a school assembly. The administration only wanted to do what was best for the Tolais. What the so-called Mataungan Association wanted was not what most law-abiding people wanted: gradual and orderly development. The administration was there to protect the interests of everyone. He pointed in the direction of the Hawaiian shirt. The administration would not be dictated to by demagogues. He asked the protesters to go home.

He was received in sullen silence. The heat was exhausting the crowd's anger. Placards became sunshades. Bare feet and worn thongs danced a jig on the hot tarmac. The car park had become a giant griddle. Then it was over; the crowd slipped quietly into shady side streets and a nearby park.

Lester turned to Gabriel. 'You're a Tolai, what do you think? Whose side are you on?'

Gabriel shrugged. 'I work in a government office. I can't take sides.'

'If you weren't working here, would you be a Mataungan?'

'Who knows.' Gabriel smiled and walked back to his desk. 'I might be.'

'What about that man in the Hawaiian shirt?' Lester persisted.

Gabriel looked at him unhappily. 'Oscar Tammur? He's in the House of Assembly.' He rolled a finger round his temple. 'Some people say he's mad, he's *longlong*.' He fidgeted in a desk drawer for his keys. 'Mr Lester, my sister is sick at home. Mr Flanagan's not here. Can I go and see her now?'

'That's fine. Please call me Lester.'

Shortly before Lester's arrival in Rabaul, the administration declared that the established Tolai local government council for the Gazelle Peninsula would be elected on a non-racial basis, thus enabling European and Asian participation.

Although the development of multiracial local government throughout the country was an administration policy supported by the House of Assembly, the proclamation of a multiracial council for the Gazelle split the Tolai population into two camps. Those who had traditionally supported the administration favoured the change. Others bitterly opposed it as a colonial plot to preserve European control over Tolai affairs and land.

Urged on by new Assembly members, truckloads of supporters travelled to meetings throughout the Gazelle, whipping up opposition to the multiracial council and calling for a boycott of an imminent election of councillors.

The town of Rabaul, however, which had its own town coun-cil and a majority of non-Tolai councillors, remained in a state of anxious detachment.

Trent, the Works Department clerk, sidled up to Lester in the compound's dining room.

'I'm going finish tomorrow, back to Melbourne. Come to my party tonight. Bring your guitar; I've heard you playing outside your donga. I'll give you a lift.'

Trent picked him up in a new Alfa Romeo GT coupé. It came into the country duty-free, Trent explained. He would ship it to Australia the next day as a secondhand car and make a profit. There were all sorts of import-export lurks if you were smart.

The party was at a neglected plank-wood home on the beachfront, hemmed between Tolai villages. A sagging veran-dah faced the beach.

'I'm Georgina. It's my mother's house,' said a woman in the hallway who watched as Lester looked curiously into musty, gloomy rooms. 'She's lived in Sydney for years. My father had a business in Rabaul. He died and she never got around to selling the place. She comes up sometimes. No one would buy it now. Villagers from along the road say they own the land.'

A portable gramophone in the living room played Simon and Garfunkel. Twenty or more European males were scattered among the rooms, drinking wine or beer. Trent introduced Lester to a few: shop assistants, bank tellers, junior company employees. No one from the administration. The guests were apparently in a social category of their own.

'Aren't you drinking?' Trent pointed to tubs of bottled beer in ice.

Lester hesitated. 'I didn't bring my own.'

'You're not a church worker, are you? The place is overrun with them.'

'No, I'm with the admin. I'm a lawyer, a prosecutor.'

'Got your hands full, then, haven't you?' Trent looked alarmed. 'A prosecutor? I shouldn't be talking to you. You'll dob me in about the car.'

'It's too late to dob you in; you'll be gone tomorrow,' Lester said, walking away.

Outside, the night was windless and rain-laden, without a glimmer of moon or stars. A storm was building out to sea. Georgina, tall, gauche and barefoot, sat down beside him on the verandah, carefully folding the hem end of her long dress around her ankles.

'It's the mosquitoes,' she explained. 'I've heard that ankles have a special scent; mosquitoes can smell them a mile away. I try smothering my ankles in perfume, but still they come.'

On the black beach sand, beyond a fringe of palm trees, someone was vomiting.

'I heard what the others were saying,' Georgina continued. 'I don't know why I have these parties. They're not my friends. Some of them I went to school with, here in Rabaul. There's really nowhere else to party, is there? They'd be thrown out of the hotels. Neighbours would ring the police if this place were in town. The police won't come out here.'

Lester shrugged, listening for a moment to the revellers inside.

'Did you hear about the Tolai protest the other day? It was right outside my office. They don't want a multiracial council. They're going to boycott the election of councillors.'

'It's about a lot more than that. If you're here for a while you'll find out.' Georgina shrugged. 'I'm sick of arguing about it. Trent told me you brought your guitar. Why haven't you played?'

'Someone asked me if I could play like Jimmy Hendrix. I thought that was a bad omen.'

'That's a pity. Do you know *The Water is Wide?* It's a Joan Baez song. I love Joan Baez.'

Georgina began to sing. Her reedy voice slithered off key and back again. She carried on for a verse or two until her memory failed and her voice trailed away. Some guests were leaving noisily. Georgina fell silent, listening.

'I don't like any of them,' she said. 'I'm glad they're going.'

'I can't believe you live here alone,' said Lester.

'This house right on the beach is rare. It's from long ago, before the Australians. Before window bars and locks were needed. The Germans built it. After my father died, my mother lived here with her precious plants and golf twice a week in town. A family from Madang lives out the back and looks after the place—and me. They've been here forever.'

Lester wondered where she worked. Before he could ask, she went on.

'Anyway, I don't stay here for long. I work in Port Moresby at the university. I come here during vacations. I lived here when I was a child, so I feel this is home. What about you? Are you a high school teacher? You look as though you might be.'

'I'm a crown prosecutor. I've just been posted here.'

'Glory me,' Georgina said with a hand pressed to her chest and a look of feigned horror.

Men's voices could be heard on the beach. Several partygoers walked up to the house. One was staggering, very drunk. They stopped on seeing Georgina.

'We found a fishing canoe on the shore,' one said. 'Donny passed out inside, on the floor. We're giving him a Viking send-off.'

'That canoe belongs to someone in the village,' Georgina said crossly. 'It's valuable.'

'We're not stealing,' another said, 'only borrowing.'

They went inside and returned carrying the insensible Donny on a camp stretcher. Trent was with them. Lester and

Georgina followed them down to the canoe at the water's edge. The men laid the stretcher on the struts of a light outrigger canoe. They debated setting the canoe on fire, as the Vikings would have, or giving Donny a paddle.

In the end they did neither. They waded waist-deep into the water and launched the canoe into an oil-black, oil-smooth sea. It floated serenely into the darkness. From far away came the low rumble of thunder.

'We should have stopped those idiots,' Lester said. 'He might drown out there.'

'That's why I hate them all,' Georgina said, turning back to the house. 'I don't care whether he drowns or not.'

Lester left the party with Trent soon after. Trent's flight to Port Moresby would leave in the morning and he was yet to pack.

'D'ya want to see how fast she'll go?'

Trent turned the Alfa Romeo onto the road towards town. A stretch of road swept past sleeping villages in a corridor of roadside palms and shrubs. Occasional villagers trudged along the roadsides, women with laden *bilum* bags making a pre-dawn start on the long walk to the market with their produce. They leapt to safety as the speeding car bore down on them.

'Slow down, you'll hit someone,' Lester said, mesmerised by speed and fear.

'I shouldn't have brought a bloody lawyer along,' Trent said, slowing the car as rain suddenly lashed the windscreen. 'Don't you like a bit of excitement?'

'It's enough to drive a man to drink,' Flanagan complained. 'I've been with the DC in the rain for an hour arguing with Mataungan leaders. They wouldn't come inside. "It's your building," they said, "not ours." They were stopped at the door by a guard. They said we hide in rooms upstairs and never come down. They wanted to meet under the trees to talk.'

Flanagan took off his soaked shirt, picked up a hand towel and wiped himself dry. Gloria, eyes averted, hurriedly handed him a fresh ironed shirt from a cupboard dedicated to Flanagan's shirts, wig and gown for court appearances.

'Is it about the council election?' Lester asked.

'First, the old Tolai council supports the new multiracial council, then it asks the admin to stop the election. Now we've had word from Port Moresby the election of the new council is to go ahead tomorrow, whatever the opposition.'

Lester turned to query Gabriel, who seemed to have lost something beneath his desk and was absorbed in finding it.

'Haven't you been keeping up, Lester?' Flanagan went on irritably. 'Haven't you been listening to the radio?'

'I don't have a radio.'

'Buy one! Listen to Radio Rabaul on the ABC. Keep up to date!'

Awaiting Lester on his desk was an indictment for the Supreme Court sittings to be held in two days' time in Kavieng, the district headquarters and main town on the island of New Ireland, less than an hour's flight on the regular Fokker Friendship service. He looked for it on the map in Flanagan's office.

Kavieng was seen as an idyllic settlement, a version of what Rabaul might have been without its unique harbour. Like Rabaul, the town had been built by the Germans, then occupied in turn by the Australians, the Japanese and the Australians again, all without any say in it by the area's original inhabitants.

The flight would leave the next day, allowing a day to meet the police and prepare for the judge's arrival. Lester packed his file and reference books into a travelling bag. Gabriel offered to carry it down to the street where Lester could hail a taxi. At the door of the building Gabriel looked around quickly, alert for passers-by, then grasped Lester's arm.

'Radio Rabaul tells lies. They say everyone must vote for the multiracial council. They don't understand.'

A brand-new speedboat belonging to the European manager of a nearby plantation vanished one night from the shore in Kavieng. It was found damaged and abandoned on another island weeks later. A local man, arrested by young constables, vehemently denied the crime. The more he denied it, the more the constables threatened him with dire consequences. Eventually, he confessed and was given a caution.

Defence counsel from the Public Solicitor's Office insisted on a *voir dire*, a legal procedure of long standing in the common law. It required a 'trial within a trial' before the judge to determine whether a confession had been made voluntarily, before it could be admitted as evidence.

Judge Prest couldn't be satisfied the confession was voluntary. As for other witnesses, the theft took place on a moonless night and no one could convince him that the identity of either the thief, or the boat, was established beyond doubt. The defendant walked free without having uttered a word in his own defence.

At the courtroom door, the defendant smiled triumphantly at the plantation manager. The manager had nursed his indignation in the months awaiting the trial. He maintained it throughout the proceedings as he sat, harrumphing occasionally, at the back of the court.

'What a bloody farce!' he shouted as he left.

John Flanagan, meanwhile, had arrived in Kavieng to inter-view villagers involved in a dispute over the title to plantation land. He met Lester at the Kavieng Hotel. Flanagan was with a European *kiap* named Beddich who'd accompanied him that day, and who seemed none too pleased at the trial's outcome.

'That didn't go so well today, did it? You look like you need a drink,' Flanagan said, offering Lester a bottled beer.

For Lester, hot and tired after a long day in a stuffy court-room, Flanagan's sarcasm was more than enough.

'I tried everything to save that damned case. Everyone knew he was guilty as hell. I think you knew I'd end up with a *voir dire*, my first one. I can't understand why they're used in a court with no jury. Why didn't you warn me?'

To Lester's surprise, Flanagan laughed.

'That was the plan.'

'Did you set me up? I find that disappointing.'

'Take it easy,' Flanagan said, patting Lester on the shoulder. 'You needed to learn what it's like on Circuit. The Public Solici-tor's troops know police recruits rehearse their stories and learn them by rote. Cross-examination of police witnesses is like shooting fish in a barrel. They win half their cases and think they're Clarence Darrow or Perry Mason for the defence.

'Finish your drink. We'll walk round to the Kavieng Club for dinner. I've asked the judge's Associate to join us.'

The judge's Associate was no longer the doddering Mr Broad, but Mali Gavera, a handsome young Papuan and soon-to-be law graduate from the new university in Port Moresby. At the entrance to the Kavieng Club, they were greeted by a smartly dressed European member, an office-bearer and man of author-ity, so it appeared.

'Welcome, gentlemen. We don't often see the court here, unfortunately. Bit of a disappointment this time, wasn't it?'

Word of the thief's acquittal had already spread.

'Is the speedboat owner here?' Lester asked nervously.

'He's taken his boat and gone back to his island. He's not too pleased, but he'll get over it. Come on in.'

As they entered their names in the visitors' book, the club member was approached by others. After a short conversation, the member turned to Flanagan.

'I'm sorry, your Papuan friend can't join you.'

'That's preposterous,' Flanagan said.

'He's the judge's Associate,' Lester added.

'I'm sorry, that's club policy.'

'Change it now. Make an exception.' Flanagan's face, normally a ruddy red, turned a shade darker.

'I'm afraid that wouldn't be popular.'

Flanagan, swelling like a puffer fish, stepped up to within inches of the member's face. Lester was alarmed.

Mali Gavera pulled Lester aside. 'I don't want trouble,' he whispered.

'Let's go back to the hotel, John,' Lester told Flanagan. 'We don't need to eat here.'

After dinner at the hotel, they continued drinking until the bar closed. Lester, who had barely touched a drink since arriving in Rabaul, fell asleep on a lounge chair. He last heard Flanagan arguing with Gavera about the speedboat case. The Associate was loudly and earnestly telling Flanagan there was no place for European justice in the islands. The culprit should have been handed over to village elders and punished under customary law.

'If there were no court,' Flanagan said, 'that manager would have turned up at the man's village with a shotgun. Besides, you'll soon be handling criminal cases yourself.'

'No, I won't,' Gavera said. 'I'm going to be a company director. I want to make money.'

5

The election of members of the multiracial council was underway when Flanagan and Lester returned to Rabaul. Mataungan leaders led a march of supporters through the town, calling for an election boycott. No more than twenty percent of villagers had voted, far less than the administration predicted. The vigorous village-to-village campaign against the new council by the Mataungans and others had succeeded.

Nevertheless, the administration declared the election a success. When the Administrator, head of the administration, came two weeks later for the council's official establishment, more than two thousand shouting protesters surrounded the council chamber in Rabaul, drowning out the ceremony and jostling the dignitaries. Altogether, it didn't augur well.

Flanagan invited Lester to an evening barbecue at his home on Namanula Hill, with a tennis court in gardens behind the house. He extended the invitation to include a game of tennis.

Flanagan was not only a sailor, but also by his own account a former champion rugby player and enthusiastic tennis player. Lester had been warned in Port Moresby that Flanagan's belligerence in any sporting contest was well known, and willing opponents were few.

'I've never played tennis,' Lester told him.

'Not a sporting type, eh?' Flanagan said.

'I can swim,' Lester said. 'And I was scorekeeper for the cricket team at school.'

Flanagan shrugged and left it at that.

The garden, lit by a string of party lights, filled with guests. Most were police officers or senior *kiaps*, some with their wives. Flanagan held court around the barbecue, tongs in one hand and a can of beer in the other. Lester helped by turning sausages and searing steaks to order. Gloria and another young woman, a friend, hurried to the house and back with side dishes, salads and drinks.

The word *Mataungan* was on everyone's lips. Protesters, jeering and jostling the Administrator at the opening of the multiracial council, were roundly condemned.

Flanagan ushered a Tolai man with greying hair to the barbecue. The guest was an imposing figure, dressed formally in a jacket and tie, the only male not in a short-sleeved, open-necked shirt. Lester had seen his photograph on a wall inside the administration offices. A veteran member of the House of Assembly, a Tolai 'big man' with influence over a large part of the Gazelle Peninsula.

'I'm Nason Tokava,' the politician said, nodding to Lester and inspecting the offerings sizzling on the hotplate. 'I hope you have enough sausages to spare a second one.'

'Nason can have as many sausages as he wants,' Flanagan said.

Nason Tokava smiled. 'And you, Lester, where have you come from?'

'Sydney,' Lester said, presenting Tokava with sausages on a paper plate.

'Ah, Sydney with the coat hanger bridge. Another one who's come up here to enlighten us backward natives, I suppose. You're on a mission to rescue us?'

'From what I've heard, Tolais don't need rescuing.'

'We need to be rescued from ourselves,' Tokava said. 'If we have no enemy to fight, we fight each other. It's always been that way.'

'Are you opposed, then, to other Assembly members who support the Mataungan Association?' Lester asked.

'They're a tiny minority. There's no support for Mataungan troublemakers away from here. Do you know that *mataungan* in our language means "be alert" or "be on your guard", as they say? I say we should be the ones on guard. It will lead to violence. That's what I've been telling the Commissioner.'

Lester slipped away to look around Flanagan's domain. Behind the house were servants' quarters, home to a Sepik family employed as his household help. Sitting outside with the husband was Gabriel. He jumped up, startled at the sight of Lester.

'Mr Flanagan asked me to come,' he said hurriedly. He pointed to his PMV on the driveway. 'I brought up things for the party. I brought Gloria and the other woman, too.'

'John should have asked you to join us,' Lester said.

'He asked me, then I saw Tokava and stayed here,' Gabriel said, looking ill-at-ease.

From the house's rear steps, Gloria shouted at Gabriel in Pidgin.

'She wants me to help inside,' Gabriel said with a sigh. 'She called me a lazy man. She's a *trabel meri*.' He waved at Gloria. '*Orait, maski, mi kam*.'

Curiosity aroused, Lester followed Gabriel into the house. Gloria and her friend were stacking dishes.

'Where's the bathroom?' Lester asked.

'I'll show you,' Gloria said wearily and led him down a corridor.

'It's a big house,' Lester said.

'Three bedrooms, two bathrooms.' Gloria evidently knew her way around. As if to head off any misunderstanding, she added, 'I help when Mr Flanagan has guests.'

Left to himself, Lester seized the opportunity to inspect. The living room was furnished with sturdy, made-to-last administration furniture in rattan or hardwood. In one corner was a hi-fi entertainment unit with a turntable and an extensive record collection. A cursory glance revealed Flanagan's liking for classical music. On the walls were Namatjira prints of the redearthed Australian outback.

The bedrooms, however, were a surprise. Furnishings in the main bedroom revealed a woman's touch. On the bedside dresser was a framed wedding photo of Flanagan in full police uniform beside his bride in a white, full-length wedding dress. In other bedrooms were children's books and toys neatly stowed on shelves and in boxes. Printed posters of fairies and unicorns were taped to walls. Photos of two young girls, not yet teenagers, in their school clothes. The girls' rooms, it seemed, hadn't been occupied for some time.

Lester walked into the kitchen as Flanagan came in from the garden.

'So, this is where you've been hiding,' Flanagan said curtly. 'Did Gloria show you around?'

'I was looking for the toilet. I couldn't help seeing the rest of the house.'

'Did you know I was married? Did you see the photos of my family?'

'I was surprised. You don't have a family photo in your office, and I haven't heard you mention them.'

'That might be because you didn't ask. The girls are at school in Australia, so their mother stays with them. They come up every year for Christmas.'

'You must miss them. Do you go back to Queensland to visit?'

Flanagan hesitated, peering through the kitchen window into the darkness. In the garden, Gabriel, perched precariously on a stepladder, was taking down the party lights. The last guests were leaving; the sound of the last car faded away. Gloria and her friend were arguing on the steps outside the kitchen door.

'I haven't been down South for a while. It's no longer home for me. This is home.'

Flanagan went into the living room and returned with a bottle of whisky and glasses. He sat down at the kitchen table, inviting Lester to join him. He poured neat whisky drinks for them both.

'Talking of home, how is the workers' compound?'

Lester shrugged. 'I'm getting used to it.'

'I have good news. An apartment is coming up on the official list. Two bedrooms, married quarters.'

'I'm not married; you know that.'

'You could have a fiancée in Australia, a young lady about to arrive at any moment. That'd do. All I need is a name.'

Lester thought for a moment, giddy with excitement and relief.

'How about Daphne?'

Flanagan laughed, a low rumbling sound from deep in his belly.

'Is anyone called Daphne these days? The only Daphne I've heard of was my great-aunt. Daphne it is, then. Thanks for your help tonight. You're welcome to stay and help me finish the bottle, or you can get a lift back to town with Gabriel.'

Outside, Gabriel was waiting with his PMV. Sharing the cabin were Gloria and her friend.

'You can't ride in here,' Gloria shouted from the cabin window. 'There's no room. You can sit in the back.'

That was the last straw, Lester thought. He had to buy a car.

6

Gloria examined the aerogramme and the postmark closely, then, holding it delicately between her fingertips, dropped it lightly on Lester's desk like a soiled paper napkin.

'It's from your mother,' she said.

Kitty had forsaken lengthy letters on scented paper in favour of cheaper blue aerogrammes. These forced letter writers to be brief, for which Kitty compensated by making her small, neat handwriting even smaller and neater.

No longer did she implore Lester to come home, accepting for the time being she'd lost him. There was chatter about daily life in and around Greenwich, and grumbling about the eccentricities of Lester's grandfather Reg. This letter, however, had no chatter and the news was unsettling.

The other day two men in suits came to the door wanting to see you. One of them waved an official-looking piece of paper. They said they might need you as a witness in a legal case and wanted to have a look around. They looked in your bedroom but didn't take anything.

I said you had gone to New Guinea. The man told me that's what they all say. I asked him who do you mean by they. People who don't want to be found, he said. Why would he say that? I didn't take to those two at all. They wanted your address. I said I hadn't heard from you since you went away months ago.

Then your grandpa came to the door. He said he thought you'd been eaten by cannibals. They didn't think that was funny. He told them to be off or he'd fetch the dog. Of course, the dog would just roll over to be tickled, but they went away. I suppose it must have been something to do with your work. I didn't want to talk about that. I know you were unhappy there and that's why you left. You wouldn't want to be bothered with it now.

Lester folded the aerogramme into his pocket, put away his files, left the building and walked down to the harbour. Near the Yacht Club was a shaded picnic table where he often spent his lunch hour alone, looking out at the yachts, imagining himself aboard and about to set sail for Timor or Tahiti. It was where he came to reflect and, if he could, to forget.

Now there was to be no forgetting.

There were few cases for the latest Supreme Court Circuit in Rabaul. Serious crimes were few, usually investigated by European police wily enough not to bludgeon confessions from defendants or lose the evidence exhibits.

Among the thefts and burglaries was the case of a manager of a car yard who had defrauded the owner by understating trade-in prices in the company books. This time Lester triumphed over Colston, the manager's solicitor. The manager was sent to the local jail in the East New Britain hinterland. After the case, the car yard owner thanked him.

'Have you a cheap car for sale?' Lester asked.

The owner smiled. 'How about that lying bastard's old one? He sold it to me to pay for his solicitor. He won't be needing it now.'

'I can't do that. People will talk.'

'They won't. You'll pay a fair price, at least on the invoice, I'll see to it. You've done me a favour.'

'I've done you no favour; that's my job.'

At the back of the yard was Lester's prize—a stylish Mercedes 190SL hardtop coupé. Although it was utterly the wrong car for Rabaul, it reminded him of the lifestyle he'd once enjoyed with Patsy, now far beyond him.

Gloria Chan, a striking blend of Chinese, Ambonese and Malay, attracted and infuriated Lester in equal measure. She studiously ignored him while at the same time forever seeking help with tedious office tasks. He longed to ask her out, as much out of loneliness as desire.

One day he seized the moment, with Flanagan in court, Gabriel on an errand and Gloria at her desk idly painting her nails and uttering sighs of boredom.

'I've bought a car,' he called from his office door. 'Would you like to go for a drive on Saturday?'

'Where to?'

'Anywhere you'd like.'

'Is that your Mercedes in the carpark?' Gloria sniffed and was silent for some time, then, with a shrug of her bare shoulders, she went on. 'I'm going to a beach party at Pilapila on Saturday.'

'Oh, that's all right then. I just thought I'd ask.'

Another long silence. Lester retreated to his desk.

'I suppose you could give me a lift,' Gloria called after him.

The party at Pilapila was in full swing when they arrived. Steaks and sausages sizzled on gas-fired barbecues. On a makeshift stage, a local band with electric guitars powered by a generator played *Creedence Clearwater Revival* hits. A wooden platform served as a dance floor for a gathering of Europeans and the mixed-race community.

Gloria immediately joined her mixed-race friends. Lester was left to watch the dancers and mingle with European drinkers around the barbecue tables. Villagers from nearby sat comfortably apart in groups beneath the palms. They clapped to the beat of the band and laughed at their children jostling for a handout of leftover sausages and lemonade.

Lester watched Gloria on the dance floor. She had let down her long black hair and danced with a glass of wine in one hand, shoes in the other. As evening fell, she showed no sign of wanting to leave, but fate intervened. There was a brawl between drunken European men. The band stopped playing, the villagers melted away and the guests dispersed.

'Take me back to town,' Gloria approached Lester and put an arm around his own. She was tipsy, her face flushed. 'Do you think I'm drunk?'

'No. Or just a little bit.'

She giggled. 'I've only had two drinks. You know us Chinese. That's all I can have before I feel funny.'

Lester had consumed several cans of beer, enough to fire his courage and desire. He saw the pink tinge of her cheeks and the fullness of her red lips. Could he possibly kiss her?

'Can I take you out to dinner?'

'I'm tired now. Can you drop me at the Ascot Hotel? I'll walk home from there. I need to walk.'

At the hotel, Lester opened the car door for her, took her hand, helped her from the car and leaned over to kiss her on the cheek. It was, he imagined, a harmless goodnight kiss. She drew away sharply.

'You can't do that. Mr Flanagan wouldn't allow it.'

'Flanagan? Why not?'

'That was trouble last time.'

She pivoted unsteadily on high-heeled shoes and hurried into the night.

On the way to Pilapila, Gloria had sat in the passenger seat, nose in the air, as though being driven in a Mercedes was her divine right. Flanagan noticed the car parked next to his Datsun Bluebird and declared that a Mercedes was unsuitably ostentatious for an officer of the Crown. Lester, though worried about being able to pay the loan instalments, was joyously in love with the car and the freedom it promised.

On the following weekend he took the bitumen road around the harbour to the settlement of Kokopo, situated on the wider waters of Blanche Bay, then across the narrow neck of the peninsula to the beach at Pilapila for a swim. From there it was on to Nonga Hospital where he hoped to find Cherry-Apsley.

Lester had never encountered anyone quite like Cherry-Apsley. He had never seen a man so good-looking: delicately tanned, a wave of golden locks and pale grey-green eyes. His clothes, hanging loosely, would have looked ill-fitting on any-one else. On him they seemed elegantly casual, adding to an air of languid grace. It was odd that he drove a weather-beaten utility. Lester wanted to meet him again, to hear for once a cultured accent, to see where he lived.

'Dr Cherry?' A Tolai nurse at the reception desk rolled her eyes in exaggerated fashion. 'He's not here. He should be here today. We don't know where he is.'

Downhearted, he returned to the administration compound. The manageress appeared outside his donga and handed him a manila envelope. It held the keys to an apartment of his own.

The apartment was one of four in a wooden two-storey building at the end of an unsealed, dead-end street, far back from the harbour. The building was named Grandview Apartments, without regard to reality.

Access to the apartment was by a front door upstairs, reached by an outside staircase. The rooms were spacious and, with louvred windows opened all round, light and airy. Better still, it was furnished in the same solid government style as Flanagan's home on the hill. Lester, thrilled, squeezed everything he owned into the Mercedes and left the compound without a backward glance.

'Do you think Daphne will like it?' Flanagan asked facetiously next day, checking paperwork for the apartment, the undertakings and indemnities, every bureaucratic angle covered, and handing it to Gloria to be filed away.

'I'm sure she will,' Lester said. 'It's very homely.'

'When's she coming?' Gloria flipped through the papers, no doubt hunting for a Daphne profile, or at least a date of arrival.

'As soon as she can.'

Flanagan followed Lester into his office with a finger to his lips. 'You'll have to do better than that,' he whispered. 'She wants to know everybody's business. There has to be a story, a believable excuse.'

There was no Daphne, of course. Daphne was a fiction, a fantasy. Lester had to be careful.

On the following evening, he heard scuffling on the wooden landing outside. Two giggling Tolai girls in tight and daringly short dresses leaned precariously over the rail, waving at someone across the street. They turned and gasped as he appeared at the door.

'Can we borrow your umbrella? It's going to rain,' one said with a cheeky grin. 'We've come from over there.' She nodded with her chin towards a settlement of squatters' shacks half hidden by jungle at the street's end. Lester, flustered and unsure of how to respond, meekly brought out his umbrella. The short twilight was quickly fading.

'Can you come with us to the pictures?' the bold girl asked. 'It's too dark for us.'

'I'm sorry, I'm busy.'

'Then can you lend us your torch?'

'I haven't one.'

The girls scuttled down the stairs, thongs flapping.

'If you don't bring back my umbrella, I'll call the police,' Lester called after them.

'If you call the police, we'll tell them you fooled around with us,' they called back, laughing, pulling each other along the street towards the town.

That night, studying his Pidgin dictionary, looking up words like 'torch' and 'umbrella', he couldn't drive the girls from his mind. Those broad, white smiles and hot brown eyes. Their lithe bodies jutting, stretching, goading under their modest coverings as carelessly, artlessly, they twined about each other.

In his bedroom, hot and restless, he stripped to his shorts. He stared through open louvres and flywire screens into an impenetrable darkness. Chittering geckos scurried up and down the wire, snatching at small white moths drawn to the window by the dull light of a bare light globe.

He turned off the light and lay down on his bed. A light rain was falling. The smell of warm, wet vegetation mingled with the itch of sulphur in his nostrils. He listened for the chatter of the Tolai girls returning.

7

His first reaction to being alone in his apartment was to realise how isolated he'd become. He hadn't known what to expect in coming to Rabaul, but he seemed to have joined George and Milo as casualties of the real world, washed up in a backwater with little hope of escape.

The European guests at Georgina's party had disgusted him; he'd seen enough of such attitudes already in Port Moresby. Many of the Europeans at Flanagan's barbecue, as at the Yacht Club, banded together to run down the Indigenous people they were supposedly in the country to support. His start as a prosecutor wasn't promising, and Flanagan's low opinion of him was obvious.

On the other hand, he couldn't give way to despair and return to Australia—not for some years at least. He'd been through tough times before and would have to make the best of it.

Yearning for company and conversation, he again visited the Yacht Club. Flanagan had sponsored him for membership, though he made no secret of looking down on members who couldn't tell a yacht's sheets from its stays. Flanagan, at a corner of the bar with Inspector Macleod and other off-duty police, waved him over.

'If it isn't the fairy godmother who saved us from a wicked car salesman,' Macleod sneered.

Flanagan turned to leave. 'You needn't stay with this lot, Lester. Come home for a drink.'

'I'll stay a while,' Lester said loudly. 'Outside, where the air's fresher.'

Lester brought his beer out to the courtyard. At a table on his own was Darryl Cleary, no longer in a paint-stained shirt and red bandana but looking dapper.

'You look wonderful,' Lester said, sitting down with him.

'You look positively Byronic, dark and brooding.'

'I'm only brooding because I can't stand the talk in the bar.'

Cleary sighed. 'I wouldn't last five minutes in the bar. Out here they can't touch me. They can't throw me out because I've paid my membership years in advance. Once in a while, I dress outrageously in my best boating ensemble. Look at me: deck shoes, knee-length shorts, polo shirt with a yachting emblem, ready to sail away. A Francis Chichester of the South Seas. I do it to taunt them and put them all to shame. Good to see a fellow exile. How are you adapting to life in paradise?'

'To be honest, I'm finding it hard to settle in. I expected the Europeans in town to be more...'

'More what? They're Australian. It's a society constructed in our own image. You must get out more. In the villages you'll find the heart.'

'I'm still nervous about heading off the beaten track.'

'It's less dangerous than drinking all night at the Yacht Club.'

'I've heard rumours about threats by the Mataungan Association.'

Cleary waved his hands, a gesture encompassing the world beyond. 'A strange revolution is brewing all around us, but it isn't directed at us. The Tolai are fighting each other. We're bystanders really.'

'You don't think much of your fellow Europeans?'

'There are three sorts of Europeans here,' said Cleary. 'Functionaries, missionaries and mercenaries.'

'And which are you?'

'Oh, me? I'm none of those. I'm a butterfly fluttering about, landing where I please, where the nectar is.'

'Alas, butterflies don't live long.'

'Oh well, that's me. A brief, glorious fling.'

Light rain started to fall, chilling the air. Lester shivered in his light cotton clothing. He wanted to go back to his apartment, lie in bed under a blanket and imagine himself back in the cottage in Greenwich, an open fire in the living-room hearth, Kitty sewing in the corner, his grandfather dozing by the fire and the dog basking beside him. His frustration begged for release.

'I'm a total outsider. I'm not in the admin's inner circle. I'm not at home in the bars and clubs. Sometimes I wonder how I got here. I ask myself if it was simply a cosmic accident.'

'After ten years in this place I confess to wondering the same,' Cleary said, rising to leave. 'Don't think of suicide. Come to a play tomorrow night; I designed the sets for it. There's a last-night party afterwards to which you are hereby invited.'

'I don't know. I've been to a couple of parties already and didn't enjoy them.'

'Weren't you living at the admin compound? You've been dwelling with the dregs. Get away from them immediately! Rabaul's a party town. No television, B-grade movies in a shed and government propaganda from Radio Rabaul. What else is there to do? I promise this party will be different.'

The Kulau Theatre catered for a European population starved of cultural nourishment. The company of amateurs gallantly attempted plays by Thornton Wilder and Noel Coward, though occasionally presented entertainment less challenging and more widely appreciated.

The Princess and the Swineherd was a play for schoolchildren of all ages and every race, presented in a large school hall. The children watched in delight as the plot unfolded and magic tricks were revealed, cheering and clapping when the princess discovered that the swineherd was a prince in disguise. A rival suitor for the princess, spirited and effortlessly at ease on stage, was Anthony Cherry-Apsley.

The party afterwards was hosted at home by the play's director, Richard Crosset, a willowy, limp-wristed bank manager. Crosset swooped on newly arrived guests and fawned over a coterie of young, male Tolai companions. He praised the cast and backstage crew extravagantly, as was expected. He gave thanks to the school for the use of the hall and to the good Reverend Clapin of the Methodist Church for the loan of his heavenly daughter Josie.

She was the quiet one front of house, he said, pointing her out in a corner of the crowded living room. She collected the tickets and calmed a restless audience when, as often happened in Rabaul, the town's power supply failed, leaving the hall, the cast and the audience in darkness.

Cleary introduced Lester to Crosset with a theatrical flourish.

'Richard, meet Lester Chettle. He thinks Rabaul is dull. I'm sure he'd prefer Hawaii.'

'Oh, my goodness!' Crosset seized Lester's hand. '*South Pacific* the movie. Mitzi Gaynor as Ensign Nellie. Those wonderful scenes with colour filters. How can we compete?' He smiled encouragingly at Lester. 'You look interesting. Can you act? We're always looking for actors.'

'I was last in a play at primary school. I was a talking dustbin,' Lester said, looking about the room. 'I saw Dr

Cherry-Apsley on stage. I didn't know he was an actor, too. Is he here?'

'Ah, Prince Etienne. He's on the verandah still trying to woo Princess Clare de Lune.'

Lester found Cherry-Apsley, now alone, gazing into the garden, still in costume, tights and a loose-sleeved, pirate-style shirt open to his chest. Traces of pink makeup bordered the collar. He approached hesitantly, wondering if the doctor mightn't want to be disturbed.

'I'm Lester Chettle. You were my star witness a while ago, do you remember? I've been looking forward to seeing you again. I heard you were out here wooing a princess. Can I call you Anthony?'

He stopped short; it had all come out in an unseemly rush. Cherry-Apsley smiled and held up a calming hand.

'Of course I remember. Please call me Cherry, everyone does. The princess is married to a policeman, so wooing her would be courting disaster. Enjoying the party?'

'So far in this town, all I hear is talk about the dreaded Mataungans. It's refreshing to hear something different.'

'The only thing theatre people ever talk about is each other.' Cherry beckoned to a woman nearby. 'Josie, come and meet Lester. He wants to talk to someone who doesn't talk theatre.'

The woman was slight enough to be called thin by anyone so unkind. She was in a plain, armless cotton dress, possibly homemade.

'Josie Clapin,' she said, proffering her hand with a smile. 'I'm a teacher...sort of. And you?' Her eyes were dark, her gaze direct and accent recognisably Australian.

Lester shook her hand. 'I'm a lawyer, sort of...'

'Lester's a crown prosecutor,' Cherry said with mock solemnity.

'I've never met a prosecutor,' Josie said. 'Aren't they meant to be intimidating?'

'You should hear me in court,' Lester said. 'Hardened criminals turn to jelly.'

While Cherry went in search of drinks, Lester learnt more about Josie Clapin. She was twenty-two and grew up in Rabaul, but her later secondary schooling, then teacher training, had been in Australia. Her father was the minister of a Methodist parish congregation at Raluana on the road to Kokopo. 'He's been there for yonks,' she said.

She spoke with her arms self-consciously folded about her chest. A cropped, boyish hairstyle made her look even younger than her age. Lester had noticed her earlier talking to young Tolai guests who'd helped backstage.

'Are you a friend of Cherry's?' she asked.

'I've barely met him,' Lester said, 'but I'd like to be.'

'I think you'd like him. He's English, you know. Are you? You don't have a dinky-di Aussie accent.'

'I was born in Australia, but my family's English. The accent sticks to you.'

'We're both Pommies, then,' Cherry said, returning with beers and a soft drink for Josie. 'Hearing you in court, I thought you might be. Has she asked you yet if you attend church? She's always out for converts.'

Josie pressed Lester's arm; a darting movement quickly withdrawn. 'Come to our service tomorrow. I'll be singing with the choir from Raluana.'

'She sings like an angel,' Cherry said. 'In Kuanua, too. But don't let her drag you to church. Why don't you join me at Taliligap tomorrow afternoon? Josie will be there, freshly cleansed of sin.'

'I'd love to,' Lester said.

'Wonderful. Come, Josie, I'll drive you home.'

8

The Burma Road wound uphill to a ridge formed by the rim of the giant Rabaul caldera. Cherry's fibro bungalow at Taliligap was set in grassy grounds beside a large, single-storey fibro building that appeared empty and neglected. The bungalow, peeping from beneath a wreath of scarlet bougainvillea, looked over Vulcan and across Blanche Bay to Rabaul, twenty kilometres away. Here, the worst of the town's heat and stifling humidity was left behind.

Cherry was waiting for Lester on the verandah, dressed stylishly in a cream linen suit. Beside him were Josie Clapin and a woman Lester hadn't seen before. They were reclining in large cane chairs, enjoying the sight of town lights flickering to life.

'You're late, Lester old sport,' Cherry said, rising from his chair. 'Nice car you have there.'

'I missed the turn-off. I stopped at a village for directions.'

Cherry laughed. 'I'm glad they didn't eat you.' He pointed to a table on the verandah. 'Adele and I have nearly finished the rum. Help yourself to what's left.' He nodded towards the women. 'I brought them up this afternoon. Josie, you've met. Adele Florian, you haven't. Adele, *viens rencontrer mon ami Lester*.'

'Pleased to meet you, Lester.' Adele waved lazily from her chair. Her brief scarlet shorts and a frilled blouse knotted above her waist were in startling contrast to Josie's modest dress. Lester took in her broad, deeply tanned shoulders and wild, raven-black mane. He was struck by the allure of a woman confident of her ability to draw men's glances.

'Adele's from New Caledonia,' Cherry said with a flourish in her direction. 'She sailed in on a yacht. She's working at the Cosmopolitan Hotel in town. We go diving together.'

Lester walked to the verandah edge and looked over the grounds.

'The gardens are well looked after,' he said. 'The building next door looks like it hasn't been used for years. I wonder why.'

'I know why,' said Josie. 'Before the war, it was a sanatorium. Patients with tuberculosis were sent there to die. Their spirits are still here. That's why the gardens are looked after. It's to placate the spirits.'

'No one dares live here except me. I can't even get household help,' Cherry said. 'I don't mind the spirits.'

Adele, meanwhile, had left her chair and slipped into the bungalow. 'Cherry, have you finished talking? *J'ai faim.*'

'She's hungry and I've been ignoring her,' said Cherry. 'I'll have to fix dinner.'

Lester followed Cherry inside. A refrigerator and gas stove took up a corner of the large living room. No sign of food or cooking utensils. Cherry disappeared.

Adele curled up on the sofa with a magazine, shook her head and grimaced. 'He'll ask neighbours in the village to cook us something. He often does that. He'll be a while. Come and sit down.'

Josie came in from the verandah. 'Mosquitoes are biting me to death. I should go. Lester, will you take me?'

Lester hesitated. 'Cherry's our host, shouldn't we wait for him?'

'No,' Josie said crossly.

'Don't leave me alone in the dark,' Adele implored. 'It's too lonely up here.'

A long afternoon's ration of rum and Coke had left her sleepy-eyed. Her English came with a pronounced French accent, which intrigued Lester. Josie, on the other hand, pointedly took no notice of her, wandering over to a bookshelf, where she chose a book and pretended to read it.

'Cherry told us you sailed here,' Lester said, sitting down beside Adele. 'Is your yacht still in the harbour? I often go down to see which yachts have come and gone.'

Adele shrugged. 'It left for Thailand a long time ago. I met the owner in Noumea. An American sailing the world with his wife. She wanted a rest, so he told her he'd sail on without her. I told him I crewed on boats in Noumea. He said: "OK, you can crew for me. I'll toss a coin. Heads, we sleep together; tails, you sleep in the sail locker."'

Cherry, returning with a tin dish of chicken and rice, laughed. 'That's her story. She won't tell me who won the toss, but the real winner was me.'

The road to the coast descended into warm, damp air that fogged the car windows. Josie, in the passenger seat and wrapped in a cardigan, barely spoke. At the dinner table Lester had watched her frowning, fidgeting, withdrawn. She was wearing a pale blue sleeveless dress with a bow around the collar, a modest concession to fashion. She'd wanted to impress, he thought. Adele had cruelly upstaged her.

'What's wrong?' Lester asked at last. 'You've been very quiet.'

'She's so *coarse*,' Josie said. 'I can't imagine what he sees in her.'

'You mean Adele? I think I can imagine.'

'I mean, lying around on the sofa like some vamp.'

'Has she been with Cherry for long?'

'I don't know. I do know she sees him in town. And they go diving with air tanks. I suppose that's more exciting than listening to me. He's a doctor, he should be more discerning.'

They turned down the coast road towards Kokopo, around a bay that mirrored the moon, behind the hump of Vulcan, through sleeping villages and past shuttered trade stores. Despite Lester's coaxing, she was stubbornly quiet. Then she sat up.

'Do you remember Cherry saying he was glad you weren't eaten?'

'He wasn't serious.'

'Do you know why the place is called Taliligap?'

Lester, eyes on the road, shook his head.

'Long ago, a Tolai man called Talili and others killed four Fijian missionaries, cut them up, cooked them and passed the pieces around to be eaten. In the Kuanua language, *Taliligap* means the place of Talili's blood, though it was more about the missionaries' blood, wasn't it? They don't do that sort of thing anymore—I mean, eat people. The missions put a stop to it.'

'I'm glad to hear it,' Lester said. 'And relieved.'

Josie hadn't finished. 'Wasn't it clever of Cherry to say that? I wanted to laugh.'

'You should've laughed; you're far too serious.'

'Then I must be less serious in future,' Josie admonished herself.

Lester found himself in sympathy with her. The obvious tension between her and Adele for Cherry's attention set him wondering.

'Have you known Cherry long?'

'Only since rehearsals for the play began. I helped him learn his lines. He's terrible; he knows them but twists them around. Somehow, he gets them right on the night. He came to hear me sing at a church fete. When I said I spent a lot of time at Malmaluan near Taliligap, he said I could come along on Sunday afternoons to listen to his records.' She sighed, then with an impish smile added: 'My father would never allow it if he knew.'

Something in her smile, Lester thought, something in the way she spoke about Cherry suggested there was more to Josie and Cherry than met the eye.

'At your age your father shouldn't be telling you what you can't do.'

Josie shrugged. 'Well he doesn't *specifically* tell me, but I'm his only daughter, his only child. So long as I stay with him there'll be boundaries.'

'Why don't you move out? Go away. Travel.'

'He's quite old and unwell. He thinks I'm on this earth to look after him. Besides, I don't want to travel. I love it here.'

While talking she had become animated, sitting up in her seat. She returned to what seemed her favourite subject.

'When I come to Taliligap, I sing and Cherry plays the guitar. He joined a music class at school and learnt to play so that he didn't have to play rugby.'

'I have a guitar, too.'

'Next time you come, bring it.'

At her father's house she leaned towards Lester, kissed him fleetingly on the cheek, jumped from the car and flitted across the front garden, sandals in hand, without looking back. It wasn't until he was on the road heading for town that he noticed her folder of songbooks on the passenger seat when it slid down to the car floor.

An uncomfortable feeling stirred within him, beyond sympathy, beyond a sudden attraction, unfamiliar and strangely exciting. The first faint twinge of jealousy.

As the dry season progressed, the nights became cool enough to sleep under the lightest of bedcovers. Open louvres in Lester's upstairs apartment welcomed the heady scent of frangipani blossom and the smell of copra being processed into oil from the Coconut Products factory nearby.

In the evenings he ate alone, experimenting with vegetables from the market and Asian recipes with rice or noodles from a cookbook supplied by Gloria. Aside from learning Pidgin and Kuanua phrases, he passed the time listening to records bought at the town's music store and played on a secondhand record player.

He thought more and more about Cherry and Josie. He longed to see them both again, but reaching out to others in friendship was a skill he'd never mastered. He'd always wanted, and waited, to be asked, an affliction that brought him misery and seemed without cure.

Meanwhile, it was evident from its inauspicious beginning that a multiracial council was not going to bring together a polarised Tolai community. According to Flanagan, the lull in protests was due to all sides retreating only to consolidate their positions.

The Mataungan Association had formalised its structure in a particularly European way, appointing a chairman, secretary and other office-bearers. The patron was Oscar Tammur, the House of Assembly member for Kokopo and the firebrand orator Lester had heard in the admin carpark.

Members of the association were active in the villages, urging people not to pay the new council tax. Instead, the Mataungans collected subscriptions where they could, promising to hold the money in trust for the reestablishment of the all-Tolai council, something Flanagan said the administration would never countenance.

'I'm Dave Hersch, remember me?'

The portly figure who sat down breezily with Lester at the Yacht Club was vaguely familiar. Lester had been hoping to see Cleary but was grateful for some company.

'Didn't I see you at John Flanagan's barbecue? You're from the *Post Courier*? I'm Lester Chettle.'

'I know. I saw you in court at Lorengau. I was up the back.'

'I remember now. You fell asleep.'

'I was fagged out,' Hersch sighed. Perhaps weariness had returned at the mere thought. 'You handle prosecutions on the Islands Circuit?'

'Have mercy on me. That was my first case.'

'You're new to the Islands Circuit; I'm new to the Islands newsbeat. I'm on my first trip, around the traps in a week. Let's have a drink.'

Hersch left for the bar, returning with stubbies of SP Lager. The evening was still and sultry, threatening rain. His dark cotton shirt showed darker sweat-stained patches. He patted beads of sweat from his face and neck with a hand towel he kept in a bag beside him.

'Can't get used to this heat,' he said. 'My last stint as a foreign correspondent was in Indonesia. It was hot and humid, but not as bad as this.'

'This is supposed to be the dry season; it's worse in the monsoon,' Lester said. 'My leather shoes turned green with mould. How was Indonesia?'

'I was a stringer in Jakarta for Canadian papers when the communist PKI led an uprising against the Sukarno regime. I spent three years there up until late last year. I saw and heard things you wouldn't want to believe.'

'Why did you come here?'

'After all that, I couldn't go home to dreary Toronto, could I? Instinct tells me this part of the world might be next. So here I am.'

'There's trouble over the local council. Not quite a revolution, is it?'

'May be, but the natives are restless, as they say. I've just come back from Bougainville. There's rioting over a land grab for a copper mine. A whiff of separatism, even independence, is in the air. That's where the real action is. Have you been there yet?'

'No. If there's a murder, I guess I'll be going.'

'It's amazing! Rugged, beautiful, extremely hot—and the people are as black as a policeman's boots.'

'If you're counting independence movements, aren't the Papuans against a forced marriage with New Guinea?'

'So it seems. I'm watching West Papua as well. There's been a so-called Act of Free Choice for the West Papuans set up by the UN. The whole thing was a sham. Refugees are flowing over the border. I want to get up there and hear their stories.'

As empty stubbies multiplied on the table between them, they talked about Hersch's adventures in Indonesia, life in Sydney and Toronto, and the dismal purgatory that was Port Moresby. Lester took a liking to this Canadian and his voluble enthusiasm.

He drove Hersch to a house in the back streets that he shared with another reporter. Hersch was impressed by the Mercedes and the story of how Lester had acquired it. As the car pulled up, he patted Lester on the shoulder.

'Maybe we can help each other. You must know what's really happening in Rabaul these days. I'll keep you posted about politics in the capital. Is it a deal?'

Lester smiled but didn't answer. Too late, he realised the perils of consorting with a man like Hersch. Within days, the story of Lester's Mercedes appeared in the *Post Courier*, with a photo of the car in the admin carpark. Flanagan was incensed.

With no judge available, the next Islands Circuit was postponed. Lester had time in the evenings to go through Josie's folder of songbooks and sheet music. Her taste was in folk music, popular at the time. He'd listened to it for years.

Two weeks later, Cherry rang with an invitation to visit Taliligap again. Josie would be there. On no account, he was told, would he be welcome without his guitar.

They spent the afternoon experimenting with songs from Josie's collection, an easy musical rapport between them. Though Lester and Cherry could sing in tune and play an accompaniment on guitar, it was obvious that Josie was the talent. Her singing voice, honed by years in church choirs, was strong and true. They played into the evening.

'I'm glad you're driving me home and not Cherry,' Josie said, curled up in the passenger seat. 'He's a reckless driver. I close my eyes and pray all the way.'

She had complained of the cool evening air at Taliligap and wanted to return to the warmth of the coast. Lester looked across at her face in the soft glow of the dashboard lights. She'd barely stand out in a crowd, Lester thought, her features regular yet unremarkable. But, as Cherry had remarked behind her back, she was too pretty to be a missionary.

What attracted Lester was her beguiling smile, so near to perfect but for an upper tooth slightly out of line. He found himself at times staring at her, waiting for her smile to reveal it. He wanted to make her laugh, all because of that one tooth.

'He does drink a lot,' Josie added after a while.

'It's mostly Coca Cola,' Lester said.

'And buckets of rum. Doctors shouldn't drink. He drinks wine, too, and whisky when he's with that woman.'

'You mean Adele? He told me she works on Saturdays at the hotel in town. She doesn't seem to come up to Taliligap often.'

'Oh, she does,' Josie said scornfully. 'He'll wave us goodbye, hop in his ute and drive down to pick her up, late at night. They spend the night in his bed then go diving on Sunday. I've seen the empty drink bottles. I think she steals from the hotel bar.'

Josie's focus on Cherry was beginning to annoy Lester. Resentment stirred, but he held his silence. As the curving expanse of Blanche Bay passed by, a desire welled up within to feel the cool, dark waters against his skin.

'I'd like to learn to dive,' he said. 'There are so many reefs and wrecks to explore.'

Josie uttered a sound somewhere between a cough and a choke. 'The wrecks are too deep; it's too dangerous. I've told Cherry not to take the risk. That awful Adele urges him on.'

That was enough for Lester. He could foresee a relationship developing between Josie and Cherry beyond music and Taliligap. He wanted to share Josie's attention and affections; he wasn't going to be the third one of three and remain on the fringe. He had to compete.

'I'll ask Cherry to teach me,' he said.

Salvagers in Rabaul, brown, nuggetty, salt-seasoned men, made money from diving on the wartime wrecks of Japanese ships at the bottom of the harbour, stripping them of their brass and scrounging for other treasures. They rented out scuba tanks and operated air-compressors. The wrecks and coral reefs fringing the Gazelle Peninsula teemed with marine life.

Cherry had quickly befriended a professional diver and was fascinated by his stories of daringly deep dives. In the bungalow at Taliligap was a shelf lined with Japanese crockery bowls he'd pilfered from wrecks he'd dived on around the coast. Lester feared Cherry would be too busy to teach him during the week but phoned the hospital.

'Absolutely delighted!' Cherry crowed. 'I have plenty of time. I don't sleep well, never have. I take night shifts at the hospital. In truth, I lead a life of shameful indolence. Meet me at Pila early in the morning. I'll bring the gear.'

On the beach, Lester listened as the equipment and principles of diving were explained: the effects of breathing compressed air at depth, the danger of nitrogen narcosis, the safe depths and decompression times for returning to the surface. In shallow water, he practised clearing his face mask and slipping out of the harness that held his air tank if he became entangled. He learnt the most important rule of diving: never dive alone; always have a companion close at hand.

There was little to see underwater at Pilapila, but Cherry promised to take him diving with Adele on the islands off-shore. They'd show him reefs of kaleidoscopic colour and astonishing variety.

The promise was soon overtaken by events.

9

'**D**on't move, stay here!'

Flanagan burst from his office and hurried into the corridor outside. Gloria was open-mouthed. Lester, bewildered, checked the clock. Still early in the day.

'Something's happened. Where's Gabriel? He'll know.'

Gloria was already tidying her desk, sweeping a collection of charms and ointments from her desk into her handbag.

'Gabriel's not here now. Said his mother's sick. He's left you his office keys.'

'His mother's sick—can you believe him? There's always someone sick in that family. Do they all have malaria or something?'

'I don't know.' Gloria made for the door. 'You'll have to ask him.'

Cherry rang excitedly from the hospital.

'Don't you know what's going on? It's all over the hospital. The local staff have gone home. Mataungans have stolen the keys to the council building. The leaders have been arrested. There's a large crowd on the council's doorstep chanting anti-European slogans. Police are everywhere. I'm heading back to Taliligap until this blows over.'

Lester was left alone in the office, the silence uncanny. He rang Police Headquarters. No one answered. The telex machine in Flanagan's office began to buzz, spitting out coils of print. From the window he could see the carpark, a hectic scene of police and admin vehicles coming and going at speed.

Flanagan's office door was open, and Gabriel's keys were on a side table. One cabinet protected the admin's secrets: files on the Mataungan Association and a plethora of intelligence updates and situation reports ('sitreps') from troublesome areas of the Gazelle Peninsula. The sitreps were compiled daily by police, *kiaps* and other intelligence sources, and were reputedly notorious anthologies of scuttlebutt.

There was also a stream of cable telegrams to and from Port Moresby, and to and from Canberra. The cables, normally guarded zealously by Flanagan from prying eyes, gave orders to the police and legal advice to Flanagan: when to advance, when to retreat, when to hold the line, when to arrest, prosecute or compromise. The political confrontation was orchestrated from afar.

Lester sat down to read them all.

For the next few days, the town was in tumult. Mataungan leaders mustered thousands to demonstrate noisily at the town's sports park and other sites. The leaders declared they'd taken the keys as a protest and wouldn't return them until the multiracial council's proclamation was revoked.

The DC declared law and order on the Gazelle must be preserved. Military transport aircraft descended to decant police reinforcements from elsewhere in the country. The police presence in Rabaul swelled from two hundred to one thousand, a quarter of the country's entire strength.

Detachments of riot police patrolled the streets at night. Hundreds more marched through the town in a show of strength, with a helicopter escort hovering overhead. At roadblocks, police checked incoming vehicles and searched for weapons. The police band played stirring martial music in the park.

Charges of stealing the keys, possessing stolen goods and obstructing the council were laid and the main suspects arrested. The council locks were soon replaced, but the council was unwilling to meet for business and wouldn't talk to the Mataungans.

Hearings would be in the District Court before a stipendiary magistrate, with Flanagan prosecuting. Lester helped to prepare the cases. Flanagan, normally a pipe-smoker, was chain-smoking cigarettes, annoying both Gloria and Gabriel who regularly fled to the courtyard to gulp fresh air. Gloria told Lester this happened whenever Flanagan was stressed.

For the townsfolk of Rabaul, the events came as an enormous shock. Rumours and idle chatter in clubs and around dinner tables had become reality. Outwardly, little changed. Shops along Mango Avenue resumed selling, restaurants kept serving, trade stores sold their cheap Chinese wares. Golfers played golf and bowlers came out on bowling greens. Footballers, tennis players and basketballers carried on with their sport. Yachts still plied the harbour in weekly competitions. But the town could no longer argue that the dispute had nothing to do with them.

'I'm impossibly sober,' Cherry said cheerfully as Lester arrived at the bungalow. 'I've been on standby for emergencies. I might have to rush off to the hospital.'

'You're dramatising. It's all quiet on the front line.'

'All quiet? There's a mighty drama and you're in the middle of it! Aren't you excited?'

'I'm exhausted.'

Inside, Adele and Josie laid out the table for an evening meal. Adele had brought lobster pieces, salad and bread rolls filched from the hotel kitchen. Josie had been at a Methodist lay training centre at Malmaluan nearby. Cherry poured glasses of wine for them all.

'I see the Mataungans have drafted a Nigerian lawyer from the university to defend them,' he said to Lester. 'I hear he's an Ibo. They say he's been touring the villages in tribal robes and is greeted like royalty.'

'His name's Okorie,' Lester said. 'He organised rallies for the Ibo cause in Australia. I knew law students who marched with him.'

'Why didn't *you* join them?' Adele asked.

'I wanted to pass my exams.'

'Adele would've been there if she could,' laughed Cherry, putting an arm around her shoulders. 'She's a born and bred revolutionary.'

'I saw the marches last week,' Adele said. 'People were angry. At first, I thought it was just about a little local council, then I saw it was more. It will be an uprising against colonial rule.'

'I saw them too,' Josie said. 'I thought it was awful. Where I live the people don't support them. They have no respect for the village elders.'

Adele gave a disdainful grimace. Josie took no notice but smiled brightly at Cherry.

'And what's an Ibo exactly? It sounds derogatory, like they say "Abo" in Australia.'

'There's a civil war in Nigeria,' Cherry said. 'The Ibo people of Biafra want to secede from the rest of Nigeria. Untold thousands have died. Dear Josie, what a blissful cocoon enfolds you.'

Lester started. 'How d'you know so much about Africa?'

'His uncle was a doctor there,' Josie said.

Cherry nodded. 'He was in charge of a medical district in Nyasaland. Before I left school I spent a long holiday with him. I loved everything about it. At medical college in London I took extra courses in tropical medicine, so I could go back.'

'Why didn't you?'

Cherry shrugged. 'Nyasaland became independent Malawi. My uncle left. It wouldn't have been the same.'

'Colonialism is to blame for the trouble in Africa,' Adele said. 'And in the Pacific.'

'The Wind of Change in Africa is coming our way,' Cherry said. 'It can't be stopped.'

After dinner and more wine, they tried out Josie's new reel-to-reel tape-recorder—purchased for her choir with church funds, she admitted, but serendipitously she was its custodian. They played, sang and listened to replays until Josie declared she was tired of listening to herself and packed the recorder away. Adele, overcome by boredom, was asleep on the sofa.

Josie walked unsteadily to the Mercedes for the drive home and stumbled onto the front seat.

'You had a glass or two of wine,' Lester said. 'That's why you're all over the place. I bet that's not in the Methodist handbook.'

Josie was quiet for a while, then punched Lester on the arm. 'I'll have you know I'm a bit lapsed,' she said. 'I'm not so *fervent*, not so *committed*.' She lay back and closed her eyes.

She had long, beautiful eyelashes, thought Lester, casting sidelong glances. Those small things about her attracted him so much: the warm and open smile, the eyes dark and searching. No makeup needed. A pity those eyes lingered so often on Cherry.

The pre-trial proceedings opened a week later. The hall that doubled as a courtroom overflowed with villagers, most of them men in laplaps, packed on benches and cross-legged on floors. A patchwork of faces filled windows and peered through open doors.

The presence of Oscar Tammur at the rear of the court made it clear the crowd was no accident; this was a Mataungan cohort, strategically assembled. Squeezed into a corner were representatives of the Australian press, Dave Hersch from the *Post Courier*, senior police and admin officials. Tension filled the room, an air of impatient expectancy.

Flanagan was the prosecutor. Lester, who'd been researching the case law, sat behind him with Gabriel at his side. The three defendants, nonchalantly guarded by a police constable, walked in through a rear door and sat to one side of the court bench. Okorie, their counsel, followed, then joined Flanagan at the bar table.

Seeing Flanagan in an open white shirt, Okorie draped his suit jacket carefully over the chair behind him, placed a satchel bulging with books on the table, looked slowly around the court, waved to the assembled multitude and sat down amid a hushed, awed murmuring. White lawyers came and went, but no one had ever seen a black one, let alone one dressed in a sleek, dark suit like a foreign president.

The last actor in this piece of legal theatre was the magistrate, a man improbably named Quentin Featherstone. His style and reputation were common knowledge. In a land of singlets, shorts and thongs, he dressed fastidiously in long-sleeved business shirts with outsized cufflinks and flowery bow ties. He was known for long-winded judgments in the simplest of cases, and for believing he had an unparalleled knowledge of native lore and customs.

Seeing him for the first time, Lester wondered what vagrant breeze could have wafted him to Rabaul, a town without a scrap of elegance or refinement.

The court was called to order; the magistrate read the charges to the defendants, translated into Pidgin by the court interpreter. They were asked to plead.

'*Yu kalapim dispela law o nogat?*'

'*Nogat,*' the defendants said in unison.

Not guilty. A happy babble arose around the crowded courtroom. This was the battle they'd come to see.

10

The following full trial lasted seventeen long days. Again, hundreds were at the court on the first day to watch and listen. Proceedings were laboriously translated into Pidgin. Defence counsel Okorie must have felt his second appearance needed to be even more dramatic, for he strode into the hall and down to the bar table in traditional Nigerian national dress, much to the excitement of the crowded courtroom.

Flanagan's face swelled and reddened, though he could hardly object. There was no formal dress code for the District Court, beyond respectability.

The facts of the case were scarcely in dispute. The council keys had been taken, the council chambers locked, officials threatened and keys of council vehicles removed. Okorie began his cross-examination of the witnesses in flamboyantly theatrical fashion, questioning memories, motives and possible coercion.

This proved the last straw for Flanagan. He launched a string of vehement objections. Magistrate Featherstone eventually intervened, telling the Nigerian to moderate his style.

The weakness of the prosecution case, however, was evident even before the case began. The prosecution had to prove the keys were stolen. Was there an intent to permanently deprive the council of the keys? The council locks were immediately replaced, so loss of the original keys no longer mattered.

The defendants claimed they hadn't been properly consulted about the establishment of a multiracial council. The previous all-Tolai council had been running well for nearly twenty years. The Tolai Cocoa Project, wholly Tolai-owned, was a successful business enterprise that would be handed to a new expatriate-controlled or manipulated council. Their arguments had been ignored, so they had carried out a symbolic act in protest, a token demonstration of popular dissent.

When the trial drew to a close, Featherstone delivered a judgment more than one hundred pages long. He believed the defendants had an honest belief in a claim of right to the keys. He recounted an ancient claim of right that enabled Scottish Nationalists, who burgled the historic Stone of Scone from Westminster Abbey, to get away scot-free. He laughed at his own pun.

He berated the administration for establishing the multiracial council in the face of growing opposition, and for insisting on a prosecution that was doomed to fail. Charges against the defendants were dismissed without a conviction.

Gabriel had attended every day of the trial, sitting among his Tolai brethren and taking a keen interest. When the crowds melted away, he helped Lester carry the voluminous material generated by the trial back to the office.

'What did you think of the trial?' Lester asked.

'We Tolais are very grateful to Mr Flanagan and yourself,' a beaming Gabriel said. 'You let the Mataungans win. The professor from Africa talked for us. He understands. He brought us new ideas.'

'He's not a professor,' Lester protested.

'The professor told us it's not about the council and it's not about the cocoa. It's about you Europeans being here. It's about the land.'

Both Lester and Flanagan were furious the administration had insisted on a prosecution with little chance of success. Flanagan, however, was committed to the administration's cause. As for Lester, the seeds of doubt were sown. How could such a trivial incident have led to the presence of a thousand police in town?

Having avoided Dave Hersch during the trial, Lester was later waylaid at the Yacht Club. The journalist was sweatier than ever and in a state of nervous exhaustion. 'I've had more front page stories these past few weeks than in the rest of my career,' he boasted over an evening beer.

'A pity it's the *Post Courier* and not the *New York Times*,' Lester said.

'What can you tell me? It was a public relations disaster, wasn't it? Score Mataungans one, admin zero. The Australian press are giving only one side of the story, of course. For them it's a thousand police beating up the poor villagers.'

Lester shrugged. 'We weren't on a winner from the start, that's all I can say.'

'I've been in the clubs, met a few planters. They're scratching their heads. What's all the fuss about? Give the Tolai their old council back. And the Cocoa Project? The planters are happy with it as it is. They just want to get on with their lives. No marches, no police roadblocks.'

'If only it were that easy. The Tolai factions are bitterly divided.'

'My colleagues in Port Moresby tell me there's little enthusi-asm for the Mataungans in the Assembly. All the members can see is the country breaking apart. The Gazelle, Bougainville...'

'That's the Canberra line, too. The administration is under orders to hold it. No compromises.'

'Tell me what's happening on the inside. I hear rumours that the Administrator wants to stop the university from appoint-ing African lecturers who can stir up trouble. Is that true?'

'I can't comment on rumours.'

'What about Featherstone's judgment? Is it a magistrate's job to lead the Mataungan cheer squad? What did they think of that in Canberra?'

Lester laughed. 'John Flanagan warned me to stay away from you. If I say a word, I'll be on the next plane back to Sydney. I'll buy you a beer and you can tell me what's happening in Port Moresby.'

11

Late on the Saturday afternoon, following the trial, Lester appeared on Cherry's verandah with a suitcase.

'I've come to stay for a few days,' he said to Cherry. 'I hope you don't mind.'

'Have you been fired?'

'No. A holiday. Three whole days. I haven't had a weekday off for six months. I need a rest.'

'I'm not surprised,' Cherry said. 'Welcome to my guesthouse. Four bedrooms, no beds. Only me, the manager, has a bed.'

'I've borrowed a blow-up mattress; it's in the car. There's liquor in the boot and all manner of groceries. Your fridge will be bare.'

Josie followed soon after. She'd been at Malmaluan and was dropped off by a PMV.

'Where's Adele?' she asked, glancing inside.

'I don't know,' Cherry said. 'She's been following that Mataungan case. I heard she met that Biafran lawyer chap who was staying at the hotel. Maybe she ran off with him.'

Josie pulled a face. 'That'd be nice.'

'Easy on. She's had a hard life and needs nurturing. She needs to be understood.'

'I understand her perfectly,' Josie said. 'I've seen her wandering about the market in pink hot pants. Tolais don't like that; it offends their modesty.'

'I've been with her in town, too. She's followed everywhere by lustful brown eyes. That's how much they're offended.'

'Stop it!' Josie jumped to her feet. 'I don't want to talk about her. We're here to rehearse. I want us to play at a church hall opening in a week's time.'

'We're not a revivalist group,' Lester objected.

'It's a place to start,' Josie said. 'Can you bring me a rum and Coke?'

Later they strolled through the garden as far as a cliff edge where the land dropped into the jungle below. Across the harbour, wisps of smoke and steam arose from the flanks of Tavurvur into a pink evening sky. Josie collected flowers and sweet-smelling frangipani blossoms to decorate the dining table. Lester cooked an evening meal of tuna cakes and salad.

Over dinner and wine, Cherry offered more about Adele. She was part Creole, part Kanak, born into a poor family and one of five children. Before coming to New Guinea, Cherry had worked at a hospital in Mauritius.

Adele often spoke of the independence struggles of her forbears on Mauritius and nearby islands. The French had hung on grimly to the island of Reunion, as they had in New Caledonia. Adele was an ardent anti-colonialist, the product of a never-ending struggle to throw off the colonial yoke.

The night grew late; Josie was yawning. She'd heard more than enough about Adele.

'Stay the night with us,' Cherry said. 'You can have Lester's blow-up thing and he can sleep on the sofa. Plenty of old hospital blankets next door. We'll guarantee your virginity.'

Josie pointed an accusing finger. 'Don't be rude. I can't stay here. I'm not going near any old hospital blankets, and it's haunted by spirits at night.' She took Cherry's arm. 'Lester's your guest, so you can take me home.'

By the time Cherry returned, Lester was fast asleep on the sofa, his blow-up bed forgotten.

The following afternoon, Cherry took Lester snorkelling at a popular diving spot known to Europeans as the Submarine Base. A reef forming a narrow band around the shore of a sandy cove ended abruptly in a sheer reef wall that dropped to a depth of one hundred and fifty fathoms before meeting a steep sea floor plunging far deeper.

Cherry explained that during the Pacific War, when constant American bombing made the supply of Rabaul by surface ships impossible, Japanese forces unloaded supplies from submarines that surfaced at night alongside the reef. They squirreled them away in caves and tunnels dug into the hill close by.

The afternoon was windy. They swam out with fins, snorkels and masks to hover at the edge of the reef wall. Cherry pointed to the ghostly shapes of patrolling sharks far below. The sight of the reef wall vanishing into an indigo abyss gave Lester the unnerving sensation he was about to fall from a high mountain ledge as the water would no longer support him. He turned quickly for shore. Cherry followed.

'Did the sharks frighten you? They're no bother. They won't come for you.'

'No—the reef disappearing into the void. I felt dizzy.'

'That's why you should see it first from the surface; we can dive next time. The wall is fantastic.'

On the far side of the cove, small wind-driven waves broke on the reef and surged through a sandy gap. Lester left his snorkelling gear on the beach, waded into the gap and bodysurfed the waves to shore. Cherry, watching from the beach, applauded as Lester joined him again on the sand.

'Where did you learn to do that?'

'I grew up in Sydney, remember?'

Cherry slapped a hand to his forehead. 'Good Lord, how could I forget? Sydney with the world's best beaches.'

'Here's a deal,' Lester said. 'Teach me to dive and I'll teach you to bodysurf. We'll go to Pila in the monsoon, when the waves roll in.'

They lay on beach towels in the sun, the breeze baking the salt on their skins. A restless sea beyond the reef dazzled in the late afternoon glare. Apart from the rustling of palm fronds behind them, the cove was an oasis of silence and solitude. Lester felt the stress of past months ebbing away.

'Put your shirt on,' said Cherry, 'or you'll end up like a boiled lobster.'

Lester gazed at Cherry beside him, a slim and golden Adonis in shorts and sunglasses. His envy must have been obvious, for Cherry raised an arm in the air and inspected it closely.

'Don't ask me why I tan so easily. My mother was the same. She was Hungarian. She claimed to be from the aristocracy, but she may have been a gypsy, for all I know. Aristocratic families were hunted down by the communists after the war and scattered to the winds. She has no papers.'

'According to Josie, you're an aristocrat yourself.'

'My father's a baronet. I have an older half-brother called Gordon, so he inherits the title—unless, of course, I can prove he was born out of wedlock. His mother was my father's first wife. He divorced her to marry my mother and caused a local scandal. I have neither a title nor a manor, so I don't know why Josie's so excited.'

'She's your number one fan, that's why.'

'But when I took her home last night, all she talked about was you.'

'And when I take her home, vice versa.'

They both laughed.

'I know this much,' Cherry said. 'She doesn't think much of men in general.'

As the sun slipped behind a hill, they went around the shore to see what traces of the Japanese base remained. In the shallows, rusting girders of a crane emerged from the sea like the humped skeleton of a whale. Dug into a cliff behind were tunnels, their entrances clogged with silt.

'Have you been to Yamamoto's Bunker in town?' Cherry asked.

'Not yet. I hear it's a little war museum.'

'All the Gazelle is a war museum. There's layer of history half-buried or submerged all around us. It reveals itself piece by piece.'

Well after dark, they returned to town. Cherry left to spend the night with Adele. A disgruntled Lester drove to Taliligap alone, too readily abandoned by his companion for a woman's embrace. He was seething with envy; life wasn't fair. It would be a long night with a leaking blow-up mattress and spirits of the dead for company.

Even the drinks cupboard was bare.

At Taliligap was a roadside store, a small tin cube with a door and serving window, selling flour, sugar and tinned goods, the basic necessities of village life. Was Lester a friend of the doctor, the Tolai owner wanted to know. The doctor was a good customer. The doctor would drive the villagers around in his utility and take them to the hospital.

Lester bought soft drinks from the store, fruit and vegetables from the village nearby, and was given mangoes for free. He made a tropical fruit salad for breakfast and began browsing through Cherry's bookshelf. F Scott Fitzgerald's *The Great Gatsby* and Graham Greene's *The Heart of the Matter*, George Orwell's *Burmese Days*, treatises on tropical diseases, a diving manual, a travel guide to Mauritius, a picture-book history of Warwickshire with its rolling green farmlands and English cottages.

He looked up to see a slight figure in a print dress coming across the lawn. Hurried, birdlike steps, slightly splay-footed, a *missionary walk,* as Cherry had described it, full of purpose, doing God's business. Josie hopped lightly up the steps to the verandah. At the sight of Lester she stopped short, astonished and confused. Lester felt the uncomfortable thud of his heartbeat.

'I was passing by and saw Cherry's ute,' she said. 'I didn't expect to see it; I thought he'd be at the hospital. I thought I'd just say hello...I mean, see if he was all right. Is he here?'

'He's gone to work. He borrowed my car.'

'Oh, God. You let him?'

'He promised to take care of it.'

'I forgot you were staying here. You probably want to be alone.' Josie turned away but halted at the door. 'Could you give me a lift to town?'

'In his ute? I don't know where the keys are. Are you in hurry?'

'Yes...no, not really.'

'Then stay and talk to me. Have some breakfast.'

Josie sat down at the table. Lester plied her with food: fruit salad, cooked chicken pieces, bread smothered in a layer of avocado, a freshly boiled egg. She began eating eagerly, her eyes averted.

'Where have you been staying? Don't they feed you?' Lester asked.

'I was at Malmaluan, and yes, they feed me...sometimes.'

'Not enough, I'd say.'

'I'm only a visitor really.'

Afterwards they sat on the verandah in the comfortable embrace of the old cane chairs. Awkward minutes passed in silence. In the garden, two sturdy young men, in laplaps and wielding sarif knives, arrived to cut the grass. They called out a greeting.

'You're sitting in Cherry's chair,' Josie said. 'He always sits there.'

'Well, he's not here. Please tell me more about yourself.'

'About myself?'

'At least promise you won't mention Cherry again this morning.'

Josie had recovered her composure enough to smile. She placed a hand on her chest. 'Cross my heart, I promise.' Again she fell silent.

'Is your past a dark secret?' Lester teased.

Another long pause. 'You know what?' she said eventually. 'I think the three of us learn about each other by going round in circles. I've worked it out. The first one tells the second one something about the third one. Then the second tells the third about the first, and the third tells the first about the second, and so it goes around. Together we're like a three-legged stool that never quite balances.'

She leapt to her feet, bowed for imaginary applause, then fell back into her chair. 'It's so hot. Can I have a Coca-Cola?'

Lester fetched a can of Coke from the fridge.

'I know you're a teacher and work for the Methodist Church, but you dart about like a hummingbird—here, there and gone again.'

'I don't teach much, except for music. I help at Malmaluan, and with teacher training at our new college at Gaulim, which is miles away in the jungle. Just getting there is an expedition. I prepare lesson plans and type them up and get things printed in town. I help my father in the parish. I'm a sort of paid volunteer, if you like. And it's the United Church, no longer the Methodist Church. Is that enough?'

'It's a start.'

Lester gazed at Josie. Her cane chair was like a giant basket in which she had folded herself, knees to chin, barefooted, her sandals on the floor. Framed by the verandah's bower of bougainvillea, she was quite unaware of being transformed—the month of July, perhaps, in a calendar of beauties.

'Do you realise we've never been with each other alone?' he asked.

'Should I be worried?'

'No.'

'I know you're a decent man. You're a lawyer who puts criminals in jail.'

'I've been mostly unsuccessful so far.'

'Cherry, I mean that doctor who can't be named, says you saved a waiter at the New Guinea Club. You stand up for the right things.'

Lester smiled. 'I'm glad that's settled, then.'

'I really must go.' Josie leapt to her feet, slipped on her sandals and ran inside. She soon returned, dangling the utility keys for Lester to see.

'I know where he keeps them. Inside the kitchen cupboard in a tin, away from thieves.'

On the way to town, Lester's Mercedes passed them at speed, heading towards the Burma Road turnoff to Taliligap.

'He didn't even see us,' Josie groaned. 'He's a demon behind the wheel.'

'Yet you forgive him,' Lester said, 'for running off to Adele after he leaves you. And when he makes fun of you. He's eight years older than you, too. Have you fallen for him, warts and all?'

Lester regretted his words immediately; jealousy had urged him on.

For a time, Josie remained silent.

'I'm sorry I said that,' Lester said.

'Then I forgive you, too,' Josie said. 'I'm a forgiving person. And he doesn't have warts. He's the kindest person I know.'

Her answer was no answer. That night he dreamed she was performing a dance around him, teasing seductively as she twirled.

12

The House of Assembly established a Commission of Inquiry to investigate the most appropriate form of local government for the Gazelle, given other longstanding Tolai grievances, particularly over land.

Prompted by Canberra, the administration appointed as chairman a prominent Australian lawyer with little background knowledge or experience of the Tolai people. The chairman berated Mataungan leaders for haranguing the Commission and making outlandish demands for self-government. The colourful and impassioned Oscar Tammur was threatened with a charge of contempt.

When the report was made public, its findings were all too predictable. The multiracial council had not been given a fair trial and the administration should continue to support it.

As for the Mataungans, they made their feelings clear by organising a march through Rabaul. Thousands of supporters carried placards calling it The March for Justice, and loudly demanded the resignation of everyone from the Minister in Australia to the DC in Rabaul.

The Commission's report was a catalyst for the violence that was to follow.

On a peaceful Sunday morning in early December, a convoy of trucks bearing Mataungan supporters fanned out to villages in a hunt for prominent council members and their supporters. Villagers were threatened and some physically assaulted, including some who were dragged from their churches. The most seriously injured needed hospital treatment. In some villages, the Mataungans were themselves confronted by council supporters. Fights broke out and more were injured.

The admin was once more caught flat-footed, but there was now an overwhelming police strength in the Gazelle. It was quickly mobilised to suppress the violence and restore calm. Mataungan leaders were again arrested. Over succeeding days, many more supporters were charged with assault and offences against public order.

To the chagrin of Flanagan and Lester, a prosecutor from the Department of Law in Port Moresby was flown in to conduct the prosecutions, while the Mataungans generally represented themselves.

Most didn't dispute their part in attacks; they sought justice of a different kind. Their spirited, if sometimes wayward, arguments failed to sway the magistrates, there to exact retribution on behalf of angry council supporters.

Convicted offenders were given sentences of up to six months and flown out of town to serve their sentences on the New Guinea mainland, part of an administration strategy to douse the sparks of rebellion, but it sowed the seeds of further discontent.

Saturday morning, a week after the Mataungan rampage. Doldrum weather had come to Rabaul. Flanagan's yacht, named *Belle Marie* after his elder daughter, lay at anchor and becalmed under a gloomy sky pressing down upon the harbour. Lester sat in the cockpit beneath an awning slung over the boom. His T-shirt was wet through with sweat.

The yacht was a wooden-hulled, broad-beamed classic design of the 1950s. The tropic sun had weathered it beyond its years. The boat's idiosyncratic ways infuriated Flanagan, but nothing could dampen his devotion to *Belle Marie*. Despite his efforts to maintain it, any sail, spar, stay or shroud was prone to failure at any moment while underway.

He'd persuaded a reluctant Lester to help him make a repair at the top of the mast. Lester would haul him up the mast on a bosun's chair and lower him slowly and gently to the deck. Flanagan's repeated warnings to heed his instructions perfectly had made Lester nervous, but it was too late to back out.

Somehow the hauling lanyard jammed, stranding Flanagan halfway up the mast for half an hour before the lanyard was freed. Lester was treated to a barrage of expletives for which Flanagan was notorious at the Yacht Club.

Still grumbling, Flanagan opened stubbies of beer in the cockpit.

'Should've waited for somebody from the club to help me. I asked around; no one was free.'

By now, Lester was well aware of his foibles. Flanagan could no more understand how his yacht could fail him than why no one would volunteer to help him fix it. It was the same at the office. He could never accept that any criminal case he prosecuted could be lost except through some malevolent agency beyond his control.

'The lanyard hitch wasn't my fault,' Lester said.

'Then I don't know how it could have happened.'

'The Secretary for Law is here,' Lester said, anxious to change the subject. 'I thought you'd be entertaining him this morning.'

'He's at the DC's residence. They want to remove Magistrate Featherstone. I told the secretary on the phone it wasn't a good idea. Featherstone's a fair-minded man; we don't want a hanging judge in Rabaul.'

'Why did he sideline us from the prosecutions? Did he tell you?'

'For our own safety. Because we live here and might be threatened.'

'You believe that?'

Flanagan snorted. 'Don't you see? We're the country bumpkins. If they're on a winner, they send counsel from Port Moresby. If the convictions are suspect, we'll be left to fight the appeals. We get the losers.'

Still fuming, Flanagan left in the yacht's dinghy to take back the borrowed bosun's chair. Lester leaned back in the cockpit and listened to the water lapping against the hull. He opened another stubby and drained it greedily. The ice-packed liquor was soothing, cool in his throat.

He wondered if Flanagan would return or leave him to swim ashore. Putting up with a superior whose irascible temperament was so unlike his own was a cruel blow. He drank another stubby, then another.

At least, he thought, Flanagan did have redeeming quali-
ties. He was a fair-minded lawyer and not a racist. His regard for
the country and its people, and for the Tolai in particular, was
heartfelt and sincere.

Asleep on the sofa at Taliligap, Lester was stirred by a hand on
his shoulder, a kiss on his forehead and the scent of a sweet,
fruity perfume.

'Wake up, sleeping beauty,' Adele said.

He opened his eyes to a vision of figure-hugging shorts and
an open white blouse. Her chest had brushed against his when
she kissed him. At times he envied Cherry to distraction.

'Where's Cherry?'

'I don't know. I had to catch a PMV from town. It was full of
men sitting in the back. Their eyes undressed me all the way.
C'était terrible.'

'I drove up this morning. No one was here, so I lay down.'

'Then you've slept for hours.'

Footsteps sounded on the verandah. Cherry and Josie came
into the living room carrying cardboard boxes marked as medical supplies.

'Where've you been?' Adele demanded.

'So sorry.' Cherry put down his box. 'I picked Josie up at
Malmaluan and we went to Toma. A spur of the moment thing.
There was a stoush between Mataungans and council supporters. A Mataungan turned up and asked me to patch up his
injured comrades. If they went to the hospital, he said, police
would be waiting for them. I was told not to report it. Not a
threat, exactly, but I took the hint. I put it down in my notes as
a traffic accident.'

'I helped with the dressings,' Josie added.

'Oh, *la dame à la lampe*,' Adele sniped.

'What?'

'She means Florence Nightingale,' Cherry said.

'What would she know about Florence Nightingale?' Josie asked.

'I wanted to become a nurse, once.' Adele shrugged, rising to go outside. 'I read about her.'

'I saw you in a Mataungan march, right up front,' Josie called after her. 'You were carrying a placard.' She waved an imaginary placard energetically above her head. "Colonists Go Home" it said in big, black letters. I think it was misspelled. In any case, that wasn't what the march was about.'

'That *is* what it's about.'

Josie rounded furiously on Adele. 'That African was behind all this violence. He came back to Rabaul right before the attacks. The Mataungans held a sing-sing for him and treated him like a god. You were with him. You're stirring up trouble. Why don't *you* go home and stir up the French instead?'

'It's you missionaries stirring up trouble. You don't want change. You have the land; you have the churches. You want control. You tell everyone the councillors have God on their side. Religion has poisoned these people.'

Cherry looked at Josie and sighed. 'I should've warned you. She eats, drinks and sleeps Franz Fanon. She keeps pan-African social-ist tracts under her pillow. She reads them like you read the Bible.'

Josie, still unpacking dressings and suture kits, had grown increasingly defiant.

'Are you taking her side? Don't you dare.'

'I do take her side. Well, in a way. I need to keep her in check or she'd blow us away with Marxist-socialist nonsense. I have to stop her from setting fire to buildings.'

Josie shook her head in frustration. She looked to Lester for support. He hadn't wanted to be drawn into the argument, but her distress, her anger, had become his own. He spoke into a strained silence.

'We can't just pack up and go. Parts of the country still don't want independence yet. They're not ready.'

Cherry waved this aside. 'That's part of the colonial strategy, old sport. Divide and rule. Encourage the go-slows. Force them into conflict with nationalist movements.'

'You've been reading Adele's books, stealing them from under her pillow.'

Cherry's eyes fixed on Lester, a pitying look for someone whose ignorance could be forgiven but not ignored.

'My uncle in Nyasaland thought the British would be there for ever. We should've gone long before, when the Mau Mau troubles in Kenya began. What a bloody mess that was! Wherever we ruled, we were eventually outwitted. We spent too much time worrying about boundaries and constitutions. None of it mattered in the end; they thanked us for neither. Take heed, Australia.'

The argument died as quickly as it had flared. No one was willing to continue. They wandered onto the verandah. Josie and Adele were uncommonly silent. Cherry brought out drinks on a stainless-steel trolley which, he claimed, had once carried instrument trays in the old sanatorium.

'I'm going to the Duke of York Islands next week,' he said to Lester as he handed drinks around. 'I want to visit the health centre. I'm borrowing the Health Department's speedboat. Come over on the government workboat at the weekend. I'll take diving gear for us both. You can use Adele's.'

'Aren't you going, Adele?' Lester was cautious, trying to sound caring.

'I have to work at the hotel.'

'How disappointing for you,' Josie said.

'Perhaps Josie would like to come?' Lester turned hopefully to Cherry.

'Our singing nun?' Cherry smiled. 'Why not, if we can keep her off the rum. She's had two already.'

'I shouldn't have had another drink,' Josie said, struggling with her words. 'You make them too strong. I feel peculiar.'

'I'll take Josie home,' Lester said.

Seizing the moment, he asked her in the car. 'Josie, are you free? Can you possibly miss one church service? Will you come? It would just be the three of us.' It left his heart racing; so simple to do, yet so maddeningly difficult.

He needn't have agonised. She'd love to, she said, well before he'd run through the possible attractions. She hadn't been there since she was a girl, before she left for school in Australia. She must've been only thirteen then. Would they sleep in the *haus kiaps*? How brilliant!

He was already on the workboat when Josie, in baggy shorts, a short-sleeved shirt and broad straw hat with ribbons, tripped briskly along the jetty, an overnight bag over her shoulder. It was a particularly hot, breathless December morning. A cluster of racing dinghies lay becalmed, waiting for a wind eddy from the surrounding hills to stir limp sails.

Lester helped her, lifting her bodily down to the deck. He wanted to press her coolness, her freshness, to him, but she slipped away, clambering over the cargo and onto a vacant space on the boat's cabin roof. She waved at Lester to join her.

'I sat up here when I was a girl,' she said.

A party of four Japanese men hurried along the jetty and onto the boat as it cast off on its daily run. They sat together at a table on the rear deck, shaded by a canvas awning. They pointed excitedly and took photographs as the boat slipped past the Beehives.

Josie picked her way over the cargo and disappeared below deck, reappearing minutes later with a long-sleeved shawl to ward off the sun. She beckoned to him, pointing behind her.

While Lester had been staring to sea, the Japanese party had undergone a transformation. No longer were they businessmen in white shirts and ties, but Japanese soldiers in worn, grey uniforms of the Pacific War, with puttees, jungle boots and crumpled peaked caps.

On the table were maps of the harbour and the surrounding terrain. One was studying the passing shore with binoculars, calling out to those whose heads were bent over the table. Lester guessed the maps marked wartime fortifications—gun emplacements perhaps, and unit lines.

The Japanese opened boxes among the cargo and began to assemble dwarf-sized shovels, screwing steel grey handles into steel grey blades. They unrolled a bundle of clear plastic bags the size of a sugar sack.

'Graves,' whispered Lester to an open-mouthed Josie. 'They must be looking for bones, for their dead comrades, to take them home.'

'They should let them be.' Josie gripped Lester's arm tightly. 'I can't breathe here, I'm suffocating.' She pulled him away, back up to her perch on the cabin roof, and sat down, placing a hand dramatically on her chest. 'Their dead don't deserve to go home.

Those evil, godless people, why are they allowed here? They've done enough harm.'

Josie was upset by the presence of the uniforms. She sat silently at Lester's side as the workboat, beyond the harbour, eased into a long, gentle swell. The Duke of York Islands lay pancake-flat on the horizon, each bristling with palms like an upturned hairbrush. The constant chatter of the Japanese, the clumping of their boots as they clambered about the deck for vantage points with their maps and binoculars, seemed to bounce from the sea's oiled surface and reverberate around the boat. The sun's heat was intense, a searing, white-hot ball.

At the mission settlement of Mioko, Cherry, in a white shirt and shorts and still managing to look like an old-time mission-ary, was waiting for them on the jetty. Around him were the naked, glistening bodies of children diving from the jetty's end. He waved a broad-brimmed straw hat as flamboyant as Josie's.

They set off from the mission in the speedboat Cherry had arrived in the day before, uncomfortably boxed between the clutter of medical stores and diving equipment. Skimming over shallow, opalescent reefs, they crossed a bay to reach a village on a smaller island.

The village was set back from the shore and separated from it by a grassy playing field. The *kiap* rest-hut was close enough to the water's edge to haul the boat up alongside. Cane chairs on the verandah were weatherworn and unravelling. Inside, the hut was bare except for sleeping mats on the floor. Heavy wooden shutters were propped open with blocks of wood. A galvanised tank dripped sweet rainwater from a leaking tap.

Curious children seemed to spring spontaneously from the sea, sand and shade trees to watch them. Tired of their constant attention, Lester crouched like the hunchback Quasimodo and chased them, bellowing, across the field. They fled, screaming, torn between delight and terror.

Josie set off to buy vegetables and fruit in the village. After unloading the medical stores, Cherry and Lester took the boat out to the nearest reef to dive.

Beneath the surface, sunlight spearing through limpid waters set fantastic coral cities afire with colour. Shoals of fish hovered like silver clouds above coral ledges. Far below, sleek shapes of larger fish patrolled a channel in a stately procession. Reef sharks, grey, sinister silhouettes, slipped in and out of a dense blue fog where the sunlight dimmed.

Lester followed closely behind Cherry's slow-moving flippers, gliding along the reef edge in a wake of bubbles, captivated by the elaborate sculpture of the coral, peering into every nook and cranny, under ledges and through Gothic coral arches.

At the far end of the island group, they dived on two rusting Japanese tanks, clearly visible on the sandy bottom. Their stark, alien shapes, softened under a gradual encrustation of coral, would in time be indistinguishable from the natural reef. From between the steel tracks of one tank Lester winkled out a rock lobster by hauling on its waving antennae. Cherry went ahead with his speargun, looking for the rest of the evening meal.

That night they feasted with Josie on boiled lobster and reef fish wrapped in banana leaves and cooked with taro and corn over hot stones. They built up the fire to keep mosquitoes at bay and settled down around it with a bottle of wine between them. Thunderclouds had built up over the mainland, a constant rumble in the sky like distant artillery. A moist heaviness in the air seemed to muffle their voices. The rainstorm, the battlefront, was approaching.

When Lester told Josie about the Japanese tanks, she quicky turned around and stared into the darkness behind her.

'Those Japanese men—I'd forgotten them. They frightened me! People in the village told me they came across from Mioko on the workboat. They're somewhere around here digging up bones.'

Cherry sat up. 'A war graves party? I'd like to meet them. They're staying here?'

'I think they brought a tent. One man tried to sell them the bones of a pig buried under his house in the village. Why can't those Japanese forget the war? Everyone else has.'

'They can't be allowed to forget,' Cherry said. 'They tortured prisoners and starved them to death. They ill-treated the Tolais and the Chinese who stayed. They murdered missionaries and burnt churches. They were a plague. That's what should be remembered.'

'My father would have agreed with you,' Lester said.

'Your father? Did he fight in the war?'

'My parents were in Hong Kong before the Japanese invaded. My mother was evacuated to Australia just before I was born. My father spent the war in an internment camp.'

'I had no idea,' said Cherry. 'How is he now?'

'He died when I was fourteen.'

'Oh Lord, I am sorry.'

'I'm sorry too.' Josie rose and put an arm around Lester's shoulder, drawing him closer.

Lester paused, hesitating, poking the dying fire with a stick. His father had rarely spoken about his internment. Kitty, however, had in time befriended other internees in Sydney and sought their own experiences. After Charles died, she had tried to explain to Lester the reasons why Hong Kong's years of brutal subjugation under the Japanese had changed him into a bitter and withdrawn person.

Lester had never before felt an urge to tell anyone in Sydney of his father's internment. He hadn't even shared this family background with Patsy. In an era when talk of the war was muted, who would have listened? Here in Rabaul, however, echoes of the Japanese occupation were everywhere.

He told them about a building next to the camp site, used as a hospital during the battle for Hong Kong. The Japanese came on Christmas Day. They murdered doctors. They bayonetted wounded soldiers in their beds: British soldiers, Indians, Canadians. Nurses were raped and mutilated. Many bodies were cremated on the spot.

'The Japanese were as cruel in Hong Kong as they were here,' Lester said.

'How horrible!' Josie took her arm away abruptly and turned to Cherry. 'Look what you've done. You've made us all sad. I was so excited to come. I was happy that we'd be together, just me and the two men I love best. I'm determined to be happy. Come and sit beside me.'

The men looked at each other, too astonished to speak. Cherry meekly obeyed. Josie, between them, draped her arms around them both. They filled plastic cups with wine. Josie proposed a toast.

'To our eternal friendship,' she raised her glass. 'And to no more talk about the war.'

A bruising rain began, driving them inside as thunder rolled and lightning crackled overhead. A sudden, violent wind tore at the thatched roof as they secured the window shutters. Lester lay under his mosquito net strung from the roof of the hut and listened to the wind battering flimsy matted walls.

The storm passed and the hissing Tilley lamp burnt low. Cherry was asleep. Lester could see Josie's silhouette behind the adjoining mosquito net as she shrugged off her outer garments and wriggled, arms high overhead, into a cotton nightgown. A peepshow, a fragment of sheet-and-lantern theatre remembered from his childhood.

He watched her kneel in a short prayer. Who did she pray for, he wondered. The souls of the dead Japanese? She was tantalisingly close, but the net was there not only to keep out the mosquitoes. Tomorrow, perhaps, would bring an opportunity to be alone.

Josie shook him awake, peering under his mosquito net, hair tousled and eyes wide. 'I hear noises outside,' she whispered.

Lester sat up. He could see nothing beyond Josie in front of him. The Tilley lamp had gone out; all was in deepest darkness on the verge of dawn. The air after the rain was cool and damp. He shivered and reached for his shirt. He heard Cherry's rapid breathing, the floor creaking as he crept close.

'Quiet and listen,' Cherry hissed.

Outside there was murmuring, then padding footfalls, first on one side of the hut, then on the other. Lester slithered from under his net.

Josie grasped his arm. 'They're all around us.'

'I'll get the speargun.' Cherry's voice was hoarse and not quite steady. 'Where did I leave the bloody thing?' He crawled on hands and knees to the other side, scrabbling in a pile of diving equipment brought from the boat.

Lester held Josie to him, their heads touching. They crept to the side of the hut and slowly raised one of the shutters. Shadowy figures were gathering around the hut.

Josie was distraught. 'Why? Why would they harm us? Just yesterday I was in the village. They know me.'

There were more low voices, a growing crowd.

Cherry handed Lester a diving knife. He pulled back the rubber slings of his speargun and cocked it. With the others behind him, he pulled open the front door and jumped onto the verandah, speargun ready at his hip.

About fifty villagers surrounded the verandah steps. Some carried kerosene lanterns on bamboo poles. For a moment there was a confounded silence. Cherry seemed snap-frozen. A woman screamed in fright. Then, as Lester and Josie's heads appeared from behind the door, the singing began:

'Good King Wenceslas looked out
On the feast of Stephen
When the snow lay round about...'

'It's Christmas Eve tomorrow,' Josie cried. 'Oh, God!'

The Tolai head parishioner, grey-haired and dignified, approached them with a wary eye on Cherry's speargun. He held out an empty tin.

'Merry Christmas, my good friends. Can you spare a donation for repairs to the church?'

Lester's hope of time alone with Josie was soon dashed. Early next morning she announced she was duty-bound to assist her father with the Christmas services. The workboat would be calling at the village and she could take it.

Lester and Cherry came to see her off. She wasn't the only passenger. The Japanese party trooped behind her along the jetty, their plastic bags bulging with bones. They'd exchanged their uniforms for loose Hawaiian shirts, as if they'd come from a Sheraton hotel hidden behind the palms.

There was also a group of suspected felons arrested by the local police, three men handcuffed to one another and again to a constable at each end. If the boat rolled over, Lester thought, they'd drown as one.

Lester and Cherry spent the day among the islands exploring reefs and exhausting the air in their tanks. A rare afternoon breeze sprang up, stiffening as the day wore on. At sunset they started on the return journey to Rabaul, almost two hours away. Lester nursed the diving equipment as Cherry, standing at the wheel with his fair hair flying, steered the speedboat at full tilt into the heaving swells. The light aluminium hull leapt the crests like a giant silver mackerel and yawed wildly into the troughs. They whooped as the spray lashed them both.

A swollen moon, a homing beacon, rose over Rabaul's volcanoes, coating the waves with sparkling sequins. A wake of green phosphorescence trailed behind like a peacock's tail. Lester was exhilarated, awed at the night's wild beauty. And brought on, he knew, by Cherry's sublime confidence as he taunted the sea with the same abandon he brought to driving on land.

Members of the war graves party, they learnt later, were spotted as they left the jetty in town. A band of Australians chased them along the street, hurling empty beer bottles. The Japanese, clutching their bones, fled to the sanctuary of their hotel with the pursuers hot on their heels.

13

Christmas brought a sigh of relief in Rabaul and an uneasy peace to the villages. Mataungan crowds abruptly materialised, marched through the streets and were herded away from the town centre into parks to protest. The police presence was highly visible and reassuring. The courts were in a long summer recess. Christmas gatherings were enjoyed in homes, hotels and clubs; businesses stayed open. To all appearances, life in the town had returned to normal.

Christmas Day crept up on Lester. He found himself alone in an apartment on a day no different from any other. No Christmas tree, tinsel or baubles, no cards or presents, no calls from friends. He felt lost in the absence of Cherry and Josie. He realised at once how much he now depended on them for companionship.

Josie was hosting a Christian work party from Australia. On a previous visit, Josie told them, the party had set about inexpertly constructing a nondescript building that had since fallen down. Their mission this time was to rebuild it.

Cherry and Adele left on a yacht for a week's sailing around islands to the north of New Ireland. According to Cherry, the yacht's owners were two French women. With Adele, that made an all-French, three-woman crew. Cherry was a supernumerary and Lester, consumed by visceral envy, could only imagine how Cherry's week would be spent.

He visited his usual haunts hoping to find Cleary or Hersch but was disappointed. Flanagan's daughters had come up from Australia for Christmas holidays. Flanagan had promised to invite Lester for a Boxing Day barbecue. The invitation never arrived.

He spent the next few days in his apartment drinking beer and reading Joseph Conrad novels borrowed from the town's modest library. Conrad's literary works were described in a preface as trials of the human spirit in an indifferent world. This matched his mood entirely and left him even more despondent.

On New Year's Day he answered a knock on the door. Gloria stood on the landing outside.

'I've brought you a Christmas card,' she said. 'It came to the office. It's from your mother.'

'Thank you,' Lester said. 'You should be on holiday. You needn't have come just for that.'

'Can I see your apartment? Is it comfortable? Is it suitable? Mr Flanagan says I'm responsible for officers' accommodation.'

'I'll show you around.'

Gloria peered into every room. Lester suspected she was looking for any trace of the long-expected Daphne.

'You still cook for yourself,' she said, inspecting the kitchen and shaking her head.

'You must come to dinner sometime,' Lester said, ushering her out.

He sat down, opened the envelope and drew out a card with a snowy landscape, prancing reindeer and a Christmas tree laden with bright red globes. He placed it on the sideboard. Inside the card was a letter.

Lester dearest

Thank you for the money. You know how much Reg and I appreciate it in the mail every month, though the mail is always slow. Reg says it must come down by canoe and it's a wonder it isn't stolen. We're just keeping our heads above water. Reg's British pension runs down here because it's frozen. I'm not old enough yet to get the pension. The arthritis in my hand is getting worse so sewing is painful and I have to take tablets. Reg isn't well, his hip's gone and he can't take carpentry work anymore. He's been a few days in hospital. The dog has taken to its bed in sympathy and won't move.

It sounds very dangerous there with riots and things. I hope you keep the doors locked at night. With Reg being away in hospital I went to a nice Christmas dinner given by the church. Do they celebrate Christmas up there? Reg says not likely as they would all be heathens.

There are letters for you from solicitors. You told me not to worry about letters from lawyers because you were no longer in Australia, so I've thrown them away.

We miss you very much...

The exchange of letters between Lester and his mother had slowed from weekly to monthly, and may have slowed further but for the need to send monthly money orders by post. He'd tried to paint a picture of life in Rabaul but concluded that the pages may as well have been blank, for all she absorbed.

This letter, however, gave rise to some serious soul-searching, with Kitty's underlying accusation of neglect. He'd even forgotten to send a Christmas card. He was also concerned for his grandfather Reg, who'd given him more affection than his father ever had. Why had he really been in hospital? Kitty, with English stoicism, was inclined to understate adversity.

Even more unsettling was that lawyers and police knew where he'd lived and were still sniffing around for evidence of wrongdoing. He fervently wished they'd leave his mother alone and move on. Only then would he be fully free to enjoy his work, his friends and life in Rabaul.

PART 2

Rabaul 1970

14

The calm that settled over the Gazelle after the violence in December lasted less than a month, disrupted by the visit of Gough Whitlam, leader of the opposition Labor Party in Australia.

This visit was part of a countrywide tour. The Labor Party was well aware Australia lagged behind Great Britain and most of Europe in divesting itself of colonies. Long-standing criticism also came from visiting missions sent by the United Nations to observe and report on Papua New Guinea's political development.

The fanfare of Whitlam's arrival confused Tolai supporters on both sides not familiar with the distinction between prime ministers and opposition leaders. The parliamentary delegation was accompanied by personal staff and the press, making a large entourage, driving about town in a fleet of government cars.

More than ten thousand cheering, chanting, singing Mataungan supporters welcomed them at an open-air rally. Whitlam, an imposing figure and rousing orator, told the crowd the Labor Party, if it came to power in Australia, would lead them to self-government and independence within a few short years.

He expressed his delegation's admiration for the Mataungans' organisation and leadership.

His dismissive, at times insulting, view of the role of expatriates, whether planters, businessmen or administration officials, turned many expatriates against him and stoked resentment among supporters of the multiracial council. To the Mataungans, however, he was the Great Liberator.

The monsoon brought the heaviest and most frequent rains of the year. Short, violent squalls filled floodwater drains in minutes. Playing fields became lakes and rivers ran along roadsides. Fallen coconuts and palm fronds littered roads. Between rainstorms, the air was still and cool, the harbour a sheet of smoked glass reflecting sour skies.

The storms brought strong surf to Pilapila Beach. On a day when the surf was running, Lester received a call from an excited Cherry, freshly home from his yachting adventure. They agreed to meet in the afternoon for a surfing lesson.

Lester was a good swimmer, having learnt during long summers at the Greenwich Baths. He'd been to Bondi Beach often enough to pick up the rudiments of bodysurfing. Cherry's swimming style, on the other hand, was vigorous but untrained. Even with swimming flippers he found it impossible to pick up the smallest waves. He struggled and was left behind in the foam. He persevered until he was exhausted and lay down on the sand.

'It's like learning to ride a bicycle,' Lester told him. 'Just when you think you'll never learn, the next minute you're wondering why it took so long. Watch the village kids out there and you'll see how easy it is.'

'I'll get there in the end.' Cherry waved him away.

Resting on the shore as the day's heat abated, they watched as cheeky, duck-diving, chattering Tolai children frolicked in deeper water where the waves were larger. Water droplets clustered on their short, tight curls like specks of silver. A shake of the head sent a sparkling spray into the air. They rode the largest waves as if born in the sea, leaning an arm on a short wooden strip from a fruit crate and careering fearlessly down the smooth wave face, shrieking, popping up again like corks in the churning backwash with broad grins and teeth as white as the foam.

Lester realised how much he treasured being alone with Cherry. Cherry's attitude to any activity he undertook had no middle course, no reserve. He had energy to spare. When they were together, Lester often felt, oddly, extra energy flowing into his own body.

Walking further along the beach, they came upon part of a tree trunk standing upright on the sand, washed up long ago and stranded beyond the tides. Three truncated branches forked from a central limb, smooth and bleached to the colour of bone. It gleamed in the setting sun.

'It's a driftwood sculpture,' Lester said. 'An abstract piece.'

Cherry took hold of a branch and wheeled the trunk around. 'Now there are two arms and legs. It's a human figure, something by Henry Moore.'

'It's speaking to me,' Lester said. 'I've got to have it.'

They heaved it onto the tray of Cherry's ute. Back at Grandview Apartments they hauled it laboriously up the staircase and into Lester's living room, then stood it against one wall. It reached to nearly his own height. The wooden floor creaked beneath its weight.

Cherry looked around him. 'I haven't seen your apartment. It's nice. Very spacious.'

'It's for married officers. I'm meant to have a fiancée called Daphne whose arrival is forever imminent.'

'I like that. Actually, I'm surprised you're still single. A little bird told me you turn thirty soon.'

'I think I know that little bird. And it's twenty-nine, not thirty. Anyway, I could say the same about you, and you're older than me.'

Cherry ignored him. 'You get airmail letters,' he said, pointing to a small pile on the sideboard. 'Does she write to you, your phantom fiancée?'

'They're from my mother. Do you get letters from your family?'

'Lord, no, they think I'm somewhere in Africa.'

The answer startled Lester. Before he could inquire further, Cherry jumped elsewhere. 'Have you met your neighbours?'

'A Hungarian called Szabo lives opposite me. At least his name sounds Hungarian. He comes and goes in a ute filled with diving gear, but he doesn't talk.'

'Szabo? Everyone in the diving business knows him. He's a dangerous man.'

'Dangerous? Should I lock the doors at night?'

'He works as a mechanic in town, but he makes his own explosives.'

'Then there's Bilson,' Lester went on. 'He lives below Szabo.'

'Who's Bilson?'

'A *kiap.*'

'A scourge of the Mataungans? Do you know him?'

'I've only met him once; he's rarely home. Like all the *kiaps,* he rushes about frantically trying to calm things down.'

'Who lives beneath you?'

'A middle-aged lady. I call her the captain's wife, but I think her name is Norma. Bilson says she's so thin, her bones rattle. She doesn't talk either. I see her every afternoon lying on a banana chair in the garden, under the big mango tree. She reads novels and drinks prodigious quantities of gin and tonic.'

'Where's the captain?'

'He's another I've rarely seen. Bilson told me he's in charge of a coastal trading ship that wallows around plantation ports, overloaded with sacks of copra.'

Cherry moved over to the window to peer into the garden.

'The captain's wife won't be there now,' Lester said. 'It's well after dark.'

Cherry stared silently into the night. When he spoke again, his tone was apologetic, even supplicatory.

'Could I possibly come and stay for while? The hospital's understaffed; everyone's away on holidays. I haven't told them I'm back in Rabaul. They'll try to find me at Taliligap, but I don't want to go back yet.'

'You can have the second bedroom. It even has a bed and bedsheets, thanks to my accommodation officer. She thinks I'll soon be a family man.'

Lester was overjoyed to have Cherry to himself. At times when Adele and Josie were present together, he wished they weren't. They became the focus of Cherry's attention, and he was relegated to the background. His jealousy went beyond Josie's obsession with Cherry. It was a conundrum he couldn't resolve, and it was beginning to plague him.

Next day, the waves at Pilapila were gentler and Cherry floundered less. As they returned to their clothes on the beach, two teenage girls in bikinis approached them. They were sisters, sharing the same stringy brown hair and freckles. The taller and elder stopped before Lester.

'Are you Lester Chettle? My dad says you are. He saw you when he brought us here. I'm Mary Flanagan, and this is Lucy.'

Lester looked around. 'Where's your father?'

'He's coming back for us soon,' Mary said. She pointed to the masks and swimming fins on the sand. 'Can you take us snorkelling? Our dad said we can't go alone. We have our own masks.'

So, these were the daughters from the photograph in Flanagan's bedroom, Lester thought. How quickly they'd blossomed from children into teenagers with budding breasts and a cheeky sexuality. He needed to be wary.

'I've been in the water for hours already,' he said. 'I'm tired out.'

'I'll take them,' Cherry said.

The Flanagan daughters were out on the nearby reef with Cherry when John Flanagan, in shorts and a T-shirt, came striding over the sand. Lester jumped to his feet, ran to the reef edge and called them in.

'Who's that fellow?' Flanagan asked Lester curtly, pointing to Cherry. 'Do you know him?'

'That's Anthony Cherry-Apsley from Nonga Hospital—the doctor in that New Guinea Club case. Your girls are safe with him.'

With the merest nod to Cherry, Flanagan clapped his hands and called, 'Come, girls, time to go home.'

'Can't we stay longer? We want to talk to Mister Cherry,' Mary said plaintively. 'He's fun, for a doctor.'

Flanagan merely swept his daughters away. From a distance, he called back to Lester, 'I'll see you in the office tomorrow. There's work to do.'

'Not a friendly chap,' Cherry said when they were out of earshot. 'Is he your boss? Looks a bit volatile. Never even introduced himself.'

'It's just his manner,' Lester said, annoyed and embarrassed. 'He's an ex-policeman. I feel sorry for the girls. From the way they looked at you, they're completely smitten. You've won two young hearts and Daddy doesn't approve.'

Szabo's apartment adjoined Lester's. It, too, was accessed by an outside wooden staircase with a small landing. When Lester and Cherry returned in the late afternoon, Szabo, bronzed and fearsomely black-bearded, was leaning on his landing rail smoking a cigar.

'Want to join me for a drink?'

They were astonished to see his living room given over to a collection of glass tanks filled with seawater. The walls of this watery kingdom vibrated to the hum of tiny pumps, making the water fizz and bubble. Tanks sparkled with the darting, flashing shapes of small reef fish.

This was his hobby, Szabo told them. His English was laboured, his accent heavily East European, his voice like the rumble of a ship's engine far below deck. The fish were rare. They awaited sale to a Chinese merchant who packed them in plastic bags onto an aircraft, eventually to find their way—the few that survived—into home aquariums in Hong Kong or Singapore.

With the beer flowing freely, he warmed to his story. As the number of tanks grew, his wife's tolerance of his hobby diminished. She'd left for Australia long ago. Would his friends like to see the divorce papers? She was a gold-digger; she was grabbing all he had. But she'd never get his fish tanks. He'd kill her first.

Lester and Cherry continued to drink after returning to Lester's apartment. Since his return, Cherry had barely mentioned his yachting trip to Kavieng. The late hour, however, was ripe for revelations.

'I know what you want to hear,' Cherry sighed. 'Sorry to disappoint you, there's no story of debauchery to tell. There was no sex at all.'

All the gear for trans-ocean travel had left little room on the boat, and no chance of privacy. Despite an obvious intimacy between the two women yacht owners, one took a fancy to Adele, which angered the other; the other took a fancy to Cherry, which made Adele jealous.

The three women argued, resulting in the owners deciding to cast Adele and Cherry ashore at Kavieng. In a change of heart, they anchored instead off a plantation on the coast nearby and stayed for a week before sailing back to Rabaul.

Leila, the plantation owner and manager, was a woman in her forties who was both French and Jewish. Starved of the company of compatriots, she'd fed and royally entertained the visitors. According to Cherry, Leila had tried to interest him in attending to her emotional needs, inviting him to return and stay at any time.

'It was all very complicated and unsatisfactory,' said Cherry. 'I'm done with yachts and yachting.'

'And done with French women?' Lester laughed, wondering how much to believe.

Cherry shrugged. 'Well, perhaps not Adele, though she's not talking to me just now.'

'I'm not surprised.'

'It's your turn now.' Cherry grinned.

'I've nothing to report. I swam, read and played my guitar.'

Silence for a time. The drinks cupboard was bare. Cherry sighed again.

'Then it's back to you, me and Josie, the Taliligap Trio.'

'The Taliligap Trio?'

'Josie decided on the name. I hadn't the nerve to object.'

'She was right to be upset that night on the island; we disappointed her,' Lester said. 'All that talk about the war. Then we waved her off to Rabaul on a boat with Japanese bone-hunters and a conga-line of felons. We have to apologise. We have to get back together.'

'Let's make a pact,' Cherry said. 'While Josie's with us, the word *Japanese* will never again escape our lips.' He rose but turned at the bedroom door. 'You *must* pay a visit to Yamamoto's Bunker.'

15

On a wet and blustery Saturday afternoon, Lester took up Cherry's suggestion and went in search of the Bunker.

Only four years after Rabaul was devastated by a volcanic eruption, it was overtaken by the Pacific War. Off the main street and opposite the New Guinea Club was a dingy underground chamber, popularly known as Yamamoto's Bunker. This was on the questionable ground it had once been used by Admiral Isoroku Yamamoto, Commander-in-Chief of the Japanese Combined Fleet, while on an inspection trip to Japanese bases.

Late in 1941, an Australian garrison of less than fourteen hundred men, a battalion of soldiers whose average age was eighteen and a half, with two anti-aircraft guns, two naval guns and a handful of outdated aircraft, was left to defend Rabaul and its prized harbour against the southward thrust of a mighty Japanese war machine.

The town was softened up by bombing. Despite a few brave encounters, the Australian air defences were quickly overcome. A Japanese invasion force of more than forty ships and one hundred aircraft descended on the hapless town. Five thousand Japanese troops were put ashore in a score of landing craft. The

Australians put up a short but spirited defence before breaking up and retreating into the hills. The retreat was far more
costly in lives than the invasion had been—an abysmal episode
in Australian military history.

Within hours of their landing, the Japanese secured a
prime base from which they hoped to invade mainland Papua
New Guinea and control the whole of the South-West Pacific
theatre.

As the tide turned against the Japanese in the Pacific, the
town became, instead, a defensive fortress and a target of Allied
vengeance. For almost two years it was ceaselessly harassed by
air attacks until no Japanese ship or aircraft could find haven
there. Twenty thousand tons of bombs razed the town and pitted the countryside. To avoid the bombing, the Japanese went
underground, digging tunnels into the volcanic hills.

The Gazelle Peninsula was gradually surrounded by Allied
bases in West New Britain, Bougainville and the Admiralty
Islands. It was blockaded and totally isolated. When the Australians returned to Rabaul in August 1945, a stranded garrison of
nearly one hundred thousand men was there to surrender, having been in occupation for three and a half years. In the town,
not a stick was left standing.

There was little to see in the Bunker, a few battered relics,
maps and fading photographs. The dim, dank ambience and
Japanese inscriptions on the walls conveyed to Lester the same
menacing air he had felt while staying on the Duke of York
Islands.

Following the December violence, Flanagan was engulfed by
an admin machine that huffed and puffed against the constant

irritant of the Mataungan Association. An influx of *kiaps* and other more mysterious government agents swelled the admin's forces.

A parallel organisation arose, devoted to intelligence gathering and answering to no one but secretive bureaucrats in far-off Port Moresby and Canberra. The business of these agents was spying and rumour mongering. Key words such as *confrontation*, *infiltration*, *informants* and *intimidation* appeared abundantly in their reports.

Flanagan loved the meetings: the intrigue, tactics and strategic planning. That left Lester to look after the office and the criminal circuits. For Lester, returning to an airconditioned office was a welcome relief. How easy it would've been, he thought, to succumb to the unrelenting heat and humidity and lie about all day like the captain's wife, in a state of tropical torpor. He needed the challenge of court work.

Gloria dropped the files for the next Circuit on his desk: cases in Rabaul and Bougainville to prepare. It wasn't long before Flanagan's bulk loomed in the office doorway.

'Not much there,' Flanagan said, pointing to the case files. 'Should be a couple of easy wins.' His way of saying that only an idiot could bungle them. Lester expected this but wasn't to be put down.

'How are your two lovely young ladies?' he asked with a smile he hoped would be disarming. 'How grown up they are, how mature.'

'Grown up? Mature? Nonsense. I can't look after them. I can't control them. They get bored too easily. They're begging to be led astray. I'm sending them home to their mother in Brisbane.'

'That's a shame. They told my doctor friend at the beach they loved it here: swimming, cycling, sailing, visiting the market, catching up with friends from primary school...'

With a stifled splutter, Flanagan interrupted.

'I enquired at the hospital about your doctor friend. Too charming by half, I was told. Charms the hospital staff. Charms his way out of hard work. His name came up in an intelligence report. Apparently, he has a troublesome girlfriend from New Caledonia. And he's been bandaging up wounded Mataungans.'

'He's a doctor, how can he refuse to treat someone who's wounded? It's his ethical duty.'

'That depends. I'd like to remind you that you're a crown prosecutor. You need to be careful of the company you keep.'

Flanagan walked back to his office, pulling repeatedly at his left ear, one of his odd gestures signifying annoyance or displeasure. Gabriel, at his desk in another corner, had no doubt heard the conversation. When Flanagan's back was turned, Lester looked across at Gabriel and pulled vigorously at his own ear. Gabriel's hand flew to his mouth to cover a smile. He knew all about Flanagan's peculiar mannerisms.

According to Hersch, who landed in Rabaul breathless and sweaty, only to take off next day for another trouble spot, Whitlam's visit to Papua New Guinea had played out on the front pages of Australian newspapers. Not only had the Labor leader stirred up the Mataungans but nationalist and would-be secessionist groups elsewhere in the country. He had repeated, to all in Australia who would listen, that if elected, he'd hasten to grant self-government and independence within his government's first term.

For most Australians, the political debate brought back a dimly perceived vision of jungles and coconut palms somewhere to the north of Australia, where their troops had fought a war and for which, surprisingly, they still seemed to have some responsibility. But for the first time, Australians living in Papua New Guinea caught an unnerving glimpse of the future. Their days as colonial overlords were running out.

'Young man, help me,' Norma called from the garden where she lay on a banana chair in the shade. Beside her on a stool were a bottle of Gilbey's gin, a collection of empty bottles of tonic that circled the gin like satellites and a plastic ice bucket. Spread open on her bosom was a romance novel with a dusky, muscled male in a pirate costume on the cover. After an afternoon's steady consumption of gin, Norma was unable to raise herself from the chair.

Lester helped her into her apartment, next door to Bilson's. Although she called Lester 'young man', she was by no means an old woman, but twenty years in the tropics had taken a heavy toll. She screwed up her eyes as she tried to bring into focus Lester's face on the far side of her dining room table. Her hands shook as she lit a cigarette. Her fingers, Lester noticed, seemed set in a permanent curl.

The captain was away, she said. Lester's fleeting glimpses had been of a large man driving away on a ridiculously small motorbike, his legs bent out at right angles like outriggers.

In the captain's absence, Norma spent her days at the Country Women's Association and played bingo. She had worked once, she told Lester. Oh yes, she had been a secretary, but something had mysteriously knotted up her fingers. She had gone to work one day and couldn't get them to move. She couldn't type. The fingers hadn't moved since.

Anyway, she was leaving soon. It had been fun once, living in Rabaul. It wasn't any more. All her friends were going. The natives were taking over. They were incompetent; they were uncivilised.

They sent a native from Port Moresby to take over her friend's husband's position in the Department of Agriculture. The man had defecated in an office wastepaper basket because he couldn't find the toilet. That was enough for her friend, and more than enough for Norma. She was just waiting for her own husband. He was on his last trip.

According to Bilson, it was always the captain's last trip. He'd been on his last voyage for many years. Norma was trapped in her banana chair under the trees, dreaming of dusky pirate kings.

Another week passed before Lester heard again from Cherry. The long-awaited reunion with Josie would be at Taliligap at the weekend.

'Oh, Chugger!' Josie cried from the verandah as he arrived. She ran to greet him with a beaming smile and a hug as strong as it was unexpected.

'Chugger?'

'That's what they called you at school,' laughed Josie. 'Chugger Chettle. Cherry told me.'

Lester called out to Cherry, lounging in his verandah chair, drink in hand. 'I told you not to tell her that.'

'I told her not to call you that,' Cherry said.

'I forgot,' Josie said, kissing Lester on the cheek. 'I've forgotten everything.'

That was the end of the cloud that had hovered over them since Christmas, if it had ever really existed.

'Is Adele here?' Lester asked.

'She's at home in Chinatown, sulking,' said Josie. 'Cherry told me their romantic yacht trip didn't work out.'

To be so close to her now, to hear the conversation between her and Cherry, the easy familiarity and sharing of each other's secrets, was difficult for Lester to bear. Since they last saw her, she'd been an organiser for the work party, she told them, a fetch-and-carry person running around in the sun.

She was no longer so thin or pale. The cropped hairstyle was gone. Her dark hair was now sun-streaked and more abundant, falling naturally over her forehead. Her clothes no longer looked they'd come from a trade store or charity shop. Lester was astonished at her transformation within a few short weeks.

In her absence he'd dreamed of her often. At times she was simply sharing music and laughter on a Sunday afternoon, but there were nights when they were back in the *kiap* hut at Mioko, where she would undress for him beneath a mosquito net and beg him to join her. He'd suddenly awaken, hot, ashamed and with a tormented longing for her to be beside him.

His gaze must have rested upon her too long. She studied him for a moment and smiled. 'Have I changed, Lester?'

Lester groped for a reply. 'You have. You're positively... blooming.'

A ridiculous response, but Josie was unfazed.

'You've changed, too. All that diving and swimming. Cherry says you ride the waves like a dolphin. That must be exciting. The lifeguards do it in Sydney, don't they?'

Her tone was affectionate, gently mocking. She unpacked her tape recorder and they listened to popular songs she'd recorded. She'd decided to take control of the repertoire, she said. She wanted to play in places other than church halls; she fancied a restaurant or hotel garden, so they had to be polished and professional. At Taliligap, they would rehearse longer and lay about—by which she clearly meant drink—less.

'Steady on!' Cherry said.

'I want to accomplish something,' Josie said. 'I don't want to be the ticket girl at the back of the hall, or everyone else's helper for the rest of my life. I'm not a doctor or a lawyer like you; I'm a nobody.'

'You're a music teacher,' Lester said.

'I want to *be* the music, not *teach* it. And especially not teach it to Tolais who can sing in harmony from the cradle.'

'Then I agree to anything you say,' Lester said, ever eager to gain favour.

Josie, grinning, clapped her hands. 'It's decided by a majority, two to one.'

Cherry shrugged. 'Make it unanimous. Now, before our abstinence begins, let's have a drink or two to celebrate.'

Long after dark, Lester drove Josie home. She wound down the passenger window as the Mercedes began its descent from the ridge, complaining she needed to feel warm and smell the sea. Lester was thrilled to have Josie to himself for a time, however brief.

His yearning to talk was thwarted. Heavy rain began; clouds blanketed the moon. The narrow, winding road was treacherous at night, made more so by occasional PMVs weaving erratically uphill.

'Close the window or we'll be soaked,' was all he could say.

'I like getting wet!' Josie said, putting an arm out of the window, then her head, forcing Lester to pull her back. Rainwater dripped from her hair and ran down her cheeks. She's had more rum than was good for her, Lester thought. She was excited about her plans for the Trio. Suddenly she turned towards him, gripping his arm.

'Why did that ghastly politician come?'

'You mean Gough Whitlam?'

'Horrible man! He ignored our elders, our pastors, our church. They said he calls himself an atheist, even though he was brought up a Christian. He praised the Mataungans. Their leaders are Catholics, but the United Church is the true Indigenous church. Our bishop is a Tolai; their bishops are foreigners. We were here first. Then the Catholics came and caused trouble from the start, chasing converts.'

'Josie, please let go of my arm, I can't drive.'

Josie sank back in her seat. 'Do you care?'

'Of course I care. I was as shocked as you were. But he's not the Prime Minister.'

'Adele believed he was the Prime Minister, so Cherry said. So did many people in our parish. He confused them. He encouraged them to believe it. Why aren't you prosecuting the Mataungan leaders? Isn't it treason or something? You're allowing the violence to go on.'

Josie's words came out in a passionate flurry. Her cheeks were flushed. Lester wondered if tears mingled with raindrops from her hair.

'The leaders *are* being prosecuted. We have to be careful not to turn them into martyrs.'

'They're the wrong kind of martyrs,' Josie said.

As they turned onto the wider, less perilous coast road, the rain eased. With the warmth and sea air Josie's anger seemed to drain away.

'You're such a good listener,' she said after a silence. 'Cherry doesn't agree with me and doesn't listen. He thinks independence can't come soon enough. Did you know, when he was a medical student in London, he had an African girlfriend? She was from Ghana or somewhere. He said countries like Ghana and Tanzania became independent ten years ago. He thinks Africans are far more sophisticated.'

'Perhaps, but that's why the admin isn't rushing things. What happened to the girlfriend, did he tell you?'

'Her father, the ambassador, found out. It caused a diplomatic incident.'

Cherry had already told Lester of the glorious attributes of his African girlfriend. No doubt had revealed all this and more to Josie. He could tell stories that could convince anyone who listened to them.

16

The success of the Mataungan campaign to boycott payment of taxes to the multiracial council led to a dramatic
reduction in council revenue. Road projects stalled and census
patrols, vital for health and education reasons as well as for tax
collection, were disrupted. The administration, left squirm-
ing between a rock and a hard place, embarked on a raft of tax
prosecutions against prominent Mataungan supporters.

Meanwhile, prosecutions before a magistrate for the December violence continued. Lester was in the Rabaul office with Flanagan and Carstairs, a seasoned prosecutor from Port Moresby.
Flanagan, deposed as the lead prosecutor, was morosely lend-
ing assistance. Lester's criminal cases for the Islands Circuit
were to begin the next day. Listening to Flanagan and Carstairs
arguing incessantly about the minutiae of witness statements
and degrees of assault, he couldn't resist intervening.

'Why do I get the feeling we're losing battles, one after
another, as well as not winning the war?'

'What do you mean by that, exactly?' Carstairs demanded.
He appeared even more pugnacious than Flanagan.

'Tolais at the market think the admin has declared war on them. A hanging judge, riot squads, police roadblocks, stopping produce from getting to the market, harassing stallholders and so on. As for taxes, they say forcing them to pay is pointless now; there are thousands of defaulters, more than enough to fill all the jails in the country.'

'And what do you say?' Flanagan asked.

Lester shrugged. 'I'd have to agree with them.'

Carstairs turned to Flanagan with a wry smile. 'I think your man is batting for the wrong team.'

Gloria appeared at Flanagan's side, announcing breathlessly, 'Judge Prest is on the phone.'

Flanagan sighed and left his office to take the call.

'You don't see the wider picture, Chettle,' Carstairs went on. 'You live in a bubble here. This is about one law for the country. We can't make special deals for the privileged few, and that means the Tolai.'

Before Lester could respond, Flanagan returned.

'The judge is going to Bougainville first, then coming back here. He'll stay at the judge's house. Go with Gabriel and Gloria. See if it's shipshape.'

When they arrived at the judges' residence, nothing needed to be done; Gloria had made sure of that. The bungalow boasted a level lawn and a glorious vista of the harbour. Lester settled into an armchair outside to take in the view. Gloria came out to join him.

'I wish I lived here,' Lester said.

'She's not coming, is she?' Gloria busied herself with a cloth, cleaning and polishing a second armchair that no amount of cleaning or polishing could restore.

'Who's not coming?'

'Her. Your fiancée.'

'It looks like she won't be.'

'Gabriel told me you have a girlfriend, the daughter of a Methodist minister.'

Lester was taken aback. 'She's not really my girlfriend. And how did he know?'

'He knows everything. He has eyes and ears in every tree.'

'He has no business telling you about my private life.'

'You can't bring her here. That's what happened to Mr Rollinson. He was in your office before you. He used to bring girls up here when the house was empty. Mr Flanagan found out and sent him back to Port Moresby.'

When Gloria went inside, Lester sought out Gabriel, chatting with the cook at the back of the bungalow.

'Gloria told me what happened to Rollinson,' Lester said. 'Did you know about that?'

'I knew.' Gabriel smirked. 'Sometimes he brought women here. Sometimes he brought Gloria. That made *planti trabel*.'

If there were totally unspoiled fragments of civilisation remaining in the twentieth century, the tiny island of Sohano, at the head of the Buka Passage, was certainly one of them. The Buka Passage separated neighbouring Buka Island from the northern end of Bougainville.

Judge Prest and the court party took a boat for the short journey from the airport on Buka to Sohano, then toiled up a hill to the admin guesthouse, perched near a cliff edge at the sharp end of the island. Like the bridge of a great ship, it looked over the sapphire-blue waters of the passage. The island itself, with its early-colonial-era buildings, parklike surrounds and giant rain trees, had barely changed from before the war, despite having been occupied by Japanese forces.

The sole case for trial was a charge of murder. Lester met with the local *kiap* and police to ensure that witnesses and the defendant would be rounded up to appear the next day.

According to Flanagan, this duty was often overlooked in sleepy outstations.

That afternoon he joined Mr Tomkins, the judge's Associate, for a swim at the base of the hill, where a gap in the narrow coral shelf was sheltered from a strong current flowing through the passage. They were followed down to the water by excited children with the rich, dark-chocolate skin that readily distinguished the people of Bougainville from those in other parts of the country. The children watched in awe as the corpulent form of Tomkins floated in the shallows, belly-up, pale and gleaming under the bright blue sky.

Like the now-superannuated Mr Broad, Tomkins was English but, relatively speaking, younger and more animated. He told Lester he'd once been a colonial civil servant and later a court official in Malaya before it merged with neighbouring states to become Malaysia.

A reservoir of such Englishmen, relics of the Empire, seemed determined to remain in a colonial setting somewhere in the world.

Three police constables dawdled around the doors of the wooden courthouse. One pointed to the man, slight, dark and middle-aged, accused of beheading his mother with an axe. He lay alone under a tree fifty yards away, fast asleep, his feet resting on the cross frame of a bicycle propped against the tree. The judge was delighted and took a photograph.

No argument about the facts, with witnesses to the sudden and violent attack. The defendant sat on a courtroom bench accompanied by a constable. When interviewed, he'd remained silent, revealed no motive and shown no remorse. He paid little attention to the proceedings.

With his head tilted and eyes closed, he seemed to be listening to the breeze whispering through the open windows. Occasionally he listened to the interpreter's translation of a witness statement and nodded. The interpreter's words might as well have come from another world.

Eventually, the judge stopped the proceedings and peered closely at the accused. '*Het bilong yu i pen?*'

'*Pen nogut tru,*' the defendant said, nodding vigorously and grimacing.

'This man has a bad headache,' the judge declared. 'I suspect he may have a brain tumour. Has he been examined by a doctor?'

Was there a doctor on Sohano, or even on Buka Island? Was there a neurologist? How could you be examined for a brain tumour in this far-flung corner of the Pacific? The judge knew that perfectly well.

'No, your Honour,' Lester said.

Arrangements were made to take the man, in police custody, to Port Moresby for a diagnosis. He'd been brought from a village far away, so few spectators were present. The case was adjourned indefinitely.

The court party trooped back to the guest house, leaving the police, the *kiap* and his staff scratching their heads. It had promised to be an open-and-shut case. Who would have thought to look inside the man's head?

The trial in Sohano ended a day earlier than expected, so the judge ordered a workboat to carry the court party through a scattering of idyllic islets lying south of Buka Passage and down to Soraken, an extensive plantation on the main island of Bougainville. There, the judge had played a part in the Pacific War only months before its end.

When they arrived, the plantation station and its tiny port seemed deserted, with plantation hands sleeping soundly in the haze of afternoon heat. Eventually two young workers, rubbing their eyes, took the judge and reluctant members of his party on a tour to find old foxholes and trenches.

The judge recounted the advance of his platoon on the Japanese stronghold around the plantation, but struggled to find and point out the old landmarks. He scratched his head often as he looked about. Where once had been a thousand Japanese troops close by with their barges, field guns and ammunition dumps, now were only grass and coconut palms.

He found a chicken coop where his field headquarters had been. Once he had heard the whine and thump of artillery shells, the crack and stutter of small arms and the shouts of men in battle; now, only the drowsy hum of insects. Where was the tree from which he had spied on a Japanese camp? Was it this one, fallen and now rotting at the water's edge, or that one in the distance, a leafless skeleton framed against the harsh sun?

Lester felt pity for the judge as he struggled with his memories and sense of place. The judge told them of his fear at night, waiting for the raiding Japanese; of the close friend who'd died in his arms. And in the end, he said, it had all been pointless. The war had already been won.

'We've a booking at the Steakhouse restaurant!' Josie was bubbling with the news. 'I went with Cherry to see the owner while you were away. We played a tape of our music. It's only a trial; we can come early on Friday nights.'

'A free dinner for three and a bottle of wine,' Cherry added.

'I'm working in town at the church's printing press,' Josie said. 'Some educational things. There's a meeting room where we can rehearse. I can stay in town, too, so we can meet twice a week.'

They were enjoying drinks on the lawn outside the Cosmopolitan Hotel on Saturday afternoon. Adele, at work behind the bar, brought out sandwiches and cake. She sat down on Cherry's knee and placed an extravagant kiss on his cheek.

'No payment,' she said before running inside. 'They owe me overtime.'

'She seems to have got over the sulks,' Lester said.

Cherry smiled. 'We've been on a dive together. She's fine now.'

'I'm *so* glad,' Josie said. 'I thought she might do herself harm or something. She's so *intense*.'

Lester looked across the table at Josie, dressed for an outing in a frock both elegantly simple and daringly above the knee. She was in town, he thought. Cherry was at Taliligap and still attached to Adele. Here was his chance to ask her to dinner at the best hotel in Rabaul.

His elation was soon smothered by doubt. Dining with her alone would upset a delicate balance in the relationship between the three of them. He was afraid Josie might refuse.

'What exciting crimes have you been dealing with?' Josie asked. 'We missed you.'

'A murder in Bougainville, a rape in the Duke of York Islands.'

'A rape case there? I can't believe it.'

'The three men in handcuffs, who came back on the boat with you on Christmas Eve, raped a sixteen-year-old girl.'

Josie's hand flew to her cheek. 'Surely not. They looked like boys to me. Is she all right? Was she hurt?'

'She wasn't hurt. She didn't struggle. They led her to a quiet spot in the bush and threatened her with a bush knife. They took her in turn.'

'What'd be the point of struggling with three strong, armed men? I hope you sent them to jail forever.'

'It's not me who sends them to jail. I asked the judge for five-year sentences. He gave them less than half that.'

'They'd have got ten years in England,' Cherry said.

'Their lawyer said people in the village thought she was promiscuous and should be taught a lesson. A meeting of village elders fined the men eight dollars each and gave the money to her family. The police only found out later through some garrulous old woman in the village. The judge said he took all that into account.'

'That's disgusting!' Josie said. 'That's the trouble; it's all about men. The rapists are men, the elders are men, the police are men, the lawyers are men, the judges are men. Women count for nothing.'

Lester and Cherry tried in vain to calm Josie's agitation. All she wanted to talk about was the lowly status of women in the village and in her church. So much denigration, she said, so much violence against women who dared stand up for themselves.

As evening came, they went their separate ways, Cherry to Taliligap, Josie to the home of a church pastor in town. Though only a street or two away, Lester insisted on driving her in the Mercedes. He opened the car boot and brought out a woven basket the size and shape of a soccer ball, closed by a lid and dyed in a decorative pattern. So-called Buka baskets were much sought-after for their quality and design.

'I bought it for you in Sohano,' he said. 'Don't tell Cherry.'

Josie cried in delight. 'A secret, I promise. I'll fill it with little things, my treasures.' She pulled Lester close and kissed him. Her breath, with the sweet scent of rum and Coca-Cola, was warm on his cheek.

'It's been a long time since anyone's given me a present,' she said, laughing. 'It's so long that I've forgotten when.'

Repercussions of the December violence continued to haunt a tetchy John Flanagan. As he predicted, appeals were mounted in the Supreme Court over the original convictions for assault by Mataungan leaders and supporters.

The truth was summary justice had been handed down by the magistrate in the glare of publicity and in the heat of the moment. Several convictions were overturned and the defendants set free. To add insult to injury for the Rabaul Prosecutor's office, among the defendants released was Gabriel Toporo.

Flanagan had ordered Lester to assist him in court by putting forward spurious reasons why the appeals shouldn't succeed. Lester gritted his teeth and did so, certain the judge would dismiss them with withering criticism.

'You knew that'd happen, didn't you?' Lester asked Flanagan bitterly as they left the courtroom. 'You put me up as cannon fodder.'

'I call it character building,' Flanagan said. 'It'll stiffen your spine.'

'And save your bacon,' Lester muttered under his breath, in no mood to forgive him. Flanagan made sure it was Lester's name, not his, that appeared in the newspapers.

To make matters worse, Flanagan stormed into the office brandishing a copy of the *Post Courier* and flung it onto Lester's desk. An article published the text of a telegram Mr Whitlam had sent to a freed Mataungan leader:

> *You have won a victory, not only for yourself and your people, but also for the rule of law and for justice itself. This judgment stands as a crushing answer to those who vilified your colleagues, your people and their aspirations.*

The curious thing was that despite Lester's humiliation in court, the experience had a positive effect. Some local police officers now saw him as a prosecutor who was at least valiant in defeat. Moreover, the Supreme Court judge sent him a note:

> *Mr Chettle, you made the best of a bad hand. Well done.*

In the glow of rare praise, Lester was left to ponder whether he might yet be a better lawyer than Flanagan would ever be.

17

The southeast trade winds in May brought some relief to the heat and humidity in the afternoons. Palms along the seaboard swayed and waved their fronds in protest at the breeze; whitecaps flashed in the open sea. Around the harbour, dinghy sailors set brightly coloured spinnakers for a downwind run home.

In town, it was the Frangipani Festival season, a spectacle of colourful floats and costumed dancers. In a bounty for Matupit, a village with no arable land, it was time for megapodes to lay their eggs deep in the warm volcanic sands around Tavurvur. Eggs harvested by the villagers were sold as a prized delicacy at the market.

In addition to Sundays at Taliligap, twice a week in the late afternoons, the Taliligap Trio met to rehearse their songs. A pause in court circuits brought Lester time to spare. Cherry could do night shifts, and besides always appeared to have time to spare.

Lester suspected Flanagan's information on Cherry was well founded: Cherry worked when he felt like it. Josie, too, had a routine of church-related activities, vague and little explained, though she could always be in town for rehearsals.

Lester couldn't get enough of their company. At the same time, their relationship was frustratingly limited. Cherry often slipped away to be with Adele while Josie felt duty-bound to be at home in the evenings for her father. There appeared to be a tacit agreement that rehearsals were purely a professional arrangement.

Though Lester longed for more connection, more intimacy between them, the intimacy ended when they all went home. Josie he missed the more, but for the moment he could only dream.

Climbing the long-dormant Mother volcano was Cherry's idea, restless and looking for fresh challenges. He set out with a reluctant Lester in pitch darkness on a Saturday morning in order to arrive at the summit at dawn. The reward was a spectacular panorama of the town, the harbour, the islands stretching to New Ireland and, looking inland, the cloud-kissed Baining Mountains.

On Monday, Lester limped into the office under the gimlet eye of Gloria.

'What happened to you?' she demanded, as if she had the right to know.

'I climbed The Mother on Saturday. Two thousand three hundred feet and two hours to the top. It nearly killed me.'

No reaction from Gloria, nor from Gabriel, reading a newspaper. Lester, somewhat deflated, went on. 'The view was magnificent. Gabriel, haven't you seen it?'

Gabriel shrugged. 'Tolais don't go there. Why would anyone go there? There's nothing there. We know where everything is, we don't need a lookout. Do we think we'll lose an island? Will it drift away when no one is looking?'

'There's a trig point at the summit for surveys,' Lester added lamely.

Gabriel snorted. 'Europeans put it there. They measure everything they see, draw it on a map, divide it into squares and take it from us.'

'Tolais don't go there because of the *Kaia*. They're frightened of disturbing the spirits,' Gloria said in a condescending tone.

Gabriel ignored her and went back to his newspaper. Gloria, however, hadn't finished.

'Only Europeans go there. They have to look down on everyone else.'

Not long afterwards, Cherry appeared at Grandview Apartments with two sets of scuba equipment in his utility.

'It's time to carry out my side of the bargain, in return for my bodysurfing lessons. It'll be a proper diving adventure.'

They drove to a village north of the town, then carried their equipment to a strip of black sand and coral reef nearby.

Lester adjusted his face mask, champed down on the mouthpiece of his regulator and followed Cherry over the coral shelf. A buoy bobbed over deep water where the shelf fell steeply away. A line trailed down from the buoy to the bow of a sunken Japanese freighter, clearly and eerily visible below them. Cherry pulled himself swiftly hand-over-hand down the line. Lester struggled not to be left behind. In this silent world the hiss of his air bubbles enveloped him; the hollow sound of his breathing from the air tank rang in his ears.

Lester was using diving equipment rented from Szabo but was without a depth gauge, air-pressure indicator, reserve tank or emergency supply. The weight belt had only two small lead weights to counter the natural buoyancy of his body. He was hard-pressed to keep up with Cherry, who seemed to glide down the rope without effort. He could feel the hard thump of his heart against the chest harness. He was in a turmoil of fear and excitement. It was just a guided tour, Cherry promised. They'd be at a serious depth for only a few minutes.

The wreck, lying on a steep incline, loomed before them. Cherry waited for Lester at the bow, pointing out features on the ship: a gun turret encrusted with coral; the black hole of the forward cargo hatch.

Lester felt menaced by the ship's bulk, as if at any moment it might topple and crush him. The hull was home to a bewildering assortment of marine life: humble minnows and powerful rays, ugly stonefish, spine-bristled lionfish, gawping, pot-bellied groupers. They stared out from, or darted into, every possible bolthole.

They continued down over the foredeck to the midsection. A yawning hole in the superstructure and twisted metal told of the ship's likely fate after being bombed while fleeing an air attack on the harbour and then grounded on the reef.

At one hundred feet, Lester's heart was pounding. He could no longer see the surface light; all around was a diffuse and darkening blue. He was reluctant to follow Cherry's black fins as they disappeared below the deck, terrified of being left alone. He entered the long passageway of the crews' quarters following the faint, darting beam of Cherry's torch. He could make out cabin doors as he passed, still descending. The corridor roof seemed to press down on him.

At last, the passageway ended. He headed up, kicking free of the fear of confinement that had gripped him. He grasped a ventilation pipe to steady himself and looked around. Where was Cherry? Still inside? His heart missed a beat. At the same moment, or so it seemed, his air gave out. One last deep, sucking breath; the next was choked.

He knew instantly he'd been breathing too hard and had used a half hour's air in fifteen minutes. He couldn't see the surface. He was going to drown! He couldn't think, couldn't remember what to do. He started up but checked himself, agonising. Stay with your companion, your buddy!

Then he caught sight of Cherry, emerging from behind the bridge on the other side. Lester swam frantically towards him, lungs bursting, slashing a hand across his throat, the divers' sign for lack of air. Cherry grasped him by the shoulder, pulled out his mouthpiece, replaced it with his own and kicked his way upwards. Lester was hauled to the surface like a limp rag doll.

Once on land, he lay back on the warm sand, hungry for the sun's heat on his trembling body. He heaved in great gulps of air. After making him comfortable, Cherry left for his utility, returning with two fresh tanks of air, one on each shoulder, bent double under their weight.

'We're going back down,' he said, dropping a tank at Lester's feet.

Lester was sitting up, shaky but composed, staring out to sea. He raised his hands. 'You're on your own.'

'You might need decompression time. You'll never dive again if you don't go back now.'

Cherry gave Lester his own equipment: a new regulator, air hose and pressure gauge, a full weight belt. They stopped at the forward cargo hold where sunlight filtered down and ascent was possible on a single breath.

Lester watched as Cherry slipped down through a large open hatch into darkness, reappearing with two artillery shell casings sheathed in coral growth. He'd found the ship's forward magazine store virtually unpilfered. He went back several times for more, piling them on the foredeck. The casings were packed with thin, dark sticks of cordite. Together they ferried the casings, two by two, to the beach.

'Szabo collects the stuff for fishing,' Cherry said. 'So do the villagers. Just stuff it in a tin. In the end they'll blow the reefs to pieces, along with a few hands and arms. I see the results at the hospital.'

He separated the cordite and placed it carefully into his rucksack.

'For that Hungarian pirate?' Lester asked.

'And for me,' Cherry said. 'Help me load the truck.'

Lester, returning to gather the clothes and towels, lingered for a last look at the place where he'd nearly drowned. It seemed so peaceful, so benign; a strip of sand crossed by shadows, a smooth and gentle ocean like a film of blue plastic, tautly stretched. The buoy bobbed like a soccer ball no more than a stone's throw from the beach.

He felt again Cherry's hands grasping him, thrusting them both to the surface in a froth of bubbles, corks in a sea of champagne. A tingling shiver swept through his body: the joy of being alive.

He found Cherry sitting by the utility, head bowed in his hands.

'Cherry, what's wrong?'

'You nearly drowned.'

'You saved my life.'

'I let you dive with that madman's gear. His tank was probably half-full. I left you alone. I'm so sorry.'

'We should've gone down to the deep end first and come up gradually. That would have been safer, wouldn't it? I wouldn't have run out of air so far down.'

'I know. I made every mistake in the book.'

'I'm over it now. Things turned out all right in the end.'

'For once,' Cherry said bitterly.

The terrifying moment of his choking, his horror of being trapped in a watery tomb, returned as nightmares for days after the dive. As much as Lester loved the sea and surf, any enthusiasm for exploring the deep was doused.

Cherry appeared chastened at first, but his usual ebullience soon returned. The shared experience of rescuer and rescued only strengthened the bond between them, more so because they kept it a secret. Yet it troubled Lester that Cherry's mood on the day became so sombre. For a moment, he had angrily turned upon himself.

After their first appearance at the Steakhouse, the Trio returned to Grandview Apartments to celebrate.

'All those stairs outside,' Josie said, puffing at Lester's apartment door. 'Why did we have to come up by the fire escape? I nearly twisted my ankle.'

'It's not the fire escape, it's my front entrance,' Lester said.

'It's the fire escape as well,' Cherry added, following Josie inside. 'And that's what you get for wearing high heels.'

'They aren't high heels, not proper high heels!' Josie said.

'You looked wonderful tonight,' Lester said, guiding her to the sofa.

Josie sighed, sat down, took off her shoes and rubbed her bare feet. 'I can't wear shoes like that.'

'You can't wear a black cocktail dress on stage and sing in bare feet,' Cherry said. 'You need to look elegant...and taller.'

'Did I look like that?'

'You did, but bare feet would be fine,' Lester said, bringing drinks. 'Take no notice of him.'

Josie stretched out on the sofa, draping herself over Cherry in a coquettish way.

'Where's Adele tonight? Are you going to fetch her?'

'She's working late at the hotel,' Cherry said.

'She works so hard...so much cleaning and washing up. it's slave labour, isn't it? No proper visa either, I suppose.'

'Now you're being cruel,' Lester said, vexed to see Josie nestling, eyes closed, against Cherry's chest.

Cherry idly stroked her hair, her cheek. 'I'll take her home,' he said. 'I know where she's staying. I'll pick up Adele if she's still at the hotel.'

'Isn't one woman a night enough for you?' It was meant to be a joke, but Lester's resentful tone betrayed him.

Cherry laughed. 'Take it easy. I'm taking Josie home, not to bed.'

'Are you diving with Adele this weekend?'

'Diving? No, I've given it up.'

'I hope I had nothing to do with you not diving anymore.'

'Time to move on, old sport. Time to explore something new! From underwater we'll go underground. I've met an Aussie Irishman, Pat Connell. He owns a tavern not far from Taliligap. He was here with the Australian army when the war ended and hasn't left since. He'll help me locate some Japanese tunnels.'

'You're the explorer, not me.'

'I'd like you to meet Connell anyway. Come up to Taliligap one Saturday and I'll take you to the tavern.'

Lester put a finger to his lips, pointing to Josie as she stirred and stretched herself awake. Cherry nodded and understood; Josie wouldn't be told.

Lester had heard of the tavern and its legendary owner. Both had something of an unsavoury reputation in town, but he was intrigued. He made sure Josie wasn't listening.

'When can we go?'

'Not next weekend. Josie said we're to play at a village somewhere inland. A big occasion.'

'Why am I always the last to know?' Lester complained.

'You'd have to ask her,' Cherry said. 'I'm only the messenger.'

On a misty morning they journeyed up the Burma Road and over the ridge, past tidy hamlets with hedgerows of bougainvillea and hibiscus, croton clusters and frangipani trees, along avenues bordered by coconut palms, past the broad sward of a disused wartime airstrip, to a village at the edge of the Toma plateau, nestling beneath a canopy of giant rain trees—a cool, shady vault, a place of shadows, an enchanted glade.

The village was celebrating the opening of an aid post. Following the opening ceremony, a village choir sang traditional songs and Methodist hymns. The children sang Beatles songs: *Yellow Submarine* and *Ob La Di, Ob La Da.* The lyrics were indistinct but boisterously delivered to howls of laughter from the crowd. The Trio followed with songs from their varied songbook. It wouldn't have mattered what they played; their audience loved all music.

Late in the afternoon, the villagers brought out their own string band, one of the finest in a field where competition between villages was fierce. The band was an all-male group of six, laden with guitars and ukuleles, sticks and a slit drum. Their songs began with a high, keening note from one of the singers that swept into a champing, clattering, syncopated rhythm from the instruments, a sound like a fast-moving, rocking train, and voices in harmony with fresh, simple melodies endlessly repeated.

The visitors ate chicken and taro basted in coconut milk and cooked in an earth oven. They stayed on until early evening. Josie sat down among the women from the church choir, cuddling plump, brown babies one after another. Cherry was surrounded by children. A boiled egg appeared magically from his empty shirt pocket and a coin from behind his ear. The children ran their fingers through his fair hair and poked hands down into his shirt in their hunt for treasure. As he writhed at their tickling, they laughed in delight.

Lester wandered off to explore, walking through the cluster of thatch and matting houses in the village square. He came unexpectedly to an adjoining clearing where a group of men, standing beside utility trucks or sitting on grass mats, were talking together.

They fell silent as he approached. He was conscious of the sudden quiet, of eyes fixed on him, hard and suspicious. He saw Gabriel Toporo walking towards him. Like the others, Gabriel was bare-chested and in a laplap, his mouth stained by betel juice to the colour of a vivid, red-raw sore. Men stood aside to let Gabriel through. He was not subservient here.

'Lester, how are you?' Gabriel spoke in English, loudly for all to hear, extending his hand in welcome. He turned to the others and spoke in Pidgin. 'It's a work friend of mine, a visitor for the aid-post opening.'

'*Singsing gutpela tru,*' one man said with a smile. He broke into a tune the Trio had played. A falsetto voice, imitating Josie. The others laughed, dissipating tension.

Gabriel put an arm around Lester's shoulder, leading him away in the direction of the village.

'It's *samting nating*,' he said. 'It's about land, that's all. Always trouble about land. We Tolais argue about it all the time. It's what Tolais do best. You're safe here, don't worry.'

Later, at Taliligap, Lester, shaken by his encounter, stood silently at the bungalow's verandah rail and gazed at the moon-lit harbour. Adele, who'd hitched a ride from town, held fast to Cherry as he lay, legs outstretched, against the bungalow wall.

Josie complained of feeling dizzy and had gone to lie down. She hadn't expected to see Adele at Taliligap.

'Where did you go today, Lester?' Cherry's voice came drowsily from behind him. 'You vanished into the forest.'

'I ran into a Mataungan gathering. It gave me a fright, but someone from the office knew me.'

Adele sat up at once. 'Gabriel Toporo?'

'You know him?'

'I've been to a few meetings. He talks like a lawyer. He's their legal adviser.'

Lester laughed. 'Legal adviser? He licks stamps and puts files away.'

'He's done well!' Adele said. 'He's in the enemy camp right under your noses. He's a member of the Mataungan executive. Didn't you know?'

'I do know. But this is a political dispute; lawyers aren't the enemy.'

Adele jumped to her feet.

'Oh yes, you are! Your laws uphold this bourgeois adminis-tration. Your laws handed German land to Australians after the war instead of giving it back. Your laws support plantation com-panies who own it now. Your laws give people institutions they don't want, foreign institutions run by foreigners.'

Cherry pulled her gently down beside him. 'Lester's one of us, Adele.'

'They aren't my laws,' Lester said. 'The House of Assembly makes them.'

Adele scowled. 'You know what I mean. Lawyers write the laws for politicians. If you believe in justice, you should be on the right side. Don't laugh at Gabriel because he hasn't got a law degree. Work for the Mataungans, like me. Like Cherry.'

Adele cooled as quickly as she'd boiled. She rose, went to Lester and ruffled his hair.

'I know it's not you; you're just doing your job.'

They were quiet for a while. Lester brooded, numbed by Adele's rounding on him so vehemently. He hadn't realised the extent of her sympathies, or of her involvement. He'd have to be more careful. He shrugged and turned to go inside.

Cherry followed him in.

'Don't get upset. You're the best friend I ever had. You're frighteningly honest; that's why I like you. I don't think of you as a lawyer at all, and I mean that as a compliment.'

18

'**W**here were you yesterday? Gloria asked Lester. 'You should've been at work.'

'I stood on a sea urchin on the weekend. The spines went into my foot, and it swelled up. The pain was unbearable; I had to call a doctor.'

'That's why I never swim in the sea. Put papaya juice on it, that's what my mother says.'

'Thanks for the sympathy.'

Lester smiled benignly at Gloria. The doctor was Cherry, who bathed the foot in vinegar, fished out the broken spines with tweezers and dosed him with antibiotics purloined from the hospital pharmacy.

'I rang you yesterday to say I wouldn't be in. No one answered. Where's John? And where's Gabriel? Is there a funeral somewhere, yet another relative perhaps?'

'Mr Flanagan's coming back from Port Moresby this morning. Gabriel wasn't here yesterday either. I don't know where he is.'

'So you went home early?'

'I'm not going to stay if nobody else is here. What would I do?' Gloria resumed flicking through a fashion magazine.

For Lester, it was going to be one of those days. He was tired; tired of the heat outside that sapped his will to work, tired of dull days at the office between Circuits that were rarer, now that police and *kiaps* were distracted by the Mataungan threat, tired of Gabriel's frequent absences and Gloria's antipathy to toil of any kind.

Cases were trickling in for the next Circuit, humdrum burglaries and assaults. He sat down with a sigh to go through witness statements and prepare the indictments.

Late in the afternoon Flanagan appeared, thrusting his way into the office, breathing heavily and dragging a bulging suitcase. He sat down heavily to catch his breath.

'More bloody land files. I had to lug them up the stairs.'

'Gabriel should've helped you,' Lester said.

'Gabriel doesn't work here anymore. I've sacked him.'

Flanagan wiped his brow and retreated to his office. He emptied a pile of folders from his suitcase onto his desk. More of the same already cluttered his office: thick, bound with white tape, crammed with yellow, curling pages marking the passage of many years. He called Lester into the office.

'I've got an impossible job.' He waved his arms about the room. 'Look at this. All Tolai land claims. The Public Solicitor pumps up their hopes and we're forced to dash them, again and again. Do I want to do it? No, but we have to hold the line. I've been in the Supreme Court arguing about a couple of local plantations. One of them is called Vunapaladig. Have you heard of it?'

'No.'

'You soon will. There'll be trouble when the decision is known, I'm sure of it.'

'What happened with Gabriel?'

'Gabriel was spotted at a Mataungan meeting at Vunadidir. You ought to know, you were with him. You were seen walking together with his arm around your shoulders, the best of buddies.'

'That was pure chance; I was there for a village concert.'

'Keep away from Gabriel Toporo. Don't get mixed up in it.'

'I don't intend to.'

'The police found out he's been copying confidential papers from my cabinet on our photocopier. He had a stash at his home.'

'I thought he was trustworthy.'

'So did I. I've known him for years. I was always wary, but I thought he might be a bridge between us and them, if you know what I mean.'

Flanagan sat back in his chair and reached for his pipe. Soon the air in the office would be tainted by pungent tobacco fumes. Gloria would be breathing through a perfumed handkerchief. Flanagan gestured again at the files that lay in stacks on his desk, on the floor, in office corners.

'If you're going to stay on, learn about what's really behind all the trouble. You can start by going back a few years and reading the High Court's decision in the Varzin case.'

The conflict over ownership or occupation rights to land was a sore that had festered since German times.

The Australian Administration's land policy in Papua New Guinea had started on the right footing: customary land was vested in the Indigenous people and not in the Crown.

The policy had two basic shortcomings. First, land could be acquired by the government for development if it were deemed 'waste, ownerless or vacant'. However, for the Indigenous inhabitants, and in the heavily populated Gazelle in particular, the idea any land might be ownerless or vacant was inconceivable.

Second, land could be acquired for necessary economic purposes.

The administration set up a system of land registration that conferred titles to particular parcels of land. That meant an inevitable conflict with customary tenure.

There followed a convoluted history of large German land-holdings expropriated, registered under the new system, then registered again after the Japanese occupation during which all records were lost. All the while, the post-war Tolai population was rapidly increasing and the pressure to find more land was building.

The Australian Government's position was to stubbornly seek resolution of land disputes through the court system. Cases dragged on for years. Claims that land had been illegally or improperly acquired generally came up against a brick wall— the existence of a registered title overrode any claim of custom-ary rights, however meritorious.

The so-called Varzin Lands was a relatively undeveloped area of the Gazelle hinterland, a typical example of alienated land with a restored registered title. A claim by the customary owners was fought through the courts for twelve years. When the country's Supreme Court found in favour of the claimants, the Tolai people celebrated. That decision was overturned by the High Court of Australia.

Having their hopes raised by Papua New Guinea's highest court, only to be dashed by a superior court in far-off Australia, was a bitter blow to the claimants.

Connell's Tavern occupied a vantage point on a ridge near the village and administration outpost at Vunadidir. Early on a Saturday evening, Lester drove up to the timber and woven-walled building. Cherry met him at the door. With him was the eponymous owner, Pat Connell.

'Always glad to meet a new customer.' Connell spoke with a lugubrious Australian twang. 'Often they don't come back.'

Connell looked ill, Lester thought, baked brown and shrunken, rheumy-eyed. Above the bar inside was a framed photograph of a different Connell and a comrade-in-arms, both in army uniform, lounging, grinning, squinting from beneath slouch hats in the sun's glare, white webbing belts hugging slim waists.

Cherry grasped Lester's arm. It seemed he'd been drinking with Connell for a long time. 'Come and see the sunset! It's Pat's tourist attraction.'

They took their drinks outside to a sloping lawn behind the building. Beyond, the broad Warangoi valley reached out to the Baining Mountains. A brief, spectacular sunset was unfolding, the sun settling behind the ranges among pillows of pink cloud hanging over forested mountain tops.

Smoke from scattered villages and mist from the moist, cooling forest mingled over the valley in a soft purple haze. Here and there, gigantic fig trees mushroomed above the forest canopy like medieval watchtowers. As the light faded, the mountains closed in, leaving only an outline in the clear night air.

The mountain ranges were barely explored, Connell told them. They still harboured shy and mysterious tribes. Stories, still fresh, were told of the feared Mokolkols who raided sleeping villages and crushed skulls with heavy stone axes. As Connell proudly declared, his tavern was at the edge of the civilised world.

'At the edge?' Cherry laughed, clapping Connell on the back. 'This place is far beyond it.'

They returned to a table in the tavern's dining area. The tabletop was hidden beneath a layer of papers: area maps, supply routes, tunnel plans, military manuals, intelligence reports.

'Pat Connell's collection.' Cherry was barely able to contain his excitement. 'He brought it all out.'

Lester picked through them with pinched fingers, wrinkling his nose. 'They're damp and greasy; they smell of war.'

'They've been stored in the generator shed for years. Connell used to collect war salvage. He explored Japanese tunnels.'

'Weren't the tunnels cleaned out after the war?'

Lester glanced idly at a small pile of maps, stained and barely legible, some in Japanese script. Cherry unfolded a map carefully, smoothing it down on the table.

'See the coloured flags? Each flag shows the headquarters of a Japanese army or navy unit. There'll be a network of tunnels in the area of the flags. Storehouses, workshops, living quarters, hospitals, a movie theatre. Whole cities underground!'

It came from Cherry in short, fizzing bursts. He ran a careless hand through his hair. A rotting scrap of paper could become a mysterious cuneiform script, the secret formulae of an alchemist, a Dead Sea Scroll. This was Lester's introduction to Cherry's new obsession.

19

After the barnstorming tour by Gough Whitlam, posing as the next Australian Prime Minister, it was inevitable a visit by John Gorton, the incumbent Prime Minister, would follow.

Gorton, too, toured major centres around the country. His overarching message was a plea for unity, declaring that his government was ready to hand down powers and advance the country towards self-government. However, it was unwilling to countenance the separation or uneven development of any part.

His government wouldn't impose a timetable for self-government against the wishes of the majority. This was a message warmly, sometimes enthusiastically, received elsewhere, though it did not go down well in either Bougainville or the Gazelle.

A crowd of ten thousand jeering Mataungan supporters greeted Gorton on his arrival at Rabaul airport. Over eight hundred police were assembled in Rabaul. Many lined up at the airport fence to keep the crowd at bay. Helicopters and speedboats were on hand nearby for a rapid evacuation of Gorton and his entourage if necessary.

Later, at an official reception for Gorton at Queen Elizabeth Park before a smaller, more receptive crowd of council
supporters and schoolchildren, he repeated his message and
offered a referendum on the multiracial council.

Lester, who was at the park, was astonished at the armed
security surrounding Gorton. Rumours said he'd been issued
with a pistol. Lester swore he'd glimpsed a pistol-shaped bulge
in the Prime Minister's sock as he alighted from his ministe-
rial car.

Days later, Flanagan invited Lester to an evening barbecue
at his home. A game of tennis between Flanagan and Hersch
ended as Lester arrived. He joined the players, both tomato-
faced and sweating, as they walked to the house.

'Who won?'

'I did,' Flanagan said.

'He challenged every point of mine,' Hersch said. 'He
wouldn't let me win.'

Twilight bathed the ridge on Namanula Hill, a brief magical half-hour as the air cooled and filled with the smell of
woodsmoke from nearby cooking fires. While the tennis players
showered and dressed, Lester helped himself to drinks laid out
on the verandah.

In the garden, five chairs were arranged around the barbecue. The missing guests, an attractive woman who looked to be
in her thirties, together with a young girl, arrived when the barbecue was well underway.

'Carol Begley,' Flanagan said, waving barbecue tongs in the
woman's direction. 'And that's her daughter Tracey. Carol's
coming aboard as my office assistant. She'll replace Gabriel.' He

smiled at Lester. 'I asked her along to get to know us. She'll see what a fine, easy-going pair we are.'

Flanagan apparently knew Carol Begley well. A New Zealander, she had lived in Rabaul for some time and had been a partner in a business of importing parts. As to parts of what, exactly, she was not forthcoming. The business partner was not her husband, and her marital status was unclear. Tracey, seven years old, was at a primary school in town.

As they enjoyed Flanagan's barbecue specials, Hersch recounted his latest travels. He'd followed Prime Minister Gorton around the country, ending up in Bougainville.

Gorton had a different message for everyone, Hersch said. A referendum here, no referendum there. Even in Rabaul he had a message for each side, which in the end satisfied neither.

'It's about to get worse,' Flanagan said. 'Squatters are moving in on plantations that were to be allocated as settlement blocks.'

'Squatters have been a feature of the Gazelle for years,' Hersch said.

Flanagan brushed this aside. 'We're trying to move them off with eviction notices, but more and more are coming. There's going to be trouble. Police reinforcements are flying in.'

Flanagan and Hersch fell into a heated discussion about the perennial land problem. Hersch clearly now preferred Flanagan as an informant on local issues. Carol, meanwhile, joined Lester.

'I don't know much about these things,' she said. 'We business types mind our own business. I heard my Tolai predecessor was sacked.'

'He was a senior Mataungan.'

'Everyone I know is worried about the Mataungans. John told me he wanted someone who can be trusted. I told him I have a friend in the police. I told him I have an ear for what's going on, but I wouldn't tell a soul.'

Carol laughed. She seemed confident and at ease in company, Lester thought. She'd been keeping up with the others, drink for drink, and was a little tipsy. Without warning, she leapt from her chair in alarm.

'Where's Tracey? She's gone!'

No one had noticed Tracey slip away. The others rushed in all directions to look for her. She was soon found, snugly wrapped in a blanket and asleep in a corner of the fibro shack that housed the Sepik staff. She was bored, she said, and no one would talk to her.

She heard the children playing and had gone to join them. She'd helped them make beaded wristbands to sell at the market. She proudly showed off a wristband around each wrist—a short, dramatic finale to Flanagan's barbecue.

Josie slipped into the Mercedes with a sigh of relief. Behind them the restaurant lights still beckoned. Diners were coming and going. Another trio, all male, was unloading guitars and an amplifier from a van. Josie had taken to wearing lipstick while on stage and was checking her image in the car mirror, wiping the lipstick off with a tissue. Her gaze, reflected in the mirror, fixed on Lester.

'Father will be waiting for me at home. He can't possibly see me like this.'

'You don't need makeup,' Lester said. 'You look fine without it.'

'The owner said it looks more professional. Of course he means sexier.' She paused for a moment, frowning. 'We're going well, aren't we? Despite the trouble around, that is. There aren't so many going out to dinner.'

'We need new songs,' Lester said. 'Most people at the restaurant are regulars. They'll tire of the same repertoire.'

'Let's jazz it up. We could try samba rhythms. I'll sing *The Girl from Ipanema* and rattle my maracas.' Josie shook her hands vigorously and made maraca-like noises.

'All those jazz chords? They're beyond me,' Lester said.

He drove in silence through the town and onto the road to Kokopo. Josie, however, seemed buoyed by the night and in the mood to talk.

'I love this car,' she said, patting the dashboard. 'With you driving, I feel safe.'

After waiting in vain for a response, Josie went on. 'Are you cross with me? Do you mind driving me home and having to drive all the way back? Cherry can always drop me off on his way to Taliligap. He drove me last week.'

'Do you feel safe with him?'

'No, it's terrifying. Anyway, I don't ask because I know he wants to stay in town with that woman.'

Inwardly, Lester was fuming. Every mention of Cherry stoked the fires of jealousy.

'I love this drive,' he said. 'A tropical moon over the water, palm trees lining the shore. It's even better when you're with me.'

He knew how trite it sounded, and how clumsy. He looked anxiously at Josie, waiting for her reaction. Her gaze, and evidently her thoughts, were fixed on the harbour. She pointed into the darkness.

'Do you see those lights that seem to be floating out there?'

'I've been told they're villagers out fishing in their canoes.'

Josie nodded and closed her eyes, summoning the past.

'I had my own canoe, once. It was tiny and as light as a toy. I'd paddle out and sit in the harbour for hours on windless nights like this, fishing, watching the lights of the other canoes, listening to the talk from all about.'

'Did your father allow it?'

'Strangely, he did. He knew where I was.'

Josie fell silent, as if listening to voices of the past, before going on.

'My canoe and I were inseparable. I felt so much a part of it then, the harbour, the fishing, the village gossip. I used to wonder what I was. Was I a white Papua New Guinean like one of those poor albinos? My skin was so fair that I wanted to rub earth on it to make it darker. Isn't that weird?'

'A childhood idyll. Do you still go fishing?'

'One night, I dreamed I was sitting in my canoe when the voices faded away and I was drifting alone far out to sea. I shouted for help, but no one could hear me. The dream frightened me; I never went out again.'

As Josie was speaking, the car pulled up at her father's home. Lester was hoping for a goodnight kiss, however brief. Instead, Josie opened the door and climbed out. 'Come inside,' she said. 'I want you to meet my father.'

The Reverend rose from his office desk, littered with papers, took off his glasses, rubbed his eyes and reached out to Lester for a handshake. He looked older than Lester had imagined, with a body that sagged into his clothes.

'You must be from Josie's singing threesome. The doctor? The titled Englishman?'

'No, that's the other one. I'm the lawyer, the commoner.'

'Ah, yes. Well, I thank you both for helping Josie spread the message of the Gospel. Her voice is a divine gift.'

Josie was laughing behind her hand. Obviously, she'd been less than candid about her singing career.

'I'd make you a cup of tea,' the Reverend went on, 'but I need to get on with preparing for the Sunday service. My daughter will look after you.' His hand waved vaguely in the air, ushering Lester away.

Josie made tea for them both in the kitchen and set down a plate of stale biscuits from a tin long forgotten in a cupboard.

'I'd love to offer you a drink, but it's a dry house,' she said. She leaned across the kitchen table and took Lester's hand. 'I'm sorry about my father. He's not very...' She paused and gazed at the ceiling, searching for a word. 'He's not very forth-coming. At least not at home. He's quite different among his parishioners.'

'And he doesn't welcome boyfriends?'

'I'm his only child, a daughter without a mother. Besides, he needs me.'

'I wondered about your mother. There's a photo in his office of a young woman holding a child. Your father's standing beside her. Is that you and your mother?'

'She died when I was six. They married and came here with the church when I was three years old. They were sent to West New Britain. My mother died of an infection after she fell and spiked her leg on a stake. There were no medical facilities there that would've saved her. That's the hazard of missionary life.'

'It must've been a terrible shock for you.'

'Strange to tell, I have the vaguest memories of my mother. She was young, only thirty years old, and quite beautiful. That's how I'll always remember her.'

'That must be some consolation, at least. I wish I could remember my father in the same way.'

Josie, eyes wide, brought her hands to her cheeks. 'Oh no, I've talked too much about me. Tell me more about your father.'

'No, no, I want to hear more about you.'

Josie grinned and pointed to the sink. 'Then help me wash the dishes; my father never does. He'll cook his own meals if I'm not here, but he never washes up. That's women's work.'

With the dishes done, they sat again at the kitchen table to talk. Eventually their voices attracted the Reverend's attention, for he appeared, looking displeased, at the kitchen door.

'Oh, are you still here?' he said to Lester. 'I thought you'd gone long ago. I'm off to bed. I'm sure Josie must be tired, too. I'll bid you goodnight and goodbye.'

Josie walked Lester, arm-in-arm, to the car.

'I'm sorry about my father,' she said again. 'Perhaps I shouldn't have brought you, but I wanted you to understand. I've never brought Cherry; he doesn't seem curious about my past and doesn't seem willing to share his own. I don't know why he holds back; I *do* ask him.'

'He's the same with me.'

Acting on impulse, Lester drew her close and kissed her. She was surprised but didn't resist. She smiled and blew a kiss through the window as he drove away. Her smile, and the lingering taste of her kiss, stayed with him all the way to town.

Josie had grown up without a family to call her own. After her mother died, she was brought back to Rabaul for school and was looked after by housekeepers and what she described as 'the church family' until she was fourteen. From there, she went to Brisbane for the remainder of her schooldays, living with her aunt, her mother's sister.

The longer she was away from Rabaul the more homesick she became. She was given the money to return once a year but leaving for flights back to Australia was the hardest thing she'd ever done.

According to Josie, her father could not imagine life without a woman's care, even if it meant his daughter's sacrifice. His own duty was to higher things: the missionary work to which he had been called by God and the saving of souls from both animism and Catholicism.

She would have liked to see him remarry a parishioner, brown or white, it didn't matter, but his only passion was for learning the language and culture of the Tolai people he lived among. When Lester asked why she devoted herself to his care, she simply shrugged and said, 'He expects it of me.'

No wonder, Lester thought, she saw the freedom and companionship she shared in the Trio as an escape from the stifling embrace of the church.

Despite his asking, she volunteered little about the years she spent in Australia. Her reluctance gave rise to more than curiosity. This element of mystery about her only increased his desire. He longed to embrace her, make her smile, and offer his comfort and support. Had he fallen in love with her? That, he thought, was a question he didn't dare answer.

It wasn't long before Cherry lured Lester again to Connell's Tavern. They stayed until only the regulars remained around the bar, managers from plantations and admin outposts, most of them unmarried and lonely, drinking until the bar closed in the early hours.

Music from Connell's amplifiers boomed over the valley. Lester, across a table, poured a glass of cola from a bottle at Cherry's elbow. A startling howl came from outside, close by.

'It's only a customer.' Cherry waved the sound away. 'It's a full moon.'

Lester, curious, walked out into bright moonlight. A young European swayed dangerously at the edge of the lawn where it dropped sharply into the valley. He bayed at the moon and was answered by howling dogs in villages far across the valley floor.

'That's what I call music from the heart.' Pat Connell, at once chuckling and coughing, was at Lester's shoulder.

'Has he gone troppo?'

'Naw, he's all right. There's an animal spirit in all of us. I hear the Eskimos do it in Alaska.' Connell scratched an unshaven chin. 'A lonely sound, isn't it? We're all bloody exiles. None of us belongs.'

'Will you leave one day?' asked Lester.

'They'll have to carry me out, mate. Hasn't the doc told you? I'm on the way out anyhow. I won't desert my mates, the ones who are still out there.' Connell pointed towards the ranges. 'Too many others have forgotten them back in bloody Canberra.'

'What mates are you talking about?'

'Didn't they teach you anything in school? About Lark Force? About the Japs and the fall of Rabaul, the political bloody stuff up? I suppose not, who'd want to know? It's long gone.'

'I saw your photograph over the bar. Did you serve here during the war?'

'Yep.'

Connell shrugged and went inside. Lester stretched out on the grass, looking up at the stars. Despite evidence of the war all around Rabaul, his schoolboy knowledge of the wartime campaigns in New Guinea stopped at the Kokoda Track.

He was conscious of Connell's return and heavy breathing beside him. Connell eased himself to the ground, cigarette in one hand, a glass of whisky in the other, arms raised stiffly above his head like a marionette. His whole body must be in pain, Lester thought. He smiled and refused an offered cigarette.

'I know every inch of it out there,' Connell said, fumbling with the cigarette packet and his shirt pocket. 'I walked it all. I was with the native troops. I arrived when the Australian Fifth Division landed, late in '44. We cleared the Japs out, right up to Wide Bay and Open Bay, over the back of the mountains.

'That's when we found out about what really happened to Lark Force in '42. They were the blokes defending Rabaul, only about a thousand of them. It was every man for himself when the Japanese overran the place. Our blokes had no chance. They died like flies in the swamps and the jungle, looking for a way out. Or they were mown down by Jap raiding parties out looking for them.'

Connell drained his glass. He paused to light another cigarette from the ember of the last.

'There's a track through those mountains, a mule track. The Japanese made it. Bridges over the rivers, steel matting through the swamps, right to the coast. I walked over it, once. Bloody hard going, even with the team I had with me. You can imagine what it was like for our blokes who had to hack and crawl their way through, without food or drink, not knowing where they were headed most of the time.

'And blow me down, d'you know what's at the end of it now? A Jap logging camp at Powell Harbour, right on the coast, shipping logs off to Japan. They're back again with knobs on. It makes me wonder what our blokes died for.'

Connell flicked his cigarette butt onto the lawn and wandered off. Lester returned to Cherry's table and the collection of military maps and manuals. They were among the last customers. Cherry was far from sober, his head bowed over the table, eyes half-closed.

'Well, it's the bloody doctor and bloody lawyer together,' said Whittaker, a plantation manager with heavily blotched skin. He swivelled on a bar stool to face them. He turned to a man next to him. 'Which one do ya need, Ted?'

'He's a prosecutor, that one,' Ted said, pointing at Lester. 'Better mind your P's and Q's. He'll lock you up.' He wiped spittle from the corner of his mouth with his forearm.

Whittaker raised his voice. 'Lawyers' jabber, that's what confusing the Tolai, turning them on each other. Multiracial this, self-government that, lawyer words they don't understand. They need to know who's boss. The people around here understood German justice. You, lawyer-man, why can't you put these Mataungans in jail?'

'What for?' Lester asked.

'What *for*?' Whittaker whined. 'They're camped all over my plantation. Bloody roadblocks, the lot. I'm getting death threats and what do you idiots do? You let them go. You'll ruin it for all of us.'

'I hope so,' Cherry said, looking up from the table.

'What's your problem, doc? You're a Pommy bastard, you should know better. Look what's happening in Africa because you wouldn't stand up to them. Smith, Rhodesia, terrorists and all that. The same thing's going to happen here.'

'Sooner the better,' Cherry said.

Whittaker, a stumpy man, took a threatening step towards the table. Cherry stood up, rolled up a sleeve, adopted a boxer's stance, danced from one foot to the other and prepared for battle. Whittaker retreated.

Lester couldn't help but smile at the absurdity of it; four of them arguing in a ramshackle tavern at the end of the world, with the villages around deep in slumber. He guided the glowering Cherry towards the door, bundled him into the car and drove him home to Taliligap.

He arose late on the following morning to find Cherry asleep on the sofa. Leonard Woolf's novel *The Village in the Jungle* lay open on his chest. As he awoke and sat up, it fell to the floor. Lester picked it up and studied the blurb.

'Woolf? The Bloomsbury Group? I know that much.'

Cherry, in the throes of a hangover, groaned and rubbed his temples.

'Was I reading that? I found it in the library. It's about British justice in a village society in Ceylon. Nothing is as it seems. The white man's language is unintelligible, and his decisions are incomprehensible. You should read it.'

'I will, after you.'

Cherry waved towards his bookcase. 'Read Orwell's *Burmese Days* as well, and Graham Greene's *Heart of the Matter*. They're part of my little collection, the White Man Dying genre. They're about Europeans unravelling in far off hellholes. The collapse of the Empire, the failure of colonialism.'

Cherry stood up and stretched, made his way unsteadily to the frig and brought back bottles of beer.

'It's too early for that,' Lester said.

'I have a raging thirst.'

'Drink water.'

Cherry fetched a jug of water and glasses from the kitchen. He was like that, Lester thought. At times he listened to no one; at other times he folded completely to the advice of others, apparently recognising a need for self-preservation. The water seemed to revive him.

'Those writers served in the places they wrote about,' he went on. 'Orwell even caught dengue fever in Burma, so they sent him home. I hope that won't happen to you.'

'You never know,' Lester said, reminded of Flanagan's antipathy. 'I could be sent home anytime.'

'You should read these stories. They apply to you and your superiors, the judges, the *kiaps*, everyone in the colonial apparatus.'

'Thanks for the lecture,' Lester said. 'Those books are from an era that's come and gone. It's different now.'

'Different? Look at Connell and the others up at the Tavern. How different are they? They hate it yet they're addicted. They can't leave.'

'You're still angry about last night,' Lester said. 'People are aware of your attitude. Baiting them will only lead to trouble.'

'Trouble? The trouble is if I stay too long, I'll end up just like them.'

20

As Flanagan had foretold, Vunapaladig, a large undeveloped plantation property, became the next arena for a full-scale conflict. The administration had recently purchased it from the registered company owners for redistribution as settlement blocks, to relieve the land shortage.

Over the years, the undeveloped land had been freely used by both Tolai and Baining people for hunting, gardens and access to fishing beaches. The admin established a local land board to decide who would be allocated settlement blocks. However, kinship groups claiming customary ownership wanted nothing but the return of their traditional lands to them.

A challenge to the admin's title had long ago been mounted in the Supreme Court. The customary owners knew such challenges were, following the Varzin case, almost certain to fail. Squatters moved in on the land. Now, for the first time, the mounting frustration of the landless Tolai was harnessed by the Mataungan Association. They mustered supporters in their thousands.

Very early on a Monday morning, Lester awoke to the revving of a Landcruiser in the garden, and the driver shouting for Bilson. Lester hurried onto his balcony to see Bilson emerging from his apartment with an authoritative swagger and a holstered pistol. This was Bilson in his moment: the *kiap* overlord. Lester, always on the sidelines, relying on secondhand accounts in the inevitable aftermath of prosecutions, now wanted to be a part of the action.

'What's happening?' he called down.

'Trouble near Vudal,' Bilson shouted. 'Mataungans, villagers, thousands of them. They're armed.'

'Hold on, I want to come.'

Bilson laughed. 'You'd be a bloody nuisance. You'll get a hatchet in your back. Go back to bed.'

It took several days for Lester to put together what happened. Most of the information came from Bilson, a little from Dave Hersch, whose presence as a journalist was tolerated, even welcomed, by the Mataungan leaders.

Hundreds of police, heavily armed, faced off against villagers with an assortment of makeshift weapons: sticks, slings, clubs, hatchets and machetes. The DC and Police Commissioner met Mataungan spokesmen on a bridge across the river that divided the sides. Neither side would give way.

The posturing, with insults shouted across the river, continued through the afternoon and the next day. Eventually, more than seven hundred villagers, including Oscar Tammur and other Mataungan leaders, were rounded up and removed. From then on, a large police contingent was stationed on the land. For the time being, a crisis was averted.

The confrontation failed to yield a single acre of land but was another propaganda coup for the Mataungans. Both local and Australian journalists talked to both sides, yet reported it in dramatic terms as another instance of colonial might against moral right. In fact, much of the Mataungans' chest-beating and invective was for the attention of journalists' ears and cameras.

A serious situation, but at times not as serious as it seemed. Hersch told Lester that on a hot day and at the height of the confrontation, a Mr Whippy truck rolled up, playing *Greensleeves* loudly. It did brisk business selling ice cream to those on both sides of the river.

The town breathed a sigh of relief and business resumed as usual. Dinner parties heard stories of the hinterland: roadblocks, the officious patrolling of armed police and threats of violence from groups of Mataungan supporters on the road. However, the trouble was in parts of the Gazelle most Europeans in town rarely visited.

In the meantime, Carol had been busy in the Prosecutor's office. She had taken over Gabriel's space. Gabriel's small desk had been replaced by a desk nearly as large as Flanagan's. On it stood a brand-new typewriter, paper trays, other office paraphernalia and a framed photo of her wandering daughter. Papers on her desk hinted she'd taken over much of the typing. Gloria sat glowering in the other corner.

'I'll be typing the court papers,' Carol said with an air of authority. 'And I can take dictation if you like.' She smiled at Gloria, who didn't take dictation.

Flanagan offered his dismal opinion on the Vunapaladig confrontation and its unsatisfactory outcome. With land disputes, Flanagan was in his element.

'It's not the end; it's the end of the beginning,' he said. 'It's another Varzin. It can only end in tears.'

'Court cases aren't the answer, are they?' Lester said. 'We've boxed ourselves into a corner on land policy. Even if we buy back land, what happens? We split it into freehold blocks that often aren't handed out to the traditional owners. That's yet another source of conflict.'

If Lester was looking forward to an argument, he was disappointed. Flanagan sat back in his chair, shaking his head. He rubbed a hand over his eyes and forehead. He was long overdue for leave.

Lester was in two minds about taking over. He had ideas of his own on the way forward. On the other hand, he doubted that anyone would listen.

'There aren't any mosquitoes tonight.' Josie lazily waved a hand at the night sky. 'The breeze has blown them away.'

The three were stretched out side by side on the Taliligap lawn, under the stars, all drinking wine. Cherry reached for the bottle of wine beside him and refilled his glass.

'You've had twice your share,' Lester said. 'Leave some for us.'

'What do you mean? Everything in moderation, as Aristotle said.'

'Is that so? According to Connell, his customers drink so much that mosquitoes bite them and fly straight into the nearest wall.'

Josie raised herself on her elbows. 'Connell? Is that the man who owns the tavern at Vunadidir? It's a terrible place. Police recruits from Tomaringa go there on Friday nights to drink. Then they fight. I've heard the furniture is destroyed every weekend and has to be put back together.'

Lester laid a hand on Cherry's shoulder to remind him to keep quiet about Connell. The Trio had rehearsed most of the afternoon and into the evening. Josie had brought a picnic dinner to eat on the lawn.

'I often lie out here just to smell the grass,' Cherry said. 'After the grass-cutters have been, and the rain, it reminds me of England. Sometimes I feel homesick.'

He rose and wandered with his glass of wine to where the garden edge fell away from the ridge.

'Look at Vulcan out there.' He indicated the dark mound with his wineglass, spilling some. 'An enormous Christmas pudding, ready to explode.'

Lester and Josie hastily joined him, fearing he might stumble over the edge. They stood together looking over the bay and distant lights of town.

'I never tire of the view,' Josie said. 'I could live here if it weren't for the spirits.'

'And the mosquitoes,' Cherry added.

'John Flanagan told me a Vulcan story,' Lester said. 'The last eruption thrust up the seafloor and joined the island to the mainland. Before it had even cooled, the new land around it was planted with village gardens, but the admin immediately claimed it as waste and vacant. After the war, the land was to be licensed as a racetrack.'

Josie was incredulous. 'A racetrack? Horse races on a volcano?'

'The claim was fiercely contested,' Lester went on. 'The admin eventually handed it back. John said it's the only land dispute he knows of where the Tolais had a win.'

Silence. Then Cherry spoke.

'It's strange. I dreamed only last week that Tavurvur and Vulcan erupted again. I was sitting here watching, as if it were a gigantic fireworks display. Tongues of boiling lava spewed out of Tavurvur's cone, spread down the sides and swept the town into the harbour. The harbour bubbled up and Rabaul disappeared in clouds of ash and steam. I remember feeling it was a fitting end to the troubles Europeans have caused since they arrived.

We shouldn't be here, and nor should Rabaul. We've disturbed the natural order.'

'If that's the way you feel, why don't you go back to England?' Lester's tone was sharper than he intended.

'On some days I do want to go back,' Cherry said. 'If only I could.'

'Oh, don't go,' Josie said, taking his arm and bringing him close. 'I couldn't stand it.' She turned him around and, arm in arm, led him back to the bungalow. 'Drive me home, Mercedes man,' she called to Lester, lagging behind. 'I'll leave this dreamer on the sofa.'

In the car, Josie looked quizzically at Lester. 'It's funny. Neither of you talked about the trouble near Vudal last week. Where were you when the squatters moved in?'

'I was ordered by a *kiap* to stay at home. What about you?'

'At Malmaluan,' Josie said. 'It was frightening! Truckloads of police and Mataungans roaring along the roads. Helicopters buzzing in the sky. Everyone was terrified. At the church, my father said, they prayed for peace. I helped print leaflets to hand out, pleading for peace, but the police wouldn't let us near. Our own Bishop Gaius went to Vudal to meditate.'

'Meditate?'

'I mean *mediate*. He's a wonderful man. Thanks to him, there was no violence.'

'And thanks to the prayers?'

'And the prayers. Now you're poking fun at me. What about Cherry? I looked for him when I was passing Taliligap. He wasn't there.'

'He told me he tried to reach the bridge at Vunapaladig. He took his medical kit but was turned back at a roadblock. He wouldn't have been needed anyway.'

'He was in an odd mood tonight, don't you think? I mean, a bit distant.

'A bit drunk, you mean. He drinks too much.'

Josie waved the remark aside. 'I wonder if there's something going on with him. Is it Adele? She doesn't come up now, does she? And telling us he can't go back to England, why would he say that? I thought he was happy here.'

'I don't know how much he's told you about the family in England; perhaps that's the reason.'

'He's told me lots,' Josie said, winding down her side window as usual to greet the warm coastal air. 'His father and brother ignore him, his sister fled to America at the first opportunity and his mother is utterly eccentric.'

'It's no wonder he doesn't want to go back.'

'He made it sound so final.'

Lester nodded. 'Occasionally I have the feeling when I'm talking to him that he's stranded. He hardly mentions his past and doesn't seem to have a plan for his future.'

Josie lay back in her seat with a sigh. 'If he's stranded, then I'm glad he's stranded here. If he's not in the past and not in the future, I'm glad he's with us in the present. He lives in a little piece of paradise with two best friends who love him.'

Lester was quiet. Yet again the conversation was all about Cherry. Nearing her home, Josie sat up again and grasped Lester's arm.

'I almost forgot! Crosset's putting on another play for schools. He wants to do *Aladdin and the Magic Lamp*. I'll be the assistant stage manager.'

Lester smiled. 'Congratulations. Promoted from the ticket box to raising and lowering the curtains.'

Josie ignored him. 'Crosset wants Cherry to play Aladdin because this time Cherry gets to win the princess. That's only fair, don't you think?'

'He's Crosset's darling.'

'You're only envious. I told him there has to be a part for you, too. He said you can be a palace guard.'

'A starring role. How thoughtful of him. Does Cherry know?'

'It's a secret. Don't say a word; I want to tell him myself.'

The car drew up before the Reverend's house. Giving Lester a quick peck on his cheek, Josie lunged for the car door, preparing for a furtive run across the garden. Lester held her back.

'Am I just your chauffeur? Until you kiss me properly, I'm not going to let you go.'

Josie fell back into her seat. A rosy glow crept into her cheeks. After what seemed to Lester an unnatural stillness, she turned to him.

'It's late. Father will be anxious. He's always bloody anxious.'

Her words for a moment startled them both.

'I didn't mean that,' Josie said. 'I mean, I never swear.'

Then she laughed. The out-of-line molar that so attracted him, that made her looks unique, that drew attention to her eyes, her lips, the curl of her eyelashes, was there to see. She took his head in her hands and kissed him strongly on the lips, enough for him to feel her passion, and for him to return it. She sat up and opened the car door again.

'There now, chauffeur,' she said, stepping out. 'You've earned a bonus.'

21

When Flanagan departed for Australia on leave, Lester moved into the house on Namanula Hill. In the absence of Flanagan's daughters, he took over the younger daughter's bedroom. Posters of the Beatles and Jackson Five now adorned walls that once featured unicorns and fairies. Nothing in the house had been moved or put away; it was as if Flanagan had just stepped out for a morning stroll.

It was a relief to leave behind the sweltering heat in town and the sounds emanating from Szabo's apartment next door. At Grandview Apartments there was no escaping the daily hum of filtered fish tanks and the screech of metal grinding tools. Nor was there relief at night from laughter, squeals and grunts as the Hungarian entertained women from the settlement along the street. In the quiet surroundings and cooler evenings on Namanula Hill, Lester could enjoy Flanagan's collection of classical music. It showed a taste surprisingly refined in someone so hard-nosed.

Lester inherited a challenging situation in the office. The subterranean rivalry between Carol and Gloria soon surfaced; arguments about demarcation of duties had to be managed. Carol decided to replace Flanagan's filing system, consisting of stacks of folders in various parts of the office and on the floor. Folders that Flanagan and Gloria had happily identified by size, age, colour and location, were now to be stored in cabinets and catalogued in a manner only Carol could comprehend. This was to be a surprise for Flanagan on his return, she declared. He'd be delighted.

Another consequence of Lester's temporary promotion was to be swept into the upper echelons of the administration in Rabaul, advising on the law-and-order situation of the day.

The admin again ordered police to serve summonses for unpaid taxes. Most Mataungan supporters refused to appear. Police vehicles, arriving in villages to arrest defaulters, were stoned. Those convicted refused to pay and were given jail sentences. This high-cost strategy resulted only in overcrowded jails. Lester's quiet advice that the administration revisit the whole issue of council representation was ignored.

He came home one evening to find Dave Hersch sitting on the verandah steps. The journalist was obviously well-known to the Sepik family behind the house, for the back door was open and he was enjoying a tinned beer from Flanagan's fridge.

Hersch, as usual, had been doing the rounds of troubled parts of the country: the border with Indonesia, then Bougainville to witness more protests against the mine, then Rabaul, where the latest administration efforts to negotiate with the Mataungans had come to nought.

'What was the point of peace offerings when the courts had become the admin's weapon of choice?' Hersch complained. 'It just made enemies of the *kiaps*, the police and the entire legal system.'

They sat on the verandah drinking into the evening. The Sepik husband invited them to share a meal of tinned corn beef and rice with his family. The conversation in Pidgin flowed freely. Many Sepiks had low-paid occupations in town, and many more laboured further afield on plantations.

Relations between Tolais and Sepiks were poor; large groups frequently clashed, most recently at football games in town. The Tolai were *bikhets*, their Sepik hosts said, and the Mataungans *pait tumas long gavman*. That they were an arrogant lot, always fighting the government, was an opinion widely shared throughout the country, and neither Lester nor Hersch could disagree with it.

'How good it is to be back in Rabaul,' Hersch said as he walked with Lester to his hire car. 'Think yourself lucky to be here. I hate going back to Port Moresby. It's a ghastly place, teeming with vagrants in shanty settlements, awash in crime. No one's safe.' He waved his hand at the flowering gardens. 'You're surrounded by tropical splendour. You're safe at night despite the Mataungan troubles. The Sepiks here are standing guard.'

'The Sepiks and a quarter of the entire country's police force,' Lester smiled.

'The Mataungans aren't all bad,' said Hersch. 'I met Oscar Tammur for a chat in Port Moresby. He's no bow-and-arrow warrior from the jungle. He's been a teacher and a mechanic in the Australian army. I asked if he was inspired by the socialist claptrap of that Nigerian lawyer, Okorie. He said he left the thinking to clever people like John Kaputin. He told me his inspiration was Gough Whitlam and the anti-Vietnam war protests in Australia. He was just a simple man, a voice to rally his people.'

'Thanks for the biography,' Lester said.

'I mentioned your name,' Hersch went on. 'He knew about you, and the doctor from Nonga. He said you go out to the villages with your guitars. He said you were a regular guy.'

'That feeling won't last. He's refused to pay his council tax. A warrant's just been issued for his arrest. I'll probably see him in court.'

They laughed together at the element of the absurd in the whole council affair.

At the car, Hersch put an arm on Lester's shoulder and drew him closer.

'Don't tell Flanagan I was here. We're no longer talking.'

'What happened?'

'I crewed for John on his yacht, in a race. There was an incident.'

'You can't say you weren't warned,' Lester called as Hersch drove away.

Late on a Sunday morning, a knock on the front door. Gloria, dressed in a startling blue *cheongsam* adorned with flowers and peacocks, was on the verandah. From a large, embroidered bag she produced a booklet of tickets.

'I'm selling raffle tickets for the Kuo Min Tang. We celebrate the Double Tenth next month, you know.'

'I didn't know,' Lester said, his eyes drawn to a length of thigh exposed by the split-sided dress.

'You have to buy a whole book,' Gloria insisted, following Lester inside. 'And one for John as well.'

He went to his bedroom to fetch his wallet. When he returned, she was prowling the living room, scrutinising pictures on the walls, in no hurry to leave.

He gave her money and took the tickets. 'You've come here to inspect, to see if I've stolen anything.'

Any irony was lost on Gloria. Again she rummaged in her bag, this time taking out a framed photograph of herself posing with a smiling Flanagan, arms casually draped around each other's waists. She was in shorts and a bikini top, her face partly hidden by sunglasses and a floppy sunhat.

It was no different from countless holiday snapshots taken on palm-fringed beaches around the world. In this case, however, it was no further away than Pilapila. She pushed aside other photographs standing on the sideboard to make room for her own.

'What a happy couple you make, the boss and his secretary together.'

'He's in Australia to arrange a divorce, I know. One day he'll take me to Australia. He said so.'

'And the photograph is a reminder?'

'He made a promise.' Gloria turned for the door with a satisfied look, mission accomplished. 'Can you drive me to town now?'

Twice a week for the next two weeks, the cast of *Aladdin* assembled on the verandah of Flanagan's house late in the afternoon, to read through the play. Crosset plotted the production. Josie, brisk and businesslike, clipboard and script in hand, prompted and took notes for the director. After rehearsals there were barbecues in the garden to which the Sepik family next door was invited, and games of tennis late into the twilight.

Lester relished these days, with laughter at rehearsals and on the tennis court, in a world apart where no one thought it important to talk politics or worry about the Mataungans.

Josie glowed, played tennis surprisingly well and looked lithe and cool in white shorts and shirt. Cherry was, as always, gracefully at ease in company. Even Lester felt an urge to be near him, to be noticed by others simply by association. He knew Josie felt the same.

At the last play reading, Darryl Cleary appeared with drawings for the set design. He looked oddly stiff in the regulation white shirt, shorts and long socks of a civil servant. He greeted Lester with a hearty hug and theatrical sweep of his hand.

'My,' he cried, 'haven't we moved up in the world!'

'Only temporarily,' Lester said. 'Then it's back to the devil's sauna in town. Why are you dressed like that?'

'I've been at the DC's residence,' Cleary said grandly. 'I was summoned to a meeting of very important people. Foolishly, I thought I might be asked for my thoughts on the Mataungan debacle but no, they wanted to commission a painting. From *me*, can you imagine?'

'Who were the important others?' Lester prompted.

'I'm not sure, but they looked important. I felt a palpable *frisson* when I walked into the room. A judge, I think, and a lawyer from Port Moresby who looked rather regal. The DC said he was the Secretary for Law. Do you know him?'

'No, not personally. He arrives and is swept up the hill in a big black car. He doesn't talk to underlings.'

'Ah, well,' Cleary said. 'You know what they say here: those who live on the hill talk to no one but the gods. There's to be a new court building for Rabaul; they wanted a painting for that. It's a pity, but I need the money. I told them I'll paint anything they want. They discussed a portrait of the Chief Justice. The DC, bless him, suggested something with a local flavour.' Cleary smiled. 'That gives me mutinous ideas.'

22

Flanagan returned to the Prosecutor's office with renewed enthusiasm. He praised Carol Begley's filing system. Gloria stared, open-mouthed, in anguished disbelief. He looked over case files for the next Circuit and handed them to Lester with a smile.

'I met the DC at the airport. He wondered if the workload was too much for you. He suggested we might need an extra hand, someone with a little more experience.'

'How considerate of him.'

'He noticed some happenings in my garden while I was away.'

'I invited the cast of a play we're rehearsing. We danced naked around the barbecue.'

Flanagan had no more appreciation of irony than Gloria.

'Singing, acting, all these arty activities. No wonder you always need a haircut and don't own a comb. I'm surprised you've any energy left for work.' He laughed unsurely and headed for his desk.

'Did you enjoy your holiday in Australia?' Lester called after him. 'How are the wife and family?'

No answer.

The New Zealand owners of a visiting ketch, having heard the Taliligap Trio playing at the Steakhouse, invited them for a sailing trip around the Duke of York Islands. To Josie's chagrin, Cherry suggested Adele join them, boasting of her sailing prowess.

The yacht set off into a strong south-easterly breeze.

'It's hard going into the wind,' Jeff, the captain, explained. 'A ketch is far faster on a downwind run.'

On rounding for home the yacht came alive, spreading sails to the following wind and charging through a choppy sea. Josie, legs astride the bowsprit, clung to the guard rail, drenched by showers of spray. Cherry and Lester, well out of the way, were told of the owners' onward journey: around the mainland, through Torres Strait, across the Arafura and Timor Seas and out into the Indian Ocean, following the route of the East Indiamen in the last century to the coast of Africa.

By late afternoon, the ketch lay moored to the Yacht Club jetty, stark and spare without its full spread of sail.

'What a dazzling blue day,' Josie sighed, sitting down in the cockpit and handing out cans of beer. 'All that salty spray flaying my skin. I feel cleansed and reborn.'

'Well, if it isn't *la figure de proue*,' Adele said.

'What?' Josie asked.

'A carving, a figurehead on the prow of a sailing ship,' Cherry said, laughing. 'Usually a mermaid with large breasts.'

'Ignore Adele,' Lester said. 'Don't take her seriously.'

'I never do,' Josie said.

Cherry downed his drink, thanked the yacht's owners and departed, saying he was needed at the hospital.

'Cherry dresses like a doctor from the old days, doesn't he?' Josie stared after him. 'All in white, even on a yacht. He suits this boat, all old-fashioned teak and varnish.'

'He doesn't want skin cancer,' Lester said, feeling the heat of his own reddened arms and legs.

'He has a lovely tan...' Josie blurted, then cut herself short.

'That's from Mauritius,' Adele said.

'I know he loves his work, but he doesn't talk about it much. I mean, most doctors can't talk about anything else. He doesn't spend time with other doctors, does he? Usually they club together.'

Adele's sly smile was all-knowing. 'He'd be bored. He's a free spirit.'

'For a free spirit, he doesn't talk very freely about himself. He's wonderfully mysterious about his past. Perhaps he was engaged, a love affair that didn't work out.'

Adele took off her sailing cap and shook out a cloud of dark curls. 'I'm staying here because I'm going to marry him.'

Lester and Josie faced each other, dumbfounded.

'He's never mentioned that to us.' Josie peered at Adele intently over her sunglasses. 'Is it to do with your visa?'

'It's nothing to do with that. I want to stay. I want to help these people get back their land.'

'There's talk about you at our church. You're preaching against the church at meetings of the Mataungans. People don't like it.'

'Some people don't like it, I'm sure. Your father, for one. Your church owns plantations, too.'

Josie stood up angrily. 'You don't give these people a mind of their own, do you? Christianity wasn't foisted on them. They accepted the church. It's part of their life. The church land is their land; it hasn't been taken away from them. It isn't my church, or my father's. It's their church.'

'What happened in New Zealand, then? I tell them about that. It's the old story. The settlers had the church and the Maoris had the land. Now the Maoris have the church and the settlers have the rest. All the talk, the promises, the treaties, didn't amount to anything.'

'That's not the way we Kiwis see it,' said Jeff, the skipper, emerging from the cabin.

Adele was undaunted. 'Possession is all that matters. Take it, sit on it, don't get off. The Tolai still have a chance; they aren't outnumbered yet.'

'There aren't going to be more settlers,' Lester said. 'This is a Trust Territory. It's going to be independent one day.'

'Foreign ownership doesn't mean foreigners will live here. Their corporations will own it.'

Adele picked up her bag and stalked off along the jetty.

'That's the last time I'll ever talk to her,' Josie said.

'And the last time she'll sail with us,' Jeff added.

'I look shipwrecked,' Josie said later in the car, twisting the rear vision mirror to study herself. 'My face is sunburnt. And look at my hair, it's as stiff as a toilet brush. I can't wait to get home for a shower.'

'You're lucky I was there to give you a lift,' Lester said. 'Cherry ran off and abandoned you.'

'That's Adele's doing. He probably couldn't get away from her fast enough. She's *such* a good sailor, scampering up and down the boat like a monkey. How I wish she'd just sail away.'

'I think Cherry was worried about a patient. He seems to find it a strain to talk about his work; that's why I don't pry.'

'I'm not prying, just puzzled. The patients adore him, at least the kids do. I've seen him in the children's ward. He finds boiled eggs under their pillows and turns his stethoscope into a pet snake that can do tricks. He's a good artist, too. I've seen him sketch some of the children and give the sketches to them.'

Lester also struggled to understand Cherry's reticence. It couldn't be laziness or a lack of interest; at Taliligap, medical texts and handwritten notes were often on the table when he visited. Only rarely would Cherry mention a case that upset him, a child injured in a road accident perhaps, or a woman's death from a ruptured spleen caused by violent blows.

'I'm interviewing a doctor at Nonga soon,' Lester said. 'I'll try to find out more.'

Josie leaned into him, so close that he could breathe in the salty tang of her skin. She smiled and stroked his cheek. 'You're such a good man.'

Lester winced at a statement his mother might have made. It was the last thing he wanted to be called, at least by Josie.

His feelings had crept up on him gradually. When the Trio rehearsed together, or sang at the restaurant, he could suppress his feelings towards her. When they were alone, and every night in his apartment, his desire for her took over his mind: what it would be like to hold her, for her to gaze into his eyes as if in search of his soul.

On Namanula Hill, watching her play tennis and mingling gaily with the others, they'd flowered into passion. For the first time in his life, he felt he was in love.

Then again, he thought, how did she feel about him? Clearly, fond of him and affectionate, but *fondness* was a vague and woolly word. So far she had deflected his attempts to draw out her deepest feelings. She idolised Cherry and made little attempt to hide it.

So long as the Trio survived, the uneasy balance in the relationship between the three of them might remain. For the moment, he had to accept its limitations. He didn't want to lose the friendship of either of the others. That was all that sustained him.

Circumstances, however, were about to change.

Less than a week after the sailing trip, Cherry rang Lester from the hospital, his tone curiously flat and detached. 'Adele's gone. She's been deported.'

'What happened?'

'Police Special Branch, the bastards. They came to Chinatown before dawn. The Gestapo couldn't have done better. They pulled her out of bed.'

'Where were you?'

'In bed beside her.'

For Lester, the only surprise in Adele's deportation was its dead-of-night stealth. It brought a vivid memory of Sydney, of himself in bed with Patsy: loud banging on the door, shouts, Patsy's panicked scramble for her clothes, the shock of her being wrenched away.

'What about her visa?'

'Expired. She didn't tell anyone.'

'Was she given a warning?'

'The police bundled her straight into a police wagon and onto a flight for Port Moresby. What can I do, Lester? She'll be on a plane to Australia by now.'

'It's too late. I'll see you at Taliligap as soon as I can.'

Lester put the phone down, ashamed. Upcoming Circuit cases were a pressing priority.

A Tolai woman was savagely attacked by a plantation labourer wielding a machete. He'd accused the woman of a petty theft.

Lester rang the doctor at Nonga who'd treated the woman and would be called to give evidence. This was his opportunity to inquire discreetly about Cherry, a fellow doctor. As Lester gave his name, the doctor interrupted.

'I recognise you. I heard you playing at the Steakhouse with Tony Cherry-Apsley and that churchy girl from along the Kokopo Road.'

For Lester, this was a setback. It would have been better if he hadn't been seen as someone well acquainted with Cherry. He had to be careful.

'Oh, do you work with Tony at the hospital?'

'I see him around. I don't really know anyone who works with him. I don't know whether he's told you, but there was some trouble not long after he arrived.'

'Trouble?'

'A fight between a couple of nurses, apparently over him. I heard he was banished from the general ward. He usually looks after children or is away at clinics, or...'

'Or?'

'Or can't be found at all.'

This doctor wasn't a Cherry admirer and didn't mind who knew it. Perhaps realising he was talking to Cherry's close friend, he added, 'Of course no one doubts his competence. He has excellent qualifications from the School of Tropical Medicine in London, so I'm told. And he's not married, so he's happy to do night shifts. I'm with a patient. Must go.'

Lester couldn't ask for more. Neither he nor Josie would be satisfied with that.

The machete attack on a defenceless woman was settled by the Public Solicitor next day with a guilty plea. The following case was far different. It aroused some interest around town and among Tolai villagers and attracted a crowd at court to hear it.

A stone carving lay before Judge Prest on the Associate's table. It was weathered and pitted, grey-green with age and mould. At first glance it appeared like a newborn child lying on its back, arms folded against its sides and knees bent double. Slit eyes peered from a stone-bearded face. When stood on its feet, it crouched like a malevolent garden gnome, ready to pounce on some unwary sprite. Its name was Palikorkor.

The carving was Exhibit A in the trial of Joseph Tokat. The thief had come in the night to where Palikorkor had rested for generations, wedged in the roots of a massive *ficus* tree near the village. He'd taken the carving away and sold it for two hundred dollars to a visiting anthropologist, who knew a rare *ingiet* carving and a tenfold profit when he saw one. The theft was reported by villagers and the carving was recovered before the buyer could leave with it.

Lester wished fervently it'd been the anthropologist on trial, not the thief. In the event, it wouldn't have mattered.

The Public Solicitor's office, reading the witness statements in Port Moresby, had discovered a legal flaw. A law lecturer from the university was flown in for the defence. A sackful of books from the university library flowed over his table in the court and lay heaped around his feet. The point soon became obvious.

'You say you're the owner?' he asked the witness. 'Are you the only owner?'

The grey-haired village elder pushed himself erect with his cane and with grave dignity answered in Pidgin, 'It belongs to the *vunatarai*, all of us, the Kwara clan.'

'So, you're not really the owner?'

'Yes, I'm the custodian. I'm the eldest. The eldest man is responsible for its safekeeping, until he dies.'

'How many are in the clan?'

'Many. I don't know. They are scattered about.'

'Have you a list of who they are?'

'A list? No.'

'Would you necessarily know if someone in the clan had died or had been born? Could you make up a list at any time?'

'Anyone may say whether they are in the clan or not. We don't know all the names. And sometimes a person may not be. It's not free from doubt. It's not important to know every one of them.'

'Can you sell the stone?'

'No.'

'Can your *vunatarai* call a meeting and agree to sell it?'

'Of course not; it's not ours to sell.'

The lecturer, thick lips framed by a goatee beard, grinned insolently at Lester and wrapped himself in the folds of his gown.

'Why not?' he asked the old man.

'It belongs to the sorcerers. It's for sorcery. It also belongs to the old people, to our ancestors. They're now dead. It's owned by the dead as well as the living.'

The lecturer looked triumphantly at Judge Prest. 'Where does the Criminal Code provide for that, your Honour? Can the owners be ascertained with certainty? No. A thing can't be stolen if you can't prove who owns it.'

Lester's arguments to the contrary couldn't save the case. The judge may have thought otherwise, but he wasn't going to have a university lecturer pursuing him through the appeal courts, armed with all the precedents in the university law library.

Tokat walked from the court a free man, scratching his head and wondering what had happened. Villagers who attended the court went home baffled.

Lester walked disconsolately back to the office, the stone carving cradled in one arm, books and gown in the other, frustrated by his professional isolation in this frontier town and the lack of a proper library to research the law.

He had studied the history of the stone figures and their link to the *ingiet* sorcerers who fashioned and controlled them. A Catholic priest had been sitting outside the court, waiting to educate the judge on their purpose and their origins—in Indonesia, so it seemed, centuries ago.

Then there was the *ingiet* itself, both a form of sorcery and a secret society of sorcerers and initiates of magic, banned since German times. There were sorcerers, Lester learnt, who could change their form at will, who could call on the *tabaran*, spirits of the dead, to torment the living.

Now he was saddled with Exhibit A. The local police refused to take it back; they wouldn't hear of it remaining in the police station. He put the carving away in a drawer of his filing cabinet.

It didn't stay for long. One morning Gloria opened the drawer to find it staring up at her. She screamed and fled, vowing not to return until the stone was removed.

At length, Bilson organised a ceremony in the village square for the return of Palikorkor. Bilson was at his most efficient, rounding up curious onlookers, selecting official parties and discussing protocols. Dignitaries to the front in lines of three and clan elders at the head of each row.

He made a short speech in praise of the administration. The government had been responsible for the rescue and restoration of this precious item of village heritage. He stood at ease, long white socks gleaming below tanned knees, shoulders squared, hands crossed behind his back, speaking in ringing, text book Pidgin.

The audience clapped politely, uncertainly, and kept at a wary distance. Not all, evidently, viewed Palikorkor's reappearance with enthusiasm. Lester realised quickly, too late, the best of intentions may not end in the best of outcomes.

Bilson beamed at him as they climbed into Bilson's vehicle.

'Great public relations! Just when we need it. Shows that we're not always the evil oppressors.'

Peter Bilson was a District Officer, a senior *kiap* in the Gazelle. He knew Lester was an admin lawyer. In a flash of camaraderie, he invited Lester to dinner.

Bilson, too, was single, but had earned the right to married accommodation by virtue of his rank. Authority assumed early in his career had given him the affectations of a man of substance. He dined at the head of a table set with the best stainless-steel cutlery the local stores could provide.

Frangipani flowers floated in a bowl of water carefully placed at the table's centre, flanked by white serviettes and heirloom silver serviette rings. The courses—Campbell's pumpkin soup, a fish curry, a selection of fruits from the market—were served by a broad-nosed, stocky Sepik man in a white shirt and old-fashioned, ankle-length laplap. Between courses the servant stood stiffly at the door to the kitchen.

Fresh-faced and fortyish, Bilson was an inheritor of the *kiap* tradition of exploration and pacification. While languishing in Port Moresby, Lester had read about the legendary patrols and patrol officers of the past. In sepia-tinted photographs, tanned, rangy men looked down from ridge tops on highland valleys of eternal Spring. Clad in khaki shorts, open-chested shirts, broad-brimmed hats and stout boots, they strode through waist-high kunai grass at the head of a line of carriers and native police winding their way over the hills. The names of Karius and Champion, Hides and McCarthy were among Bilson's illustrious predecessors.

In a rambling conversation after dinner, Bilson told of his last posting on the Sepik River, a great waterway rising in the formidable Schatteburg mountains and flowing for more than a thousand tortuous kilometres through lakes and flood plains to the Bismarck Sea.

He'd lived at Ambunti and Nuku, and among the Avatip people along the Karawari River, a Sepik tributary. The Avatip were renowned for their skills as painters, potters and wood-carvers, and for *haus tambarans*, spirit houses with steep-pitched thatch roofs and fantastically painted portals. At dusk in this poor, harsh environment, mosquitoes rose from the swamps in clouds that prematurely darkened the sky. Each night was spent in fear of tormenting spirits or raiding enemies.

Around the walls of his apartment, Bilson had put up wooden carvings, basket hooks, bark paintings, masks with drooping mouths and pig tusks pierced through flared noses. He brought out two *yipwons*, strange, two-dimensional, one-legged wooden figures, from a trunk in his bedroom. He gave them to Lester. He had dozens of carvings, he explained, presented by grateful Sepik villagers wherever he went.

Only at the end of a long evening did Bilson reveal the real reason for his dinner invitation. Water from Szabo's tanks upstairs seeped through the flimsy ceiling below to drip maddeningly onto Bilson's white, starched sheets, his spotless lace tablecloth and his mirror-polished floors, a source of constant friction between them.

Szabo's sullen obstinacy and half-hearted attempts to stem the leaks rubbed against Bilson's self-righteous indignation. Bilson was determined to find some way that the might of the admin could hobble this outlandish man.

Lester told him that Szabo's plundering of the reefs didn't appear to break any law. Bilson grumbled, banging his fist loudly on the table. 'The man's cocking a snook at the administration. There must be some wrongdoing, some crime he's committing. These no-hopers, these deadbeats, are being allowed into the country. They're a plague!'

Late that night in his apartment, Lester propped up his *yip-wons* on a dressing cabinet in his bedroom. Moonlight filtering through the window threw elongated shadows of them on the wall. He watched the shadows lengthen, spreading slowly towards the bedroom window. They were imprisoned in his room, he thought, far from their spiritual home along the Sepik River and straining to be free.

Outside, taxi trucks rattled along the road to the squatter settlement. You had to watch the girls who lived there, Bilson warned. Every wretched shack was a brothel.

23

Though the Kokopo Agricultural Show was an exhibition of local agricultural products and of research for novel ones, the other attractions, from *sing-sing* competitions to amusement stalls, really drew the crowds. It had something of the flavour of a country town show in Australia.

Administration agricultural officers, known everywhere as *didimen*, mingled with plantation managers and families from inland or around the coast. Tolais from villages near and far mingled with town dwellers in a way rarely seen outside of market days.

Cherry drove the others down from Taliligap after a last-minute rehearsal. They were nervous about performing on stage behind a bevy of microphones provided by the organisers. They needn't have worried. A trio of Europeans singing popular songs was a rare event.

Afterwards, in the cool of Cherry's bungalow, they showered and sank into the armchairs on the verandah.

'It's our anniversary today,' Cherry said, suddenly sitting upright. 'A year since the Taliligap Trio was born.'

'A year that brought the three of us together,' Josie said.

Lester laughed. 'You make it sound like a marriage.'

'I have a surprise!' Cherry sprang from his chair, hurried inside and returned with a bottle of champagne in a plastic bucket of ice. 'I bought it a while ago to celebrate Adele's birthday.'

'What a shame she's not here to share it,' Josie said gleefully. 'I'll bring some glasses.'

As Cherry opened the bottle, a cry came from Josie in the living room. 'What was that? A gun?'

Cherry laughed. 'Poor thing, she's never heard a champagne cork popping.'

They drank a toast to the success of the Taliligap Trio.

'And to absent friends,' Lester added. He raised his glass in Cherry's direction. 'Have you heard from her?'

'I thought she might call from Australia, but she hasn't. I've no idea where she is and the police won't tell me. When they came for her, I felt helpless. What could I have done?'

'She wanted to marry you,' Josie said. 'She told us so.'

Cherry shook his head. 'I don't know why she said that. She knew I wasn't in love with her.'

'Then you strung her along,' Josie said, trying with little conviction to sound reproachful.

'I did no such thing. She was exciting to be with. I went on Mataungan marches with her. I suppose I nailed my colours to the mast. When the police arrested her, they said they'd have liked to put me on the plane as well.'

'I think you're sorry she's gone.'

'Of course I'm sorry. I admired her spirit, but I couldn't imagine her as a doctor's wife.'

Josie pulled a face and drank a second glass of champagne, followed immediately by a third.

'Champagne should be sipped, not swilled,' Cherry said.

'I'll drink it any way I like!' Josie carelessly flung her hand.

Lester drove her back to Malmaluan. The champagne had gone to her head, and she refused to be seen at the centre's front door. She pulled Lester around the building to find an open window with a mosquito screen and took it down.

'They all do it,' she laughed, referring to the students. 'Just push me through.' On the other side, Lester heard her tumble, but her face appeared again at the window. She grinned and kissed him. 'You're my hero, Lester Chettle,' she said.

He returned to find Cherry reclining on the verandah, propped up by the bungalow wall. Cherry often seemed to prefer the floor to an armchair, perhaps because it aided his air of languorous decadence. He flourished a bottle of Negrita rum and suggested they finish it. He gestured in the direction of Malmaluan.

'We're corrupting our virgin Josie. What an exquisite experience it is. She's dipping her delectable toes in a swamp of depravity. She reminds me of Audrey Hepburn in *The Nun's Story*. She's torn between Christian rectitude and the pleasures of the real world.'

'Who's to blame?' said Lester. 'You're the one who plies her with liquor.'

'I don't think she's quite the puritan she pretends to be.'

'Surely she wouldn't want us to be fighting over her,' Lester said. 'Or would she enjoy it? She's hard to read.'

'She seems happy as things are. I've never seen her happier than today.' Cherry shook his head. 'I have a feeling today was as good as it will ever be for the Trio.'

'Don't say that to Josie.'

'Where do we go from here?'

'We're down to a farewell appearance or two at the Steak-house. There's no other regular venue in town. Connell says we could play at the tavern.'

'Josie won't go near it. I don't blame her.'

At that moment, the verandah trembled, a short, sharp movement. Dishes rattled in the kitchen. Dogs howled in the village nearby.

'Another *guria*.' Cherry stirred from his slump against the wall.

Lester yawned and levered himself from an armchair. 'They seem more frequent lately. I woke up the other night thinking that someone had hold of my foot and was shaking me. My bed began jiggling across the floor.'

Cherry waved a hand at the bay below.

'It's a sign that the volcanoes are coming to life. Look at Vulcan sitting there, brooding. You won't believe it: *The Last Days of Pompeii* is playing at the cinema in town.'

'*Gurias* have been occurring for years. No one seems worried about them.'

'It'll happen one day. We'll be smothered like the poor citizens of Pompeii. The volcano doesn't want us here. Time's running out for us; I can feel it.'

'Take it easy,' Lester said, pointing to Cherry's bottle of whisky, which had replaced the Negrita. 'I'm off to bed.'

'I can't sleep. I'll stay out here where it's cool.'

Clutching the bottle, Cherry rose and sat down on the verandah steps. 'Connell told me about a Japanese tunnel complex that's still full of stores and ammunition. I'll try to find it tomorrow. Will you come with me?'

'I can't—I'm in court on Monday. I need to prepare.'

Cherry waved Lester away. He looked tired, Lester thought, and a touch forlorn. No Adele to comfort him now.

'Next time, then. I'd prefer not to go into the tunnels alone. They go on for ever in all directions, like warrens. You can get lost. There's snakes, bats, bandicoots and God knows what else.'

Lester laughed. 'Many thanks, then, for the invitation.'

Aladdin and His Magic Lamp was the school's play. The audience, young and old, was entranced. A swirl of swordplay and gaudy costumes. Scantily clad girls from the ballet school performed the Dance of the Seven Veils. Genies appeared from a trapdoor and thieves from cane laundry baskets. Aladdin's cave had been framed in flashing lights, but a short circuit set fire to the flimsy construction during a performance. The hall emptied in chaos and the flashing lights were destroyed.

All over the stage was the flowing presence of Cherry. An Aladdin whose looks beguiled, who could conjure yards of coloured cloth from the air and juggle the batons of the Palace Guard. Who tweaked Hassan's beard, plotted with thieves and caused Princess Badroulbadour to swoon into the arms of her maidservant.

An Aladdin who delivered his lines with honeyed eloquence, but rarely twice in quite the same words, to the despair of the cast.

The last-night party was one to be remembered, though not by Lester. As the curtain closed, still in costume as Hassan of the Palace Guard, drenched in sweat, he staggered into the wings and collapsed.

Restful silence enveloped the bungalow at Taliligap. Little could be heard beyond the occasional passing of a PMV, the chattering of children on their way to or from school and, in the evenings, the twitter of starlings gathering to roost in the palm trees. Cherry put Lester into his own bedroom while staying over on most nights at Grandview Apartments.

Dengue fever charged through Lester's body, leaving a trail of disorder and aching joints. It built up each day to a sweaty climax in the midday heat.

The afternoon breeze was a soothing balm, but the fever returned as fits of shivering during the night. He was racked with headaches and ulcers erupted in his mouth. He was too weak to get up or eat. Josie and Cherry took turns to come, heating up soup and bringing fresh sheets laundered by the charitable staff at Malmaluan.

Within a week, the worst of the fever was over. He could rise then and sit on the verandah, tormented by an itchy, angry rash over much of his body. The ulcers were slow to heal, and still he couldn't eat, sipping only soup and water.

Cherry's child patients at the hospital made him a get well card. Each had drawn an animal or a bird from the overflowing ark of the New Guinea forests. Cleary and Crosset brought flowers from the cast of *Aladdin* with a card praising brave Hassan who, despite becoming ill on stage, had soldiered on in the best tradition of the theatre.

Bilson called to see him while on his way, as he always seemed to be, to attend an important event. He briskly inspected the buildings, which were government property. He summoned the caretakers and ordered the lawns be trimmed yet again.

Carol Begley and her daughter were dropped off by her friend, a police inspector. According to Carol, he was her armed guard and protector whenever she bravely ventured beyond the town boundaries. She produced a jar of swamp-green liquid, saying it was Gloria's homemade papaya leaf juice. Gloria claimed it would cure Lester overnight. Carol, who sampled it, declared it far too bitter to drink. She also brought a get well card from Flanagan.

Lester tried to smile. The ulcers were razor blades in his mouth.

'How nice of him. Too busy to visit, I suppose?'

'John says if you don't come back in a week, he'll bring in another lawyer.'

'He's all care and compassion.' Lester painfully eked out the words.

Carol smiled benignly at the thought and nodded. 'I think so too.'

Lester had scarcely spoken to Gabriel since their encounter at Vunadidir many months before, apart from brief greetings at the market, along with a conspiratorial wink or two from him that annoyed Lester greatly.

Thus, Lester was surprised when Gabriel arrived in his PMV, accompanied by Jacob ToVailu, a man Lester recognised as a leader of the Mataungan executive, often quoted in newspaper reports of the demonstrations and, along with Gabriel, recently acquitted of assault in the District Court.

He led the men to armchairs on the verandah and fetched soft drinks before joining them.

'Thank you for your help in the court.' Gabriel solemnly reached out to shake Lester's hand.

Lester smiled. 'I wasn't in court to *help* you. How did you find me here? I've been warned to stay away from you.'

'We know you, and the doctor too, and the Kanak woman who has gone now,' ToVailu said. His tone was affable. A handsome man and a teacher, whom the administration regarded as an opponent of violence and nobody's fool.

Gabriel nodded. 'We wanted to thank you because the judge said we were not guilty of fighting at the church. We tried to stop it. We tried to lead people away.'

Lester sat up instantly. 'Do you think we tried to lose? We couldn't prove what you did or didn't do because the police investigation was poor.'

'Ah, I thought so too,' Gabriel grinned. 'That's what our lawyer from the university told us. We talked about the case together. I went to the office to thank Mr Flanagan, but a policeman wouldn't let me in. Tell Mr Flanagan we're grateful.'

'If I ever get better, I'll pass on the message.'

Gabriel raised his hand as if giving a blessing. 'You will get better. I'll send my sister IaKalit. She'll know what to do.'

ToVailu cut in. 'I also want to thank you for letting some of our people go from the tax charges. I heard you; I was there in the court.'

'They changed their minds and paid the tax. I didn't let people go, the court did. That's the policy.'

'So they weren't sent to jail, were they?' ToVailu shrugged but seemed gratified, nonetheless.

Lester gave up on the logic of his visitors. The argument, the cause, the message that the administration was vulnerable under pressure, was more important to them than legal logic, guilt or innocence. He smiled again at Gabriel as he sank back into his chair.

'You're a rogue. I'm glad Flanagan sacked you.'

'There are Mataungans working in the administration. Even among the *kiaps* we have supporters. There are many who help us.'

Gabriel rose and walked to the verandah steps, ready to leave, but turned back abruptly.

'Why don't they leave us alone? Why do the police put shields in our faces? That's a challenge to our men. Shields and clubs against shields and clubs, that's what we did before the Europeans came. The old men remember those ways. The women tell us to fight, to show them we're still men. You'll take our pride as well as our land. It will end badly.'

Lester, unnerved by Gabriel's sudden anger, sought a distraction.

'Have you met Carol, your replacement?'

'The new lady?' Gabriel's countenance softened. He giggled. 'Gloria told me the lady has a police guard because she might be killed in her bed by Mataungans.'

'I think you enjoy the reputation you have.'

'Have we killed anyone? It's in your minds only.'

Watching Gabriel as he walked to his truck, Lester realised the gulf between them. He'd struck up a friendship with a man he'd seen as a self-effacing office clerk. He'd been playing happily with a wolf's tail but was now uncomfortably aware of sharp teeth at the other end. He noted a new arrogance about the Mataungan leaders. They had control of the night.

Gabriel's sister IaKalit appeared the next day with her medicine, a posy of herbs tied with a snip of bamboo string. She stirred the herbs into a cup of hot water, then sat silently beside him until he swallowed the bitter dose. She laughed shyly, a flash of dazzling white teeth, as he grimaced.

In the following days she returned, making the long trip from town in the back of a PMV. Lester suspected Gabriel had ordered her to hover, to see whether he recovered or died, he supposed, on the principle that the potent ingredients of village medicine either killed or cured.

She pottered about the bungalow, dusting or sweeping, sometimes reading or idly gazing at Lester as he sat in a state of lassitude on the verandah. She asked him, in Pidgin, if he was a Christian.

'I'm Anglican,' he said, to humour her.

'Oh! There are none here, only European Anglicans and a few Papuans from Popondetta on the Papuan side. They sing the hymns to different tunes, and we don't like them.' She laughed at that.

She liked to read, not Cherry's books, which she glanced at and put aside, but the *Australian Woman's Weekly* and *Home Beautiful*, a collection of which, years old, had been left in the bungalow. She sat quietly on the verandah floor for hours with the magazines scattered around her, staring intently at each page, absorbed in the advertisements and glossy pictures, her brow furrowed.

There Lester could watch her, afternoon sunlight on her warm, brown skin, her face in profile: sweeping eyelashes, high, sculpted cheekbones, a small, flared nose and pink budding lips. She would bite her bottom lip gently as she read, a long-fingered hand turning the pages. Otherwise she was stock-still, an artist's model.

She wore a loose-fitting *meri* blouse and an ankle-length laplap wrapped and carelessly knotted about her waist. Hard-soled feet in thong sandals were the only roughness in that lithe and gentle creature.

One day she looked up, startled to find him gazing at her. Her eyes darted away. He could see her breathing quicken. She jumped up to the verandah rail.

'My truck is coming. I must go now.'

She ran along the verandah, thongs flapping on the boards like the wingbeats of a large bird, frightened from its cover.

Lester later learnt from Josie about IaKalit's religious experience. She'd dreamed she was in a bedroom, the sort of bedroom she'd seen in *Home Beautiful*. She was having intercourse with a man who had the fairest skin and hair, like Doctor Cherry. The man had a beard like Jesus. The bedsheets were printed with pale pink flowers. She wanted a baby like the ones she'd seen in the magazines. 'So white,' she'd murmured in Pidgin, 'so clean.'

Josie was distraught when IaKalit revealed her dream. Cherry insisted it was the fault of the missionaries. Josie wanted the magazines destroyed as a bad influence. Only Lester was amused. Wasn't a Tolai woman as entitled to dream of sheets with pink flowers as anyone else? Josie refused to answer this mischievous question. The offending magazines were not seen again.

Days later, still fatigued, Lester slumped in an armchair on the verandah. The scent of freshly mown grass carried up to the bungalow, aided by a caressing breeze. Though the fevers had subsided, the headaches lingered on. His mouth felt as if were stuffed with rotting carpet. The first drink of rum and Coke in three weeks made him giddy at first, then pleasantly lightheaded. He closed his eyes, listening to Cherry, in a chair beside him, talking about his family.

Cherry's grandfather inherited a Georgian-style house that, over generations, had never quite been finished. Beyond the grand gates and driveway was an extravagant fountain with piddling cherubs, and beyond that, an imposing building with three storeys as well as an attic and basement. No one in the family knew for certain how many rooms there were.

His father, the baronet, lived with Cherry and his Hungarian mother, though was rarely at home. Cherry's mother, a glamorous woman of extravagant tastes but little money of her own, doted on him.

Gordon, the baronet's first-born son and six years older, generally ignored his half-brother. Hannah, his half-sister and three years older, was a friend when they were young but, at least in the mind of Cherry's mother, became wildly jealous as a teenager of Cherry's fair good looks.

If Hannah and Cherry's mother hated each other, both had their reasons for hating the medieval vagaries of the aristocracy and male succession. For Hannah, an ardent feminist, it was because as a female she could never inherit her father's title. For Cherry's mother, it was because, with Gordon in the way, Cherry couldn't inherit it either. This led her to periodic fanciful plotting to get rid of his half-brother.

'You paint a grim picture of your family,' Lester said, taking another drink.

Cherry shrugged. 'The only one in that family I really liked was my grandfather. He lived in rooms at the top of the house and had his own housekeeper. He died when I was seven. To me he seemed impossibly old even then. He used to drive me in his car to the village for an ice cream. He drove everywhere at a top speed of twenty miles an hour. He often drove on the wrong side of the road because he had a theory there were fewer potholes on that side. It was jolly exciting.'

'Your driving is no less exciting,' Lester laughed.

'I used to cringe in shame every time a car overtook us, tooting its horn. I promised myself I'd never, ever, be overtaken again.'

Cherry paused, lost, it seemed, in a memory.

'Were you lonely?' Lester asked.

'I loved that house. I loved the wind sighing in the chimneys and rattling the windowpanes and those wet, wild gardens. And the books! Shelves of books on Africa, India, Burma, when all the world seemed our empire. Books overflowed in piles down the staircase. That house was my world. In a way, I've always been alone since then. I was my own companion, my own best friend.'

Cherry's voice wandered away. He seemed tired and dejected. Lester felt a surge of compassion, of love, for his friend. Aroused by the smell of grass in the air, a picture came to mind of Cherry's home in an English countryside of hedgerows and soft, misted light. It sounded as if Cherry was talking about a place to which he might never return.

He reached for Cherry's hand as a gesture of comfort. He felt closer to him than to anyone in his life. Cherry looked at him, wondering, perhaps uncertain of the intimacy, then pressed his hand to Lester's own.

'I've bored you half to death.'

'I've never been to England,' Lester said, 'but I felt I was there with you.'

'Your family's English,' said Cherry. 'It's in your blood.'

Lester shrugged. 'They're from a different England. I don't know what I am now. I still don't feel properly Australian.'

A cool rain began drumming on the bungalow roof. He found himself shivering.

'You don't look well,' Cherry said. 'I let you drink too much. Why don't you go and lie down?'

The next day Lester came outside to find Josie in a chair on the verandah, her legs propped up on the verandah rail, feet in sturdy, dusty sandals, silver anklets gleaming in the sun and skirt tucked up immodestly about her thighs. She was sucking on a passionfruit pulled from a flowering vine that twined around the posts. As ever, Lester's heart skipped a beat on seeing her.

'I didn't hear you come,' he said.

Josie fanned her face with her hand. 'A PMV dropped me at the village up the road. I had to walk the last bit. I'm so hot. Do you have a Coke?'

Lester fetched her a drink and ushered her to sit beside him. She'd brought ointment to bathe the ugly ulcers at the corners of Lester's mouth. After slaking her thirst, she inspected them closely, coolly professional, dabbing the ointment on, leaning close, her chest brushing his own. Lester, hotly stranded between embarrassment and desire, longed to reach out and embrace her.

Slowly Josie packed the ointment and cotton buds in her bag. For a time she was quiet. Then, with a nervous glance, she said, 'Cherry and I played at the restaurant on Friday night.'

'Oh?' This was unexpected, and despite himself Lester's tone was reproachful. 'He didn't tell me.'

Colour rose in Josie's cheeks. After a moment's confusion, she rushed on. 'Of course he can't play the guitar like you.'

'Do you two have something going on?'

'Oh, no, it's not what you think. I wanted to try on my own, that's all.'

'How did you go?'

'Some rowdy seamen came in. One of them shouted, "Show us yer tits, dear." I couldn't help myself; I called him a birdbrain.

Cherry threatened to hit him. There was a scuffle. Cherry punched someone and we had to leave.'

'I'm sorry for you; that's terrible.'

'Actually, it was exciting. We were both angry. He drove me home so fast, I was scared out of my wits. At the same time, I felt like urging him on. I felt somehow...liberated. He was very brave. He's a bit too brave sometimes, don't you think?'

'He says he and I are inseparable,' Lester said, 'Often I think I'm only around to keep him out of trouble.'

'No, you're his best and loyal friend. He says so.'

'You spend more time with him than I do.'

Josie smiled. 'Don't be cross. Besides, I've brought you a present.' She went inside and returned with a bouquet. 'There's a jasmine bush outside my window that catches the breeze, so you should hang this outside yours. It's the flower of love.'

'Is it a token?' he asked.

'It could be.' She gave a lingering, dark-eyed look.

Lester dropped her off at Malmaluan. That night he hung the jasmine and went to bed, delighting in its perfume and tormented by his thoughts. Was she playing him? Had she been staying with Cherry at Grandview Apartments while he was languishing at Taliligap?

At one time he'd believed her incapable of deception; now he was no longer sure.

Cherry had given Lester a medical certificate, signed by himself and of doubtful validity, for a month away from work—four weeks of enforced idleness. The illness had wound him down to the pace of the tropics where each new day drifts endlessly past, equally as hot, humid and enervating as the last. With nothing to do except read or look out at the harbour, the passage of time lost all significance.

Almost two years since his arrival in the country! He had to check and recheck a calendar to believe it. Time to return to work. He needed the air-conditioned office to revive him.

As Cherry pointed out, at least he hadn't been sent home like George Orwell.

24

In Lester's absence, the Rabaul Prosecutor's office had become the epicentre of the admin's legal battle to restrain the Mataungans and their intractable demands.

Spot fires erupted on many fronts. Prosecutions continued in the Supreme Court against Mataungan leaders for offences of rioting and assault that had occurred nearly a year ago. Prosecutors from Port Moresby assisted Flanagan with the prosecutions. The insufferable Carstairs had taken over Lester's corner office. Gloria fumed at their complaints about accommodation, meals, office supplies, allowances and the lack of office space for them to work. Meanwhile, Carol typed opinions, statements and reports as fast as she could—never fast enough. Flanagan had again taken up smoking cigarettes. Lester had apparently been forgotten.

He expressed his anguish at the administration's tactics to Flanagan, whom he suspected was also frustrated, but instead Flanagan supported Carstairs and other prosecutors who argued that from the broader perspective of Port Moresby, there was scant support for the Mataungans elsewhere in the country.

Carstairs cleared his desk, leaving Lester with a pile of left-over appeals from remote *kiap* courts and guilty pleas to the usual run of local crimes. All rather dispiriting.

A week after Lester's return to work, Josie turned up at Tali-ligap as usual on a Sunday afternoon, but in a state of high excitement. When Lester arrived soon after, she hugged him enthusiastically.

'I've been staying at Gaulim, helping the teachers. I couldn't live there any longer and be tortured day and night by insects. Baining villagers have invited a few of us to a fire dance tonight. I've been told it's spectacular. I've already asked Cherry. You can come too.'

Lester's look was sceptical. 'Is this some animist ritual? What would your father say?'

'My father's seen it. He's written about it. You should be grateful because it doesn't happen often, especially now when there's so much trouble. It's an outing to celebrate your recovery.'

The village near Gaulim, where the dance was to take place, lay in the foothills of the Baining Mountains. It was considered a dangerous excursion by the townspeople who had to pass through Mataungan strongholds at night on a narrow, pitching dirt road.

As darkness fell, they set off in Cherry's utility and joined a convoy of vehicles travelling nose to tail. The performance, in a large clearing, was already underway when they arrived. An elaborately costumed dancer swayed to the lilting chant of a male chorus. The bonfire in the centre of the clearing threw a glowing halo around the dancer's outsized mask of bark-cloth that resembled a duck's head and beak. Large red and black bullseyes on the mask stared sightlessly into the forest.

Spectators, a handful of them foreigners, formed a circle around the fire at a respectful distance. Opposite were younger men not taking part in the dance. In front of them a score of children, wide-eyed, silent and still.

Sitting close together on the ground, the Trio were soon immersed in the performance. The drumming and chanting were at once monotonous, hypnotic and compelling. The sounds defined boundaries between light and darkness, the clearing and the forest, drawing the audience and the dancer together.

One by one, several masked dancers came from the forest. Each one danced with increasing intensity before careering through the fire, shrieking, kicking at the red embers and showering the night with sparks. They seemed to take enormous strides, to leap, to fly over the fire's bright core, huge, fantastical figures appearing from nowhere, wreathed in flames.

As suddenly as they burst from the fire, they vanished into the forest. As the fire was replenished, the performance was repeated. Screeching dancers reappeared, streaming across the clearing and terrifying the children. From outside the circle, at the edge of the clearing, came high-pitched hoots of encouragement from the village elders directing the performance.

Lester was aware of Josie edging closer, her breathing audible, her grip tightening on his arm. He'd been to Tolai ceremonies at schools and churches, but sensed he was now witnessing something more primordial and unworldly, a spectacle not primarily performed for the audience.

Children clutched each other fearfully if a dancer came too close. When not dancing through the fire, the performers were silent, only adding to their sinister otherworldliness. These were true creatures of the forest, communing not with the onlookers but with other unseen presences around them, with spirits that lived in the rocks and trees, and in the deep, swift rivers.

Though the dancing would continue until dawn, the visitors, eventually exhausted, left before midnight. Cherry, driving behind the convoy, kept his eyes doggedly on the taillights of the vehicle in front. The narrow road reared and plunged abruptly, with jungle pressing on both sides. Occasionally a dog or pig detached itself from the undergrowth and stared into the headlights with bright devil's eyes.

At a fork in the road, the taillights ahead blinked and vanished. The utility slewed as Cherry braked hard. Cherry fumbled in his pocket, took out a coin and tossed. Left or right, heads or tails. When heads came up, they went left. No more than a hundred yards further on, the road ended abruptly in a cliff and a fast-flowing river below. The utility skidded to a halt on the brink.

No one spoke for the rest of the journey back to the welcoming lights of Kokopo.

The Reverend's house was in darkness. 'He's away in New Ireland,' Josie said. They settled in the living room of the comfortable plantation house. Josie slipped away and reappeared with a bottle of Negrita rum.

'I hide it in my dolls' box. I only have a swig occasionally, I promise.'

'Hail to our fallen angel,' Cherry said.

Josie brought Coca-Cola and ice from the refrigerator and made drinks, then flopped onto the sofa.

'I'm drained,' she said. 'My longest day ever. I was so frightened tonight! Listen, you can hear the ice rattling in my glass. That's my hand shaking.'

Lester laughed. 'No wonder. We nearly ended up floating down the river. Cherry saved us.'

'No, not the drive. I mean the dancers. The Baining village frightened me. I felt I was in a place that God didn't even know about. I was falling into a trance, being drawn into a dark cave, towards the heat, towards the fire. There was this terrible attraction. At any moment I could have jumped into the flames.'

Lester recalled the discomfort, not only physical, of sitting cross-legged for hours before the dancers. How swiftly and easily his book-fed knowledge of the world became irrelevant. An earlier learning, innate and instinctual, had overtaken it. His senses, he realised, had been heightened. For a time he'd been acutely aware, alert to the breaking of a twig, to movement in the shadows, to the shapes cast by the flames.

'What does it mean, the dance?' he asked. 'Apart from frightening everyone, I couldn't connect it to anything. Is it some sort of ritual?'

'My father says it's not a ritual, not a fixed thing,' Josie said. 'It's really about the Baining people affirming their culture. Otherwise, it'd be swamped by the Tolai. They believe they have a unique connection to the spirits. They dance their way into the spirit world to channel its energy, or so I was told. I don't think any outsider knows the whole story.'

Cherry, on the verge of dozing off, shook himself awake.

'I saw a church next to the village, and you're building a Christian teachers college next door. Why hasn't the church denounced it?'

Josie strangled a despairing groan.

'The Baining don't see the incongruity of believing in spirits—good ones as well as bad. The church is an extra layer of security.'

Cherry persisted. 'What would Christianity mean to them? What would the symbolism of the cross possibly mean to them?'

Lester held his breath, waiting for Josie to retaliate, but she laughed quietly, still rattling the ice in her empty glass.

'You can sneer all you like. At least the church is an antidote to sorcery. Without it, the Baining would succumb to sorcery from cradle to grave. That goes for the Tolai too.'

Cherry was baiting her, as he tended to do when the rum flowed. It was no secret that he regarded Christian evangelism as just another unfortunate consequence of colonialism.

'Now leave me alone. I'm too tired to argue.' Josie moved close to Lester on the sofa, relaxing beside him, stretching, uncurling. After a pause, she went on.

'You know,' she said, 'as I sat between you, I could sense each of you close beside me. I felt frightened yet safe, very alive, out of my skin. I imagined I could see things, shapes, far into the forest, through the trees. I remember thinking that if anything happened, if the Mokolkols appeared, we'd have grown like giants and would've run away together, striding over the treetops.'

'There was something in that smoke from the fire,' Lester teased.

'I wouldn't be surprised,' Cherry said. 'Connell told me the Baining people are infamous sorcerers. The Tolai fear them. Their sorcery is strong because they really believe in it.'

'I've an admission to make,' Josie said. 'I tried marijuana once at a teachers college in Australia. It gave me the oddest feeling. I don't know whether it was the smoke tonight, but for a time I felt myself being absorbed into a kind of shared consciousness. I've never felt like that in church. I wonder if there's a pagan spirit stirring inside me; after all, I've lived here nearly all my life. The people here live their lives surrounded by spirits. I'm becoming more superstitious. I don't disbelieve any more. Like them, I try to accommodate both worlds.'

She smiled and rose to leave the room, pausing to kiss Cherry's cheek. 'I wonder how long they last, the effects? I'm going to bed.'

The Steakhouse rewarded the Trio's last appearance with a free dinner, a best wishes card signed by the staff, a framed photograph of the Trio on stage to be hung in the restaurant and three bottles of champagne.

'Our Last Supper,' said Cherry. 'Who'll be the betrayer?'

Josie frowned. 'Don't be sacrilegious.'

Lester pointed at the champagne bottles. 'There's a bottle each.'

'I don't want mine.' Josie gazed unhappily around the room.

'You could raffle it for the church,' Lester said, hoping to cheer her.

'Champagne for the Methodists? Sometimes I despair of you both; you gang up on me. I think I want to go home.'

Cherry opened a bottle and filled a glass for each of them.

'We can still sing together, can't we?' Josie asked. 'I mean, go back to villages and events.'

Cherry shrugged. 'I can't keep up the rehearsals anymore. It's too time-consuming.'

'We'll stay together, won't we?'

'Of course we will. Taliligap is our refuge from a brutish world.'

After dinner, Cherry suggested tossing a coin for Josie's bottle of champagne. The winner would have the champagne; the loser would drive Josie home.

'I can't believe I'm hearing this,' Josie said. 'I'm traded for a bottle of champagne?'

'He's joking,' Lester said. 'I'll take you home.'

Josie jumped up from the table. 'I have things to do in town tomorrow. You can drop me at the pastor's house. I'm going to the bathroom.'

Lester watched her flounce across the room and vanish behind a door. He glared at Cherry across the table.

'What's the matter with you tonight? You were cruel to her.'

'I know. I should've put it the other way round.'

'The winner takes Josie? That's ridiculous. You're still raffling her off.'

'I couldn't resist,' Cherry said, looking down and toying with his glass. 'She's so brimming with goodness that occasionally I feel an urge to annoy her. I can't stop myself. I'll apologise. I'll make it up to her, I promise.'

They waited for her in silence.

'Did I tell you?' Cherry said. 'Connell's been in hospital. His prognosis isn't good. Only months if he doesn't dry out now. He won't try, I know. He tells me to bugger off.'

'Josie won't be praying for him, will she?'

Though Lester's remark was tongue-in-cheek, Cherry responded with a rare sombre look.

'He's beyond divine assistance. I feel guilty about drinking with him. I should've forced him to stop, but I wanted him to help me.'

'And did he?'

'The tunnel complex I told you about is near Bitapaka. He's given me directions. We can go on the weekend.'

'I don't particularly want to.'

'You can't possibly refuse again.'

'What do you hope to find there?'

'I don't know. I suppose I don't care. The quest's the thing, isn't it?'

Lester groaned. 'Well, there's a first and last time for every-thing, so this will be both.'

A waiter clearing the table told them Josie had left the res-taurant to walk home. Lester, in his car, found her walking alone and in darkness on a deserted street nearby. Tears had streaked her cheeks. She sat beside him, resolutely silent, for the short drive to the pastor's house, and left him without a word.

Lester was angry with himself for not reacting more strongly to Cherry's taunting her. He seemed unable to challenge Cher-ry's sometimes wayward behaviour. In his own mind it left him looking weak and caring little for a woman he believed he was in love with.

Something about Cherry, Lester thought, some unhappi-ness, some hurt, occasionally surfaced as bitterness. Cherry had spoken of his upbringing as lonely, though he seemed to view his childhood through a lens of nostalgia rather than unhappiness.

He shared Josie's suspicion that a chapter of Cherry's life he hadn't revealed hobbled his ambitions. Lester longed to explore it with Josie, but it was proving difficult to track her down. If she wasn't at Malmaluan, she was at Gaulim, and if not there, she was in a village somewhere talking to the women. She could easily avoid contact if she wanted to. She was obviously furious with them both.

Far along a narrow road to the Japanese tunnel complex, Cherry, in the utility with Lester, pulled up at the lush gardens of a war cemetery at Bitapaka. They dawdled among the simple, serried graves of Allied servicemen, reading the inscriptions. The graves were for Australians, New Zealanders, Indians and Fijians who hadn't returned to distant homes and families. The beautiful, remote and lonely memorial moved them both to a sad silence.

Further down the road, Cherry turned onto a track weaving between palms and an undergrowing layer of cocoa trees. Plantation labourers from the New Guinea Highlands, sullen, stocky men clad in filthy shorts and carrying long bush knives, watched from the shadows.

On foot and laden with Cherry's equipment, they set off through a carpet of fallen cocoa leaves into the forest gloom. Five minutes' walk brought them to a tunnel entrance, a crude arch portal, greening with mould. It appeared far older than its thirty years.

Cherry squatted down with his maps, books and equipment. Clad in khaki shorts and a shirt plated with pockets, he looked every inch the English gentleman explorer. He put ordnance manuals, water bottles, candles, matches and biscuits in a canvas bag. A wartime American army helmet hid his fair hair. He gave Lester a torch and a cheap plastic helmet.

Cherry studied a hand-sketched map of the area and another of the tunnel system, as far as had been explored. The maps were borrowed from Connell who had bought them from an earlier treasure hunter. On the area map, it was clear the site had once been a large, fortified Japanese encampment.

Armed with their torches, they entered a cool, dank world through the narrow portal. The tunnel gave way to a sizeable chamber from which corridors branched off in every direction. Branches led to other corridors, to staircases carved into the earth, to dead ends and smaller chambers. To Cherry's chagrin, all were empty. The air was rank; ventilation shafts had been sealed. Bats skimmed and whirred above them.

One tunnel, left untouched, had sheltered a major field hospital, complete with operating theatres, servicing army units in the area. This was what Cherry wanted to see. Steel bed frames lay along the walls, barracks-style. Light fittings dangled from the roof.

A few faded photographs of an idyllic Japanese countryside were pasted on wooden panelling. There was a hospital smell of ether, and of something else more putrid, slowly leaking. Lester sat down wearily on a bench sculpted from pumice. It felt cold under him, like a carving in dark grey ice.

Cherry, meanwhile, darted from chamber to chamber. His flashlight flickered in a firefly's dance around walls and along rows of shelving, accompanied by exclamations, stumbles and curses. Jars, phials and stainless-steel medical instruments piled up on the floor of the ward. Full medical kits in tins, complete with labelled medicines and syringes, were added. Lester and Cherry packed their bags full for the return journey.

'Let's get out,' Lester urged. 'It smells of death. I'm suffocating.'

When he emerged into the light and the fresh, scented air of the glade, he glanced at his watch. They'd been underground for two hours. Laughing at each other's dirt-spattered faces, they washed themselves and their clothes in the nearby creek and lay naked on the soft leaf floor until their clothes were dry.

An elated Cherry hurled his utility along the road, scattering villagers as they dawdled home from schools and gardens. Lester prayed that among the pantheon of Tolai spirits was a guardian to protect them from Cherry's madness behind the wheel.

Work wound down in the Prosecutor's office. Courts closed for the Christmas recess. Rumours circulated that the Mataungans were collecting money illegally for a trading company of their own, to run cocoa-processing facilities in opposition to the fermentaries belonging to the multiracial council. The council was reportedly closing down its services due to lack of tax revenue.

Ignoring ominous rumblings around them, clubs, hotels and businesses in town held Christmas functions as usual. In the villages, churches prepared for Christmas celebrations.

Shortly before Christmas came news that the DC, a long-serving *kiap*, was leaving Rabaul. His departure was lamented by everyone who knew him, whether Asian, European or New Guinean, for he was held in high regard as a man of integrity who looked to find solutions through patient negotiation, rather than force. However, more often than not, this approach was summarily rejected in Port Moresby or Canberra.

Flanagan treated the Prosecutor's office to Christmas dinner at the Kaivuna Hotel. Its three solid storeys on an entire corner block made it the most imposing building in town and the only establishment, aside from the New Guinea Club, where patrons thought to dress for dinner. This was certainly the case for Carol and Gloria, who'd dressed as if for a night at the opera.

Their competition for Flanagan's attention was plain: a daring split-sided skirt versus a plunging neckline. They took turns in gazing fondly at Flanagan and glaring at each other.

Flanagan, in an expansive mood, with his loud voice and laugh, attracted the attention of other diners who knew him. To Lester's surprise, he was introduced as an up-and-coming prosecutor with a bright future. He was sure the flattery was intended solely to discomfit him.

Towards the end of the evening, Flanagan turned a beery, glassy-eyed gaze in his direction.

'You're overdue for leave. If you want another contract, you'll have to take it now, outside the country, too. Go home for Christmas.'

Go home for Christmas? Lester was immediately struck by a vision of Sydney in the summer, the harbour and the surf, salty sea breezes cooling bodies in the brilliant light, streets and gardens garlanded with the purple bloom of jacaranda trees.

But there was no going home for Christmas. For all he knew, he was still wanted for questioning by the CIB. He imagined police waiting for him at the airport. He could contact no one for information about the case or ongoing lawsuits, least of all Patsy. Any contact with her would surely arouse suspicion.

'I've decided to go to Hong Kong,' he said.

Flanagan's mouth opened and closed like a gasping trout.

Carol squealed with excitement. 'Oh Lester, take me with you!'

Of course she had no intention of going anywhere. She'd edged ever closer to Flanagan during the evening; they were holding hands under the table.

Only Gloria was silent, but as they left the hotel she took Lester aside, looking around furtively to check whether she could be overheard.

'Your friend the doctor, I've seen him in Chinatown. My Chinese friend tells me he gambles with Chinese men.'

'Gamble? You must be mistaken. His girlfriend used to live there.'

'The Kanak? I know her, she left. My Chinese friend says he comes alone at night.'

Lester had no explanation to offer. Gloria rummaged in her bag and produced an airmail letter. 'It came to the office.'

Lester raised his hand. 'Don't tell me; it's from my mother.'

Kitty's last letter hinted that preparations were underway to welcome him home for Christmas and forever after. Reluctantly, he'd written to let her down as gently as he could, having already made airline bookings to Hong Kong. He wanted to see the internment camp where his father had been held. He thought she'd understand his need to make sense of his father's apartness from their lives. He took the letter home to read.

Reg and I are terribly upset to hear that you won't be home for Christmas again this year. Why would you want to visit Hong Kong? It ruined your father's health and his mind. Reg says they don't celebrate Christmas in Hong Kong because they're Chinese. I told him that's rubbish, the Hong Kong Chinese celebrate everything. I've put up a Christmas tree with decorations and we'll get together with the next-door neighbours and the dog so that's better than nothing.

A lady turned up at our door telling us she is your friend Patricia. She looked glamorous I must say but older than you by a few years I would think. We told her you were still in New Guinea. She brought you a Christmas present, a small wooden box she said was Japanese. It's to hold your cufflinks, but I've never seen you wearing any. We were told to keep it in a safe place until you returned. I asked Patricia if she had heard from you. She laughed and she said no, she'd been away for a year seeing the world.

Reg being a carpenter couldn't resist fiddling with the Japanese box until it opened. He found a key to a deposit box and a note about shares you bought with

Patricia in a mining company. It said the shares had made you both a lot of money.

Reg's health has taken a turn for the worse. He says it's because his Fulham football team was relegated to third division last year. He doesn't get out much and I have to do a lot of looking after him. We both wish you were here to help...

At least in one way, thought Lester, reading the letter, Patsy had been both prescient and steadfastly honest.

He'd promised Kitty, hand on heart in an earlier letter, to be home for Christmas Day, but thoughts of his upcoming holiday soon overtook his guilt. Leaving Rabaul was made easier by the absence of Josie and Cherry over Christmas and New Year. Josie would be with earnestly energetic Christian work parties from Australia. Cherry would spend his Christmas break with the French plantation owner near Kavieng, though he hadn't mentioned this to Josie.

The prospect of the fabled colony, an exotic Asian city he'd only imagined, aroused both excitement and a vague sense of familiarity.

Occasionally, Kitty had opened her scrapbook to show him photos of her Hong Kong days. Both a singer and a seamstress, she'd joined the Gilbert and Sullivan Society, sewed costumes and sung in the chorus. She led a life of gaiety with a constant round of social events the taciturn Charles Chettle apparently took little interest in.

Lester waited impatiently to leave.

PART 3

Rabaul 1971

25

Returning to Rabaul after the pulsating energy of Hong Kong, Lester took time to adjust to a place where time and motion slowed to a crawl. Norma, lounging in her banana chair, and Szabo, smoking cigars on his landing, seemed not to have moved since he left.

The following day brought a monsoon storm, a furious barrage of wind and rain that swept away the humidity and refreshed the air. He drove to Pilapila on a road dangerously strewn with fallen palm fronds and coconuts. The breeze that raised whitecaps on the harbour sent convulsive shivers from the opposite shore out to sea. The tide was lower than he'd ever seen it, exposing slabs of inshore reef leached of their undersea colours.

Under a grey sky, the beach itself was almost deserted. He sat on the sand and watched villagers pottering gingerly over sharp coral, filling their woven carry bags with mussels, crabs and small fish that were trapped in coral pools by the receding tide. He bought a bag of baitfish and crabs to cook at home from children eager to sell.

The long flights had tired him. He lay back, gazed at the lazy drift of clouds and dozed off, only waking when two giggling Tolai girls tickled his bare feet with a gull's feather. When he sat up abruptly with a shout, they ran off laughing along water's edge, long-limbed and lissom in their faded shorts and T-shirts. So carefree, Lester thought, so innocent of the world beyond the beach, their village, their school, their church.

In Hong Kong, he'd wondered if he really wanted to return to Rabaul. He could easily have traded his ticket for a flight back to Sydney. On the beach at Pilapila, listening to the girls' laughter filled him with a sudden, fleeting euphoria. Here, he too could be free and unburdened, with a future still uncharted, a rare friend he cherished and a woman he was in love with. He wasn't willing to let those jewels go.

Gloria was alone in the office, wrestling with her typewriter, when Lester came in. The office furniture had been rearranged for no discernible purpose. His desk and chair that had faced one way, now faced the other.

'You should have an electric typewriter like Carol's,' he said.

'Carol said I don't deserve one.'

He helped Gloria untangle the keys, for she feared damaging her nails.

'Where is she? And where's John?'

'Mr Whitlam from Australia is here again, causing trouble. John refused to stay while Mr Whitlam is in town. He went away in his boat.'

'And Carol?'

A fierce scowl from Gloria. 'Carol went with him.'

'What about the furniture? Why has it all been turned around?'

'Hah. She said it was good for the new year; it would give us more energy.'

'Did you approve?'

'Of course not! Before, we have back to the mountain and face the water, good *feng shui*. Now we face the mountain and have back to the water, bad *feng shui*.'

Lester smiled. 'Bad? I hope not.'

'Mr Whitlam's gone now, so John will come back. You liked Hong Kong? Lots of pretty girls. You try?'

Lester thought of the bar that, out of loneliness as much as curiosity, he had visited in Wanchai. He'd soon departed, alarmed at the amount of money that would be siphoned from him.

'No, none were as pretty as you.'

His answer appeared to satisfy Gloria who nodded and resumed typing. He read the reams of telexes that had flowed in since he left. The Mataungan Association had begun the process of setting up a parallel government for the Gazelle. It foreshadowed another busy year for prosecutors. He left early to go home.

Gloria called him at the door. 'Did you bring Hong Kong presents?'

'Tomorrow,' he said.

Flanagan and Carol appeared the next day, beaming and relaxed. They might well have been cruising the Pacific on a liner. In truth, they'd travelled on *Belle Marie* no further than the Duke of York Islands.

Prompted by Gloria, Lester handed out his gifts from Hong Kong. To Carol and Gloria he gave each a jade bracelet and a hand-painted fan, realising at once that cheap sandalwood fans abounded in nearby trade stores. For Flanagan, a traditional, long-stemmed Chinese pipe. Flanagan wrongly concluded that his present was an opium pipe. He handled it as if it might be both contagious and illegal.

Gloria scrutinised her jade bracelet, then began scratching it with a fingernail and rubbing it between her hands.

'Maybe a fake,' she said. 'Maybe not real jade. I'll take it to my friend in Chinatown. She knows.'

Only Carol seemed genuinely touched. When Flanagan stepped out of the office soon after, she came over to Lester to thank him. It was an opening he couldn't resist.

'How was your yachting experience? Did John boss you around?'

Carol's laugh was deep-throated and assured. 'No one bosses me around.'

'I mean, was there a lot of swearing?'

'He was as gentle as a lamb. The only time I heard him swear was when he got up in the night to wee-wee over the side. We'd anchored in a little cove and had a few...well, quite a few...drinks. I heard him stumble, then a loud splash as he fell overboard. There was a lot of swearing then.'

With the new year came a new chapter in the Mataungan saga, their cause boosted by Gough Whitlam's second visit within a year, although this time Whitlam's tone was considerably less inflammatory.

As one journalist put it, Whitlam's three-day sojourn in Rabaul must have been mostly for sightseeing, since no one other than the Mataungan Association showed much enthusiasm for meeting him. After his disrespectful and dismissive attitude on his first visit, the Gazelle multiracial council refused to have anything to do with him.

Again a crowd of Mataungan supporters, thousands strong, greeted him at the airport. Whitlam largely ignored the admin-heavy welcoming party while ostentatiously meeting and greeting Mataungan leaders, later provocatively offering Oscar Tammur a lift in his official car.

However, his message was more nuanced, encouraging the Tolai to resolve their own differences, despite others of his delegation continuing their hard-line anti-colonialist rhetoric around the country.

In terms of national politics, momentum for self-government was building. Even among the rump of Europeans and Chinese most resistant to change, there was a grudging acceptance that Papuans and New Guineans would soon take control.

Rabaul was in the vanguard of change. It was easy to see and hear around town that commercial confidence was waning, while frustration grew at the admin's stubborn perseverance with the same old policies.

A week after Lester's return, Cherry rang to say Josie had returned from wherever she'd been and wanted to see them both at Taliligap.

Pleasingly for Lester, nothing at Taliligap had changed: not the bungalow, the gardens nor Cherry in his cream linen clothes. Josie was there too, leaning against the verandah rail, hands carelessly hidden in the side pockets of a stylishly flowing, pale green dress. The missionary look was long gone.

His heart thudded wildly at the sight of her. He hugged her hungrily, feeling the soft folds of the material as her body yielded to his own. He'd dreamed of her every night since his return.

For a time, they sat quietly in the living room, clearly wondering how to begin and what to say. Lester, sensing the mood, brought out his presents from Hong Kong: a cloisonné bowl for Josie, a wooden model of a Chinese junk for Cherry to assemble. He gave his impressions of the city, of being caught up in its vibrancy as well as its chaos. He told of his visit to the site of the internment camp, and the photographs he'd seen of internees on the day of their freedom, some of the men as thin as prisoners of war in Changi.

'It must have been terrible for your father,' Cherry said. 'You told me once that he found it difficult to relate to you. I've heard that soldiers who marry and go off to war come back to find themselves responsible for a family and can't accept it.'

'I'm glad I saw where he was interned,' Lester said. 'It was another world. He had to adapt to survive. What he never adapted to was life in Australia.'

He was tempted to leave the subject there, but the truth was gnawing at him for release.

'I've never told you how he died. His body was found at the bottom of a cliff near our house in Sydney. The coroner found it was misadventure. I sometimes noticed him standing at the cliff edge, staring down at the rocks below. I know in my heart he jumped.'

A moment of stunned silence, then Josie reached out to rest her hand on Lester's arm. 'How awful.'

'I can understand it now,' Lester said. 'He was a colonial official living a high life in Hong Kong. Money and respectability were everything in his life. In Sydney, he was a struggling Pommy immigrant with poor prospects. Nobody had much sympathy for him.'

'You've changed since you've come back,' Josie said. 'I think you're more at peace with his death.'

'We've all changed,' Cherry said. 'It's a symptom of the times.'

'You make it sound like an illness,' Josie laughed.

'Rabaul has changed too,' Lester said. 'There's a difference in the air; I can't really define it.'

'The Tolai are more nervous,' Josie said. 'The Mataungans have upset the order. No one knows what's coming next.'

'The Wind of Change is upon us,' Cherry said. 'Let's celebrate staying together for as long as we can. I'll bring out the drinks.'

Indeed, things had changed for all of them. Josie had surprisingly matured. Her stance, her movements, were no longer nervously birdlike but had the confidence she'd always shown when singing.

She told them she'd grown tired of an overbearing Christian fellowship, of constantly having to publicly reaffirm her devotion to God. Her faith was personal and practical, rather than devotional. She preferred to spend her days with village women, encouraging those with education to make use of their skills beyond village life.

Cherry told them he'd spent two weeks in New Ireland on Leila the Frenchwoman's plantation, loafing, fishing and swimming with village children in a nearby river.

He'd also taken over Adele's accommodation in Chinatown, a single room with toilet and kitchenette above a trade store. Of course he'd still live at Taliligap, he said, but the times when he was on call at the hospital, he wanted to stay in town. At other times he couldn't be bothered to drive all the way home.

Lester desperately wanted to drive Josie down to the coast, to talk to her alone and be given his chauffeur's reward. His hopes were dashed by a horn sounding on the road outside.

'I almost forgot!' Josie jumped to her feet. 'That's our bus. I'm taking people back to town. They'll be on the plane to Port Moresby tomorrow. I have to go.' She leaned over Cherry, still sprawled on the sofa, put her arms around his neck and kissed him on the forehead.

'Thank you for everything,' she said. 'You're the perfect host.'

The two men, suddenly robbed of Josie's company, were left to drink on their own.

The bungalow at Taliligap was becoming a miniature war museum. All around were scraps from the Japanese occupation: ceramic bowls, tin water bottles, rusted pistols, a bayonet, a field telephone and other pieces of Japanese equipment. A table by the living room window was covered in maps and plans. By the wall, a case of anti-aircraft shells. In one corner, a stack of large brass shell casings, cleaned and polished. Medical items brought back from Cherry's expedition with Lester. He'd been ferreting in other tunnels since then.

'You seem hell-bent on collecting munitions,' Lester said.

'They're for Szabo. He defuses old munitions using an American army intelligence manual with half the pages missing. If I were you, I wouldn't be living next door.'

'Thanks for the warning.' Lester thought of Bilson, fuming below. An anonymous tip, a note under his door, perhaps.

'He's packing explosives for me, too,' Cherry went on. 'Connell's been telling me a few stories. A Japanese general, Hitoshi Imamura, was in charge of the Rabaul garrison. Connell says his underground headquarters in the hills have never been found.'

'And the explosives?'

'If I find Imamura's hideout, I may need to blow my way in.'

'Dangerous. And it'll attract attention.'

'No one goes where I'm looking; it's too steep to be planted. Old tunnels are everywhere. The trick is in finding the right one.

'Anyway, the locals don't take much notice. Unexploded ordnance underground sometimes blows up. An old man told Connell it's set off by the spirits of dead soldiers who'll go on fighting underground for ever.'

Cherry's look and manner had grown in intensity as his enthusiasm mounted. He refilled his wineglass constantly, a reflex action that made Lester uneasy.

'You needn't invite me to join you,' Lester said.

Cherry shrugged. 'It doesn't matter, I'm all right on my own. I take a couple of Tolai lads with me to stay with the ute. They'll know where I am. Hang on, let's share another bottle.'

'No more for me.' Lester waved the offer away. 'I have to drive home.'

Cherry smiled. 'Always the steadfast, law-abiding, risk-averse lawyer.'

A siren sounded, far away.

'There's the police siren,' Cherry said. 'They're off to another confrontation somewhere. It seems so pointless, doesn't it? The admin is only buying time to pull out. They aren't going to bother with solutions now.'

He wandered slowly out to the verandah steps with the wine bottle and sat down. As Lester joined him, Cherry pointed to a host of fruit bats speckling the evening sky, winging inland with a heavy, clumsy beat.

'Here come the enemy bombers, right on time,' he said. 'That's what I'd have called them when I was a boy.'

'In many ways you're still a boy,' Lester said, half-hoping Cherry wouldn't hear.

'I hope I always will be,' Cherry said with a smile.

Cherry wasn't done with surprises that night. He still had things he had not wanted to tell Josie but was more than willing to share with Lester.

His activities on New Ireland had extended beyond loafing and fishing. He'd enjoyed the Frenchwoman's bed. The two of them had joined neighbouring planters in the evenings for card games that began with fantan and soon escalated to poker.

He had, he claimed, won an island. No larger than a football field or two and planted with coconut palms, it was barely a hundred yards offshore, an appendage to a plantation owned by a Chinese businessman from Rabaul. Cherry was free to sell the coconuts to Leila or the Chinese plantation owner.

For Lester, the news was unsettling. Cherry's life seemed to be slowly and steadily taking a different course. Outwardly, he was still the same, full of warmth and pleasure in their company. But he was, unconsciously perhaps, drawing away.

On the other hand, Lester thought as he drove home, it presented an opportunity. Josie would be unhappy if she discovered Cherry's dalliance with a woman ten years older. Moreover, she openly disapproved of his drinking, his association with Connell and his fascination with Japanese tunnels. It upset her, too, that he had little respect for the Christian mission in Papua New Guinea or anywhere else.

Lester longed to have the hold over Josie that Cherry had. He agonised over whether Cherry took her to bed, trying to convince himself she lacked the earthiness of Adele and seemed wary of such intimacy. Besides, Cherry had praised her as possessing a childlike innocence, a quality he said he admired and would never spoil.

26

For some time, the Mataungan Association had been running a three-pronged attack against the administration. The first prong was the campaign against the multiracial council. The second was the dispute over ownership and control of the all-important cocoa fermentaries. The third was ongoing demands for the return of alienated plantation lands. Once the Association determined to take over political control of the Gazelle, they coalesced into a full-frontal assault.

The multiracial council issue came to a head early in the new year. This council was in its death throes. Finally, the administration relented, passing a proclamation to revoke that council and restore its all-Tolai predecessor—a so-called solution that pleased no one. The council members maintained they were still the legitimate local government. The Association, on the other hand, proceeded with plans to establish its own form of village government.

At the same time, the Mataungans moved to take control of the multiracial council's network of cocoa fermentaries scattered through the Gazelle Peninsula. They'd been a very successful revenue earner for the council.

Mataungan supporters in their hundreds advanced on several fermentaries in turn, felling trees and barricading the roads, forcing their closure. The admin deployed riot police, also in large numbers, to remove them. There were inevitable clashes, but to the credit of the police, they maintained their discipline and restraint in clearing the roads and dispersing the protesters. However, there was no sign the fermentary issue might be settled.

The flow of criminal cases for the Supreme Court in Rabaul dried up. The police, preoccupied with tax evaders and charges of obstruction, which they took to the lower courts, were slow to prepare cases for prosecution. Lester, with little to do, had time to observe the blossoming romance between Carol and John Flanagan.

For an hour at a time, Carol would sit on the opposite side of Flanagan's executive desk, notebook in hand and her pencil conspicuously idle. Flanagan told stories that made her laugh, and occasionally gasp. At other times she was the tale teller, with Flanagan paying rapt attention to every word and airy gesture.

Carol's assumption of control over the office administration mildly annoyed Lester, but put Gloria into a state of perpetual dudgeon, seeing her substance slowly leaching away.

Carol had taken over collecting the mail, followed by inspections of the judge's house and organising Circuit bookings. The electric typewriter on Carol's desk chattered constantly. Lester wasn't sure whether he felt sympathy or pity for Gloria. He provided her with scraps of typing, to be filed in a cabinet and never seen again.

'Here's a couple of cases for you in Kavieng,' Carol announced one morning, dropping the files on Lester's desk. 'One is for a shooting by a couple of *kiaps*. John has drafted the charges for you. I'll book your flights for next week.'

Carol's patronising attitude couldn't pass without a riposte, however lame.

'Did the Flanagan girls come up for Christmas? He hasn't mentioned it.'

'No, they didn't come this time.'

'That's a pity. They could have met your daughter Tracey.'

'John said they're too old now. There's hardly any young Europeans here, and no parties.'

Gloria, listening intently, cut in. 'They had mixed-race friends from school. Many friends still here.'

'I talked about it with John. Friends grow apart as they get older. Tastes change. They prefer their own kind. We agreed it was for the best.'

Gloria waited until Flanagan left the office with Carol to lunch at the Cosmopolitan Hotel.

'You see?' she hissed at Lester. 'She thinks she's superior, and mixed race like me are second class. I might like to hit her.'

'That's not a good idea.'

'Your friend the doctor is different. I think he lives in China-town now.'

'Only when he stays in town. He rents a flat above a shop.'

'He owes money to some Chinese,' Gloria added in an ominous tone. 'Not good business Chinese. Bad trouble Chinese. They're like jellyfish, they float under the water, you can't see them, then they sting you. Aaagh!' She clutched her bare arms in a fine imitation of agony.

Lester had rarely visited the area known as New Chinatown. Cherry's flat, like Lester's own, was reached by a staircase at the rear of the building. Cherry, lately home from the hospital, greeted Lester at the door wearing a sumptuous blue silk jacket embroidered with dragons and fastened by knot buttons. He'd also swapped shoes for traditional black slippers.

'Do I remind you of Hong Kong?' Cherry posed, arms outstretched. 'The wonderful establishment below me is a Chinese Aladdin's cave. It has clothes. It has everything I could wish for.'

Lester smiled. 'I'm reminded of an Englishman trying to look like an old-time Chinaman.'

The flat's only window opened onto Ah Chee Avenue and the harbour beyond. A hint of incense and the smells of Chinese cooking wafted from the part of the ground floor where the Chinese owners lived. Cherry, primed with newfound enthusiasm, opened bottles of beer for them both.

'I love living in Chinatown. It was fate that I took over this place before you went to Hong Kong. I've been here for Chinese New Year: dragon dances, firecrackers, drums. The noise, the colour! Not as exciting as Hong Kong, of course.'

'You must love the food, then.'

'I eat nothing but noodle dishes now.'

'I hear you like more than noodles. You've taken up gambling.'

Cherry ignored the remark and sat down heavily on his bed. Apart from a clothes rack, a small Laminex table and two chairs, the bed was the only furniture to be seen.

'God, I miss Adele. We slept together in this bed.'

'Until the police turned you out of it.'

'I wouldn't say this in front of Josie, but Adele was a great lover. So gymnastic.'

'I'd like to see Josie's face if you did tell her.'

'The truth is, Adele wasn't entirely faithful.'

Lester raised his hand impatiently.

'Cherry, I haven't come to hear about your love life. I'm told you're spending time with people with a bad reputation. As a friend, I've come to warn you. Keep away from them.'

'Oh, that? Just a bit of fun, old sport. The odd afternoon, before I go on night shift at Nonga. I feel lonely, so I join in a game. It's quite harmless. I can take care of myself.'

'I hope so.'

Cherry grinned. 'You and Josie are my conscience; you'll keep me out of trouble.' He rose to fetch fresh bottles of beer. 'Bring your drink downstairs. We're dining with the owners; they have the best Chinese food in town.'

Lester was pleased to get away from the constant preoccupation with Mataungan issues to the untroubled surroundings of Kavieng. He looked forward to arguing a challenging case of a shooting on a quiet night in small settlement on the New Ireland coast.

Two bored young *kiaps*, patrol officers, were drinking vodka and orange juice on the verandah of their bungalow. One suggested a round of target practice with his own revolver and a paper target on the verandah table. A stray bullet ricocheted through the thatched wall of a village house seventy yards away and wounded a teenage schoolboy. The *kiaps* were charged with acting together to cause grievous bodily harm.

They were stoutly defended by private solicitors from Rabaul who contested the ballistic evidence, the seriousness of the injury and all points in between. In the end, only the *kiap* who owned the gun was convicted.

The same *kiap* who had lamented the outcome of Lester's speedboat case in Kavieng caught up with him as he was walking back to the Kavieng Hotel.

'Ralph Beddich. Remember me?'

'How could I forget?'

'Great result for our fellows. Great defence counsel. Took you down a peg or two, didn't they?'

'That's not the way I see it,' Lester said, still vexed by Flanagan's insistence on more serious charges. 'It was a fair result.'

Beddich hurried on. 'I'm taking a couple of schoolkids who gave evidence back home tomorrow. Why don't you come along? See where it all happened. Beautiful place. I'll take you out to one of the islands.'

'I'm sorry; I have to return to Rabaul.'

'So, what did you think of the guys you prosecuted? You've got to feel sorry for them, don't you. They're the last of the line. The days of European *kiaps* are over; no more are being trained. Their careers will be cut short.'

'Shooting a schoolboy wouldn't help, would it?'

Beddich shook his head sadly.

'Every young *kiap* wants to be posted to the Highlands, pacifying, mediating, stopping tribal battles, building roads and bridges. Instead, they've ended up in a place where nothing ever happens. The roads and airstrips were built years ago. The locals garden, fish and sing hymns all day.

'Their only complaints are that the Chinese take their fish and the Japanese take their trees. They're things they can't control. No wonder those two were going quietly mad.'

Lester arrived back from Kavieng on a Saturday morning. A taxi dropped him off at Grandview Apartments. Cherry's utility was in the driveway.

'The doctor's here,' Szabo called down from his apartment's landing. 'You come too.'

Lester unpacked, changed from his court clothes and knocked on Szabo's door. Szabo admitted him warily, to the sound of door bolts being drawn. Where fish tanks once stood in his living room was now a large worktable piled with shell casings, fuses, firing pins and other components of explosive weaponry. An acrid smell of metals and acid assaulted the nose. Szabo cleared a space at the table and brought chairs, bidding his guests to sit. Stubbies were produced from a garden bucket half-filled with ice cubes.

'Szabo found a propeller,' Cherry said. 'It's on a Japanese freighter at the bottom of the harbour, half buried in silt. Four tons of bronze worth a small fortune, two hundred feet down.'

'Too bloody deep,' Szabo grunted, fiddling with a blasting cap.

Cherry was the go-between, the interpreter of Szabo's grunts.

'He'll bring it up somehow. He has to blow it off the shaft first.'

Lester looked anxiously at the boxes around him, breathing in the air with its awful energy compressed within the apartment walls.

It's all right,' Cherry laughed. 'The explosives are at his workshop.'

Lester had seen Szabo's workshop in town, a yard that seeped oils and battery acids into the soil and neighbouring streets.

'I should tell the police,' Lester said, only half in jest.

'Go ahead and see what happens. Where else are the police going to find a decent mechanic to fix their vehicles? Szabo's the best in town.'

Between Cherry and Szabo existed a friendship based, in Lester's view, on a mutual disregard for danger. Perhaps it was no coincidence that each had a Hungarian mother.

'I know why you're here,' he said to Cherry. 'It's madness to be fooling around with this stuff. You're a doctor, not an explosives engineer.'

'Don't worry,' Cherry said. 'Szabo's my tutor.'

'That's what I worry about.'

'Relax. I came to see Szabo about something else. He's getting married, did you know? He wooed a beautiful Tolai girl. When's the wedding, Szabo?'

'Next week.' For a moment Szabo came to life, looked up from his tools, the wires, the brass bits, the screws. 'You must come. Everybody must come. We'll all get drunk.'

Later, Lester invited Cherry to stay on at his apartment, but he was anxious to return to Taliligap with a collection of what Lester suspected were homemade explosive charges. As he watched Cherry's utility drive away, Bilson emerged from his own apartment and stopped him.

'I see you've been visiting our Hungarian neighbour.'

'The fish tanks have gone. You must be pleased that water no longer drips from your ceiling. Now his hobby is making explosives.'

'I can't stop him. He doesn't keep explosives, as such, in the apartment; I checked with police.'

'He does at his garage.'

'Then he'll only blow himself up. Besides, the Gazelle's riddled with unexploded ordnance and the Tolais collect it. It'd be unfair to make an example of him. We're more worried that the Mataungans will booby-trap the fermentaries.'

'Are you that worried?'

Bilson snorted. 'They're bolder every day. More squatters, more blockades, attacks on police serving tax summonses, police vehicles stoned, petrol bombs. It's an insurrection and we're powerless to stop it.'

'The police seem to be in control.'

'It used to be the job of us field officers to keep the peace. No one listens to us anymore. We're finished here.'

'I've just come from New Ireland. I've heard the same from *kiaps* there.'

Bilson laughed. 'They're in the land of the lotus-eaters. What would they know?' He threw up his hands and jumped into his Landcruiser.

27

The Methodist church, neat and freshly painted, stood on a lawn running down to the sea. Szabo the groom looked almost human, scrubbed clean of grease and beard trimmed, standing by the altar in a white shirt cleaving to his midriff. A gold chain around his neck would have held a ship at anchor.

At the church door in a full-length bridal dress was Bonnie, demurely wringing her hands, her tight-pressed curls studded with fresh frangipani blossoms. The air about her carried their sweet perfume. She offered Lester a shy smile as he arrived. Lester recognised her at once, one of the two who had taken his umbrella.

Young women from the squatter settlement near Grandview Apartments formed a giggling church row, dressed in a wildly varied assortment of European fashion and wearing high-heeled shoes either too large or too tight. Lester had wondered about Szabo's choice of a bride, but Cherry assured him that Bonnie wasn't a prostitute but a church worker who saved fallen women from sin.

The visiting minister was annoyed, arriving to find hens roosting on the altar table. Also, the service was going to be late.

The bride and groom were present; the best man and the choir were nowhere to be seen. Guests, many from the nearby village, filled the wooden pews.

Faces suddenly clustered at the open shutters, voices chattered outside. Lester looked over their heads towards the shore. A figure was running, prancing, through the shallows. A fleeting silhouette against the sun, in and out among the palms. Cherry, the best man, in a white tuxedo and black formal trousers, appeared at the church door, hot and flustered. Trouser legs rolled up to the knees and shoes in hand, he dripped water down the aisle.

'Late,' he panted to the front row. 'Short cut. High tide. Sorry.'

Outside, a flurry of dust and vehicles. The choir poured into the church, agitated and dishevelled. They'd been singing at a wedding further down the coast road. In the rush to return there'd been an accident, a brush with a vehicle from another village. Blows were exchanged. One man held a handkerchief to a bloody nose. It made no difference to the singing; their harmony was divine.

Late in the day, sharing a whisky nightcap with Cherry at his Chinatown flat, Lester remembered Cherry's island, the prize, so he claimed, in a poker game.

'I thought of you and your island while I was in New Ireland. Have you set foot on it yet?'

'Unfortunately, I haven't. And won't. Hard won and easily lost at the card table.' Cherry drained his whisky glass and poured another. He rose from his chair unsteadily, filled the glass with ice blocks from the refrigerator and sat down again. He'd been drinking solidly since returning from the wedding.

Lester persevered. 'It was just a pipe dream, wasn't it? I can't believe you'd really have visited.'

'You're wrong, you know. I wanted to build a shack there. I was going to sit all day on the verandah and count my coconuts.'

'That doesn't make sense. You're a doctor who specialises in tropical medicine. You work at a hospital that treats tropical diseases. Isn't that why you came here?'

'I came for adventure,' Cherry said, gesturing grandly with open arms to encompass the world. 'You know me. Africa, Mauritius, the Pacific, tracking the sun from west to east.'

'Josie and I wonder why you no longer seem as dedicated as your colleagues. You've changed. You aren't looking after yourself. Something is bothering you. I wish you'd tell us; we're your closest friends.'

Cherry waved a hand. 'What about you? You spend your time running down the colonial legal system. Why are *you* here? Why aren't you in Sydney doing what city lawyers do?'

Both stared silently into their whisky glasses, as if each had inflicted a knife wound on the other and were unable to believe it. Lester felt short of breath. An unbearable weight pressed down on his chest. He had to speak to relieve it, to confess.

'I'm here because...well, because, in a way, I'm on the run.'

'Good Lord, you robbed a bank?'

'Partners in the law firm where I worked ran a tax-dodging, money-laundering, insider-trading sideline and were caught.'

'You were innocent, of course?'

'Of course, but the authorities closed down the firm and hounded everyone in it. I thought a change of scene would be good for me.'

Cherry laughed. 'So you're here prosecuting criminals?'

'Don't tell a soul or I'll strangle you. Now it's your turn.'

Cherry left his chair to sink down on his bed. 'I'll tell you one day. It's complicated and I'm tired. I'll just sleep here.'

Not long after the Szabo wedding, Lester received a rare telephone call from Josie at work. He hadn't heard from her since their last meeting at Taliligap more than two weeks ago. Nor had Cherry, so it seemed. They'd long agreed she was hard to reach if she was tied up with church business, as she called it, and away from home.

She'd been the keenest of the Taliligap Trio, the one insisting on regular rehearsals. Without her, the bond between the three as a group, a gestalt relationship as Lester saw it, was fraying, even if the individual friendships weren't. He couldn't put aside his fear of being the one who might suffer.

'Where are you?' he asked Josie. 'You sound upset. Has something happened?'

'I'm home at Raluana. Cherry said I could stay at Taliligap anytime, so I turned up yesterday with my bag. When I walked in, I caught sight of Cherry in his bedroom—with a woman.'

A long pause. A sniff.

'Josie, are you there? Are you crying? Tell me.'

'They were in bed together.'

'What did you do?'

'I sneaked away. It was the French woman from Kavieng, I could tell. She looked old enough to be his mother.' Another long pause, a plaintive voice. 'Can you come and comfort me?'

'I'd love to, but I can't. I'm leaving for Bougainville this afternoon. I'm in court tomorrow.'

'Oh, I see.'

'I'll be back in a few days and come to you straight away. Don't do anything silly.'

The line clicked as Josie hung up.

Cherry's sexual promiscuity had been exposed! An opportunity to take pride of place in her affections had arisen yet couldn't be grasped. Lester cried aloud.

Carol, also in the office, stared at him, alarmed.

'Just a stitch in my side. It's gone now.'

In the courtroom at Kieta, the axe was passed from hand to hand, from witness to counsel and counsel to the judge. All were within a single bound of the murderer. Each examined the axe casually, feeling its weight and solidity, testing the haft and the blade, wondering, perhaps, how it would feel to behead a man with a single blow.

An enterprising police constable had cleaned and sharpened the steel head, ignorant of the significance of bloodstains and hoping, no doubt, a sharp and shiny axe was a more impressive murder weapon than a blunt and rusty one.

There was no issue, however, about the murder weapon or who wielded it. The only issue was motive. What thoughts had passed through the mind of the ebony-hued Bougainvillean as he swung the axe at the neck of his neighbour sitting beside him at an open fire?

It was a curious coincidence that the circumstances were so similar to the murder case in Sohano. Perhaps, thought Lester, an axe was the murder weapon of choice on Bougainville. Here, too, the defendant sat passively awaiting his fate, watching through the window as a water truck passed back and forth, spraying down the dust along the road beside the courthouse.

The smell of wet earth filtered through dusty louvres, mingling with diesel fumes from huge earth-moving trucks thundering past in convoys and making the courtroom tremble. Kieta, a modest township and the administrative centre of Bougainville Island, was being swallowed by a Gargantuan operation to disembowel an area inland for its copper.

Mountains of mining machinery dwarfed the assortment of government offices and fibro houses that hugged the harbour. Trucks churned the streets into mud on wet days and coated the buildings in copper-coloured dust if it was dry. Men from the mine, hulking, big-booted and bearded contractors, strode through the town with the arrogance of conquerors.

Judge Butters hurried the murder case to a close. The dead man's pig had damaged the defendant's garden. Despite months of entreaty, no compensation had been paid. There were old wounds, too. Bride price for a daughter hadn't been handed over by the dead man's family, nor any return in kind for traditional gifts. A dam of resentment had burst one night, without warning, by the fire.

The judge gave the murderer seven years in prison. With a remission for good behaviour, he would be out in five. He thanked the judge gravely, smiling shyly as he was led from the court. No wonder, Lester thought, the man was happy. Five years was well worth it. Five years of good food, a useful trade learnt and savings to take back to the village. The cancer in his life had been cut out for ever by one deft swing of an axe.

Struggling to stow his books and robes in the bobbing speedboat, Lester almost missed her. Ribboned hat in hand, she was picking her way delicately along muddy boards laid down as a footpath, past the bank and trade stores on the main street. She wore a white dress, with an airlines bag slung over her shoulder. As usual, she seemed protected by an invisible shield against the outside world of heat and dirt, emerging unscathed from clouds of diesel fumes belching from rumbling trucks.

'Josie!' Lester called, his heart racing.

She ran lightly across the road and down to the shore. 'Here I am! Where are you going? Where are you staying?'

The court party was headed for the small island resort of Arovo, a brief trip offshore. The resort, newly built, had not yet officially opened but, as the judge explained, the owners were thrilled to welcome a judge and his entourage as trial guests. They'd be more discerning than a boatload of beefy truck drivers.

Lester was equally confounded and delighted by Josie's unexpected appearance. She smiled at the judge.

'I'm a friend of Mr Chettle. I'm here on business for the United Church, but I haven't a place to stay. The hotel in town is booked out.'

'Then you must stay with us,' the judge said.

'You're a convincing liar,' Lester whispered in Josie's ear as the boat slipped away. 'I never knew you had it in you.'

Apart from Josie and the Circuit party, another guest was on the island, Meredith. She'd come upon Lester and Josie as they walked hand in hand along the pearly water's edge. She'd seen them before, she said, in Rabaul, singing at the restaurant.

She was dark-haired, heavy-hipped with large, languorous brown eyes. She spoke oddly, in sudden disconnected pronouncements. She seemed to view them as minor celebrities, welcome strangers who'd come to brighten her stay, and was determined to enjoy their company. She invited herself to dinner.

Voices echoed in the empty dining room with its high-arched roof of thatch and pillars exquisitely carved by Woodlark Island people, far off to the south in the Solomon Sea. Trainee waiters tumbled over each other in their eagerness to serve.

Judge Butters, who'd taken on the Circuit cases at short notice from Judge Prest, presided at the table. His temper was improved by the unexpected presence of two attractive women guests. Beneath the jowls, under the lines and scars of countless court battles, a handsome and much younger man was lurking.

His voice boomed across the table. He gave Josie lingering, salacious glances and was vexed to see them ignored. He praised Lester extravagantly, hoping to win her approval by indirect means. The defence counsel was plainly flabbergasted; to hear the judge praise a prosecuting counsel was virtually unknown. Josie smiled at the judge, and at Lester, and toyed with the great red lobster on her plate, picking and sucking daintily at its bony extremities.

Aware that his crablike male advances were not appreciated, the judge turned his attention to Meredith, testing the waters with some ribaldry, titbits from the unpalatable diet of rape cases on Circuit. He leaned across the table towards her, as if confiding a secret.

'It's often hard, among the people of the Highlands, to obtain evidence of an erection. There doesn't seem to be a word...'

'I was raped once,' Meredith interrupted flatly. 'Gang-raped. My husband's friends did it.' Her manner was placid and impassive; she might have been giving a passer-by the time of day. 'I should never have married. Now they've given my child away, my only child. It's the custom when there are too many children among a large family.'

'Are they Christians?' Josie asked, aghast.

'In this country Christianity begins and ends at the church door.'

'That's not true!' Josie said.

'Well, it doesn't extend to the home. That wasn't what I wanted. I didn't want to be cut off entirely from my world. I mean, he had a house and a car. He worked at the mine.' She fastened her cow's eyes upon the judge. 'I really married him for the sex. Do you know that a black man can prolong a climax for five times as long as a white man? It's no myth, I've researched it in depth.'

Silence around the table as she turned away and lit a cigarette. Smoke curled up to the wooden rafters and seeped into the thatch. The judge's jaw had dropped into the overlapping folds of his chin.

Only Mali Gavera, the Papuan Associate now assigned to Judge Butters, knew where to look. His eyes never left the charms that Meredith revealed through her white lace top.

After dinner, running, chasing each other along a sandy shore, Lester and Josie fell together onto the sand, laughing at Gavera's eyes riveted to Meredith's bodice and the judge's dead-fish stare.

Beside them, a two-man outrigger canoe was pulled up on the beach.

'I asked the staff if I could borrow it,' Josie said. 'Just for a paddle. Come on.'

The canoe slid away from the island into a motionless, silk-smooth sea. A crescent moon peeped over the horizon. Josie wielded a paddle expertly from the bow; short, clean strokes with long pauses between them, allowed the canoe's momentum to keep it gliding smoothly over the water. Her bare arms gleamed in the moonlight; her dark, sleeveless top blended with the night and the sea. She seemed to Lester almost bodiless, a wraith.

'It feels so good to be paddling again,' she said as they slipped silently past the shore. 'A canoe is something I can control, like riding a horse.'

The island they were circumnavigating was at most a ten-minute walk from side to side in any direction.

'Look! We're back where we started already. Let's go in,' Lester said, trying to hide his impatience.

'Let's stay a while.' Josie's voice was a near whisper. 'It's so peaceful out here.'

The canoe came to rest, water lapping gently against the wooden hull. Josie put the paddle down and turned to Lester behind her.

'You haven't even asked why I'm here.'

Lester laughed. 'I haven't had a chance, have I? But I couldn't be happier. I'll accept it as a miracle.'

Josie's voice trembled. 'I felt betrayed when I saw Cherry with that woman. I'm trying to save him from himself, but she's stealing him away.'

'Saving him from what, exactly? Aren't you just jealous?'

'I don't know. I don't want him to change. He was so delightful when we all sang together. Now he gambles and admits it openly, and he's obsessed with that old war.'

'Tell me one thing. I want an honest answer. Are you in love with him?'

Josie sighed. 'I knew you'd ask me that.'

'Yes or no will do.'

'Then it's both and neither. I don't know what it is about him. I know he's absurdly good-looking. I can't resist staring at him or running my hand through his hair. I can't resist putting my finger in the little cleft in his chin. But it's not that.'

'I feel inferior already.'

'Don't be silly.' Josie paused, gazing at the lights of Kieta winking in the distance. 'It's more that I feel so confident in myself when I'm with him. People say "Oh, you're a friend of the fair-haired doctor". Or, "You used to sing at the Steakhouse," as Meredith said earlier. I've never had that feeling before.'

'Has he taken you to bed?'

'That's the first thing a man *would* ask, isn't it? You're all the same. No, he hasn't.'

'Do I, the ugly one, still have a chance?'

Josie sighed. 'Sometimes you make me angry, you're so cynical. You both are. Don't force me to choose. Cherry needs me, and I need you.'

'I'm flattered. Why do you need me?'

Josie laughed and handed the paddle to Lester. 'I need you now; I'm tired of paddling. Go on, take me in. I've been thinking about what Meredith said. Do you think there's any truth in it?'

They made love, with mutual surprise and delight, in the unaccustomed luxury of a guest suite, on Lester's double bed and to the purring sound of an air-conditioner. Neither, it seemed, had known exactly what to expect, but the sensual exploration of each other's bodies and their coming together was without shyness or hesitation.

Afterwards, they sat at a table by a window looking out on the sea and distant lights on the main island. Liquor and soft drinks were on hand from the bar fridge, courtesy of the management.

For a time, they were content to drink without talking, in the embrace of an emotional release.

'You're a good lover,' Josie said eventually. 'I think you're experienced. Cherry told me about your sexy blonde girlfriend in Australia.'

'The rat. Why can't he keep a secret?'

'Am I too thin to be sexy? Tolai women say I'm a *bun kaka-ruk*, a scrawny chicken.'

'Nonsense.'

'Were we good...together?'

'Wonderful.'

'I was so worried; it's been a long time.' Josie paused, finished her courtesy bottle of wine, opened another and looked gravely across the table at Lester. 'I shouldn't say this, but you aren't *quite* the first.'

'I realise that now. I was surprised. I know I've no right to be.'

'I had a boyfriend in Australia when I was nineteen.'

'Only one? I'm sure you had others chasing you.'

Josie didn't answer. She was drinking quickly now, her face flushed.

'When I saw Cherry with the French woman, I decided then and there that I wanted to have sex. Not with him, but with you. Not at Taliligap, not at your apartment next to the brothels, but somewhere romantic, somewhere secret and secluded. I'd never have dreamed of this.'

She yawned, stood up unsteadily, pulled Lester back to the bedroom and onto the bed, undressing them both as she went. Once again, he enfolded her in his arms, kissed her bare shoulders, held her firm, small breasts in his hands, felt the softness of her stomach, urged their hips together. Not long after, they were fast asleep.

'Have you *spent your sex*?' she whispered to him near dawn, as he lay, barely awake, on the bed. It seemed odd to him, a line lifted from an old church guidebook to righteous behaviour. Unready to answer, he was rescued by a knock on the door, a call to early breakfast before packing to leave.

Outside, he saw Mali Gavera walking hand in hand with Meredith. No doubt, somewhere along the line of guest rooms on the beach, she'd put the judge's Associate to a test for which no fantasy could have prepared him.

28

Carol heard about the incident first. Flanagan confirmed it after lunching at the Yacht Club. A European police inspector had assaulted a Doctor Cherry-Apsley in the Cosmopolitan Hotel lounge. In Carol's version, the inspector had stumbled upon Cherry in a steamy embrace with his wife. Cherry suffered facial injuries but hadn't gone to the hospital, instead fleeing in a taxi to Chinatown. He hadn't been seen at the hospital for days.

At the office, the story was relayed to Lester by Carol, with relish, while nearby Flanagan wore a knowing smirk. As for Gloria, who overheard the conversation, this was a fate that awaited any wife-stealer and gambler.

As soon as he could get away, Lester drove to Cherry's flat in Chinatown. Cherry was no longer there. That evening he drove up to the bungalow. He found Cherry lying on the sofa propped up by cushions, a glass and whisky bottle on a coffee table beside him. His nose was stuffed with gauze swabs and heavily plastered. An icepack rested on his forehead. He took it off to reveal a blackened, swollen eye socket, the eye almost closed.

'You look as though you've gone five rounds with Muhammed Ali,' Lester said, while thinking the injuries were less severe than Carol had described.

'No, just a dumb policeman.' Cherry sounded as if he had a heavy cold.

'I've come to see if I can help.'

'No need, old sport, I'm self-medicating. Better every day.'

'What's happening to your life? In Chinatown people told me Chinese men were looking for you. They thought the men bashed you up and that's why you left in such a hurry.'

'I owe a bit of money, but I've arranged a loan to pay off the debt. I'm finished with gambling.'

'What about the inspector's wife? I heard about what happened. I know the man; he's the archetypal jealous husband.'

Cherry lay back with a sigh and gazed at the ceiling. 'A terrible misunderstanding. Regrettably, no one believes me except Josie.'

Of course she would, Cherry thought. 'Tell me,' he persisted. 'Tell me about the wife.'

Cherry sat up and cast a sorry, black-eyed look around the room. He pointed to the whisky. 'Fetch a glass, pour yourself a drink.'

The woman's name was Rosa, and she was originally from the Philippines. Cherry had treated her in hospital for a bad gash that might easily turn septic. He'd met her a few times since at the hotel just to check on her recovery.

'I heard you were canoodling with her on a hotel sofa,' Lester said.

Cherry shrugged. 'What can I say? I was only comforting her. Then that brute of a policeman appeared, breathing fire.'

Once upon a time, Cherry's account could be trusted. That time was passing, at least for Lester.

'Has Josie been looking after you? Has she been staying here?'

'She comes and goes. She likes it here; it's better than a dorm at Malmaluan.'

'Tell me you haven't slept with her.'

'Why? Have you? She told me she met you unexpectedly in Kieta. She said she was on church business. I don't know whether to believe her.'

'Tell me.'

'I haven't slept with her. We talk, I drink. We share our thoughts on spiritual subjects. She gives me a goodnight kiss and goes to bed in the guest room. She wears the most old-fashioned flannel nightie you could imagine. As if it's any of your business, which it isn't.'

'I worry about her welfare.'

'For God's sake, she's twenty-four now. She's more than capable of looking after herself.'

Cherry, visibly annoyed, swallowed his whisky and poured himself another. He seemed in pain from his wounds.

'You should be taking aspirin,' Lester said, trying to make peace.

Cherry smiled and held up his glass. 'Whisky's better, that's my medical opinion.'

After a long pause, he went on.

'I'll tell you what we talk about: violence against women. I see so much of it at the hospital. Rapes, bashings, broken bones, ruptured spleens. She wants to do something about it. She says doctors and nurses should speak out, but they don't.'

Cherry left the sofa, walked gingerly onto the verandah and lowered himself into an armchair. Lester followed, about to ask him why he was in such pain. Cherry was a step ahead.

'He hit me so hard that I fell and hurt my hip on a coffee table.'

The air quickly cooled as darkness fell. A misty shroud settled over the hilltop, followed by heavy rain, unusual in a dry season already underway.

Lester fetched a blanket for himself, another for Cherry, as they huddled under the verandah's eave. Calls could be heard from the road as villagers got out of a PMV and hurried to nearby homes. To Lester, the world outside was dissolving, leaving them both in a void without form or boundaries. It was cold enough to set him shivering.

'You should understand something about Josie,' Cherry said eventually. 'Did she tell you what she suffered in Australia?'

'I know she was at school there, and at teachers college. I know she had a boyfriend. I think she hated life at the college.'

'She did, and I can tell you why.' Cherry sat up, gripping the chair arms tightly. 'She was raped one night at a house party. Some college students forced her into a room upstairs. She says she doesn't remember much of what happened.'

Lester's heart raced. Why hadn't she confided in him?

'What? She told you this?'

'She mentioned the rape case on the Duke of York Islands you told us about, and how helpless the young woman must have felt, when all of a sudden, she began to cry. Mind you, she'd had a few glasses of wine and *in vino veritas,* as the saying goes.'

'Did she call for help? Did she call the police?'

'She was too ashamed, she said, and confused about what exactly took place. You're the lawyer. Ask her yourself. Cross-examine her if you want.'

'We must have been stupid not to suspect something. She often seems standoffish about men. You sneered at her behind her back for being so full of Christian virtue.'

Cherry, brimming with indignation, tried to rise, wincing in pain at the effort. 'You're the one who called her Mary Poppins without the magic.'

'That wasn't me, that was Cleary. He thought she disapproved of his lifestyle,' Lester said.

'It doesn't matter. Neither of us deserves her, but I need her more than you do.'

'Speak for yourself.'

'I'm very protective. She's the one person in my life who overlooks my faults. I'm sure we'll disappoint her in the end, both of us.'

'Let her go,' Lester said. 'You'll only hurt her.'

'What does she really mean to you? Are you in love with her?'

Lester hesitated, caught in a quandary, unwilling to disclose the depth of his feelings.

'I'd rather be with her than with anyone else.'

Cherry's laugh was mocking. 'I wonder if she feels the same.'

At that moment a thunderclap, close and startling. Lightning flashed overhead. The bungalow shuddered. The rain redoubled, beating a deafening tattoo on the tin roof.

Just as suddenly, the power went down and the rain stopped, leaving silence and darkness all around. Lester, who'd planned to stay, picked up his bag and left. At the car door he turned to see Cherry still in his verandah chair, staring from his one good eye into the night.

As the Mercedes wound down to the coast, Lester's anger and frustration dispersed in the warmer air. The act of driving calmed him and gave him time to reflect. He was profoundly shocked by Cherry's account of what had happened to Josie.

He wished she were beside him in the car as she usually was, but it was too late to call at her home, and unwise to do so if her father was there.

In two years of friendship with Cherry, he couldn't remember another argument between them, let alone the bitterness that crept into their quarrel that night. That it was fired by jealousy he understood, though at least in Cherry's case it seemed less to do with sexual tension than emotional need.

Cherry seemed so confident of his hold over her. Perhaps he assumed his charm would always win out. In Lester's mind, however, the charm was waning and the good looks were taking a battering. One thing was clear: to avoid embarrassment, Cherry wouldn't return to work until no scar on him remained. Lester was glad of that. No way would he desert a friend who'd saved his life, but it was time, he decided, to have a break from his company.

Next day, at the office, he tried to reach Josie. Wherever she'd gone, it was beyond the reach of a phone call.

Since their night together at Arovo, she was constantly in his thoughts. He yearned to enjoy the intimacy between them again. Perhaps she was somewhere in the hinterland doing good deeds. Or she merely wanted some time to herself. Either way, her unexplained disappearances were becoming harder to bear.

He thought of writing her a letter, of baring his soul, then backed away. It might have led to the end of his friendship with her and Cherry both. He lacked the courage, and that made him more frustrated than ever.

Beyond the walls of the administration building, and beyond the self-contained expatriate confines of the town, the Mataungan

Association, urged on by the demagoguery of Oscar Tammur and the articulate persuasiveness of John Kaputin, pressed on with the election and swearing-in of a council of their own.

The new, non-sanctioned council, the *Warkurai Ni Gunan*, would take control of the cocoa fermentaries, raise taxes and provide services in areas of the Gazelle under its sway.

There were large crowds and festivities for the formal launch of the council on the Mataungan stronghold of Matupit Island. The administration, now supporting the restored all-Tolai council and doggedly pursuing tax defaulters, seemed powerless to stop it.

29

At last, Rabaul had several general criminal cases to make a visit by a Supreme Court Circuit judge worthwhile, and for Lester to again feel useful.

In the most serious case, a Chimbu man from the New Guinea Highlands was convicted of raping a Tolai woman near a plantation where he worked as a labourer. The man's innocence was doggedly argued by counsel from the Public Solicitor's office. Only as it ended did Lester notice Josie sitting at the rear of the courtroom. She'd reappeared in Rabaul as quietly and mysteriously as she'd left.

Later, outside the court, she was seething. Why, she wanted to know, did the defence counsel argue the sex may have been consensual, when it most certainly wasn't? Why was the man's confession, which she'd heard in court, rejected, only because the Tolai police officer interviewing him used some of the wrong words in the caution? The plantation manager said unmarried plantation workers often caused trouble with village women; why wasn't that relevant?

Lester tried to explain but Josie remained inconsolable, at least until he offered her a lift home to Raluana. Once settled in the car and driven beyond the town, she seemed to calm down. Lester reached across to put a comforting hand on hers.

'I heard what happened to you in Newcastle.'

Josie ripped her hand away. 'I suppose Cherry told you. I don't know why I told him.'

'He didn't have the full story,' he said, 'because you started to cry. It must have been a ghastly experience for you.'

Josie didn't respond, instead gazing from the passenger window as the road wound around the bay. Stirred by a strong sea breeze, the harbour waters glittered in the late afternoon sun. Lester understood her reluctance, her silence. Not until they were approaching her home did she speak again.

'At school in Brisbane I lived with my aunt. Her daughter, my cousin, was the same age as me. I adored her; we went everywhere together. We agreed that boys of our own age were hopelessly adolescent and inferior, so we banished them from our lives.'

'That didn't last,' Lester said, prompting and teasing at the same time. 'At Arovo, you told me you had a boyfriend.'

'The first and only one. He was a student at college like me. One night he took me to a student party. He coaxed me into drinking vodka with his friends. Three of his friends took me upstairs to a bedroom and sort of raffled me off.'

'Oh, Josie! The Steakhouse. Raffling the champagne. We were idiots.'

Josie waved the Steakhouse away.

'I was so woozy at the party, I was barely aware of what was happening. I remember one stayed and the other two left. The next thing, I was on the bed with him, and he was pulling my clothes off. I can't remember much else except I think he had sex with me, or at least he tried. I'm sure I resisted, but at the time I felt it wasn't me it was happening to. I was like a horrified spectator looking on.'

'Why didn't you go to the police?'

'Why? For a start it was dark in the room, and I couldn't see them clearly. I didn't know them either. When I came downstairs, they'd gone.'

'What about the boyfriend?'

'I'm sure he could have identified them, but he ran away too. I'm not certain which one was on top of me. It would've been my word against his, wouldn't it? Besides, I was too ashamed. If it came out, they'd say I was a Methodist Church girl who got drunk at a party. How'd that have sounded? It would've destroyed my father.'

Her voice faltered. Lester took her hand again.

'I understand completely.'

'I prayed but it didn't help. I kept wondering why God would punish me, not them. From then on, I didn't want to stay in Australia and go through the ordeal of a trial. I wanted to go home to Rabaul where I thought I could forget it ever happened.'

'Has it poisoned your opinion of men in general?'

Josie smiled and hugged herself.

'Now I only like men who are older than me. Mature men. A doctor and a lawyer, what more could a woman need?'

'Are you serious?'

'Sometimes.'

'Then that's a good start. I hope you've been able to put it behind you, as much as anyone could.'

'Of course I haven't forgotten. I tell myself I'm a different person now. If anything like that were to happen again, I'd pursue that man to the ends of the earth.'

The Mercedes pulled up at the reverend's bungalow. Josie told Lester to wait while she looked through the front windows. She put a finger to her lips, then indicated he should follow her quietly inside. Her father was asleep on the sofa, mouth open, grotesquely askew. His glasses hung limply from one ear; a book lay open on his chest. Goaded by the ceiling fan, a strand or two of greying hair flayed his bald patch.

His illness was no secret. Malaria and hepatitis had undermined his health, if not his faith. It was common that missionaries of his generation offered themselves up to the tropics with hope that a belief in God was the only necessary prophylactic.

'I won't stay,' Lester said. 'I don't want to wake him.'

'He sleeps the sleep of the just,' Josie said. 'He won't wake up. We'll leave him. Come down to the shore, I want to show you something while it's still light.'

A little further along the road, a small village nestling in thick vegetation hugged the shoreline. In a clearing by the water's edge, two men were making a *babau*, a bamboo fish trap. A completed trap, an oval-shaped cage of woven bamboo strips over a frame of bamboo hoops, stood higher by half than Lester and, at its centre, was greater than the width of his outstretched arms. At one end of the trap, a narrow neck and tunnel allowed fish to enter. Small fish could escape the cage; larger fish chasing them could not.

Lester had heard about traps of this kind which, at least in New Guinea, were unique to the area. He marvelled at their size and the skill in their making. Josie obviously knew the men well, chatting to them easily in her blend of Kuanua and Pidgin.

'They've known me since I was a girl,' she said. 'They asked me why I don't fish anymore with the women. I told them I'd rather build myself a fish trap. That made them laugh.'

They sat down on a log by the water's edge to watch the makers. Josie pointed to a raft of stout bamboo poles some distance from the shore.

'They attach a trap to the poles and anchor it down with stone weights.'

'Simple, elegant and effective,' Lester said.

Daylight waned; the brisk breeze died away. With the slow and methodical work of the men, and the quiet conversation between them, the unhurried pace of village life settled over the clearing. Lester felt his body relax as if gentle hands were massaging his limbs. Josie took off her sandals and bathed her feet as the ripples washed over them.

In that moment, unaware of eyes upon her, she reminded Lester of an Impressionist painting he'd seen of a young woman, portrayed as equally unaware, bathing her feet in a brook. Was it by Camille Pissarro? He had been keen on Impressionist art at school, a long time ago.

He put an arm around her to bring her close and kiss her. She gave herself freely, then pushed him away, laughing.

'Those men are staring at us. They don't approve.'

Lester turned to see the men, again engrossed in framing the bamboo trap. Josie groaned at his bemusement.

'Kissing in public—such a public display of affection—it's not done.'

'I'm sorry, I couldn't resist. I'm ignorant; you understand them. You're half Tolai already.'

Josie sighed. 'Sometimes I wish I were. I wish I really could understand them. Father has spent a lifetime trying, but it's complicated. One thing I do know: I don't miss Australia at all.' She sighed again. 'I don't know where I belong.'

'I'm not surprised you don't miss Australia.'

Josie was silent for a time, gazing out to sea. Her arm rested affectionately on his shoulder.

'I'm glad I told you I'm not a virgin. I wanted to let you know in my own way. At Arovo the time, the place, seemed right.'

As the short tropical twilight gave way to night, they walked back to the house. The Reverend, now awake, met them at the door.

'It's getting late,' he complained to Josie. 'I was wondering when you'd come home; it's past dinner time.' He looked quizzically at Lester. 'And who's this?'

Josie rolled her eyes and winked at Lester.

'It's my friend Lester—the lawyer, remember?'

The reverend nodded doubtfully and shuffled away. Josie took Lester's hand.

'He remembers you perfectly well. He's a curmudgeon at times.'

They cooked a meal of fish and chips from frozen packets in the refrigerator and ate in the kitchen. The Reverend ate in his study. Josie led Lester to the living room sofa.

'The dinner was blissfully domestic,' she said with a mischievous smile. 'I wish I could go to bed with you, right now. That'd be perfect—and perfectly impossible.' She nodded towards the study.

'Wait for your father to go to bed, then sneak back to town with me.'

'Sometimes I wish for things, sometimes I dream of things I can't have. I don't want to have a secret relationship with you. What if Cherry finds out?'

'I'd handle that.'

'I couldn't.'

Lester fought back his frustration.

'Have you seen Cherry lately? Have you been with him?'

Josie stiffened, taken aback by the sudden edge in his voice. She put a calming hand on his arm.

'I've seen him only once, to tend his wounds. He has a cupboard packed with ointments and things; he nicks them from the hospital. He's been very sore, though he won't tell me what happened. He said awful Pat Connell was coming to stay with him, so I haven't been back since.'

'The last time I saw him, we had an argument. Over you, actually.'

For a moment Josie seemed nonplussed. Perhaps, thought Lester, it had suddenly dawned on her that by encouraging both men, then fending them off, she had created a predicament. She stood up, shaking her head.

'You carry on like brothers—childish brothers. You shouldn't be jealous. I've told you already I don't feel I have to choose between you, and you're not going to force me, either of you.'

'I adore you, Josie. I couldn't force you to do anything.'

Josie walked away, peered into the Reverend's study, went into her bedroom and returned with a triumphant look, holding up a small bottle of Bacardi rum.

'Father's forgotten us and gone to bed. I souvenired this from the bar fridge at Arovo. I really need to drink it now.' She went into the kitchen and came back with drinks. 'Rum, lemonade and lemon juice,' she said. 'It's a cocktail called daiquiri. Cherry told me Adele the barmaid used to make it at the hotel.'

'How far this innocent sheep, a missionary's daughter, has strayed from the fold!' Lester raised his glass. 'To you, Josie.'

Josie followed suit. 'To us.' She drained her glass, blinked, gave a little shudder and sank back on the sofa, fidgeting, seemingly wrestling with an urge to speak. She sat up and looked at Lester intently.

'If you return to Australia, will you go back to your girlfriend? Cherry said your law firm was full of crooks, and you came here to get away from the law.'

Lester's heart sank. The curse of the tree-legged stool.

'Don't listen to Cherry. I came here for adventure.'

Josie laughed. 'That's exactly what he said about himself. I don't know whether I should believe either of you.' From the kitchen she fetched a second hotel bottle, this time whisky, refilled the glasses and began sipping it neat. After a pause she blinked and shook her head as if to clear it before speaking.

'This is a day for shedding secrets, isn't it? I shouldn't tell you, but Cherry got into trouble at a hospital in London and had to leave. That's why he went to Mauritius.'

'Did he tell you this?'

'No, he told Adele, probably when they were drunk together in bed. It was just before she was deported.'

'And Adele told you?'

'She said she only told me because she thought I was too good for him and should leave him alone. What cheek!'

'Did she give any details?'

'No. I thought she made it up.'

'Somehow her story makes sense to me. It's why he's been a loner at the hospital.'

Josie, frowning, gazed up at the ceiling. 'I've never asked him about it, but when I last stayed at Taliligap, he woke up at midnight with a shout. He'd had a nightmare about being chased around London by an angry mob.'

She downed the last of her whisky, kissed Lester and lay back on the sofa. 'I think I've ended up with a couple of fugitives. I can't cope with that now. I'll have to go to bed.'

Pat Connell died at Taliligap two weeks after coming to stay. The funeral, being in the tropics, took place soon after. In a country where solemnity was never far from farce, it was no surprise the funeral procession reached the cemetery gates before someone realised the coffin was empty. Connell's corpse had been forgotten.

While the mourners sat down and fanned themselves by the roadside, the hearse returned at speed to the morgue for the body, then resumed its place at the head of the procession as if nothing had happened.

A wake was held at Connell's Tavern. It was assumed that the tavern, already looking dilapidated, wouldn't outlast its namesake.

Once Connell left to stay with Cherry, creditors, patrons and neighbours helped themselves to whatever liquor and furniture remained, although, as he breathed his last, he revealed to Cherry that a stash of liquor lay hidden beneath the floor for just such an occasion.

Cherry maintained his friend and mentor had received the best of palliative care and died peacefully and without pain. Josie believed he'd been heavily sedated by alcohol and substances smuggled from the hospital.

Cherry caroused well into the night with the tavern's regular barflies, not least the plantation managers who'd apparently forgiven him. Lester, still the faithful protector, stayed sober enough to drive him home to Taliligap.

They filled the boot with books, maps, notes and other documents found in Connell's rooms behind the tavern. Cherry swore they were left to him in Connell's will, though no will was found. They proved to be a treasure trove of material about the Japanese occupation. Lester slept over at the bungalow, while Cherry sorted through Connell's bequest in a state of frenetic excitement before leaving for his hospital shift at dawn.

Later that morning, Lester awoke to the clatter of dishes being washed at the kitchen sink. Josie had dropped in only to tidy up the bungalow, or so she said. It was certainly a chore ignored by Cherry while Connell was there.

'I'm *so* glad Connell's gone,' Josie said, bringing tea and toast to the table for breakfast. 'I saw him here one day with Cherry, still drinking. I've never seen anyone so ill; it must've been just before he died. His body looked as if it was turning itself inside out. And his eyes! Do you remember those awful comics we used to read at school where someone's eyeballs leap from their sockets?'

'Whoa! Was he really that bad?' Lester put up his hands, pretending to fend her off.

'He filled Cherry's head with stories about the war. Look around, the place is full of war junk. Cherry brings things home like a dog bringing in old bones from the garden. That Connell was a bad influence.'

Her vehemence seemed to surprise Josie herself. She smiled and blushed, avoiding Lester's startled look, then intently began buttering her toast.

'Poor Connell,' Lester said. 'Have you no Christian compassion for an old war hero?'

'None.'

Lester pointed to the mound of books and documents in a corner of the living room. 'His influence lives on beyond the grave. Those are all about the war, the tunnels, the war crimes trials. Cherry spent all last night reading them.'

'Then please help me to stop him. He's lost interest in his work. He's besotted with that woman in New Ireland. She's much too old for him. Crosset wants to cast him in the pantomime later this year, but he says he's done with the theatre. Help him find something new.'

Josie's agitation, the dark eyes wide, the colour in her cheeks, only made her more desirable than ever. Lester leaned

over the table to kiss her, then led her by the hand and unre-
sisting, to the sofa.

'I want to make love to you, Josie. Here. Now.'

She drew him close in an embrace and gently, slowly, traced
the contours of his face with her fingers. 'I want you too. But not
here, not now.'

'Why not? We're all alone. It's our chance.'

'I couldn't. It's Cherry's home. It would feel like a betrayal.'

'How about a luxury suite at the Kaivuna?'

Josie laughed, draped her arms around his neck and fixed
her eyes upon his own. 'That would be wonderful. But right
now, could you possibly drive me to town?'

Lester knew better than to cajole her. Her desire, however
fervent, was a fragile thing. Still, his voice held a hint of bitterness as he pointed to the Mercedes outside.

'The chauffeur's at your service, madam. Your limousine
awaits.'

Lester returned to spend the rest of the weekend at Taliligap.
Cherry arrived from his hospital shift in the late afternoon and
immediately took to drinking Bacardi with a supply of ginger beer he discovered in the kitchen cupboard. As always, he
greeted Lester like an old comrade in arms, but soon fell to rum-
maging again through Connell's papers scattered on the living
room table.

'Still searching for Imamura's hideout?' Lester asked.

'No. Connell told me about something more exciting. Help
yourself to a drink, sit down with me and I'll explain.'

At Connell's funeral service, Lester had learnt a little about
Connell's war record and his post-war service as a military

provost. Nearly two hundred war crimes trials were conducted in and around Rabaul by Australian military courts. Connell had attended many trials as a guard.

According to Cherry, Connell became delirious in his last days. He rambled about a particular trial, that of General Imamura. As the Commander-in-Chief of Japanese army forces in the region, Imamura was held accountable for the crimes of his subordinates. He was convicted and sentenced to ten years imprisonment.

Connell could never forget that trial, Cherry said. It was one of the last and longest. The prosecutors, Japanese defence counsel, translators, stenographers and judges were all exhausted. Rain drummed incessantly on the tin roof of the makeshift courthouse, so no one could be heard without shouting. The stench of frogs and giant snails, crushed by trucks and rotting on the road outside, was unbearable.

There were no witnesses, only paper statements from other trials read over to Imamura and painstakingly translated. A hundred of them, a record of humiliation, torture, beatings and executions. Connell admitted it had been hard not to become numb to it all by then.

One subject raised in the trials had piqued his interest. An infamous Japanese doctor named Hirano, from the 24th Plague Prevention and Water Purification Unit, had carried out bizarre medical experiments on prisoners of war. The doctor was never charged with a war crime and his experimental exploits went unpunished. This angered Connell, so he decided to follow them up for himself.

It was rumoured that a secret underground hospital complex and laboratory were established near Imamura's headquarters. Connell's search for the facility was unsuccessful. He thought the tunnel entrances had been sealed and camouflaged, though he never gave up hope that someone else, younger and able-bodied, would continue the search.

That someone was Cherry.

Cherry's account, in a voice both soft and persuasive, transported Lester back to the time and place of Imamura's trial, but he couldn't understand Cherry's enthusiasm for resurrecting events that most would rather forget.

'So you've decided to have a go? Why on earth would you? The war ended decades ago.'

Cherry left the table, hunted in a box in a corner of the room and returned waving a sheet of paper.

'In medical school I read about gruesome experiments the Japanese performed on prisoners of war. I want to find what outlandish things they might have done here. If I found what Pat Connell was looking for, it would be my Holy Grail. I'd tell the world. I need something to keep me going.'

'You have us, your friends. You have your medical career.'

'My medical career mightn't last, old sport. Besides, I promised Pat I'd try.' Cherry held up the paper he'd brought. On it was a rough, hand-drawn map. 'He drew this for me. I think it was the last thing he ever did.'

'Enough,' Lester said, heading for the verandah. 'I need some air.'

'I'm hungry,' Cherry said. 'Let's walk to the village. I'll order chicken and rice for two.'

'Don't you ever cook?'

'Not if I can help it,' Cherry said.

They set off along the road into a spectacular pink twilight. Frangipani trees along the way lent a sweet fragrance to the air. Children appeared from nowhere to join them, pulling them by the arm to the roadside store. Cherry bought them bottles of lemonade and more for himself. 'To tame the Bacardi,' he said.

Lester struggled to reconcile the tranquil beauty of the evening with Connell's macabre tale earlier in the afternoon. Cherry's preoccupation with such a morbid subject seemed to reflect a rising despondency with his life in general.

30

J ack Emanuel, the new District Commissioner, was regarded by the administration as an outstanding officer whose experience and fluency in both Pidgin and Kuanua made him particularly suited to mediate in the long-standing dispute between warring factions on the Gazelle Peninsula.

By now, clashes between Mataungan supporters and the police, involving blockades of fermentaries, were close to a daily occurrence.

Emanuel's belief in his ability to speak directly to Tolai people led him to adopt a highly personal style, visiting villages by day or night, and often alone, to talk to village leaders to gain their confidence and trust. Their trust, however, was hard to win, for he had approved the use of force against squatters and protesters in the past.

As if to remind the Tolai of his attitude, a contingent of one hundred and sixty heavily armed police, led by senior officers and including Emanuel himself, descended on Matupit Island on a Sunday morning to serve a summons on a Mataungan leader for a minor offence of obstruction.

A serious fight ensued between angry villagers, using petrol bombs, stones and knives, and police, who responded with tear gas and shotguns loaded with birdshot.

Lester, enjoying a lazy Sunday at Grandview Apartments, heard Bilson's Landcruiser roaring away. As this now happened regularly, he took no notice. He was unaware of the day's events until he received a telephone call in the afternoon from Cherry, in a state of high excitement.

'I've been at the airport. Matupit islanders stormed it in their hundreds. Skirmishes everywhere. Lots of injuries, police too. Gabriel picked me up in Chinatown and took me. He said children in the village nearby were screaming, blinded by tear gas.'

Lester, imagining the scene, was stunned. 'Were you able to help them?'

'I washed their eyes and exposed skin. I told them to throw away the clothes they were wearing. That's not all. Some men showed up with shotgun pellets in their legs. Luckily, I had my medical kit and took most of the pellets out. Some were too deeply embedded.'

'Couldn't you take them to hospital?'

'They wouldn't go; they thought police would be waiting to arrest them.'

'I'm impressed. You sound as if you need a drink. Shall I come round with a bottle?'

'I'm exhausted. I think I'll lie down instead.'

The Matupit Island incident brought the Mataungan conflict to the very edge of Rabaul town. The scale of the violence shocked residents of all races.

Only days later, the Supreme Court in Port Moresby brought down final judgments on two of the most contentious issues in the conflict. In the first case, the court confirmed the existing council tax was validly imposed. In the second, the claim of Tolai villagers to customary ownership of Vunapaladig was inevitably defeated by the existence of a registered title.

These losses proved a bitter pill for the Mataungans. In desperation, they took one last stand to seek restoration of customary rights. The new flashpoint was a longstanding dispute over Kabaira, a tract of plantation land also held under an unassailable registered title, thus sunk irretrievably in the same legal sinkhole as Vunapaladig. Most of the undeveloped land had been occupied without incident by villagers for more than fifty years.

Encouraged by the Mataungans, villagers repeatedly removed survey pegs and resumed land previously occupied, part of which was earmarked by the administration for a future power station.

Although Flanagan would have argued the administration's case in court, his sympathy in land cases was with the villagers.

'Self-help's the only option for them now,' he told Lester in the office.

'The admin won't step in to assist?'

'That's the policy. They don't want to set a precedent.'

A sudden rumbling sound swept through the building. Cabinets rattled; loose objects danced on desks.

'*Guria!*' Gloria jumped wildly to her feet. 'A big one!'

'There's no need to panic.' Carol waved a dismissive hand in Gloria's direction. 'It's the season.'

Gloria's face showed incredulous scorn. 'The season? A *guria* season? Are you talking about the weather? It's the *Kaia*, the volcano spirits! Tolais at the *bung* say the fighting has disturbed them. All the time fighting. It's the government's fault. We Asians, we foreigners, are afraid.'

Lester stepped in to separate the combatants. 'I've heard the Chinese have had their bags packed for years. They're forever ready to leave.'

'Nothing about the Chinese would surprise me,' Carol said.

Lester, with his hearty dislike of Carol's flat-vowelled New Zealand accent, her permed hair like a deflated beehive and her air of superiority, retreated to his office and closed the door. Gloria, still seething, followed him.

'They're moving in together, John and her!' Gloria's voice trembled with anger. 'I heard them talking. He's a bigamist!'

Lester shrugged. 'Not unless he marries her. Besides, they seem suited to each other.'

It was the wrong thing to say, and he was immediately remorseful. He liked Gloria and at times still guiltily desired her, despite her shows of disdain.

He was about say something to placate her when she pulled out an envelope addressed to him and hidden in a folder she held. Inside was a printed card, in English and a stylish copper-plate script: an invitation to Gabriel Toporo's wedding.

'I've got one too,' Gloria whispered. She pointed gleefully to Flanagan and Carol. 'Those others haven't.'

The wedding was held in a Methodist church at a staunchly pro-Mataungan village close to Matupit Island. The ceremony followed the traditional Christian playbook: Gabriel, resplendent in a formal suit and tie, his bride in a white full-length dress and bridal veil. The service was only a Christian confirmation of their union, behind which lay a complex traditional settlement involving kinship groups and bride wealth.

Lester, officially warned away from Gabriel and his Mataungan connections, was wary of staying for long at the garden reception. Cherry, also a guest, had no such qualms.

He called Lester over to where Gabriel was holding court with several Mataungan leaders whose names and faces were familiar due to their notoriety and frequent appearances in and around the court.

Gabriel turned to his fellow Mataungans and spoke in English.

'These are my good friends. Lester was my friend when I worked at the government building. Dr Cherry here is a doctor who helps us. He treated our people who were hurt by tear gas and shotguns.'

'Where are your guitars?' Jacob ToVailu, one of the group, asked. The others laughed.

'Lester brought his guitar all the way from Australia,' Gabriel said. 'He thought there were no guitars in New Guinea.'

More laughs, but Lester was anxious to deflect the attention. He patted Gabriel on the back.

'Celia made a beautiful bride, and you look like a Wall Street banker in that suit.'

Gabriel smiled. 'A banker? Foreigners say I'm a gangster.'

ToVailu, suddenly agitated, cut in.

'Mr Lester, you're a lawyer. If we are gangsters, where are our guns? Your police fight us with bullets and tear gas. Why do they use such things? Why does the DC carry a gun?'

'They're not my police; I don't give them orders. The bosses in Port Moresby worry about the violence of your supporters. You have a responsibility, too.'

'I saw petrol bombs being thrown at police,' Cherry said, coming belatedly to Lester's aid.

'One policeman had a hole burnt in his shirt,' another in the group said. The others laughed again.

'We're not the ones to blame,' Gabriel said. 'We sent a letter to the United Nations. We told them we are finished with colonial rule; we want self-government now. We said twelve people were wounded by shotguns at Matupit and our children were made sick by tear gas spreading everywhere. Maybe they were trying to kill us.'

An excited ToVailu added, 'Emanuel was to blame as well as the police. It's the second time he's ordered shooting our people.'

The group muttered their assent. Gabriel turned to Lester and held up his hands.

'This talk is wrong on my wedding day. We should be happy. Come, both of you, and meet my family.'

Lester looked around Cherry's flat in Chinatown, their rendezvous after the reception. It seemed even more cramped and cluttered than before: clothes scattered, empty beer bottles, a makeshift shelf of medical books, maps, diagrams and notes from Connell's collection. More of the same overflowing the table onto the floor.

'You dragged me away,' Cherry complained. 'I was enjoying myself.'

'I couldn't stay,' Lester said. 'I'm in enough trouble with Flanagan as it is. Besides, you're the hero. I'm the punching bag.'

Cherry, now infatuated with all things Chinese, brewed a pot of herbal tea, claiming it would excite his energy, cure his insomnia and balance the elements of *yin* and *yang*. He persuaded a sceptical Lester to try it. Lester baulked at the bitter taste and sipped as little as possible. Cherry recalled his part on the day of the Matupit riots.

'I was angry,' he said. 'Isn't it a war crime to use tear gas against innocent people?'

Lester shrugged. 'Tear gas is used against rioters everywhere.'

'Not against children.'

Cherry cleared the table of papers and poured more tea for them both. 'Sorry there's nothing to eat. I'm a tad short of cash at the moment. I live on fruit from the market and noodles from the noodle palace downstairs.'

'You still have money for drinks,' Lester said, pointing to a row of empty bottles along a wall.

'I took a lot of liquor Connell left behind at the tavern. It's all gone now. To make things worse, the damned police came to the hospital yesterday. They're charging me with passing a dud cheque.'

'You? I can't believe it.'

'Neither can I, old sport. I swear I thought the money was there. I never look at my bank account. It's only a couple of hundred dollars and I'll make it good. For God's sake, this is New Guinea! Everyone owes money to someone else.'

'What are you going to do?'

'I thought you might see me through. I'll pay you back from my next pay.'

'Do you owe gamblers? Was it a gambling debt?'

'You can't be serious. You can't pay gambling debts with a cheque.'

'I'll write you a cheque tomorrow. I promise it won't bounce.'

They laughed together at that.

'Come downstairs to dinner,' Cherry said. 'At least noodles are something I can afford.'

31

A Fokker Friendship emerged from the grey cloud mantle above the airstrip. Spray streamed from the wheels as it landed. Passengers disembarked to the dying whine of turbines and hurried towards the terminal, caught in the unexpected thunderstorm. Among the passengers was Judge Prest on his regular Circuit visit.

The last passenger to leave the plane was assisted down the landing steps and into a waiting wheelchair. The woman trundled herself over the long stretch of tarmac to the terminal, hunched against the rain. No one moved to help her. Airport staff huddled under the terminal awnings. The hostesses passed her, running together, a flurry of arms and legs beneath a borrowed raincoat.

Lester left the delegation that had gathered to welcome the judge and helped the woman through to the luggage collection area.

After seeing the grumbling judge to his waiting car, Lester noticed the woman had wheeled herself out of the terminal. She was waiting by the roadside with a large black bag across her lap, shivering under a layer of thin cotton clothes wetly plastered to her body.

'Is someone picking you up?'

'It's OK. The hotel bus is coming soon.'

The woman opened the bag and rummaged. She brought out a hand towel and slung it awkwardly around her neck. Lester draped it properly around her shoulders.

'Thanks,' she smiled. 'I'm pooped. Today I've travelled all the way from Sydney. Before that, I came all the way from the States.' She offered Lester a limp, damp hand. 'I'm Beth—wet, cold and tired out.'

Beth was comfortably established in an air-conditioned ground floor room at the Travelodge Hotel when Lester visited next day. The room opened onto the hotel's swimming pool and had a separate entrance to the street behind the hotel.

'Not many Americans come to Rabaul,' Lester said. 'Only old warhorses on a pilgrimage.'

'Well, that's me, at least by proxy. I'm on my father's pilgrimage. He was in the US Navy in New Guinea during the war. He never got to be an old warhorse. I was told he died here.'

'I'm sorry.' Lester wished he'd bitten his tongue.

'Don't look so sad,' Beth laughed. 'Wait for me at the pool, I'm going for a swim.'

She emerged from her room without her wheelchair, lanky, flat-chested, spider-legged, walking slowly to the pool and settling beside him on a lounge chair. Her eyes were shaded by dark sunglasses. Bony hips poked through a faded pink, frill-edged bathing suit. A cloud of tightly curled, light-brown hair hovered above pale, hollow cheeks and a slash of bright red lipstick.

'My hair is the one thing I'm proud of,' she laughed, struggling to stuff the springy strands under a bathing cap that seemed to be growing little plastic flowers. 'That, and the urge to keep on going, no matter what.' She eased herself from the chair and lowered her body into the pool's shallow end. Holding on to the side, she kicked the water into a froth with her legs, grinning like a child in the bath. 'My daily therapy. The Ethel Merman hour.'

She soon tired and Lester helped her climb from the pool.

'I'm sick of pools,' she said. 'I'm sick of chlorine and things that are square. Square rooms and square swimming pools, that's my life. I'd just love to swim in the ocean all the way to the horizon.'

The next evening, Cherry appeared at Grandview Apartments to collect his cheque. Apparently, the need was urgent. Lester was keen to talk to him about Beth and her condition.

'From what you've told me,' said Cherry, 'she has multiple sclerosis. She needs your help. She's pretty brave to be here.'

'I'm happy to help. It's just her attitude. She's demanding.'

'She's American, one of the chosen few for whose use and entertainment this world was created.'

'She's from Minnesota, up near the Canadian border. She told me she flies all over America from one lot of relations to the next.'

'She's overshot the runway this time,' Cherry said. 'Perhaps she thought this was Hawaii.'

'Her father was a lieutenant in the US Navy during the war, an airman in one of the naval squadrons. His aircraft was shot down over the Solomon Islands. She was six years old when she last saw him.'

'What happened to him? Does she know?'

'That's what she's come to find out,' Lester said. 'She's given me newspaper clippings and a letter from the naval authorities in the US. The letter said he was missing, presumed dead. If he survived, he'd probably have been taken prisoner and sent to Rabaul. That's all she has. Please take them; see if Connell's papers can add anything.'

Cleary, in a laplap and paint-spotted singlet, met them on the verandah of his thatched village house. Lester wheeled Beth from his car and helped her walk up the steps. Cleary took her hand and kissed it with a flourish.

'Welcome, Elizabeth, to the home of Darryl the dauber, painter of the humble coconut palm in all its many moods.'

Inside, paintings covered the woven walls and lay in stacks on the floor: village scenes in lashings of oil; brown Gauguin-esque bodies in showers of frangipani and poinsettias. Other canvases depicted birdlike dancing figures in skirts of bunched leaves and tall, conical masks topped with feathers.

'Palm trees and *duk duks*,' Cleary offered as Beth peered at the figures in the dim light. 'My specialities.'

'*Duk duks*?' Beth queried. 'They look sinister to me. Are they sorcerers?'

'It's more like a secret society, a male initiation thing. The village invited me to join, at the lowest level of course. It's unusual that they would ask a foreigner. They must be short of *tambu*.'

'*Tambu*?'

'Shell money—traditional currency.'

'I've seen it at the market. Lester took me yesterday. It seems as good as dollars there.'

'It is, but its true value is for ceremonies. It has to be accu-mulated. It's like their gold reserves. I'll show you my gold.'

Cleary opened a Chinese chest embossed with dragons. Inside were strands and bundles of white shells, the size of dried peas, strung together in the old measurement of fathom or half-fathom lengths.

'They think I'm a big, fat man who must be rich, so they've set a high price for entry. I've had to collect the stuff for years.'

They moved to chairs on the verandah. Cleary brought out a bottle of Riesling wine and glasses. Lester was pleased to see Beth seated by Cleary's side as an eager seeker of knowledge. He'd seen her vigour ebb and flow with the vagaries of her con-dition. She was unpredictable, sometimes grumpy, sometimes graciously appreciative, but always exacting company.

The hut trembled on its base of thin wooden posts. Bare feet padded up the steps, belonging to two teenage boys from the village, laplaps wound firmly around slim hips and their short, dark curls blonded by peroxide. They stopped, clutching each other at the sight of Cleary's guests.

'Samuel...Daniel.' Cleary introduced them airily. 'Aren't they silly, these biblical names?' He dismissed them with a wave 'There's Coke in the *liklik bokis-ice.*'

In response to Beth's questions, Cleary talked about Tolai beliefs and customs; of the co-existence of animist beliefs and introduced Christianity; of spirit beings symbolised by the cre-ation within the clan or *vunatarai* of *tubuans*, spirit-mothers who gave birth to other masked spirits, the male *duk duks*. They were symbols of power and authority, feared in the villages as enforcers of the customary canons.

Beth, tired and tipsy, leant on Lester's shoulder then tee-tered down the steps and into her wheelchair. Cleary had per-suaded her to buy a painting. She clung to a rolled-up canvas small enough to fit into her suitcase. She'd adamantly refused a painting of *duk duks*, instead choosing one of a beach with a fringe of palms and Watom Island far offshore. The island loomed from the water like the back of a broaching whale.

At four o'clock the next afternoon, Lester was closing the last case of the Circuit list when the wooden courthouse began to shake. A row of casebooks, standing neatly on his table, slid to the floor. Judge Burchett, oldest of the Circuit judges, raised a weary bloodhound face to the roof, blinking slowly at the wild gyration of ceiling fans.

'We'd better, ah, adjourn, d-don't you think?' The judge, stammering, disbelieving, seemed frozen to the bench.

Police constables guarding the defendant fled from the court with shouts of *'guria'*! The defendant slipped away in the opposite direction. Lester and the defence counsel hurried outside, soon joined by witnesses and the judge's Associate.

A metal awning above them buckled and collapsed as they scrambled to escape from beneath it. On the streets nearby, traffic lurched or skidded to a halt. Like ants from a threatened ant hill, staff and customers streamed from shops and offices. In the distance Lester caught sight of the police constables chasing their escaped charge.

When the shaking subsided, Lester and the Associate ventured inside to find the judge still sitting on the bench, a lonely, petrified figure draped in a red robe. The police constables returned, panting, with the thief. There was no power and no light. The fans dangled limply, exhausted by their brief, frantic dance. Beyond the court, the town was in chaos.

Justice was suspended for the day.

Lester hurried to the Travelodge, past cars that had strayed off the road and over pavements that crackled with shop-window glass. Severed powerlines with smoking ends trailed from poles that leaned at odd angles.

The sturdy hotel had suffered little damage. Beth was sitting rigidly at the poolside, clutching the arms of a solid wooden chair. The pool, she stuttered, had suddenly come to life and launched a wave that washed up to her knees and carried away the wheelchair beside her. The chair's stainless steel was shimmering at the bottom of the pool.

An hour after the earthquake, tidal surges began. In the harbour, the sea swelled like bread rising in a baking tin. It surged over the wharves, across the waterfront and into shops on the main street. Just as quickly it was sucked back, far beyond the lowest mark of the low tide, leaving tracts of mud, stranded boats and flapping, dying fish. Contents of the supermarket, trade stores and the pharmacy spewed from the shop doors.

The town's residents, after checking their homes were safe, gathered around the waterfront to watch the steady surge and retreat of the harbour waters, a surreal spectacle in the deep red radiance of the setting sun.

At Beth's insistence, Lester retrieved her wheelchair and wheeled her down to the harbour to join them. They gazed in disbelief at the Beehive rocks, the volcanic plug at the harbour's centre, which had sheared in half. Cliffs on the harbour's far side had cascaded upon the Kokopo Road in creamy, chalky drifts. They were now massive dunes running down to the sea.

Some saw the earthquake as a sign that nearby volcanoes, dormant for nearly thirty years, might be awakening. In hotels and clubs, residents debated guarding their homes and possessions, fearing an outbreak of looting.

The surrounding villages, however, hadn't been greatly affected. The pliant materials from which buildings were constructed swayed and shivered but held together. Gardens remained to be tended, and fish still swam in the sea.

But according to Gloria, it was the manifestation of a deeper torment brought on by the conflict engulfing the Gazelle.

Lester had to calm an unnerved judge and accompany the court party for a short case in Kavieng, even though New Ireland had also been affected by the earthquake.

The judge had endured many adventures, he told Lester, not least hair-raising aircraft landings and a tribal fight outside a Highlands court, but he'd never sat in court through an earthquake.

Cherry was busy at the hospital. Josie had volunteered to help at Gaulim teachers college where new buildings were severely damaged. According to Cherry, she was distraught.

On Lester's return to Rabaul, his taxi driver told him strong aftershocks persisted. The Rabaul Observatory kept saying the continuing tremors were normal, no cause for alarm. No one was reassured. After all, the driver said, it hadn't predicted the event itself, so what exactly was the Observatory there for?

Lester, worried about Beth, called first at the Travelodge only to find her in bed and fast asleep at two in the afternoon. He'd asked Cherry to check on her while he was away. They agreed to meet later that day at the Cosmopolitan Hotel.

Cherry was already settled at the bar when Lester joined him. Heavy rain had been falling since his return and drummed on the hotel's iron roof. To Lester, the hotel and the town itself seemed dismal, about to drown in misery.

'I met Beth,' Cherry said with a grin. 'You thought I'd forget, or be drunk or worse, didn't you?'

'How is she?'

'She's quite a woman; I can see why you've taken a shine to her. The heat's not good for her. She should stay in the air-conditioning.'

Lester raised his voice to be heard above the rain. 'I wish she would, but she won't.'

'She doesn't need more excitement.'

'I was going to ask you if she could stay at Taliligap. It's cooler there. We can look after her. She's given me a carer's booklet. I can learn what to do.'

'With landslides blocking the Kokopo Road? We can't get there! I've left her some tranquillisers. She's complaining of stiffness. You can help by massaging her legs. We can't look after her if she needs a hospital. Nobody here would know what to do. She has to go home.'

'How did she react to that?'

'She didn't say anything. Just glared at me with those big blue eyes.'

'She wants to see where her father died before she goes. Did you find anything in Connell's papers?'

'I found a diary note. After the war he went with Australian war crimes investigators to a place they called Tonoro Beach. They'd been told that a group of Allied war prisoners was there, about to be transferred to a camp on Watom Island, when a bomb from an American aircraft landed on their shelter. According to the Japanese, they were all killed. Their account couldn't be verified because no bodies were found, but it's likely that American airmen were among them.'

'Her father killed by an American bomb? How did she take it?'

'She didn't take it well. She wants to see the place for herself. I found a hand-drawn map as well. Why don't you take her?'

Two days of rest revived Beth's spirits and determination. She hadn't yet finished with Rabaul, she declared, begging Lester to take her snorkelling—'glassing', as she called it—over a coral reef.

Late on the following afternoon he drove her to the submarine base. He swam breaststroke over the coral beds, piggybacking, her hands clutching his shoulders.

In a shallow area where she could stand unaided in trade store sandshoes, she peered into the water. Her hair, free of the ridiculous bathing cap, floated about her head like a waterlogged bush. A long-sleeved shirt belonging to Lester warded off the sun. He kept her away from the reef wall and its frightening plunge into the depths.

A Tolai woman passing by on her way from the market brought them a husked coconut, slicing the top with a bush knife to share the coconut's cool, sweet liquid. When they'd finished drinking, she chopped the coconut in half and fashioned spoons from pieces of husk to scoop out the white flesh.

'No need to pay,' she told them. 'I had a good day at the market.' She'd sold almost all she had brought.

'This is a perfect place.' Beth smiled, laying back on the sand.

Her face had lost its pallor in the pink light of sunset. Her beauty was concentrated there, thought Lester, as well as in the graceful fall of her neck and her slim, coat-hanger shoulders.

A twin-engine aircraft droned above them, the sound fading away slowly over the sea. Beth, aware he was gazing at her, sat up slowly and shook her head, looking down at her hands, her strength.

'I'm not a nice person, Lester,' she said. 'I'm a suckerfish. I latch on to people who wander into my life. I'm like one of those strange animals I saw this afternoon, living in a hole in the coral. If anyone comes close, my tentacles pop out and fasten on. I've lost all scruples about it. I don't want to be dependent. It's survival.'

'Wiggling tentacles attract other fish. I find tentacles irresistible.'

'Like my arms and legs?' Beth, laughing, lying on her back, waved her arms and legs feebly, swimming through the air. 'Hell, I'm so tired. Please take me home.'

In her hotel room, Lester waited while she showered and changed. She raided the refrigerator for chocolate bars, then settled into her bed in striped pyjamas. Her voice was soft and sleepy.

'I've always wanted to live beneath the waves like the Beatles, free of my wretched body. I'd drift like a jellyfish among coral gardens; no effort, no pain, just a little flip, one little squirt and I shoot along. I guess today was as close as I'll ever get. Thank you, Lester, for that.'

Lester smiled, taking her hand, smoothing the bedcovers around her.

'One last favour before I leave.' Beth breathed the words, slurring them now, eyes closing. 'Tomorrow, in the evening, I want to see where my father died.'

Lester turned the Mercedes down a narrow track to the beach, then wheeled Beth onto the sand.

'On my map, the place is here somewhere,' he said. 'There's no reef; Japanese workboats from Watom Island could load from the shore. The map says a wooden marker at the spot where the bomb fell is no longer there. It's probably buried in the sand.'

Beth shrugged. 'It doesn't matter. Can I just sit here quietly for a while?'

Lester left her and strolled along the sand until she became a small, lone figure in the distance. She was in her wheelchair and holding up a parasol, a silhouette against the setting bronze orb of the sun.

'I've been praying,' she said when he returned. 'I prayed for my father, and for all of them. Isn't this the beach in my painting? Look, there's the island over there. Somehow, I knew it would be. I had that feeling.'

She opened a plastic bag of frangipani blossoms collected for her by the hotel staff and scattered them on the ground around her feet.

Lester sat down beside her.

'There's nothing left, no trace at all, no buildings, no graves, nothing. I'm sorry this is what you came so far to see.'

'I know it sounds odd, but maybe that's appropriate,' Beth said. 'I don't even know if it happened. All I know for certain is that one day, when I was six, he walked out of our front gate, got into a car and drove away. From the window I watched him go. I never saw him again.

'It's impossible to make any sense of it, that he died here on this beautiful beach thousands of miles from America. I'd rather believe he ran off to Minneapolis or Chicago and married someone else. That'd be easier to accept, but no such luck. He was killed by mistake in some awful war that never came near his home.'

Lester called for Beth the next day, planning to take her that evening to an open-air picture show on the lawns of the swimming pool by the harbour. A sign at the pool promised a show 'subject only to tidal waves'.

Beth wasn't at the poolside and her room was locked. Lester called on the manager, who said she'd left Rabaul on a dawn flight, a charter. The manager had arranged her flights through to Sydney and had taken her to the airport himself. She was unwell yet determined to go.

'Why didn't she tell me?' Lester asked.

'There's something you should see,' the manager said. He led Lester to Beth's room. On the bathroom mirror she had scrawled in lipstick, 'Love you, Lester' within a large heart. And below, the words, 'Fuck life!'

32

Following the earthquake, shops and businesses in Rabaul shut down to restore their premises and restock. Elsewhere, buildings and homes needed repair, schools were closed, church services suspended. The respite from Mataungan threats and violence was welcome.

Lester's attempts to contact his friends were unsuccessful. Josie was still at Gaulim; Cherry was nowhere to be found. The hospital suggested he may have taken a week off, though no one was sure.

The admin building was outwardly undamaged; internally, the offices were in shambles. In the Prosecutor's office, cabinets and bookshelves had spilled their contents; volumes of law reports, textbooks and files littered the floor. Replacing them was a task delegated to Gloria, which she did with intense concentration and conspicuous care. Carol, sitting at her desk and pretending to be busy, called Lester over.

'My policeman's been transferred to Port Moresby,' she said in a low voice, not wanting to alert Gloria's keen ear.

'Are you going with him?'

'No, I'm happy here. Tracey loves it; she's made school friends.' She took Lester's arm, drawing him closer. 'I'm moving in with John.' She nodded towards Gloria with her chin. 'I thought I'd tell you first before someone else does.'

'That's great news.' Lester struggled to sound as if he meant it.

'John and I want you to come to dinner tomorrow. Just you. My new social life has to start somewhere.'

Casually wandering through Flanagan's home the next evening, Lester found Flanagan's family history had been snuffed out, with the furniture rearranged, and sporting photos, Namatjira prints and other remnants of a previous life removed. Missing from the main bedroom were photos of Flanagan's wedding. In another bedroom, books and toys belonging to Tracey had replaced those of the Flanagan daughters.

After dinner, and while Carol put Tracey to bed, Flanagan brought out the whisky and moved with Lester to the living room.

'I want to talk to you about your friend Cherry-Apsley,' he said.

The emphasis on friendship spelled trouble for Lester. All along, he'd suspected an ulterior motive in the dinner invitation.

'That cheque problem was a one-off,' he said warily. 'I'm sure he's fixed it.'

'A cheque problem? What was that?'

Lester silently cursed his error. 'Nothing important.'

'Have you been in touch with him recently?'

'Not recently, no.'

Lester was feverishly prodding his memory. Was it at Gabriel's wedding? No, it was at the Cosmopolitan Hotel after the earthquake. They'd talked about Beth. Barely a week had passed, but much had happened in that time.

Flanagan took on a solemn air, as if duty-bound to reveal a distasteful secret.

'He's been arrested on a drink-driving charge in Kavieng. Apparently, his hire car veered off the road and overturned. I suppose you'll be glad to hear his injuries are minor.'

'How did it happen?'

'He said he lost control of the car due to an aftershock from the earthquake. The Kavieng police had a good laugh.'

Lester shook his head. 'He's not himself lately; possibly he's been working too hard. Is his excuse plausible?'

'Whether or not his excuse is plausible, you'll have to stop making excuses for him. He's been giving police the run-around. He failed to show up for a hearing in Kavieng and forfeited his bail. Instead, he flew back to Rabaul. Police rearrested him here and put him on a plane back to Kavieng.'

The Yacht Club bar had reopened soon after the earthquake. It appeared no earthly power could delay the annual power-boat regatta. No doubt, thought Lester, the club was where Flanagan got his information.

'I'm shocked; I had no idea. Where is he now?'

'With that fellow, your guess is as good as mine. I'd say he's still there, waiting for his court case.'

Lester fell silent, absorbing the news. Even by Cherry's standards of late, this incident and his behaviour were bizarre. Flanagan, however, had more to say.

'I've also heard he persuaded an airline employee, a young lady, to give him a return ticket to Kavieng by showing his hospital pass and claiming he was needed urgently for a medical case. He said he was bringing vital medication. He promised to pay later by government warrant. That hasn't happened.'

'When he comes back, I'll talk to him. There could be some confusion. I'm sure we can sort this out.'

'You won't be talking to him. By the way, the hospital's had enough; they're looking into his medical registration.'

'That's absurd. He's an excellent doctor, so others tell me. I suspect some don't like his politics.'

'Whatever's the case, from now on, I expect you to keep away from him altogether. And you're not to divulge to him or anyone else what I've just told you. I'm sure you understand why. This office might be involved in a possible prosecution in future.'

Once at home, Lester settled into an armchair with the whisky bottle beside him. He rarely drank alone, but he needed to consider what to do about Cherry.

He was torn between taking the next flight to Kavieng on a rescue mission, or allowing events to take their course. Cherry might be fined or even jailed if he couldn't pay the fine. He couldn't contact Cherry directly, but in Kavieng he could talk to the police, the local hospital and perhaps as a last resort, the *kiap* Beddich. It would be a delicate mission. He had to be careful not to be seen as interfering in the course of justice.

As the whisky went down and a long night passed, memories of their time together resurfaced in snatches of fitful sleep. Their hours spent with Josie rehearsing and playing their music were among the happiest of his life. One day, however, he could never forget. He'd have drowned had it not been for the miracle of Cherry's life-saving air.

He fell asleep in his chair with his mind made up; he'd fly to Kavieng as soon as he could.

In the morning, he booked for the next flight in two days' time. The flight never took place.

Lester and Gloria were alone in the office. Through the hum of the air-conditioning came the sound of a dog howling in a garden nearby. Lester looked up from his work, a moment's premonition of the second earthquake before it began.

The building shook, gently at first, then violently. Steel cabinets tipped over as their laden drawers slid out, scattering papers. Flanagan's collection of diplomas, maps and admiralty charts danced on the walls and clattered to the floor.

Gloria screamed, picked up her bag and ran for the glass door as it cracked. Lester came after her down the staircase as it heaved beneath them. The handrail shook itself free of the stairs, eluding his clutching hand.

Outside, a storey-high water tank came loose from its base, shuddered towards them on spindly steel legs and toppled as the legs buckled beneath it. Water sluiced from the tank onto a tarmacked street undulating slowly like a great black python. Parked cars bounced along the snake's back as if on pogo sticks. Telegraph poles swayed like palms, bowed to each other and whipped upright. Power lines crackled and snapped in showers of sparks.

Lester stood rooted to the spot, unable any longer to trust his sight or balance. He was standing at the bow of a ship rolling and yawing wildly in a storm. His mind could bring nothing he saw or felt to a familiar order. He heard, far away, cries and breaking glass, barking dogs, a siren. Gloria was moaning beside him.

Just as abruptly, the movement stopped, giving way to an unnatural stillness. Lester moved gingerly lest the ground disappear beneath him. A jagged crack had opened before him in the street. He was among a small crowd that had fled the admin building. The building had survived—at least so it appeared from the outside.

He sent Gloria home and hastened to Grandview Apartments through a town strangely quietened by shock. The apartment block still stood, though more insecurely than ever. Szabo's staircase had tumbled down. Szabo was lashing a ladder brought from his workshop to what remained of the landing, twenty feet above the ground. Bonnie, his Tolai bride, was calling loudly for help from a window.

'My new lady,' Szabo said breathlessly. 'I have to bring her down. She wants to jump.'

In the garden was Norma, the captain's wife, kneeling on the grass, a mess of stringy hair and rumpled clothes. An open, half-packed suitcase lay beside her. The earthquake had rudely interrupted her afternoon binge on gin. She was weeping, shouting for the captain.

'Jack, come and get me! I've gone mad. This is the end, the very end. I'm going home! Jack! Jack!'

The captain would be a long time coming. He'd given first call on his loyalty to his ship.

The second earthquake happened less than two weeks after the first. The damage caused in New Britain and New Ireland this time was greater and more widespread. Around Rabaul, the water in the harbour rose higher and receded further, a slow, inexorable pulse of advance and retreat.

Boats were washed into the streets and cars sucked into the sea. Goods from restocked shops and supermarkets choked stormwater drains. Low-lying villages were swamped and the roofs of churches and school buildings in the hills collapsed. Damage from the second earthquake compounded damage from the first.

The DC, from his residence high on Namanula Hill, appealed for calm. Evacuation centres and tent camps were established. Extra aircraft flew a shuttle service when the airstrip was repaired, ferrying frightened families to more stable ground. Hundreds left for other towns in Papua New Guinea, Australia or Hong Kong, adding to those who left after the first earthquake. Many vowed never to return.

Australian warships appeared off the coast—to evacuate the Europeans, so the Chinese claimed, while they, yet again, would be left behind. Chinese traders, more superstitious and prescient than others, had packed their bags.

First buried by a volcano, then bombed to rubble by the Americans and finally shaken apart by earthquakes, the future didn't look propitious for a town with such an unlucky history. In the clubs, rumours again began: the Mataungans would seize this chance to advance on the town by stealth in the dead of night and murder the Europeans.

A police guard was placed on the admin building until the damaged interior was repaired and precious intelligence reports could be locked away.

At the hospital, staff prepared for the worst. A town dam had cracked and water towers all over town had collapsed. A shortage of drinking water was likely. This raised the spectre of typhoid and cholera.

Gabriel's village of Matupit, on flat land by the harbour, had been flooded. Lester took food to Gabriel, sheltering with his family and many others in a church hall, waiting for the restless harbour to settle.

Despite Lester's offer to take Gabriel's family to his apartment, they seemed satisfied where they were. Their house was on stilts and they would soon be home, little the worse for their experience.

Aftershocks continued for weeks, fraying nerves even further. The Observatory tried to scotch rumours that a volcanic eruption was imminent, and claimed a third earthquake of similar magnitude soon after the second would be almost impossible.

By this time, no one was listening.

33

The admin building, closed for a week for repairs, reopened for business. In the Prosecutor's office, the same scene: fallen cabinets and contents strewn across the floor, Gloria on hands and knees sorting volumes of the law reports, Flanagan rehanging his admiralty charts and Carol idly cleaning dust from office shelves.

They heard each other's earthquake stories. Lester had little to report except the massive driftwood piece in his apartment had toppled and cracked the floorboards. Flanagan's tennis court had cracked from side to side. *Belle Marie* had been left high and dry, but his dinghy had been swept away and couldn't be found.

Carol claimed to be suffering from nervous shock. Her daughter Tracey thought it was an exciting adventure. Gloria's family had fled to the hills to stay with friends. She was adamant that friends and relatives who had not yet abandoned Rabaul were about to do so.

As with most of the town's residents, those in the Prosecutor's office counted themselves lucky. The Yacht Club and Cosmopolitan Hotel on the waterfront were flooded, as were the supermarket and food stores, but the Tolai market was unaffected and bustling as usual. No one was going to starve.

Shortly after Lester's return to work, Cherry called on the phone.

'I'm at the airport. I've come from Kavieng. I've no money for transport. Can you give me a lift to Chinatown?'

On the way to his flat, Cherry's tale unfolded. He'd been on the road from Kavieng to see Leila at her plantation when the steering wheel suddenly shook, the car wobbled and overturned. He waited at the roadside for two hours before police and a tow-truck arrived. He might have been dying for all they cared.

They drew a straight line on the ground beside the road and made him walk along it. He was dazed and couldn't follow the line precisely, so they charged him with being drunk in charge of a vehicle. Eventually he pleaded guilty to the charge.

'Why did you plead guilty if you weren't drunk?' Lester asked. 'You could have told the magistrate what you just told me.'

'I saw the magistrate talking to police at the hotel, looking at me and laughing. Who was going to believe my story? Also, I had no money to stay on in Kavieng for a court case. The whole thing was a gross miscarriage of justice, but what other option did I have?'

Lester listened to Cherry's explanation with some scepticism.

'How fast were you driving?'

'Not too fast,' Cherry said.

'On the best and straightest road on the island? You drive like a kamikaze pilot.'

Cherry ignored him. 'I was fined a hundred dollars, seven days to pay or a month's jail.'

'Have you paid?'

'I didn't have the money. Then the big quake struck Kavieng and I had trouble getting back to Rabaul. I haven't any spare cash at the moment and the seven days are up. I was wondering if you might help.'

'Another loan? Shall I just add it to the money you already owe me?'

'I'll pay it back. Trust me, I'm a man of my word.'

At work or at home, rarely an hour passed without Lester's thoughts straying to Josie. He sought information from her father at Raluana, but the telephone line was dead and the Kokopo Road was blocked by further landslides.

He found her at last in the offices of the church, in town. The teachers college at Gaulim, a project so many years in the making and far in the hinterland, lay in ruins. What the first earthquake had begun, the second earthquake finished off. Classrooms, dormitories and teachers' quarters were damaged beyond repair.

It was without electric power or facilities of any kind. Students, teachers and volunteers had been sent away, some never to return. Only by divine intervention, Josie insisted, had no one died or been seriously injured.

Despite a flood of donations made or promised, and the certainty it would one day be rebuilt, Josie was heartbroken— the first time Lester had seen her utterly dejected. She was also exhausted, having spent the previous day in the bumpy back of a truck, dodging landslides and cracks that had opened in the ground, while taking a hazardous route through the hinterland and around the far coast to reach Rabaul.

He took her to his apartment in the early afternoon where she slept on the sofa until the evening. He cooked dinner for them both while she showered. She'd eaten nothing but bananas in two days, she told him while eating ravenously.

He gave her a clean shirt and shorts of his own to wear. Though they were far too large, the look was fetchingly gamine. She kissed him with passion.

'I must go now,' she said.

'Please, stay the night here. With me.'

'I can't. I promised the pastor I'd stay at his house. He'd be worried.'

Futile to press the point. For Josie, apparently still in a mild state of shock, the time, place and ambience had to be perfect. Lester's offer obviously failed on all counts.

She was gathering her old clothes to take with her when she asked, 'Where's Cherry? Have you heard? The whole place is so topsy-turvy. It's crazy.'

Lester felt a familiar churning in his stomach, the dreaded pangs of jealousy. He hesitated, weighing his answer. Impatiently, Josie pressed on.

'I haven't seen him since that miserable Connell died. Since then it's been turmoil, rioting at Matupit, earthquakes...'

'He's been staying in Chinatown. He treated people from Matupit who were gassed or wounded by police. He also went to Kavieng.'

'Was he with that woman?'

'Whatever his plans were, the last quake put paid to them. He's back in Chinatown now; you can see him.'

'At Adele's old flat? I'm not going there.'

'The hospital, then. He can't get to Taliligap.'

'Has he mentioned me?'

'Honestly, I can't remember. I've hardly seen him either. He knew you were at Gaulim and unreachable.'

Josie frowned and wrung her hands, displeased by the answer. Plainly, Cherry should have remembered her and could have tried harder. She rose to leave and immediately sat down again.

'Someone I talked to today told me you'd been seen around town wheeling a lady in a wheelchair. He said she'd stayed at the Travelodge for ages. Who was that?'

Lester smiled. 'Is this an interrogation? Why do you want to know?'

Josie, her face reddening, shook her head.

'I don't want to know, then. Can you take me to the pastor's house?'

She was tired, upset and with no one else to talk to, Lester thought. The three-legged stool on which she had relied for so long had collapsed, another casualty of the earthquakes.

On the landing outside, they kissed again. It felt strange and thrillingly erotic to kiss her while she was wearing his own clothes. He wanted her so much; it was an agony to let her leave. At that moment, Szabo returned in his utility.

'That man!' Josie lunged desperately for the apartment door. 'He can't see me like this—in your things!'

Safely out of sight, she calmed down. When Szabo was gone, Lester led her down the staircase to his car. On the way to the pastor's home he had an idea.

'The woman in the wheelchair? She's American, her name's Beth. Tomorrow, I'll take you on a drive and show you why she came.'

'That'd be nice,' she said limply, too tired to refuse.

Lester picked Josie up at the pastor's house. She seemed refreshed and much happier. She had shopped at an undamaged trade store in the morning for new clothes to wear and returned his own.

On the way to Tonoro he told her the story of Beth's father, offering little detail except no trace of the tragic event remained. He said he wanted to bring her to what, for Beth, had been a place of solace and remembrance.

Josie sat silently on the shore for half an hour, looking out to sea. At length she put an arm around Lester's waist and drew him close.

'It was kind of you to do that for Beth,' she said. 'She must've meant a lot to you.'

While on the shore Lester's mind had wandered back to Beth and the time, brief yet intense, they'd spent together. When carrying her in his arms down to the water's edge, she seemed no heavier than a down pillow. He was reminded of gathering up an armful of broomsticks and trying to keep them together. Her life was an exercise in will, he thought. She was determined to extract her full quota. His admiration for her spirit was unbounded.

He dropped Josie off at the pastor's house. The Kokopo Road was reopening next day and she could see her father at last. It remained unsaid, but Lester guessed she would immediately return to Malmaluan and wait eagerly for Cherry to reappear at Taliligap. There seemed no resolution to this awkward triangle of affections without hurt. He wasn't prepared for that, at least not yet.

He was glad he hadn't revealed Cherry's ongoing plight to Josie. That was up to Cherry, a long-awaited test of his honesty.

Carol came into Lester's office, sat down on his visitor's chair and opened a copy of the *Post Courier* like a town crier unfurling a royal scroll. 'Article on page three,' she announced. 'Headline: *Nonga doctor convicted on drink driving charge.*'

Without waiting for Lester's reaction, she read the article aloud in its entirety.

> *'The District Court in Kavieng has convicted Anthony Cherry-Apsley, a doctor at Nonga Hospital in Rabaul, on a charge of drink driving. The court was told that his car left the Boluminsky Highway at speed and overturned. Cherry-Apsley pleaded guilty but claimed he had lost control of the car due to an aftershock that affected the car's steering. He was fined $100, in default one month's jail. Reporting of the case was delayed by recent earthquakes in the New Guinea Islands region.*

> *Kavieng police have since charged Cherry-Apsley on 2 counts of passing valueless cheques amounting to $527.60. The charges relate to payments for accommodation and repairs to a hire car in Kavieng. No date has yet been fixed for a court hearing.'*

Carol closed the paper and laid it triumphantly on Lester's desk. 'That's your *friend*,' she said. 'I can't wait to tell John.'

Cherry called from the bungalow verandah.

'Have you come to ask for your money back?'

Lester had slipped away from the office and the midday heat in town. Cherry should have been at work, but as the hospital had confirmed, he wasn't.

'Have you read the article in the *Post Courier*?' Lester waved the newspaper in the air as he climbed the verandah steps.

'What article?'

'About your fine for drink driving. I've paid it for you. Now it's more dud cheques. "That charming English doctor, who would have thought it?" That's what I hear around town. I can scarcely believe it myself.'

Cherry took the paper, glanced at it, handed it back. 'Oh, that. It's such a mess. I don't know how I got into it, and I don't know how to get out of it.'

'I'm here to help if I can. I'm forbidden from seeing you, so I've hidden the car next door.'

'Sorry I haven't been in touch; I've been lying low. I'd rather people didn't know I'm here.'

Lester laughed. 'No one followed me.'

'Come in for a drink. Only Coke, I'm afraid. I've no money for rum.'

'I've brought the rum,' Lester said, producing a bottle of Bacardi from a shopping bag.

'A godsend,' Cherry said.

'Tell me about the mess, the cheques in Kavieng,' Lester said, settling into a chair on the verandah. 'What's more, John Flanagan told me you promised to pay for your flights with a government warrant that doesn't exist. Is that true?'

Cherry, in Kavieng again for his court case, had no money. He'd contacted Leila for help to pay his fine and accommodation, but she refused, claiming he was too fickle to trust.

In dire straits, he paid for his stay at the Kavieng Hotel and for the car repairs with cheques, hoping they'd clear on his return to Rabaul. As for the airline tickets, he believed he could charm the Treasury staff in Rabaul to issue an official warrant, but they wouldn't accept his story.

Having convinced the Kavieng police he'd plead guilty to the cheque charges, he'd managed to have his hearing moved to Rabaul and had put up his own bail, but again he'd run short of money.

'So what can I do now?' he asked Lester.

'You can't ask me to lend you more,' Lester said. 'I don't believe I'll get it back. Pay your debts now. Sell something. Sell the ute.'

'I can't, I need it to get to work. I've nothing else to sell except my medical kit. I can't sell that either.'

'Savings? Money in a bank in England?'

'All gone. I took it out to travel the world and spent it.'

'Your family? Your mother? Are you in touch now?'

'No. They don't even know where I am.'

'Would the police withdraw charges if you paid what you owe by instalments?'

'They won't. They're harassing me. They accuse me of helping the Mataungans, along with Adele. Maybe they want to deport me as well.'

'Is that it? What else is there?'

Cherry paused, running a hand through his hair. 'I'm behind in my rent for the flat. The owners are restless; that's why I've moved back here.'

'At least you're employed,' Lester said. 'Let's see what happens at your court hearing. It's time you had a solicitor.'

'I can't afford a solicitor. Can't you represent me?'

'You know I can't. You should get a character witness from the hospital to say what a fine doctor you are, and wholly irreplaceable.'

Cherry leapt to his feet with a loud snort, threw his hands in the air and disappeared into the bungalow.

'You're mocking me,' he called out. 'Even you! What hope have I?'

Lester rose to leave. He heard Cherry call after him.

'Can you leave the rum behind?'

Despite, or perhaps encouraged by, the earthquakes, the movement of squatters onto the Kabaira plantation continued. A squad of more than a hundred police, together with DC Jack Emanuel and the plantation manager, ordered a group of squatters to leave, saying the pursuit of their claim was futile.

It confirmed their view the administration would never listen and would always take the side of the white man and his plantations. Though the squatters were time and again evicted, the confrontation between police and the customary owners would inevitably be repeated. With Kabaira, the last stand had become the last straw. The stage for violence, for a symbolic and defining statement, was set.

Less than a month on from the second earthquake, and with the people of the Gazelle only beginning to reclaim and restore their lives, the statement was made.

The nineteenth of August 1971, a Thursday morning. Another quiet day in the Prosecutor's office. With no Circuit or other court work since the earthquakes, boredom verging on somnolence prevailed.

A phone rang; Carol picked it up. Then shrieked.

'Mother of God! Jack Emanuel's been murdered.'

'Wah! How terrible!' Gloria stood up, looked fearfully around as if the murderer were present, then sat down again, wide-eyed and pale.

Lester ran to the windows. *Kiaps* and police milled in the courtyard below. Engines revved. He ran down the stairs. He found Bilson talking animatedly to others. He heard the words 'stabbed', 'bayonet', 'couldn't be saved.'

Back in the office, Flanagan, muttering 'my God, my God' and pulling furiously on a cigarette, was summoned by phone.

'Urgent meeting upstairs. Security. Airport. Lester, man the telex machine. The rest of you, go home.'

Cherry rang Lester from the hospital. He'd been woken from his morning sleep after a night shift, and ordered back in case he was needed. He left his flat as the trade store owners downstairs pulled down the shutters. No doubt, Cherry said, they'd hide under their beds all day.

News of the murder, down to the grisly details, spread rapidly throughout the Gazelle Peninsula.

Apparently, a group of Tolai men had appeared on a path at Kabaira without warning, as if sprouting spontaneously from the soil. A line of fifteen, unarmed and arms folded, faced the DC and the Superintendent of Police. Their faces were whitened with lime and slashed by bold markings of red and black, colours of the *tubuan*.

Each wore in his hair a white feather on which was painted a black and red circle. Around their necks were necklaces of *tangket* leaves, a ritual sign of warning and the invocation of magical powers. The path lay between the village at Kabaira and the plantation. The air throbbed with their anger.

A heavy, stocky man called Taupa was at their head. He waved the DC away.

'The land, the title, is not clear!'

The DC approached the trembling, perspiring Taupa and pressed a hand on his arm. 'Let's go and talk,' he said.

Together they walked ahead on the path until they were lost to sight among the trees. When the DC hadn't returned after some time, the Superintendent went after him.

He found the District Commissioner's body beside the path. A trail of blood and a bloodstained Japanese army bayonet were close by. A wound in the DC's chest had penetrated deep into both lungs. He died within minutes, unable to draw breath.

Rabaul closed down in a state of shock. Within hours, villages around Kabaira were deserted, the people fearing retribution on a biblical scale. They fled into the hills, far down the coast and into the fearful wilderness of the Baining Mountains.

In the following days, convoys of trucks bristling with armed police sped along the narrow roads that criss-crossed the peninsula. They set up roadblocks and swept through villages, gathering up weapons: bows and arrows, slingshots, axes, even kitchen knives. Helicopters hung in the sky over every sheltering cove and hamlet.

The Mataungan Association offices were raided and their papers confiscated, although no connection between the organisation and the murder had emerged. The Administrator on the radio promised to root out all who were 'possessed by the demons of hate and violence'. The painted warriors on the path to Kabaira were hunted down relentlessly, identified and arrested.

Grief at the DC's death brought together, at least for a brief time, Rabaul's divided and diverse communities. Eight thousand people, Tolai, Asian and European, gathered around the Anglican Church grounds for the funeral service.

It was the culmination of two years of bitter animosity, misunderstanding and mistrust. It came on top of a succession of natural disasters that had shaken the confidence of the hardiest expatriate planters and Chinese storekeepers. The impermanence of their tenure, in every sense, had never been brought home to them so strongly.

The Tolai people, for their part, were shocked by the consequences of their anger. There was a fine symbolism in the dagger, a Japanese bayonet that struck at the heart of the Australian Administration—of greater significance than they'd intended. In its own way, it heralded an end to the colonial era.

Many of Bilson's colleagues flew in for the DC's funeral. The following evening, he hosted a dinner at his apartment. Several of his fellow *kiaps* were there, those with whom he had shared the hardships and rewards of life on remote outstations with legendary names and infamous reputations.

Lester was also invited, finding himself at the table beside Princess Clare de Lune and lamenting the end of the Kulau Theatre.

Bilson, in formal dress, presided at the head of the table. He sliced a leg of roast beef with a carving knife from a gold-embossed presentation set held proudly by his Sepik attendant.

The conversation, sombre and subdued, was about the murder, of course, whether it had been planned long before, whether the Mataungans had been involved, whether it was part of a close-knit conspiracy or the beginning of a widespread insurrection.

There were rumours the perpetrators had bought spells from Baining sorcerers to make themselves invisible to the police and invulnerable to bullets. The dinner guests pondered the future—if there was to be a future.

Lester stayed behind with Bilson to finish the whisky. Bilson hadn't moved from the table during the evening. Bilson's gaze roved slowly about the room, lingering over masks and baskets, necklaces and pig tusks, gourds and arrows, axes and shields, bowls, pots and carvings of every description in wood and stone. They covered walls and sideboards and spilled from corners. They extolled the richness and vitality of cultures in the society he had adopted as his own. They spoke to him with a compelling resonance, echoes of a timeless chant from the makers of these wonderful, sensuous shapes and textures.

'I'm leaving next week,' Bilson said flatly, breaking a lengthy silence. 'Off to the swamps of Western Papua. My last posting, I suppose.'

'Lawyers will soon be gone, too.' The words escaped from Lester's mouth unbidden, surprising himself. He was expressing sympathy, he thought.

'It's all right for the lawyers. They'll always need bloody lawyers.'

Bilson undid his tie and threw it across the room. He slumped in his chair, rubbed his cheeks in his hands, then looked up balefully at the ceiling.

After a pause, a long sigh, he asked, 'What happened, Lester?'

Bilson waited for an answer, but the question was rhetorical. He went on.

'The bloody politicians in Australia, that's what happened. They interfered in something they knew nothing about. They spoiled it all, our years of work. They spoiled the trust.

'The *kiaps* used to be on the side of the people. We were their champions. The politicians and bureaucrats changed all that. They made us their spies and enforcers. We were the enemy.

In the end we couldn't contribute to the solution because we became part of the problem.

'All those years wasted! I'm nearly forty. I love this bloody place; I have nothing else. What do I do now?'

Bilson wiped his eyes on a napkin. In the shadows, the stiff form of his Sepik manservant was by the kitchen door. Lester could see the man's lip trembling. It was true, Lester thought, what Cleary had said to him at the funeral. The day the DC was killed was the day the gods became mortal.

The coming together of both European and Tolai populations in shared grief might have been a priceless opportunity to seek a resolution of the conflict in the Gazelle. Instead, the admin all but went to war against the Mataungans.

Inflammatory broadcasts by admin officials in effect vowed revenge and stirred up anti-Tolai sentiment among the Europeans. Search-and-surveillance missions by armed police continued, combing the Gazelle, targeting Mataungan sympathisers and hunting for evidence of their involvement in planning the murder.

Police tactics left behind damaged homes and terrified villagers. The missions unearthed a few unregistered firearms and many unregistered vehicles but no signs of Mataungan involvement.

To make matters worse, the admin concurrently embarked on a new crusade to recover unpaid taxes due to the now-defunct multiracial council. No wonder the Mataungan leadership maintained its campaign for autonomy in ever more strident language.

John Flanagan, a man with a police background and a law-and-order attitude, keenly felt the death of Jack Emanuel. He was a dedicated supporter of the so-called old guard of elders on the formerly multiracial council, many of whom he knew well, and an equally dedicated opponent of the Mataungans.

At heart, he was a conspiracist, an anti-communist warrior surrounded by what he saw as the ever-encroaching threat of Communism from Indonesia, Vietnam and neighbouring countries.

From Lester's perspective, he was someone who would readily believe any hint, any whisper, of communist influence behind the Mataungans. The visits of Gough Whitlam and his Labor Party associates proved to Flanagan's satisfaction that this party was infiltrated by rabid socialists. At the Yacht Club and New Guinea Club, or among plantation owners, he wouldn't have been alone in that view.

Not long after the Emanuel murder, Flanagan came into the office flourishing an article from the *Tribune*, the official newspaper of the Communist Party of Australia. It accused the administration of fomenting a state of public hysteria over the murder and justifying repressive measures, particularly against the Mataungan Association whose aims and struggles the article fully supported. The article was all that Flanagan needed as vindication.

Gloria came through the office door, struggling with a large red suitcase, which she put down in the middle of the office.

'I'm leaving,' she said with a dramatic look at Carol. 'My family is going to Brisbane. For ever.'

She began gathering her collection of precious things from her desk, putting them in her shoulder bag.

'Goodbye,' Carol said.

'I'm sorry you're going,' Flanagan said, sounding sincere. 'I can't say I'm surprised. Many people have just had enough. You'll be owed some money. Carol will arrange it with the Treasury office. Thank you for everything you've done.'

'I'll help with your suitcase down the stairs,' Lester said, opening the office door for Gloria to leave. 'It must be heavy.'

The suitcase was empty and could have been lifted by a four-year-old child.

'Can I give you a lift?' Lester asked in the car park. 'A drive in the Mercedes?' Gloria didn't answer, so he went on. 'I suppose you'll be looking to marry some rich Chinese man in Australia.'

'Not a Chinese man; they don't look after their women. And not a fair hair man like your doctor friend. Think of my baby. A dark hair one, like you.'

'There are plenty of those in Brisbane.'

Gloria's look conveyed what might possibly have been sympathy. 'I'm sorry I didn't marry you,' she said. 'Not suitable.'

'I suppose so. We never did get off on the right foot, did we?'

She studied Lester again, frowning at his legs, his workday shorts and long white socks.

'Right foot? What foot? I don't understand.'

She pulled a handkerchief from her bag and fluttered it open, sending forth a faint, familiar perfume. She dabbed at her eyes. A taxi pulled up beside them. Lester put her suitcase in the boot. At the door of the car, she kissed him.

'Farewell, sweet Gloria,' he said as she climbed inside.

He was sad to see her leave. She'd regularly threatened to do so, Flanagan said later, but she'd never leave without being paid every cent she was owed and that might be weeks away. It was the first time she had appeared with a suitcase, but that was only to make a point.

Cherry represented himself in the District Court on the charges of passing valueless cheques in Kavieng. He pleaded not guilty, despite his promise to the Kavieng police to plead otherwise.

On the day, however, it hardly mattered. The magistrate was unimpressed by his claim that he honestly thought his funds would cover the cheques on his return to Rabaul. A flight of fancy, the magistrate said. The amount of the cheques was substantial, and Cherry already seemed in financial difficulty. He found Cherry guilty and fined him one hundred dollars with seven days to pay.

Convictions, debts and fines were mounting, but that wasn't the end of Cherry's troubles. Outside the court, police were waiting to arrest him again, this time on a charge of making a false representation with intent to defraud. It had to do with the airline tickets for Kavieng and a travel warrant that was never issued.

Lester returned to Taliligap the following weekend, concerned for Cherry's welfare. He'd barely arrived and was unloading a box of groceries from the Mercedes when Josie appeared, like a pixie, in the garden. She froze at the sight of Lester, his car and Cherry's ute on the back lawn.

'I...I didn't know anyone was here. I hopped off the PMV and thought I'd pop in to see if the place is all right. You know, earthquakes, the murder and everything. Why are the cars parked at the back? I couldn't see them from the road.'

The words gushed from her, a mix of embarrassment and relief.

'We're trying to keep out of sight,' Cherry said, appearing on the verandah.

'I haven't seen you in *ages*.' Josie ran up the steps and hugged him. 'I've called in before, but you weren't home. You must have been staying in town.'

Cherry smiled and hugged her in return, looking beyond her shoulder at Lester: *Be careful of what you say.*

A sultry grey morning darkened as the patter of heavy rain began. They sought shelter in the bungalow.

'You both forgot about me,' Josie said.

Was that petulance or self-pity? Lester wondered.

'We thought about you all the time. You weren't here. You were stuck in the jungle.'

'Events have overwhelmed us all,' Cherry said. 'But now here we are together.'

'I don't want us to stay apart,' Josie said. 'I can't stay now. Let's meet again tomorrow. It's Sunday, so I'll come in the afternoon. We have a lot to catch up on.'

The rain settled in as Lester cautiously drove Josie to Malmaluan. Failing shock absorbers jarred along a road long neglected by the failing council. Windscreen wipers came to life in unpredictable bursts. Inwardly, he cursed his decision to buy a car for which spare parts were rarer than gold nuggets. As he drove, he wrestled with a lawyer's urge to explain Cherry's plight.

'About Cherry...'

Josie, a hand on his shoulder, stopped him. 'I know about Cherry's troubles with the law. He's all tangled up. You don't have to tell me.'

'You read the newspapers?'

'I don't. Sometimes I listen to the radio. And because they know about us, people in town tell me. They ask whether I knew. Maybe they suspect I was involved in whatever it was. Anyway, I don't care. I don't believe the half of it. He's a good man, not a criminal.'

For Josie, that was the end of that.

Of late, Cherry had often been seen in shorts and a scrappy T-shirt, but for the Sunday afternoon he'd dusted off his colonial attire, signalling a return to the Cherry of a year ago, all geniality and humour as he set out the drinks.

Looking out from the bungalow verandah at the town and harbour, laid out like a picture postcard below, the three agreed it was hard to believe in the tumultuous events of the past few weeks. It was more like a vividly bad dream, suffered simultaneously by everyone and best forgotten.

Josie had brought her tape recorder and the tape of a performance by the Trio at the Steakhouse. They listened to it in the cool of the living room: the songs, the applause, the chatter of diners, the clatter of dishes.

'*Times have changed...*' Lester sang a line. '*All the good times that we had, have gone now...*'

Josie laughed. 'I loved that song. It's so sad. I never believed in it when I was singing it.' She stopped to look out at the view, shaking her head. 'Maybe I do now.' She rose from the sofa and began to pack the tape recorder away. 'At least we have the tape.'

'It's yours,' Lester said. 'You deserve to keep it.'

Josie sank back on the sofa, sighing. 'I often wonder what brought us together. I think we were lonely, in our own way.'

'Not so,' Cherry said.

'Go on, admit it. Each of us was an only child. None of us had a proper, I mean traditional, family upbringing. We had nobody to turn to except ourselves, isn't that true?'

'There's a difference between loneliness and solitude,' Cherry said. 'I've always been happy to be alone.'

'Whichever way you look at it, we were waiting to find each other,' Lester said.

The afternoon and evening meandered along with anecdotes about what remained of their families: Cherry's imploded relationship with the half-sister, a would-be artist who taught him to draw; Josie's father and his incurable messiah complex; the fantasies of Lester's mother Kitty about her thwarted career on the musical stage and more.

No one mentioned Cherry's recent convictions. They, like the earthquakes, might never have happened.

That night, Lester, the least affected by alcohol, helped Josie to the Mercedes.

'I can't go home like this,' Josie said, leaning on Lester's shoulder. 'Father might see me.'

'Then stay here.'

'No, I want to talk to you.'

Josie was unusually quiet as they drove to Grandview Apartments. No one would see them together, Lester assured her. Bilson had departed; so had Norma. Szabo was on his honeymoon with Bonnie in New Caledonia, the homeland of Adele, inexplicably swapping one hot tropical island for another.

They laughed as Josie struggled up the stairs and flopped on the sofa inside.

'I've mostly been here when I've had too much to drink,' she said, kicking off her sandals, spreading her Indian print skirt and draping herself along the sofa in the elegant pose beloved by artists. 'Do I look like a courtesan?'

Never less like a courtesan, Lester thought, and not like the vivacious Josie who'd worn a black party dress. She looked pale and tired. He made coffee for them both. Josie waved hers away.

'Something's different,' she said, looking about. 'You've got rid of that ghastly piece of wood.'

'My driftwood sculpture? It nearly fell through the floor.'

Josie yawned, her head drooping. 'It frightened me. A head-less monster.'

'Don't fall asleep. Not yet.' Lester ached to hold her.

'I'm worn out,' she said. 'All that work at Gaulim, all gone. I feel sorry for the staff, the trainees, the children who won't be taught.'

'I heard that donations are pouring in for rebuilding.'

Josie sighed. 'It will take years; this is New Guinea, remember.' A long pause, as if she were weighing up whether to say more, then she went on.

'The other day when we met, Cherry asked if I could give him a loan from the donations box. That's what he called it. He had a guilty look. How could he have thought I would? I think he's desperate.'

'He's in more trouble than you know,' Lester said. 'He's on bail for another offence. If he's guilty, he might go to jail.'

He silently rebuked himself for revealing it, but an urge to dim Cherry's halo had taken hold. Expecting her to jump to Cherry's defence, Lester was surprised Josie stayed silent. She rose, fetched a glass of water and returned to the sofa.

'He's been taking a drug called Valium because he's anxious and can't sleep. He even made me try it. He said he'd prescribed it at the hospital for a woman called Daphne. He said you'd know about her.'

'Daphne?' Lester laughed.

'It's not so funny. I think it's affecting him; he's acting strangely. Last time I stayed at the bungalow he asked me to read *The Wind in the Willows* to him before he went to bed. He keeps the book at his bedside. He told me he'd once been in a play called *Toad of Toad Hall* where he played the Chief Weasel. He seemed proud of that. Sometimes I think he's never really grown up.'

'He must be homesick; he admits it at times. He told me he mostly reads dismal books about the end of the British Empire.'

'Oh, he reads more than that. When he was younger, he read fantasy novels. Months ago, I brought him novels by Rumer Godden. I thought they were exotic and different. A kind lady leaving Rabaul gave them to me when she was leaving. He read them all.'

'I remember *Black Narcissus*. I saw the movie. Nuns in the Himalayas. Deborah Kerr.'

'Cherry said the story was about repressed sexuality. Her stories often were.'

'Do you agree?'

Josie hesitated, demurely looking away. 'I don't know what that means.'

'It means you've had too much to drink,' Lester said, deciding to save her.

'I'm going to sleep in your bed,' Josie said. 'Would you take advantage of me while I'm drunk?'

'Would you like me to?'

'I might.'

Together in his bed, unclothed in the warm night air, they embraced. Lester could feel her heartbeat against his and breathe in her fragrance, her essence of wholesomeness. He kissed her hungrily. Her eyes softened with desire as she looked at him, then she turned away, took his arm and placed it on her breasts.

'You're not going to marry me, are you?'

'Do you want me to ask you?'

'That sort of answers the question, doesn't it? I want both of us to be honest. I don't want either of us to reject the other.'

'Would you come to Australia with me?'

'No. Would you stay with me in Rabaul?'

Leave or stay? Lester dreaded the decision. 'I haven't decided about next year,' he said.

Josie pushed the arm on her breasts away.

'I think you have. We're not the people we thought we were when we met. Your future isn't here, I know it. I think in your heart you know it too.'

'Josie...?'

Lester, upset with himself, wanted to explain, but there was no response. Gently he leaned over to rouse her, kiss her. Whether or not it was feigned, she appeared to have fallen asleep.

He got up, poured himself a whisky and sat in the darkened living room, furious with himself. Why couldn't he decide about his future? Thinking about it was like peering into a dense fog. As much as he loved Rabaul, he couldn't stand much more of Flanagan's antagonism. If he wanted to be with Josie he'd have to stay, but there seemed no way to escape the triangle while Cherry remained.

A hand touching his shoulder startled him. Josie was standing there, a silhouette in the darkness behind him. She'd raided his wardrobe and was wearing a kaftan-length cotton shirt he'd bought in Hong Kong. She'd been crying.

'I can't sleep,' she said. 'And you can't either.'

'I was thinking of our future. I love you. I'd sign on for another tour—two more years—if we could live together.'

'I love you too. But is love enough? Would we be happy? Do you really want to prosecute poor villagers all your life? I know you're frustrated with your job.'

'I'd make the best of it. For you.'

'That's a devious answer. You need to think about what I want from my life, too. I have my own belief in God. I'll always work here with the church, even if I'm not a missionary type. You're absolutely godless. You're a very secular person.'

'That's unfair. I respect your belief, and the Bible. That's better than Cherry; he's a rabid atheist.'

'Oh, Cherry! Don't bring him into it; he's not your problem. I think he's closer to God than you are. He's really quite mystical. Adele was right for once; he's a free spirit looking for solace, for redemption.'

'So you won't choose between us?'

'For me, it's not a real choice.'

Josie put her arms around Lester's neck, leaned over and kissed his cheek. 'I can't say any more. Come back to bed.'

Their lovemaking was long, languorous, lingering. Josie was playful, adventurous, more so than she'd been at Arovo. She seemed to want him to forget his pain, his confusion.

'One thing I've learnt about you,' he whispered in her ear as they released each other to sleep. 'You aren't sexually repressed.'

When he woke up next morning, she was no longer there.

34

The *Post Courier* reported a slump in business and a general feeling of gloom and apprehension throughout the Gazelle, brought on by the succession of calamitous events.

The Tolai community responded with a week-long festival of Indigenous music and dance, the *Tolai Warwagira*, on the town's rugby oval. The organisers claimed more than seventy thousand people attended, the largest ever Tolai gathering in their lifetimes.

Lester, who came with Cleary and Crosset on the last day, was among the few European spectators. The Mataungan Association officially boycotted the festival, but their supporters came anyway, symbolic of the paradox created by the situation on the Gazelle. Through it all, the Tolai rituals of life, death and belonging were resilient and unchanging.

Lester was asleep on the sofa when Cleary rang from a friend's house in town, about a wake happening the next evening in a clearing near the village where he lived. Cleary would be in a dance group, a sight not to be missed.

Through Cleary's entreaty to the village elders, Lester was permitted to watch preparations for the wake in a secluded grove behind the dance ground. Dancers donned headgear of feathers and spiky leaves, adding an elaborate makeup of black dots, stripes of red clay and coatings of white lime.

Cleary, with his pale and ample torso, caused much amusement and debate. Despite his protests, his torso was rubbed down with coconut oil and plastered with a reddish-brown clay. White lime coated his legs.

Beyond the grove, several hundred villagers gathered around the dance ground. No tears or wailing; on the contrary, the crowd seemed ready to be entertained.

A group of chanting dancers, forty strong, advanced on the open area at a slow shuffle. At the head was a young man with no body below the trunk. He walked solely on his strong arms and fists, dark muscles rippling. Murmuring among the crowd, for people with severe disabilities were usually hidden away in the villages. The man's body was painted in the same manner as the others. The effect was startling, a half-man, an optical illusion, a trick of the evening light.

The dancers settled into a rhythm of shuffling steps, forward and back, to the beat of thumping bamboo drums. Relatives of the dead man came forward with palm fronds to strike favoured dancers a stinging blow across the shoulders. Occasionally, a man dashed from the crowd to fling grey powder into the face or hair of one of the dancers, or to hand up a cigarette.

As darkness fell, a second group of dancers—Cleary among them—came tramping and chanting from behind the clearing. Cleary's appearance was greeted with howls of delight. His belly jiggled grotesquely in counterpoint to the drums. The gluey clay covering ran down his body in sweaty rivulets. The dancers turned face-to-face, squatted and took hopping steps forward then back.

Tears of laughter ran down the cheeks of spectators. Cleary was a *sumo* wrestler among lean and wiry village men.

When the ceremony ended, dancers, drummers and villagers joined in the distribution of lengths of *tambu*, broken from coils the size of truck tyres, and also banana bunches and chunks of raw pork on which flies were already settling. A trade store nearby sold orangeade until the supply ran out.

Lester drove the sagging Cleary home to the village, washed him down with buckets of water, wrapped him in a sheet and propped him, exhausted but elated, against a verandah post. No one in the village had expected him to complete the dance, so his standing had risen. He had gathered a sizeable store of *tambu* for his initiation chest.

He told Lester the funeral rites had long ended; this occasion had served as a memorial, a carefully orchestrated show of wealth by the *vunatarai*, who knew to the last fathom how much *tambu* had been distributed and to whom. The gifts would be reciprocated in future. It was a stage in the cycle of obligations that marked village life.

The Emanuel murder investigation continued apace. Police interviewed scores of suspects and witnesses. Some villagers were charged with riotous behaviour, others with the offence of sorcery, allegedly employed to embolden the perpetrators. Some readily confessed to their involvement in the stabbing itself, while others admitted their support.

Flanagan and Lester read and advised on many of the statements of interview. Police officers and translators came and went from the office. On the desk, once Gloria's, was a tower of folders, statements to be tendered at the preliminary committal hearing.

Flanagan, with Lester assisting, presented the preliminary prosecution case before a magistrate in the District Court. Five defence counsel lined up for the defendants. The lengthy hearings ended with the committal of eighteen Tolai villagers on a charge of murder, with little dispute about the murder itself. The trial would be about the circumstances that led up to it, and the extent to which each was involved.

Lester's busy days, early to the office and arriving home bone-weary, left him little time to reflect on his last, fateful night with Josie. There'd been a finality in her saying she had no real choice. She was rejecting him; she was not rejecting Cherry. One thought remained stubbornly in his mind: as long as he was in Rabaul, he wouldn't let Cherry take her over.

She'd left secretly at dawn, without saying goodbye, but it couldn't end there.

John Flanagan's obsessions were not only in bringing the murderers to justice. Another was the pursuit of Anthony Cherry-Apsley. Obviously, to Lester, the cultured and, in the mind of some, louche, Englishman had got under Flanagan's skin.

As an ex-police officer, Flanagan was plainly offended by Cherry's casual attitude to the law. Equally plainly, he detested Lester's close friendship with the doctor. Was it also the doctor's charm that had excited Flanagan's impressionable daughters? Or his consorting with the Mataungans? Or dallying with a policeman's wife?

The case against Cherry for obtaining an airline ticket by fraud was serious enough to be taken to the Supreme Court.

Flanagan appointed himself as the prosecutor. He made no secret of his delight at prosecuting a case he considered unlosable, brazenly asking Lester for his opinion on the evidence. Lester dimly remembered from his student days the complicated law about false representations.

'Cherry-Apsley should have a lawyer,' he said, unwilling to be drawn.

'Nonsense,' Flanagan said. 'Besides, the man's broke. Who's going to pay for a lawyer? The Public Solicitor won't touch it, and it certainly won't be you. His goose is cooked.'

Carol was no less one-eyed about Cherry. She accosted Lester in his office.

'That doctor, the one John's going to prosecute, phoned you. I told him he's not to call here, he's not allowed. And you're not to contact him. John told me so.'

'What did he want, did he tell you?' Lester asked.

'He wanted you to meet him at the Cosmopolitan Hotel.' Carol slapped a hand to her mouth. 'You're not going to do that, are you?'

'Of course not,' Lester said.

Later he found Cherry in the hotel garden, sharing reminiscences about Pat Connell with former patrons of the infamous tavern. They'd been drinking for most of the afternoon.

Cherry drew him aside to another table. His voice, his hands, trembled with emotion.

'I've been given the sack. I've been told not to come back.'

'Just like that? No reason?'

'It's com...complicated.' Cherry fumbled. 'I'm no longer registered to practise.'

'With you these days, it's always complicated. Not registered? I don't understand.'

'I have to give up the bungalow. I was hoping I could move in with you for a while.'

'You can't. You've been indicted for fraud and Flanagan is prosecuting. You could go to jail. I don't want to join you. What about your flat?'

'My landlords are about to throw me out.'

'I'll lend you a couple of months' rent to buy them off. That's my best and last offer.'

'You're my saviour, dear Lester. Come to Taliligap this weekend. Help me move out.'

Cherry, a picture of misery, slumped in his chair. He'd treated his last patient after lunch, he said, then walked out without a word to anyone.

Lester was saddened though not surprised; it had only been a matter of time. As if Cherry's recent record hadn't been enough, travelling to Kavieng while pretending to be on urgent government business risked damage to the hospital's reputation. That his registration had lapsed or was suspended was predictable.

He wouldn't let Cherry drive himself back to Taliligap, instead leaving the utility and driving him to the flat in Chinatown. He told the trade store owners he'd be back with cash for the rent next day. Cherry followed him as meekly as a child.

After the utility was unloaded, there was barely room in the flat. Cherry's clothes and books were few. His collection of war relics, all of which he insisted on bringing with him, filled the utility's tray to the brim and left only enough room to squeeze through between the bed and the rest of the flat.

At the day's end they drove to a secluded beach north of the town. After a swim, they sat on the sand and watched seabirds wheeling and diving over a shoal of fish offshore. Cherry had scarcely spoken all afternoon.

'You've no money and no job,' Lester said eventually. 'What are you going to do?'

'I have money: back pay, holiday pay. They can't take it off me.'

Lester laughed. 'You might like to pay me back, then.'

'I will. I want to stay. I'm going to fight the registration thing. The hospital knows they won't find another doctor as good as me. Meanwhile I can get a job with the chemist in town. I want you, me and Josie to be back together.'

'Then you have to honest with Josie. Tell her you've been sacked. Tell her you're about to be prosecuted for fraud.'

Cherry looked at Lester with a mixture of disdain and disbelief.

'I'm not going to tell her. If she asks why I'm not working, I'll tell her I made a silly mistake and let my registration lapse. As for the warrant thing, she doesn't need to know. It was all a misunderstanding; I can explain it. Don't you tell her about any of this.'

Cherry picked up his snorkel and goggles and strolled over to a group of young Tolai boys gambolling at the water's edge. With his foot he drew two parallel lines in the sand thirty yards apart, called the boys to him and offered the snorkelling gear to the winner of a footrace between them. When the race was won and the prize presented, he joined Lester again on the sand.

'I love these children,' he said, waving to the group as they ran off. 'They have nothing, but they're happy. I wish I had the power to stop them from growing old. I'd grant them eternal youth.'

'Like Peter Pan?' Lester asked.

'Exactly. No one deserves to grow old. If this were Never-land, I'd stay here forever.'

They ate dinner and bought drinks at the Steakhouse. Lester, no longer heedful of Flanagan's warnings, invited Cherry to stay. Cherry was adamant about driving back to Taliligap.

It was his last day for many things, he declared as they settled on the bungalow verandah with their drinks. His last night at Taliligap, his last swim on a reef, his last dinner at the Steakhouse.

'It's not the end of the world,' Lester said.

'If I'm convicted, I'll go to jail. You said so,' Cherry said morosely.

'I've been meaning to tell you; I've lined up a solicitor to defend you. He defended a *kiap* in my shooting case in Kavieng. He's very good.'

'I can't afford a solicitor.'

'Talk to him. Don't mention me, but tell him in confidence you have a chance of getting off. Ask him to check the fraud laws here in New Guinea.'

'I will, I will.' Cherry nodded and reached for the Bacardi. After a lengthy silence, he shook his head and went on. 'I've caused you so much trouble. I ask myself again and again: how did it happen? Where did it all begin?'

Lester believed Cherry's troubles since coming to Rabaul began with Pat Connell's inexhaustible supply of liquor and bottomless well of war stories. Cherry had started to drink too much and too often.

Then came Leila, her Chinese business friends and the lure of gambling. The losses, the debts, more drinking. Nightmares that haunted him and pills he took to banish them.

'You should never have taken up with Connell,' he said.

Cherry waved that away. 'No, no, it began long before.'

'When was that?'

'I was a junior doctor at a London hospital. A child died while I was on night duty in the children's ward.'

'What? Why have you never told us?'

'I tried. I couldn't. Josie...'

'Were you responsible?'

'Everyone said so. The nurses said so; the hospital said so. There was a furore. The press got wind of it. "Scandal!" they shouted. "The son of a baronet! The son of an MP!" My registration was suspended immediately. That was too much for my father—he was mortified. Too much for me, too, so I disappeared.'

For Lester, the mystery of Cherry's presence in Rabaul, his reluctance to talk about his work, his distance from other medical staff, was now solved. The explanation was shocking, yet so logical that he was hardly surprised. As a lawyer, he itched to know more.

'Were you there when the child died? Were you involved?'

Cherry gave no answer, instead stepping down the verandah steps to sit on the lawn overlooking the bay. The night was brilliantly clear; the full moon cast a sheen on the sea surface far below. In the distance, town lights sparkled around the harbour.

'I sit here when I can't sleep,' Cherry said as Lester joined him.

'We've suspected for a long time that something was gnawing away at you,' Lester said. 'The day you saved me...'

'That day was terrible—the thought that I might have been responsible for another death. I've tried to put it all behind me. I've stuck to my job, to treating children, wanting to make amends. Still, in my head there's a voice that repeats, over and over: the past will catch up with you sometime.'

'You shouldn't have run away. Any doctor can be forgiven one mistake.' Lester flinched at his own words, aware of their cold comfort.

Cherry put an arm around Lester's shoulder. 'It's too late now, old sport. My fate awaits. Let's finish the rum.'

35

Strong aftershocks continued to rock the town and keep residents on edge. Szabo returned with Bonnie. Grandview Apartments, she complained, shuddered with each aftershock and the rebuilt staircase to their apartment was unsafe. Within days they moved to a house in town.

Lester was left alone in the building, but not for long. A new tenant moved into Bilson's apartment downstairs, a Papuan man smartly dressed in *kiap* style. His attractive Papuan wife was with him. He introduced himself as Bilson's replacement.

Several days after his arrival, the new *kiap* announced he'd be having a housewarming party. By evening, cartons of beer had arrived in wholesale quantities. The guests, young Papuan and New Guinean men in casual dress, arrived in cars and admin Land Cruisers.

By nine o'clock they'd spilled from the apartment into the garden. As the night progressed, the music grew louder, the crowd became rowdier and fights broke out. Windows of the apartment were broken; furniture smashed and tossed outside. A woman, who could only have been the *kiap*'s wife, began screaming.

Lester, witnessing the violence and destruction from his landing, ached to intervene but feared for his life. He returned inside, bolted the door, closed the louvres, turned off the lights and sat down with a full glass of whisky. Alone in the darkness, he was overcome by a feeling of bitter helplessness at this sign of things to come.

No point in calling the police. The brawling mob downstairs *were* the police.

Lester's in-tray on Monday morning revealed a letter from Sydney.

Lester dearest

I'm sorry to tell you that your grandfather Reg has passed on. It happened two weeks ago. Since then, I've been in a dither with the funeral and everything. People were very kind. One morning the dog kept barking at the door of his shed at the back and when I went in there he was still in bed and asleep. That's what I thought, but he looked so peaceful lying there and he was gone. He was 88 years old. I thought it was his smoking, but the doctor said no, he was as tough as an army boot and it was his age. His pension died with him and I have hardly any money. I was told I can get a pension here now that I'm over 60, but no one helps me apply for one. I've cleaned out the shed and I'll have to get a lodger. That's why I hope you will be home for Christmas this year. With all the troubles I hear about up there I worry about you all the time. Reg had nothing to leave behind, only a savings book and his carpenter's chest of tools. He loved those tools though I've been told they belong in a museum, but he left them for you. Of course, he also left behind the dog, which sits outside the shed all day and waits for him. Poor thing, maybe it could belong to you.

Your loving mother Kitty

He read Kitty's letter again at the picnic table by the harbour where, in his early days of loneliness and depression, he'd taken his lunch. It distressed him that his grandfather's last days, his death and the funeral, had passed without his knowledge.

He recalled his grandfather's stories of his years as a carpenter at Ealing Studios, where he claimed to have been a set designer to the stars. He'd adored Gracie Fields and learnt to play the ukulele with George Formby, the Ukulele Man. He could, and did, sing Formby's bawdy songs to Lester when out of Kitty's earshot. He'd talk about the day that Charlie Chettle married Kitty Kettle, marvelling at the alliteration. He joked about his boss, Mr Potts, calling the Kettle black.

Lester remembered, too, helping to build the shed in the back garden where Reg could smoke. Kitty had forbidden smoking in the house, insisting it would ruin her singing voice and be the death of them all.

In many ways Reg was the quintessential English working man who brought his England out to Australia and never left it.

The letter stirred feelings of emptiness and regret in Lester, although sitting beneath the rain trees and looking out at the glorious harbour, the image of his grandfather he'd treasured was already beginning to fade from his mind.

On the other hand, after three years away from home, his image of Kitty as a long-suffering and abandoned mother, was vividly clear. The ingredients of guilt, homesickness and nostalgia curdled inside him.

Word came to Flanagan from the Department of Health in Port Moresby that Cherry, on arrival in the country, had received a provisional registration to practise in a public hospital. He produced his qualifications in medicine, promised to produce his British registration papers and added a glowing reference from a hospital doctor in Mauritius.

Only when Cherry failed to pay the annual fee for the current year did the Medical Registrar realise he hadn't produced his British papers. An enquiry to London revealed he had been deregistered in Britain long ago.

'He's toast,' Flanagan said, with relish. 'Practising in Papua New Guinea under false pretences. With the warrant case, that'll be two for the next Circuit. Our dodgy doctor will have a full agenda.'

'I know nothing about any of it,' Lester said.

Flanagan's smile was mocking. 'You two are as thick as thieves. You must know more than you've told me. I'll find something.'

Next day a dossier arrived, via Port Moresby, from hospital authorities in London. Anthony Cherry-Apsley was wanted in England to answer a charge of medical negligence. While on night duty in a children's ward, a child, urgently admitted with a fever, had died later that night. The course of events after the child's admission had been disastrous—a late diagnosis, a change of nursing shifts, the wrong medicines administered, an error in the nurses' notes—all had contributed to the outcome. Cherry's whereabouts at the critical time couldn't be established, but he wasn't on the ward.

Nor, much later, could he be found for the coroner's investigation.

'Well,' Flanagan smiled, handing the dossier to Lester. 'They've found him now.'

Gone was the silk jacket, replaced by a drab brown dressing gown wrapped around him, despite the heat. The Chinatown flat was in a sorry state of disorder. Cherry pushed aside Connell's maps and notes on the table, making room to sit down.

'You look feverish,' Lester said.

'Just a cold.'

'Not malaria, I hope. Are you taking your anti-malarials?'

Cherry shrugged and fetched beer from the fridge.

'You shouldn't be drinking,' Lester said.

'My nanny, the angel on my shoulder, always looking out for me. Any news?'

'Not good news.'

'I no longer expect good news.'

'You wanted the news? You told the Medical Board you were registered in Britain when you weren't; you were never registered in Mauritius; no one has heard of the Mauritian doctor who gave you a reference and your registration here ran out months ago. Flanagan wants to prosecute you.'

With a shrug, Cherry's bearing sagged. 'I'm tired of hiding, tired of explaining. I'll plead guilty to anything.'

'That's not all. You're a wanted man in England. The child who died on your watch, remember? Flanagan's received a dossier on you. I found it difficult to read. It said you weren't even present at the time. Where were you?'

'I was chasing up a doctor in another ward.'

'They must have paged you, surely.'

'I pretended I didn't hear the call. I knew what was happening. I needed someone to help me. It was an unfolding disaster I couldn't stop. I panicked. I didn't want to be found.'

Lester's anger mingled with despair. For a moment he was lost for words.

'There's no rest,' Cherry went on. 'I can't escape; my fate pursues me everywhere I go.'

He rose and opened the fridge door; no more beer. He found a half-finished bottle of wine in a cupboard and poured glasses for them both. His cold plus the alcohol made him sway on his feet. He reached out to grasp Lester's steadying arm as he sat down. He drained his glass of wine before going on.

'Everyone, at some point, wishes they could start their life all over again. In another dimension and another time, everything would turn out for the better. I've felt that every day.'

Beyond the open window of the flat it was dark. A whiff of sulphur drifted in with the night breeze. Lester glanced at Connell's papers on the table. He picked up a loose sheet about to blow away. He recognised Connell's hand-drawn map, the possible location of Dr Hirano's underground laboratory. He waved the paper at Cherry with a look of incredulity.

'You can't be going ahead with this?'

'Why not? The earthquakes have caused landslides up in the hills. That changes everything. I'll need help. Will you come with me?'

'I'm not going near any tunnels, they're too dangerous. You mustn't go either.'

'The tunnels are my refuge from a cruel world. For me, the danger lurks outside. I'm like a mole in its burrow; I'm safe there.'

'Safe with the snakes and scorpions? The answer is still no.'

Cherry's mood veered swiftly from dejection to feverish excitement.

'Then come with me to the Highlands! Goroka. Mount Hagen! We'll smell the Highlands air, the smell of wood fires at night, just like in Africa. I want to climb Mt Wilhelm, it's nearly fifteen thousand feet high, the highest in the country. There might be snow on top.'

'I barely climbed the Mother,' Lester said.

'We'll climb it together. If you can't go on, we'll fail together.'

'You can't go climbing. You're on bail and can't leave Rabaul.'

'To hell with my bail,' Cherry shouted, leaping to his feet. 'You're always so damned negative. Go home!'

Lester hadn't seen Cherry in this state before, with wildness in his eyes, a look of desperation. Lester shrugged and rose to leave.

'Take care,' he said. 'If you need me, I'll be around.'

36

Lester had scarcely sat down at his desk before Carol slid up beside him.

'A friend in the police told me about the wild party at your place. The young *kiap* complained about the apartments. He said they were run down and unsafe. So they're going to be condemned—just like that.' She snapped her fingers in a gesture of disdain. 'He's one of the new breed, isn't he?'

'He's getting a fancy new bungalow,' Lester said. 'That's how it's done now.'

'Awkward for you, isn't it? I mean we'll have to find you other accommodation.'

From Carol's officiously eager manner, Lester guessed immediately where the conversation was heading. Carol had winkled out the truth about Daphne, the phantom bride.

'I should be able to stay on for a while.'

Carol galloped on. 'You aren't married. It'll have to be single officers' quarters. Now, if you were a *kiap* or in the police, it wouldn't be a problem; they look after their own. No one looks after people like you. Suitable accommodation in town will be hard to find.'

'I'm sure you'll do your best,' Lester said.

Carol was not to be put off.

'Perhaps you can move back to the admin compound until something turns up.'

That was the final blow, the thrust of a knife blade in Lester's back.

'What can I do for you?' Flanagan asked amiably later in the day, tapping the embers from his pipe into an ashtray.

'I've decided to resign,' Lester said, straining to screen out the emotion in his voice.

Flanagan's eyes widened. Carefully, lovingly, he scraped clean the bowl of his pipe and refilled it. 'Any particular reason?'

A particular reason? A whole bag of reasons. They'd materialised in the past few months and coagulated into one. Little point in elaborating. One particular reason brooked no argument.

'My grandfather died a month ago in Sydney. He lived at home and looked after my mother. Now she's living alone and needs help. She wants me home by Christmas.'

'Oh, I didn't know. My condolences. You should've told me.'

'I'm sorry. I only recently heard, myself.'

Flanagan took time to strike a match and light his pipe, another little ritual. The air again reeked of the tobacco that Lester now loathed. Carol, unlike Gloria, seemed to savour the smell as if it were ambrosia, perfume of the gods.

'I've been wondering if you've become disillusioned with life as a prosecutor. Is it the woeful briefs we get, or the feeling you're on board the wrong bus?'

'Neither of those.'

'That's odd. I've had the impression for a long time that you've been cheering the Mataungans from the sidelines.'

'I haven't been cheering the administration, that much I admit.'

Flanagan rose to look out from his office window. 'That's a pity,' he said eventually.

'You'll find someone else, I'm sure,' Lester said.

Flanagan sat down again, took up his pipe, sucked and blew. Wisps of smoke drifted in Lester's direction.

'I haven't had much success with my juniors, have I? With you and your predecessor, I mean. At least you were competent, but it's the company you've kept. I'd have put in a good word for you in Port Moresby, if you'd wanted a transfer. Your knowledge of Pidgin would've been useful. Not so useful in Sydney, eh?'

Though Lester had a moment's visceral pleasure in telling Flanagan of his decision, he realised Flanagan cared not a whit for whether he left, stayed or perished in a stream of red-hot lava. Not only was he a good lawyer, he thought bitterly, he was a better lawyer than Flanagan. He was comforted by the idea that jealousy was at the root of Flanagan's antagonism.

He went home that evening to the silence of a lifeless building, conscious for the first time of its shabbiness, creaking floorboards and creeping patches of mould. He lay down, feeling his energy draining from him, a feeling beyond tiredness.

It might have been the lagging effects of dengue fever, he thought, or the realisation that whatever hopes and expectations he had nourished in Rabaul would never be realised. In any case, he was unable to resist. For the first time he could remember since the long ago death of his father, he shed a tear.

Flanagan invited Lester to dinner at his home. Lester arrived to find other guests had already settled into drinks on the verandah. Carstairs, the prosecutor from Port Moresby, was there with his wife Millicent. So were the resident lawyer from the Public Solicitor's office, another defence lawyer from Port Moresby and a Sydney barrister.

Though Flanagan had told Lester the dinner was to bid him farewell, it was soon clear his presence was an afterthought. Carstairs was weighing up whether to become Lester's replacement and had brought his wife for a taste of life in Rabaul. The defence lawyers and the Sydney barrister were assessing the logistics of a murder trial with more than a dozen defendants that might last for weeks. As if the committal proceedings hadn't been taxing enough, Flanagan declared, the trial itself, when it happened, would be bigger than Ben Hur.

Only as dinner progressed did Flanagan speak a few overblown words in praise of Lester, and express sadness to see him returning to Sydney. It was then that Lester's evening began to unravel.

At the mention of Sydney, the defence lawyer from Port Moresby sat up and peered at Lester across the table.

'Haven't I met you before? I was a solicitor in Sydney. Didn't we attend a property settlement together?'

'I don't think so,' Lester said uneasily.

'Or in the magistrate's court? Didn't you work for that firm of crooks that had to close down? You know, the money launderers?'

'I remember them,' the Sydney barrister said. 'The partners went to jail; so did their accountant, a very attractive blonde, I recall. A stunner.'

The defence lawyer agreed. 'Others were involved as well. They didn't catch them all.'

Flanagan's eyes bulged. Lester, filled with sudden dread and with nowhere to hide, waved the questions away. 'I did work for them once. I had nothing to do with all that.'

Thankfully, the talk passed on to other things, including the construction of a new courthouse to be ready for the trial.

At Flanagan's request, Lester stayed on after the other guests left. He steered Lester to a chair on the verandah and handed him a glass of whisky, shaking his head.

'Well...I don't know what to say.'

'About what?'

'You've always been cagey about your past and why you came here. You're not the public service type, are you? I mean the hair, the gaudy shirts, the sports car, your choice of friends...'

'I'm here because someone sent me a fake postcard of Port Moresby looking like Honolulu. I like colourful shirts because I had a really drab childhood.'

Flanagan smiled. 'Never mind, you're having me on.'

'I suppose Carstairs is taking over.'

'He is. Look, before you go, I want to mention a couple of matters I couldn't bring up at dinner. The first is that Port Moresby told me to drop that travel warrant charge against Cherry-Apsley. It seems there's a bloody hole in the law that'll allow him to get away with it.'

Lester's feeling of satisfaction was intense, but he held his tongue.

'The second is, I've still got one charge up my sleeve. He's about to be arrested yet again, this time for lying to the Medical Board in Port Moresby when he arrived. Oh yes, and we're looking into sending him back to England to face his accusers there.' Flanagan's grin was triumphant. 'I've got him this time.'

Carol came onto the verandah to bid Lester goodbye.

'We're getting married, John and I,' she said. 'Early next year. Sadly, you'll miss the wedding.'

'Congratulations!' Lester said, taken by surprise. 'All the same, send me an invitation, won't you?'

He drove furiously down Namanula Hill, parked his car by the Yacht Club jetty and sat down on the harbour wall. Clouds drifting overhead in the moonlight cast giant shadows on the water. Yachts moored off the jetty fidgeted at their moorings. Faint voices, braying laughter, drifted across the lawns from the club. A stray dog scuffled in rubbish washed up against the stones below.

Slowly the tension in his shoulders eased and his body relaxed. He imagined easing a heavy rucksack from his shoulders to the ground. Inside, struggling vainly to escape, were toy-sized figures of Flanagan, Carol and those sneering, smug, supercilious and dismally boring lawyers he'd just left behind.

He imagined throwing the rucksack far into the harbour and watching as it bobbed on the surface, wildly at first, before it slowly sank. He felt a wave of elation and relief. For the past three years he'd been trapped onstage in a play.

Now the curtain had come down. He was free to slip away by the stage door and go home.

'I found a way in, a ventilation shaft.' Cherry's voice on the phone to Lester was unnaturally shrill. 'It was blocked so I blew it in. There's a terrible smell; I'll let it air for a couple of days. I'll go back at the weekend.'

'What was there? What did you find?'

'I dropped my damned torch, the big one. I heard it slide all the way down the shaft. I couldn't see a thing, but the shaft's wide enough for me to slide down. There could be a maze of tunnels down there. It might be Hirano's Ground Zero.'

'You're mad, Cherry. You're about to be arrested again. You're in deep trouble. You have to find a lawyer. You'll probably be jailed and deported if you don't.'

'I'm beyond lawyers. This is my priority now.'

'Have you told Josie?'

'I haven't had a chance. I think she knows already. Did you tell her? I swear I'll kill you if you did.'

'I didn't, but if I find her, I will. She deserves better.'

Cherry's anger through the phone's handset was almost palpable. 'Leave her alone! You're just a damned prosecutor like the rest of them. I'll tell Josie in my own way. Those nurses in London set me up; they covered their own mistakes. Josie will understand.'

The phone rang off. Lester, alone in the office, packed his few belongings into a box and left the admin building—the Kremlin— for the last time.

Alone that night, he ate little, drank whisky and listened to music on his record player. *Creedence Clearwater Revival* and *The Doors* at full volume reverberated through the empty apartment block. He despaired at the end of a friendship.

He was woken in the morning from his sleep on the living room sofa by a soft knock at the door: Josie, in shorts, a pink polo shirt and sandals, holding her overnight bag. His heart reacted wildly as it always had.

'Surprised to see me?'

'Surprised and delighted! You've either come to stay or you're going on holiday.'

'Neither,' Josie said with an arch smile. 'I've been staying with a church friend.' She came in, dropped her bag and hugged him warmly. 'You don't look well. I hope you aren't ill.'

'A late night, a drink too many.' Lester guided her to a chair. 'You look distressed. What is it?'

'It's Cherry. Have you seen him recently?'

'He rang me yesterday. If you ask me, he's unhinged. I've given up on him. He's going to slide down a ventilation shaft to explore a tunnel. I told him he was mad.'

'I saw him, too, the other day. He told me the same. I have a bad feeling about it. Stop him. Don't let him do it.'

'He won't listen to me.'

'Then take his car keys or something. He's acting so strangely, I think he must be taking some drug. He told me he's been driven to do it. He doesn't make sense.'

Josie, agitated and shaking, began wringing her hands. Lester reached out and took her hands to calm her.

'Did he tell you he's about to be arrested...again?'

'No. Is that why? And he's going to hide down a hole? That doesn't seem sane.' Josie uttered a desperate sound, somewhere between a wail and a moan. 'What can we do?'

'Let him go, Josie. We can't do any more.'

'I can't believe you'd say that!' Josie pulled her hands away. 'You don't know how he's suffered. He told me all he ever wanted to be was a children's doctor. The child who died in London left a hole in his heart that couldn't be healed. I'll never abandon him.'

Josie rose abruptly from her chair. Lester asked her to stay; she told him she was needed somewhere else. She wiped her eyes, kissed him lightly, picked up her bag and left, hurrying down the staircase and into the street before he could offer her a lift.

Her visit left him in emotional distress. Angry at Cherry; tired of the contradictions, tired of arguing, tired of supporting him. And angry with Josie, despite his longing to hold her and stay with her. She was blindly devoted. She would fight for Cherry, whatever might happen.

In the end he sought to allay his feelings of guilt. He might have done more, perhaps approach the police on Cherry's behalf. But to what end? Cherry's arrest would put paid to his wild dreams of underground discovery.

For Lester, the emptiness of Grandview Apartments and the surrounding silence were unnerving. He'd woken at night believing he heard strange sounds on the stairs outside. No one was there. He was intensely conscious of being alone.

For a day or two, he moped about in the apartment, anguished, brooding, torn between self-pity and vexation. A sequence of events had spiralled out of control and a framework for his life had collapsed. He had left his job, abandoned his closest friend and lost the woman he loved.

He was back where he'd started, a fugitive from an earlier failed attempt at forging a career. What could he have done differently? Was it due to a weakness of character? Or because, as his favourite Russians would say, the best of human endeavours are ultimately doomed to failure?

Eventually, he summoned up the will to venture outside. Another person he was particularly fond of, an artist who had been the first to befriend him when he arrived, might be the last to see him off.

Darryl Cleary, at home in his village, stretched out comfortably on the cool verandah floor.

'How the heat doth pare away desire,' he sighed. 'I'm worn out. Even to look upon my gorgeous Joseph gives me no pleasure.'

Joseph sat opposite, cross-legged, frowning, motionless. Parts of a portable radio and a screwdriver lay around him.

'That radio is broken,' Cleary said. 'I gave it to Joseph in working order and he broke it. I've asked him to fix it. It's only a spring come loose or something. Will he do it? No, look at him sulking.'

'I don't know how to fix it,' Joseph mumbled, staring at the floor.

'And wouldn't listen if I told him,' Cleary said. 'Not interested in the slightest. No curiosity about this modern marvel, the wireless. This magic box with string bands and symphony orchestras locked inside. Joseph is content that it remains a mystery.'

'I don't believe you could fix it either,' Lester laughed.

'That's my point. I'm growing more and more like Joseph. I'm sure it's the heat. Lethargy has consumed me. The urge to open radios and understand their workings has evaporated. So has the will to overcome, to master, to possess. I just blend and accept, take the easiest route, walk around and not over. I flow with the current like an autumn leaf in the river.

'I lie here and wait for something to happen. I am beginning, at last, to understand the Tao. My advantage is not necessarily your disadvantage. What is yours may also be mine. Things are made to be broken. Every day, the road to the village gets worse. There's no money to fix it.

'I used to get angry and shout at people, but nobody listens. When it can't be used any more, I'll sit and watch the jungle grow over it. I'll marvel at the vigour of nature and at the futility of human effort to defy it.'

'I've come to say goodbye,' Lester said.

'Mercy me! The *ancien régime* really is crumbling.'

'You'll stay on, I suppose?'

'Many friends have gone; others remain,' Cleary said, waving an arm vaguely at the surrounding village. He rose slowly and enfolded Lester in a bone-crushing hug.

'Dear man, I love you dearly, but you're a conscientious creature at heart. This isn't the place for you.'

As he walked to his car, Cleary called after him. 'Come to the new courthouse tomorrow. I'm hanging my painting.'

Cleary stood back from the wall, his hands clasped in supplication, his head quizzically to one side.

'It's fine there, do you think?' He looked doubtful. 'I value your lawyer's perspective.'

Lester studied the painting against the bare cement brick wall. A standard Cleary subject, a grove of palms and cocoa trees through which three *duk duk* figures were dancing. Two were in the shadows, the third caught in a shaft of sunlight. The eyes, large red and black circles set in the conical masks, malevolently unblinking. The foyer of the new courthouse, nearing completion, starved of light. Against the grey background the painting had a forbidding presence.

'It's a bit gloomy there,' Lester said carefully.

'Well, we can't hang it over the judges' bench, can we?' Cleary's voice was tight with frustration. Assisted by Joseph, he'd put the painting up and taken it down again in a handful of places, none of which suited, heaving and balancing the huge, heavy hardwood frame. 'There's nowhere else. That'll have to do.'

Lester stood back to look at the painting again.

'I can't help thinking there's a certain symbolism,' he said.

'What might that be?'

'The judges' laws may rule in the courthouse. Beyond these walls the *tubuan* and *duk duks* hold sway.'

'Is it *that* obvious?' Cleary groaned. 'I tried to be subtle.'

The advent of a new courthouse would be a happy coincidence. The old building, earthquake-damaged and awnings crumpled around it like a fallen petticoat, was condemned. The new building, in glass and concrete, was triangular and futuristic, shaped like a paper glider in the act of taking off, and designed by a Chief Justice wise in the ways of the country yet blinkered by judicial tradition.

A jury box for a legal system without juries and a press box for the town's sole reporter. Deep pile carpets and public galleries with padded red seats. 'At least red seats won't show the betel stains,' Cleary said.

Robing rooms for the judges. A powerful air-conditioning plant humming in the background. It would keep judges cool in their robes and wigs but send lightly clad witnesses home with pneumonia.

There was no place for the public to wander about, squat down and wait, gossip, sell beads, waylay the judge, talk to lawyers or pass an idle day. Only Cleary's sinister *duk duks* hinted that this court was not opening for business in suburban Australia.

Perhaps, thought Lester, the Chief Justice was attempting to prescribe the future. Within those robust walls, in wood-panelled rooms, on sturdy shelves filled with ageing, hand-me-down volumes of law reports gifted by the Australian Government, British justice would be impregnable, safe from earthquakes, volcanoes and enemy bombers. It would be shielded from the forces of darkness, from animism, superstition, sorcery and revenge. It would last a thousand years.

To celebrate the picture hanging, he joined Cleary for a drink in the Yacht Club garden. Festive lights and Christmas decorations already brightening the club reminded Lester of his impending departure. His tickets were booked. For Lester, Cleary's companionship had meant everything to him in these last, lonely days. Cleary's soliloquy on the Tao suggested there might be a middle way between despair and acceptance. It lightened his mood.

Cleary had completed his initiation, he said proudly. He'd been confined for a week within a pen of bamboo stakes in the bush. Each night, whooping *duk duks* crept from the undergrowth to dance and chant around him. He'd been too frightened to sleep.

On the last day, men tied him up with vines, blindfolded him and ritually beat him with switches. They tied a husked coconut to a tree branch above him so that it dangled above his head. One man uttered a blood-curdling cry and charged at him with a heavy club.

Cleary thought it was the end; he was to be sacrificed in the jungle, and no one would ever know. The club shattered the coconut, filled with chicken's blood that sprayed all over him. He thought he'd been beheaded. He hadn't been quite the same since.

Thoroughly heartsick, Lester tried once more to contact Josie at the Church's office in town. According to a church worker she had failed to appear the previous day at Raluana or anywhere else she might have been expected to be. Her disappearance was reported to the police.

Even though the era of the notorious White Women's Protection Ordinance in Papua had long passed, there lingered in the subconscious of many Europeans in the country the notion that black men were unable to control their sexual urges and would take advantage of any white woman found alone and unprotected.

The police, led by European officers, descended on villages that Josie was known to visit. The villagers, already terrified by police squads looking for Emanuel murder accomplices, feared further retribution. No one would admit to having seen her in recent times.

Eventually, Reverend Clapin told police she must have slipped quietly away, by boat, to a mission station along the New Britain coast. If so, he said bluntly, she wanted to be left alone. He couldn't say when she might return.

Boots clumped on the stairs outside. Then an imperious knocking at the door. In the blessed hour of coolness after dawn, Lester rose sleepily from his bed to open it, shivering in nothing but his shorts.

'Good morning,' Inspector Macleod said briskly. Behind him were two stout Tolai constables. 'I hope I haven't woken you.'

'You have. And I see you've brought the troops. What's this about?'

'Cherry-Apsley's disappeared. Looks like he's done a runner. He's abandoned his flat and taken his truck. We thought you might be able to help us. Do you want to put some clothes on?'

The cheeky bastard, Lester thought. He let them in and fetched a shirt.

'When did you last see him?' Macleod asked.

'Not for a couple of weeks.'

'Or spoken to him?'

'A few days ago. He was going to explore a Japanese tunnel. A hobby of his.'

'Where was that?'

'He didn't tell me.'

'There's a warrant out for his arrest. John Flanagan says you knew about it. He thought you might have tipped your friend off.'

'That never occurred to me.'

Macleod pointed an admonitory finger at Lester's chest. 'We'll be keeping an eye on you,' he said.

Macleod rang again that afternoon. They'd found Cherry's utility at the head of an overgrown track leading to a nest of wartime tunnels. The area was remote and in thick jungle. Police had searched the area and found blocked or caved-in entrances. No one had thought to look for ventilation shafts.

'Will you keep looking?' Lester asked.

'We're not going to search old tunnels,' Macleod said. 'That would be madness, especially since the earthquakes. If Cherry-Apsley's in there somewhere, he'll have to find his own way out.'

Lester spent a restless night, taunted by a vision of being trapped, buried alive, unable to breathe. Almost beyond comprehension that it could have happened to Cherry...almost, but not certain. He feared the worst.

Cherry's flat had been searched by the time Lester arrived the next day. Police had taken the keys, the trade store owners said.

He hadn't returned them and left the door wide open. Anybody could come and steal, they complained.

They were sorry to see Cherry go, a man who behaved like a Chinese gentleman and was ever courteous, though he owed them a hundred dollars. If Lester would pay the debt, he could go upstairs and look around for himself.

The unmade bed, unwashed dishes in the sink, the clutter largely untouched, a scatter of documents on the table. Few signs that the flat had been disturbed.

He sat down at the table and riffled through the documents with little interest until he came upon an official-looking document titled *Sketch of Japanese Track: Powell Harbour to Malabunga. Based on Captured Japanese Maps, January 1944.*

The track ran obliquely across the neck of the Gazelle Peninsula. Geographical features, mountains, swamps and river crossings were shown in some detail. Cherry had marked a spot in the hills near Malabunga where the track might start.

Lester remembered Connell mentioning a settlement on Powell Harbour from which logs were shipped to Japan. Could Cherry have set off on the walk with the idea of escaping by boat? Not only would it be a hazardous journey; it would be hard to get away undetected—the sort of mad escapade only Cherry could dream up. Why then would he have left the map behind? The whole idea was fanciful.

The window was open to a breeze that fluttered lacy trade store curtains. Lester, sitting, musing, on the bed, had an eerie sensation of Cherry having left only moments before.

He lay back on the bed as emotions again welled up within him: sadness at the loss of a friend as close as any brother, anger at the way he'd been rejected, even betrayed, in the end.

Eventually he dozed off in the afternoon's heat. An uncomfortable hardness at his back soon disturbed him. From under the thin mattress he pulled out an artist's folder. It held a sheaf of pencil drawings on fine drawing paper—portraits of Josie, some larger than others, several unfinished. They showed the skill of an accomplished art student.

Studies of her face down to her shoulders, drawn from different angles. A drawing of her feet and ankles, the latter adorned with silver bangles. A few were of wistful or playful poses on the verandah at Taliligap.

Every drawing seemed intimate and sensual. However, two stunned him.

The first was of Josie sitting up on the rumpled bedsheets of Cherry's double bed, naked apart from a towel pulled carelessly across her hips. In the second, she was on the sofa, dressed only in a silk Chinese robe provocatively open to her waist.

He gazed at the drawings in consternation. Josie was depicted as a teenager of fifteen or sixteen, barely on the cusp of adulthood.

The folder also held a note in Josie's handwriting, thanking Cherry for the gift of the silk robe and offering in return her own copy of Norman Lindsay's classic children's book, *The Magic Pudding*. The note was signed: 'For someone young at heart, with love.'

The folder revealed a relationship more intimate than any he had imagined.

On the way out, he asked the owners if they'd seen any recent visitors to Cherry's apartment other than the police. A young European woman came, they said, some time before Cherry left. They saw her arrive but didn't see her leave. They thought she must have stayed the night.

He shouldn't have asked the question, he knew. The answer left a hollow sickness in his stomach.

More days passed with no word of Cherry. Lester was woken one morning by an engine revving and a horn tooting in the garden below. Gabriel Toporo called Lester to come down.

'I've a box for you,' he said. He fetched a cardboard box from his utility.

Lester, drowsy from a night's dream-laden sleep and nursing a whisky hangover, opened the box. Inside were documents and notes, fragments of Connell's war archive.

'You have to look after them,' Gabriel said softly, with a secretive air. 'Dr Cherry said so.'

Lester was suddenly wide awake.

'I don't want them. When did you see Cherry?'

'I saw him at his place in Chinatown. He gave me the box. Dr Cherry, *i go pinis oltaim*?'

Lester shook his head. 'Gone forever? I don't know. He no longer works at the hospital. I no longer work for the administration. I'm going back to Australia.'

'That makes me sad.' Gabriel paused, sniffed, looked down at the ground. 'You were my good friend.'

'And you were mine,' Lester said. 'I can't stay because my mother is alone at home.'

Gabriel nodded. 'I'm sad you won't see our child when it's born and won't be at the christening. If it's a boy we might call him Lester.'

Lester smiled. 'Please, not Lester—choose a biblical name. Send me a photo and I'll send the baby a present.'

Gabriel shook Lester's hand. 'A koala bear.'

'I promise. A koala bear.'

Departure time came quickly upon him. Days of the doldrums; unbearable humidity and threatening thunderclouds. A languor made worse by idleness. A last swim at Pilapila in a motionless sea. Packing a trunk for shipping. A few mementos. The *yip-wons*, for he believed the strange one-legged spirits would follow him everywhere, whether he packed them or not. Market beads and dolphin carvings. A string of *tambu* gifted by Cleary. A dozen books.

He kept two of Cherry's drawings of Josie. The rest he returned to the folder to be left for her in town. Between the drawings he tucked a letter.

Dear Josie

I was devastated that you left so suddenly without a word of farewell. Perhaps you needed to recover from the disasters of the past year and wanted time to yourself in some place where you could be at peace. I'm sure you'll come back to fulfil your dreams.

I was jealous of Cherry's closeness to you, but on seeing these drawings I finally realised how deep your bond was with him. I believe he was obsessed by a fantasy of childhood and sought it in you. He never quite left the world of Peter Pan. It was one side of a split personality. He was right at home with the roughest of characters like Pat Connell and my neighbour Szabo yet was drawn to the ideal of innocence.

Not that any of us were totally honest with each other. I don't believe we actually told lies. Not revealing the whole truth isn't the same thing, is it?

You once said Cherry and I were a pair of fugitives. He certainly was. If you helped him in any way to disappear, be sure that no one finds out because you've probably committed a crime.

I'm leaving to go back to Australia. My grandfather died and my mother is living alone. She begs me to come home.

Wherever our paths lead, my feelings for you will never change. We were blessed to have our time together. I hope we meet again one day.

All my love

Lester

Next day, he left the Mercedes at Szabo's garage. Rust in the tropics had got the better of it, but if anyone could save it from the scrapheap, it was Szabo. He took a taxi to the airport terminal. Dave Hersch was in the arrivals area waiting for his luggage.

'On your way overseas for leave?' Hersch asked.

'It's a one-way ticket.' Lester waved it in the air. 'I'm going home.'

'Good heavens! I hoped to talk to you.' Hersch, as ever, was breathless.

'There's always Flanagan,' Lester laughed. 'What brings you here?'

'Jack Emanuel's murder—the aftermath. I thought you'd be here for the trial. I hear there'll be an Australian judge and more than a dozen defence counsel.'

'I'll read about it on Bondi Beach.'

'I sense the independence caravan's moved on,' Hersch said. 'The Mataungans have run their race. They've played their part. An election's coming up for a national parliament. A new political class is rising—Michael Somare and the Pangu Party. There'll be independence in the blink of an eye. I'll be writing about that. What do you think?'

Lester's flight was called. What did he think? He'd need both time and distance to reflect.

'I have to go,' he said. 'Good luck to you.'

'And to you,' Hersch said. 'Look out for me in Bondi.'

As the plane taxied past the airport terminal, he caught sight of a woman standing at the tarmac edge. Even in the baking heat, she looked cool in a white cotton dress and broad-brimmed hat.

He knew immediately it was Josie. Had she found the letter? Had she come to see him? She could've been there for anyone; she was often enough at the airport. If she was there for him, how did she know the right day?

She was still there, watching as the plane took off, a hand raised to shield her eyes from the sun. And there again as the plane banked and wheeled away, until she was lost to sight. For a moment he felt a wild desire to return on the next flight. The moment was fleeting; a door closed. He lay back and closed his eyes.

What did he think? Hersch had asked.

One thing was certain. Though Rabaul might limp on into the future, it would never be the same. For those who had come and gone, it was a paradise lost.

EPILOGUE

Alone on the rooftop bar of the Kaivuna Hotel, Lester looked out on a surreal landscape bereft of colour, a vista of battle-field devastation viewed through a chrome-yellow lens. Rain had fallen steadily since his arrival the day before. Spumes of ash and steam billowed from the cone of Tavurvur into a bank of rainclouds hovering above.

Beyond the hotel, the town lay beneath a quilt of dark grey ash. A fine mist rose from warm, damp streets. Rows of leafless trees pointed bare, gnarled fingers at the sky. Only a scattering of buildings remained standing—those built, like the hotel, of solid brick or concrete. Many had collapsed under the weight of rain on falling ash.

He had come on the spur of the moment, not realising how much of the town remained abandoned a year after Tavurvur's eruption in 1994. There were no shops and no transport. There were no services and no people. In the lobby were photographs of the hotel, dug out from the ashes and refurbished. The hotel's only telephone was out of order.

Late in the afternoon he ventured into the town. The streets were layered with a deep pile carpet of ash. Only the picked-over entrails of looted shops and homes remained.

He stopped before the old cinema; it had imploded under the weight of ash. Large spools of film, tossed aside by looters, trailed black ribbons across the road.

The administration building was still standing, but doors and windows had been smashed and the interior trashed. Further afield, little remained of Grandview Apartments. The volcano had succeeded in bringing down the creaky wooden structure, where successive earthquakes and demolition orders over the years had failed.

The extent of Rabaul's destruction saddened him. That night, as he lay on his bed drifting to sleep, he wondered if the ash had also buried his memories of Rabaul as it once was.

He enquired about Josie at the hotel desk.

'You mean Josie Konia? Old Reverend Clapin's daughter? She lives at Raluana,' the hotel manager said. 'I'll lend you a hotel car and driver for the day. You'd better take the inland road.'

Lester found her sweeping the verandah of the house she had lived in since childhood. She shook her head in surprise, put down her broom, wiped her brow with a handkerchief and led him to two rickety cane chairs.

'Well, I never...I can't believe it's you. Is it *really* you?'

'Have I changed that much?'

'Oh, no, not at all. I mean...'

'Nor have you.'

Nor had she, thought Lester. The alluring smile and eyes. The lightness of her movements.

'Liar!' Josie's laugh was half a sigh. 'Not a word from you in twenty-five years! What are you doing here?'

'I came to see what remains of Rabaul...and to see you.'

'It's so sad. Nothing's left of the Rabaul we loved.'

'We all knew it would happen, didn't we? We buried our heads in the sand.'

'Perhaps it's for the best.'

'You've married a Tolai, it seems.'

'What about you?'

'I'm with an old flame.'

'One old flame; now you're visiting another,' Josie teased. 'The blonde bombshell? She waited for you?'

'Not exactly. She was just sort of around when I came back.'

'I can say much the same,' Josie said. 'Father died three years after you took off. I would've been homeless, but a Tolai pastor took over the parish. I knew him well already. In the end I sort of came with the house.'

Smiling, she waved the subject of family life away. 'What are you doing now? Still a clever lawyer?'

'I'm in shipping. Large ships.'

'My goodness, you must be rich. Do you still own a Mercedes?'

'A big black one with a chauffeur.'

'A chauffeur?' Josie laughed.

'I'm kidding. No chauffeur.'

An awkward silence.

'I'll bring out tea and biscuits,' Josie said, as if aroused from a daydream.

Lester followed her into the living room. He stopped to look at a framed certificate on one wall, a degree in Social Sciences from the university in Port Moresby; beside it, a framed photograph of Josie, in a businesslike skirt and blouse, among a group of Papua New Guinean women.

'A conference on women's rights in Brisbane last year,' Josie said, noticing his surprise. 'I was a speaker.'

He returned to his chair on the verandah. Josie, it seemed, was incurious about his life in Sydney: his decision to follow his father into the world of merchant ships; the shipping company and his study of maritime law in London; his inheritance of the cottage in Greenwich.

What was the point? There, on the verandah, the last twenty-five years might not have passed at all. The view hadn't changed, the garden still lushly green, the harbour beyond a vivid blue. The volcanic ash had not carried this far.

Josie reemerged with tea and a biscuit tin.

'I remember that old tin,' Lester said. 'I hope they aren't the same old biscuits.'

'I bought these only a year ago,' said Josie, holding up a biscuit. 'Before the eruption, that is.' She fiddled with the teapot, the cups, arranging biscuits on a plate. The noonday heat was intense, the air breathless. Then, with a shrug, she went on.

'Do you remember the letter you wrote to me before you left? What you said about honesty? I've thought a lot about that. Did it matter that you found out I wasn't a Vestal Virgin? Or I found out I'd fallen for two men with a dodgy past? We had wonderful times together. We cared for each other to the very end. Sometimes honesty can be overrated.'

'I agree, though you cared for Cherry more than me,' Lester said, more sourly than he intended.

'Don't be silly,' Josie said. 'I could possibly have lived with you, but I could never have lived with him.'

She disappeared again inside, returning with the Buka basket Lester had given her long ago. From the basket she took a short loop of string-like vine, brown and shrivelled with age, tied into a loose knot in the middle.

'It's a *kuara*,' she said, holding it up carefully for Lester to see. 'A charm for a kind of love magic called *malira*. It's usually used by boys, but I was told it works also for girls.

'You hide the string in your palm. When the man you want looks at you, you pull the knot closed with your fingers. The effect on your quarry is like being caught in a fish trap. He can thrash around, but there's no escape.'

Josie dropped the charm back into the basket as if it might come alive and bite her. She smiled, a shaft of sunlight catching her face as she turned, marking the fine lines around her eyes.

'Do you remember our night together at Arovo? I held it in my hand all through dinner. I took it with me in the canoe, but I couldn't use it. I was frightened. If I'd pulled the string my life would have been different, wouldn't it?'

Lester longed to reach out to touch her, to hold her.

'Did you ever hear again from Cherry?'

'He's dead.'

'Dead?' Lester's heart skipped a beat.

'Well, declared dead. That policeman looked for him for a few days, then gave up. They were better off without him, he told me.'

'There was an inquest?'

'There was, a half-hearted one. A pompous relative came from England, I think he was Cherry's half-brother. He said he'd come to take the body home, but there was nothing to take, was there? He demanded a search of the tunnels, but the police refused.'

She gestured; nothing more to say.

As he left, she kissed him, as passionately as she ever had, and turned to go inside.

'By the way,' she said brightly, 'Gabriel's still alive and well. He lives near Keravat.'

To Lester, Josie remained as desirable, yet as enigmatic, as ever. She'd been playing Cherry and him off against each other, that much was clear, and undoubtedly she knew more about Cherry's disappearance than she let on. Things had turned out unexpectedly. Whether she wished it or not, in the end she lost both.

Gabriel's house near Keravat was grand by village standards: a tin roof, separate rooms, glass louvres in the windows. Other houses nearby and a shed serving as a trade store together made a small, sleepy hamlet.

They sat in the shade on a wooden platform under the house. Gabriel's home at Matupit had been buried under the ash. He'd been able to rebuild here because the land belonged to his clan, and he was sufficiently wealthy and influential to ignore competing claims.

They shared a meal with Gabriel's wife Celia, their two adult sons, Lester's driver and several children. Bidden by Celia, the children ran into the house and returned with soft stuffed toys: a koala, a kangaroo, a platypus, a wombat, a bilby.

'Each year you sent a toy,' Celia said. 'Now our grandchildren have them.'

After the meal Lester and Gabriel were left alone.

'What happened to the National High School at Keravat?' Lester asked. 'I passed it on the way here. It used to be a showpiece; now it seems derelict. I was told at the Keravat trade store you were a member of the Provincial Assembly. You must be disappointed.'

'Provincial Assemblies were no good. They are abolished now.' Gabriel paused and coughed; something was amiss in his chest.

'What's the use of education? At the end of the year, teachers tell the students to go home and do something useful in the village. They are told, "One day you will run the country."

'Look around you, there is nothing. When the students go home, they know they've been told a lie. They go back and break the school windows. It's all they can do.'

'What about the government?'

'Our politicians know how to sit in their offices. They know how to drive around in cars. I know because I used to be one myself. The rest of the world moves too fast. The politicians run so fast that they run away from us altogether. We elect our politicians, then they go to Port Moresby and don't come back. I hear they buy houses and live in Australia. Is that true?'

'Some do, I believe.'

'The teachers aren't paid. There are no medicines. The roads break down. The *kiaps'* work is *bagarap pinis*.'

'What about the Mataungan Association?'

'Nothing came from Mister Bayonet in the end. What did we leave behind? What did we do? Without an enemy to fight we lay down and went to sleep.'

'Are you sorry the Europeans left?'

'The *mastas* were bad for us. We had to rule ourselves.'

'At least they maintained law and order.'

'They brought their own law and order. We didn't understand their law and order. You told me once the judges were good men. They were your good men, not our good men.'

Lester rose to leave, thanked Gabriel and shook his hand.

'Do you know what happened to Cherry?' he asked. 'I think I do. You planned his escape with his girlfriend Josie. You drove him to Malabunga.'

Gabriel's smile was distant. 'Maybe I know or I don't know. It's not for me to say.'

Next morning, persistent drizzle drifted from grey, spongy clouds hovering over the town. He borrowed a plastic cape from the hotel manager and set off on foot for Namanula Hill.

Torrential rains following the eruption had destroyed houses on the ridge and swept away the lush vegetation, scouring deep ravines in the hillside, as if the surface of the earth had been peeled away.

While descending cautiously through a maze of gullies he came face-to-face with a short, plump Japanese man in a rain-coat and Wellington boots. The meeting was so unexpected that it startled them both. They jumped back in fright before grinning sheepishly and waving each other past.

Later on the rooftop bar, the Japanese man, Dr Hitashi Aso, from a volcanological institute in Southern Japan, presented his card.

'We are the only hotel guests tonight,' he said. 'We should dine together.'

Over a dinner table abounding in dishes of freshly caught seafood, Dr Aso expounded on volcanoes in Japan, Indonesia, the Philippines and elsewhere on the Pacific Rim of Fire.

'Some say volcanoes are symbols of destruction and death,' he declared, reaching across the dinner table with his chop-sticks, 'but they are really the fountains of life. Destruction and growth are like mother and child. This is the way we believe in Japan. Each time there is an eruption, we learn more about our-selves. We are wiser, we cry, we are sorrowful, then we rebuild

AUTHOR'S NOTE

The famous American author James Michener described Rabaul in the 1950s as 'the loveliest town in the Pacific.' It has a special place in the memories of people from abroad who spent time (or their entire lives) there, for its spectacular setting, vibrant Indigenous culture, tragic wartime history and world-famous diving sites.

The town was all but destroyed by a volcanic eruption in 1994.

The major events described in this book took place between 1969 and 1971. They are presented, both historically and chronologically, as accurately as possible. Other than the main political figures from Australia and Papua New Guinea (including the District Commissioners), the characters are mostly drawn from a composite of real people and freely fictionalised.

Lester Chettle's legal experiences draw in part on my time as a Crown Prosecutor in Rabaul. His background, character and journey, however, are far different from my own.

The so-called Mataungan Uprising among the Tolai people was a seminal event in the decolonisation of Papua New Guinea.

In 1969, the Australian government thought independence for the country was thirty years away. A Labor government under Gough Whitlam, elected in 1972, was determinedly anti-colonialist and openly supported the Mataungans.

Independence came in 1975, only three years later. It made news in Australia at the time, but afterwards the extraordinary nation of islands with a boundary little more than four kilometres from Australia's northern shore faded from public consciousness. Australians' interest in, and knowledge of, the country (with the possible exception of the wartime campaigns) markedly declined.

The trial of thirteen Tolai men allegedly involved in the murder of District Commissioner Jack Emanuel in 1971 took place in Rabaul over five months in 1972. They were represented in the Supreme Court by an array of senior legal counsel from Australia and Papua New Guinea. Two of those charged were found guilty of murder, a further three guilty of conspiring to murder and eight were acquitted.

Errol John (Jack) Emanuel was awarded the George Cross posthumously for gallantry in the service of the Australian Administration of the Territory of Papua and New Guinea between July 1969 and his death in August 1971.

Records of the war crimes trials mentioned in the story have largely been digitalised and accounts published in various guises under the title of *Australia's war crimes trials 1945–51* (Eds: Georgina Fitzpatrick, Tim McCormack, Narrelle Morris).

A final point: In 1969, the country was known as 'the Territory of Papua and New Guinea'. However, in 1971 references to 'the Territory' were dropped and the national name became simply 'Papua New Guinea'.

That did not immediately stop its inhabitants from referring to it as 'the Territory', but to avoid confusion I have generally referred to Papua New Guinea by that name, or as 'the country' in a national sense, and 'Papua' or 'New Guinea' when referring to that part of the country alone.

In the past, each part has been regarded separately in administrative or cultural ways, and Papua New Guineans may still refer to themselves as Papuan or New Guinean, as the case may be.

ABOUT THE AUTHOR

The author was born in Northern Ireland and migrated to Australia with his parents at an early age.

He studied law at Melbourne University and later in London. He enjoyed a lengthy career as a senior lawyer with the governments of Papua New Guinea and Hong Kong, followed by many years with the Attorney General's Department in Canberra.

Alan has written three previous novels: *Cheung Chau Dog Fanciers Society*, *Up at Killen's Corner* and *The Mine of Eternal Spring*. All three have taken as a starting point the author's own experiences. The Cheung Chau story, in particular, is regarded as a Hong Kong classic.

He now lives in Sydney, Australia, with his family.

Contact author: https://alanpierce.com.au

Facebook: https://www.facebook.com/alanbryanpierce

ACKNOWLEDGEMENTS

There are countless learned books, articles and theses on the political and wartime history of the Gazelle Peninsula and on aspects of Tolai life and culture. I consulted many. My bedrock research, however, lay in three comprehensive works: *Mangroves, Coconuts and Frangipani—The Story of Rabaul* by Neville Threlfall, *The Australian Trusteeship Papua New Guinea 1945–1975* by Ian Downs and *Hostages to Freedom— The Fall of Rabaul* by Peter Stone. Also invaluable as a contemporary source of information was the *Encyclopaedia of Papua and New Guinea*, in three volumes, edited by Peter Ryan and published in 1972.

on the ruins of the old. In the end Rabaul will be better. What do you think?'

'In the case of Rabaul,' Lester replied, 'I think they've learned from history and built somewhere else.'

He wandered for the last time through the streets of Rabaul as the sun crept over the caldera rim. In that golden moment of crisp, dewy fragrance before the doors of the furnace opened, the scene was subtly transformed. Like a mould, the first green tinge of new growth lay over the ashen carpet on gardens and playing fields.

Stubborn frangipani trees still bloomed, a scatter of white and yellow petals around their roots. The frangipani had been a wise choice as the town's floral emblem. It was as Dr Aso had said: the earth would heal itself. The volcano buried the past and new grass sealed it down.

He stopped before a solid structure partly buried in the ash. The court building had been looted. Reams of paper torn from books, scraps of statutes and legal precedents, were strewn in the foyer. In one corner, discarded as worthless, was Darryl Cleary's striking painting of the *duk duks*. He prised the canvas carefully from its frame, dusted off the ash, rolled it up gently and carried it back to the hotel.

He wondered, what had become of Cleary, and of others he had known? His years in Rabaul had long ago assumed for him a magical, dreamlike quality. But they had passed and could never be regained.

www.ingramcontent.com/pod-product-compliance
Lightning Source LLC
Chambersburg PA
CBHW020927020726
47495CB00002B/380